Born in Car
at the Roya
Akademie
secretary and concert ma...g
monic Orchestra in London and the BBC Training
Orchestra before meeting her Australian husband
on the ski slopes of Austria, marrying and moving to
Australia. There she raised a family, taught Suzuki
piano and fell in love with Australia.

After successfully organising The Suzuki 21 Piano
Salute to the Bicentenary, Anne relinquished music
teaching to run the family business and concentrate
on writing. She has written articles for a wide range
of publications and, after successfully conquering
the pain and misery of arthritis, published *Pain Free
Living: An Anti-Arthritic Cookbook*. Her first novel
Reach for the Dream became an instant bestseller.

Anne's English upbringing as the daughter of a
Cambridge University don, and her time spent in
London and Europe, provide the background for
the middle section of *Ride with the Wind*. Her husband's mother and father were born and raised in
country towns in New South Wales, giving Anne
access to first-hand accounts of life in rural Australia.

Anne has two children, a well-trained golden
Labrador and a garden that won't keep orders.
She is an enthusiastic skier, sailor and glider pilot,
and with husband Jim recently won the New South
Wales two-seater glider championship. She practices
yoga, enjoys cycling, horseriding, gardening, sewing,
patchwork and quilting. Originally dreaming of
becoming an opera singer, Anne wants to continue
to encourage others to succeed, and to write novels
that are a 'damn good read'.

She is currently working on her new saga, *Beyond
the Song*.

Also by Anne Rennie

Reach for the Dream

'The Australian Outback has provided
inspiration for some of the most outstanding and
memorable pieces of Australian literature—and to
that list can now be added Anne Rennie's story
Reach for the Dream.'
NEW IDEA

'You can . . . smell the smells, hear the birds
and taste the grit in your mouth.'
THE LAND

ANNE RENNIE

RIDE WITH THE WIND

ARROW

If you would like to write to Anne Rennie, she can be contacted at the following e-mail address:
jwrennie@ozemail.com.au

This is a work of fiction and all the characters are solely the product of the author's imagination. No resemblance is intended to real persons, living or dead.

An Arrow book
published by
Random House Australia Pty Ltd
20 Alfred Street, Milsons Point, NSW 2061
http://www.randomhouse.com.au

Sydney   New York   Toronto
London   Auckland   Johannesburg
and agencies throughout the world

First published 1998

National Library of Australia
Cataloguing-in-Publication Data

Rennie, Anne.
Ride with the wind.

ISBN 0 09 183454 6.

I. Title.

A823.3

Typeset by Midland Typesetters Pty Ltd,
Maryborough Vic 3465
Printed in Australia by McPherson's Printing Group

10 9 8 7 6 5 4 3 2 1

To Jim, Patsy and Ellie.
You are the centre of my being.

Acknowledgements

As with my novel *Reach for the Dream* I have been overwhelmed by the friendship and help I have received while researching *Ride with the Wind*. To you all I send my heartfelt thanks. In particular I would like to thank Catherine Bird for introducing me to wonderful horses, teaching me about massage and natural therapies for horses and for dragging me off to track work at four a.m.; Gai Waterhouse and Denise Martin of Star Thoroughbreds, inspiring in their energy; Dianne Minter for introducing me to Nita Marusich, assistant to Bart Cummings; and Nita who took time to explain the running of Lelani Lodge; Reg Inglis and Fiona Guth of William Inglis and Son Pty Limited; Bronwyn Hogan from the AJC; Victoria Morish of Clear Day Lodge; and Rosemary and Wilfred Mula for their generous support. To Kathy and Duncan Guy for their medical expertise; Fiona Clyne, Greg Mitchell, Peter Flynn and the whole team at Woodlands Stud, Jerrys Plains; Gloria and Graham for their hospitality at Bunnan; and John Jeffs, manager of Sydney's Randwick Racecourse who always made time to answer my barrage of questions.

I should also like to thank the following people

who shared their time and expertise: Robyn Aldridge; Daphne and Lindsay Beasley; Janet Boakes; Anne and Bill Bowen; Ray Burgess; Cara Brett Hall and the members of the Cornucopia Committee Inc.; Catherine Chicken; Heather Clarke, Elite Academy of Modelling; Marnie Colton, equine vet; Bev Duncan, Emirates Park; Chris Ferguson, Chic Model Management; Bob Forest; Yvonne Gregory; Elisa Grubler at the Swiss Consulate; Regina Hayes; Robyn Henderson; Karen from the Mounted Police; Tony and Lucy McCullagh; Justine Mitchell, Royal Prince Alfred Hospital; Elaine, Lynne and Wendy Moore; Dr Michael Morgan, Department of Neurosurgery, Royal North Shore Hospital; Alan and Michelle Page; Rod Palmisano; Nola Rennie; Jenni Rhodes, New South Wales Pony Club Association; John Small, horsebreaker and trainer; Mick Stanley; Christine Silink; Jessica and Michael Singer; Hannah and Ruth Strickland; Brook Talbot; Kim Veringa, Widden Stud, Hunter Valley; Lynne Wilding; Robin Yabsley.

My sincere thanks go to my agent, Selwa Anthony, for her continuing friendship, energy and ideas and for being there whenever I need to talk; to my publisher Linda Funnell for her excitement over the manuscript, her hard work and patience in the final weeks of production; and to my editor, Julia Stiles, for her skill, gentleness and sense of humour. Thank you to all my friends who take such an interest in my stories; to my husband Jim and my two wonderful girls who keep me sane and grounded while writing, and finally to the courageous horses who give horse lovers the world over so much pleasure.

Let your soul take flight and ride with the wind.

Part One

Chapter One

JOANNA KINGSFORD FELT the familiar bubble of excitement as she mounted Magic Belle at the stripping sheds at Sydney's Royal Randwick Racecourse. It was five-twenty a.m. on Wednesday 10 July 1974. It was also five months to the day since she started working as a track rider for her father, Charles Oliver Kingsford, Australia's leading horse trainer. Despite the predawn gloom, the sheds were abuzz with the routine activities Jo loved. Horses snorted, their breath escaping from flared nostrils in dual clouds of ghostly white. Hooves clattered against stone, bridles clinked against the metal railings of the stalls where the horses waited while strappers saddled them in preparation for exercise. As the stable foreman ordered riders to mount, stable hands busily hosed down horses returned from the track, steam rising in great clouds from their taut bodies, their glistening coats darkened by the water.

Wrinkling her nose in pleasure at the smell of fresh hay mixed with warm horse, Jo nudged forward the skittish chestnut thoroughbred, talking to her softly. Magic Belle was the third of the four horses allocated to Jo for exercise that morning, she was also Jo's favourite of the eighty-six horses in the famous Kingsford Lodge. The two-year-old's flanks gleamed eerily in the gloom, her great white blaze and two left socks making her easily distinguishable from the other shadowy horses.

'Daddy letting you ride again?' whispered a rider in his early twenties, passing too close to Magic Belle and upsetting the filly. A scruffy blow-in who had ridden a couple of times before for Charlie, Hawk was only peeved because Jo had refused his offer of a date. She ignored him.

'One day you'll be working for me—if I let you,' she thought darkly.

Slightly taller than the small, mean-eyed track worker, sixteen-year-old Jo was still shedding her puppy fat. Intense, dark violet eyes stared out of her oval face, accentuated by the violet shadows beneath; her untidy ash-blonde plait was jammed under her rider's skullcap, and her whole being exuded a vibrancy that was always evident when she was near horses. Riding, horses and track work were the loves of her life. Tossing her head, she guided Magic Belle around a pile of steaming droppings towards Linda, her partner for the morning.

Linda, holding Jillaroo, a gentle brown filly, was chatting animatedly with Jo's twin brother Rick, despite the antics of his mount Prestigee, a cantankerous three-year-old who was backing around, tossing his head and jerking at his bit. Keeping her distance from the big black colt, Jo called to Linda who quickly mounted and rode over to join her.

'Reckon you can hold her, sis?' quipped Rick, his cheeky grin resting a moment on Jo before returning to Linda as he clicked his horse forward.

'You should ask! No worries with Bella,' retorted Jo, using the horse's stable name. 'At least she's not a bolter with four left feet.' As she spoke, Rick steadied Prestigee as the colt stumbled. Known for his habit of trying to bolt to get his track work over as fast as possible, Prestigee was also renowned for stumbling at slow work. Yet let him stretch out in a race and he became the most sure-footed of animals, usually widening the gap between himself and the other horses with ease. Nevertheless he was always led out to the track by a rider on a pony. Jo and Linda laughed as they waited for Rick and his escort to go ahead and then followed at a safe distance.

A chill breeze bit into Jo's cheeks as the little party headed out towards the Randwick all-weather track. Cutting through her light grey tracksuit top, the wind whipped at her legs encased in tight-fitting jeans and knee-high leather boots. Snatches of conversation from other track workers reached Jo's ears as, shivering occasionally, she moved forward with the others along the dark cinder track which was flanked on either side by white railings, stark against the surrounding gloom. The training supervisor barked out an order. Jo shouted a greeting, the energy of horses and riders, as always, fuelling her excitement.

Across the wide expanse of greyness partially illuminated by the giant stadium floodlights, Jo could just make out swiftly moving shadows. Reaching the crossing at the half mile she and Linda waited as jockeys, hunched high over their mounts, emerged from the murky grey. Thundering past they disappeared back into the gloom, the horses' rasping breath almost as loud as the rhythm of their pounding hooves. Walking the horses smartly across the track, the cinder soft under their hooves, the two girls headed towards the trotting track in the middle of the course to put the horses through their warm-up exercises.

Normally the quietest day in the week, today was unusually busy. Jo and Linda were working left handed to give the horses practice riding the opposite way around the track. Bella was always more nervous with the left-hand canter and Jo's hand tightened on the reins as the filly shied nervously away from a pair of horses returning from the track, clouds of steam billowing from their bodies. Leaning forward Jo patted Bella reassuringly with her gloved hand, talking softly to her as the two girls set off around the trotting track at a steady pace.

Jo had loved Magic Belle from the moment the nervous, skinny yearling had come to Kingsford Lodge. Always around her father's world-famous stables from the moment she could toddle, Jo had naturally absorbed many of Charlie's special techniques in dealing with horses and their different characteristics. In awe of his ability, she had watched in admiration the way Charlie had summed up this frightened, scrappy yearling at the sale, then settled her down back home, building her confidence and her frame so that now, while still highly strung, Bella was a healthy, responsive two-year-old. When Charlie had put Jo on Bella six weeks ago for slow track work, Jo could hardly believe her luck.

'If you can train her up at slow pace work, she's yours,' her father had promised. Jo was stunned. They both knew this horse was destined for great things. From then on horse and girl had been as one, Magic Belle responding to Jo's every command, Jo in tune with the chestnut's quirks and marvelling at the horse's plucky nature.

As she and Linda continued to work the horses, warmer now from the exercise, Jo was glad the gloom hid the pride that shone from her dark, pansylike eyes. Gone were concerns of unfinished school assignments, low grades and detentions from falling asleep in class. Here was her great love. Here lay her dream to become Australia's greatest female trainer. Riding track work was another step closer to that dream. With typical Kingsford stubbornness Jo refused to accept that racing was a male world with little place for female trainers. Ever since she could stagger at the age of two she had seen a top trainer operate. Half her childhood had been spent being baby-sat by horses. Typical comments around the traps that women couldn't handle the heat of the track and were better off in the heat of the kitchen made her blood boil.

For the umpteenth time Jo felt her excitement build as she imagined Magic Belle coming round into the final straight in that mecca of all Australian races, the Melbourne Cup. Surging forward, Jo saw Bella pulling on that extra reserve, stretching out her lead against the other horses, Jo's own colours vibrant on her chosen jockey's back. She could feel the rush of exhilaration as the gentle horse strained to give that bit more. Every nerve taut, Jo watched her strides lengthen, screaming herself hoarse as Bella turned into the final straight amid the tumultuous roar of the crowd and then watched in awe as Bella pulled ahead in those final vital seconds to thunder victorious across the finishing line a clear head in front. Then, clutching her hat as she burst from her place in the members' stand, she grabbed the reins to lead Magic Belle and her jockey in the victory walk, laughter on her full red lips, tears of joy streaming down her face, the magnificent gold chalice held high for all to see. And her father Charles Oliver Kingsford, the greatest Australian horse trainer of them all, his face alight with pride stepping forward to acknowledge her triumph before the cheering onlookers. Just imagining all this made Jo's heart beat faster. Sensing her excitement, Magic Belle started to back away. With a quick sigh Jo brought her mind back to the present, settling them both down again.

'Has Rick asked you out yet?' she tossed at Linda as they settled into the second lap of the track, her stirrups pulled halfway up Bella's side, her legs bunched up almost to her chest.

'Sort of,' replied the slim, dark-haired seventeen-year-old with an embarrassed laugh.

'Are you going to say yes? You know he's batty about you.' Dear Rick. Linda was the first girl her cocky brother had seriously fallen for and he was not at all bothered that she was nearly two years older than him and a good head taller. Linda didn't seem that fussed either.

Just then Rick cantered past, reins pulled in tight, Prestigee's head bent sideways as he strained against Rick's control. The older of the twins by three minutes, to Jo Rick had always been her elder brother. From birth each had known what the other was thinking. She had not needed to tell Rick how much she wanted to ride track work. He had just understood, unlike their brother Bertie, the eldest of the three Kingsford children, who was so moody and jealous. At nineteen and studying law at Sydney University, he continued to sneer at Jo's passion for horses and the twins' involvement in their father's training stables. Jo could never understand how Bertie could be so disparaging about the very livelihood that was giving him everything he wanted: position, academic opportunity and a generous allowance. What infuriated her most was the way he kept ramming home their mother's view that Jo should choose more feminine activities. Showjumping and pony club were fine. Track work was not. Right now Jo didn't give a hang about femininity and she loved the buzz of the racetrack.

When Jo had pleaded to be allowed to help train her father's horses as soon as she turned sixteen, she had refused to accept his argument that there was no future for her on the track. In the end it had been Rick with his quirky smile, blond hair and deep violet eyes, identical to her own, who had persuaded her father otherwise. Rick recognised Jo's innate ability with horses, he also recognised that she was better than he at training them. While they both naturally assumed he would step into Charlie's shoes as head of Kingsford Lodge, Rick acknowledged that Jo had greater dedication, a greater love of the animals and a greater attention to detail. Charlie had recognised his daughter's natural aptitude too, but he hadn't taken her seriously. The real problem for him was that she was a girl. However, to Jo's great joy, three weeks after her sixteenth birthday, he had capitulated.

Kookaburras' raucous cries heralded the arrival of dawn as Jo and Linda cantered around the sandy track. Hugging the inside rail and shielded by Jillaroo, where Bella would feel more secure as other horses pounded past, Jo exulted in the rhythmic sway of the horse beneath her. Her cheeks tingled from the rush of cold air, bringing tears to her eyes and with them the sudden sense of loss she always felt as her ride with Bella drew to its end. She could hear her father yelling orders from the Pizza Hut, the octagonal tower in the centre of the racetrack where trainers watched their horses and riders perform. Jo gave a small sigh. Once more round the track and she would have to hand Bella over to Archie, her father's leading jockey, to complete the fast track work in preparation for Bella's first trial on Friday.

Light seeped slowly over the horizon, fighting for recognition against the stadium lights. Bella was fussing again over the left-hand canter. Still hugging the rail, Jo steadied her down as the cold dawn mist rose from the course and a towering grey mass revealed itself as the imposing Royal Randwick grandstand. Rick thundered by on Prestigee, the horse now less frantic to bolt as the pace work quickened. Jo smiled briefly, alert for any change in Bella's steady canter. A few paces on Prestigee stumbled.

'That horse really does have four left feet. To anyone who didn't know he could be mistaken as going lame,' Jo thought, glancing at Rick to check everything was all right. With a stab of intuition she sensed Rick was becoming unsettled.

Suddenly a sparrow flew out of the grass. Startled, Bella shied into Jillaroo. Linda swerved her mount just in time to avert a collision. Then Jo's heart lurched as out of the mist a riderless horse thundered straight towards them. Digging her heels into the horse's flanks, Jo urged Bella forward, trying to swing her out of the path of the runaway horse. Already unnerved, the sight of another horse careering towards her was too much for Bella. Whinnying in fear, ears back, eyes staring, Bella bolted. Unable to hold her back, all Jo could do was cling on, fingers dug into the thick chestnut mane, as Bella, showing the speed Jo always believed she possessed, hurtled towards Rick and Prestigee, tail flying, eating up the distance between them in seconds.

'Rick! Look out!' screamed Jo, her voice snatched

by the wind. She was almost on top of him.

Feeling Jo's terror, Rick glanced quickly over his shoulder and saw the wild-eyed Bella. Prestigee stumbled again. Cursing, Rick jerked the horse's head savagely round to save himself from being thrown off and lost his balance. The next few seconds were crystal clear in Jo's mind. Like a slow-motion film a part of her watched detached as the colt stumbled a third time and Bella cannoned into him. Rick was tossed from the saddle like a doll and came crashing to the ground as Prestigee fell and Bella ran over the top of them. Lifted by the force of the impact and thrown clear, Jo heard the snap of bone as Bella fell on Prestigee, the two petrified horses thrashing about on top of one another, before she crashed against the rail. Excruciating pain shot through her shoulder and she tasted blood in her mouth before she blacked out.

Stocky and self-assured, the great horse trainer Charlie Kingsford walked Red Star around in a circle on the cinders in front of the Pizza Hut as the dawn light gradually turned the silhouettes of riders, stable hands and trainers into people. Powerful binoculars slung round his neck, the collar of his thick jacket turned up against the chill air, a designer hat on his head—a quirk in his dress that had become synonymous with him since his start in the industry—Charlie shouted to a strapper to give the track rider a leg-up. Rapping out his instructions, he walked over to Archie who was leaning casually against the railing that circled the Pizza Hut, talking to one of the riders in his broad Scottish accent. It was turning out to be a good morning for Charlie. Rick had handled that difficult bugger Prestigee well in the canter. If ever a horse wanted to bolt his work and get home it was Prestigee, but he was a good horse and had already brought in some good steady winnings at country races. Rick had his measure, though, and horse and rider had worked well this morning.

By God how he loved that boy. Charlie's heart swelled with pride. Rick was his hope for the future, the next head of the Kingsford dynasty, so different from his elder brother Bertie. Charlie blew out his cheeks. He would never come to terms with the disappointment he felt in his eldest son's disinterest in training but he had put it behind him. He had done the right thing by Bertie and had set him up at university; in fact, he'd given all three kids a good education, something Charlie'd never had himself. Now Rick was living up to his expectations and his love of the racing industry was obvious. Overcome with a sudden rush of emotion, Charlie pulled out his mauve silk handkerchief, blew his nose and shoved it back in his jacket pocket.

Jo, too, was showing surprising talent this morning on Magic Belle. Not much to look at as a weanling, it was the horse's great blood line, plus an instinctive feeling that she would turn out right, that had convinced him to buy her. In the last six weeks Jo had brought the horse on a treat with slow track work. Now girl and horse seemed to be made for one another. He could not deny his daughter's natural talent. If only she'd been born a boy. But she'd be right. After she'd done this modelling course Nina was so insistent on putting her through, she'd find a good man, a doctor or a vet or a barrister, get married and support her husband in his practice.

'Jo's on Magic Belle, when she gets here take her up to the three-quarter and then gallop her home for the last two furlongs,' Charlie said to Archie. 'What's keeping the girl anyways?' He raised his binoculars to his eyes, searching the misty track, and his heart missed a beat. Surely that was Prestigee, only he was riderless and heading straight towards the grass.

'Someone get that horse!' Charlie yelled, pointing at the fleeing animal. Where the heck was Rick? He swung his binoculars around. There was no sign of Bella or Jo. His throat suddenly felt tight. Then he heard the track supervisor's voice over the walkie-talkie and saw the ambulance speeding up the adjacent track, closely followed by the horse ambulance. His mind blank with fear, Charlie tore across the dirt in the direction of the moving vehicles.

The track attendant who had come running down from his station at the top of the hill when he saw Bella crash into Prestigee, gave a quick intake of breath at the havoc before him. Jo lay in a crumpled heap close to the rail, her face ashen, a large bruise already rising where her face had struck the wood. Rick lay several metres away, one arm twisted in an unnatural position, blood pouring from his broken nose. Having checked they were both still breathing, he held a handkerchief to Rick's nose, one eye on the thrashing Bella. In danger of rolling towards Jo, she kept struggling to get to her feet, her lips stretched taut over her teeth in a grimace of agony. As each horse raced by, her eyes rolled in terror and she struggled further, her white socks fighting the empty air. There was no sign of Prestigee.

'Hey, this one's bleeding bad!' the attendant called as the ambulance officers arrived and came running across to the injured twins. Heaving a sigh of relief as the officers took charge, he moved quickly to Bella. Two other horsemen materialised and while one held Bella's head down, the attendant relayed a message to send for the vet.

Breathing heavily from his frantic run, Charlie arrived on the scene and watched in shock as the officer in charge quickly knelt beside Rick, checking for vital signs, then covered him with a blanket and staunched the bleeding.

'We'd better deal with this kid first,' the ambulance officer called to his assistant. 'Possible head injuries.'

'Righto. Here, take this blanket and cover the other casualty, sir,' he ordered Charlie, holding out a blanket, 'but be careful not to move her.'

Charlie accepted the blanket with trembling fingers. 'Make sure you look after that lad, he's my son.'

Pity flickered across the officer's face. 'We'll do our best, sir.'

Part of Charlie seemed to be detached from reality as he carefully spread the blanket around his fragile daughter, the deep violet shadows almost black beneath her closed lids, her lips the colour of parchment. He had seen enough accidents on the track to know the extent of injuries sustained in a fall like this one. He also knew that shock was the first big danger and, if not treated immediately, could kill before the casualty had a chance to get to hospital. He was utterly calm, a man in command of his emotions, assisting at just another track-side accident. None of this was connected to him. In a moment he'd wake up back at the stripping sheds congratulating everyone on their hard work.

Sliding a brace under Rick's neck, the officers then bandaged his shoulder so it and his neck were immobilised, thereby reducing the risk of further spinal injury. Careful to leave his skullcap in place because of the suspected head injuries, they lifted him onto the stretcher and into the ambulance. Internal injuries were the other worry. They had to get both casualties to hospital as fast as possible.

'Thanks, mate,' the officer nodded to Charlie who stepped aside from Jo. But Charlie hovered anxiously nearby, feeling hopelessly inadequate, the lines in his suntanned cheeks deep furrows.

'Go and sit with your son, sir,' suggested the ambulance officer as they repeated the process with Jo.

As she was lifted onto the stretcher, Jo gave a low moan and her eyelids flickered open for a second. Charlie's heart fluttered with relief then turned cold as he climbed into the ambulance and saw Rick's grey still face. He hardly seemed to be breathing at all.

'Please, dear God, let them both live,' Charlie muttered. Why, oh why, had he ever agreed to letting them do track work? He knew the dangers. Countless times he had seen the shocking injuries sustained by jockeys. Nina had warned him, but he had ignored her.

'Mr Kingsford, I'm afraid we can't save the horse.'

Charlie looked up startled, into the course vet's face. In his numb distress he had completely forgotten Magic Belle, the horse that was to have brought him so much luck. He glanced over to the chestnut filly. She had been allowed to stagger up and she was standing on three feet, the fourth leg dangling uselessly. Charlie didn't need to be told the suffering she was in.

'Do what you have to, Jack,' he nodded grimly to the vet as the ambulance doors closed behind him.

Horses you could buy more of, but not your own flesh and blood. How could he have been such a bloody irresponsible fool? Glancing briefly out of the window he saw the horse sink to the ground. Jack would have done it quickly and mercifully.

Charlie's hand hovered near Rick's cheek. God keep these two alive. As the ambulance drove out of the gates of Randwick Racecourse the sun spilled over the horizon in a golden blaze of glory.

Chapter Two

NINA KINGSFORD PULLED her pink angora bed-jacket closer around her shoulders. Smoothing back her chestnut brown hair and adjusting the strap on her ivory satin nightgown, she poured herself a cup of freshly ground coffee from the Villeroy and Boch china pot on the breakfast tray the housekeeper had just deposited on her lap. The gold and crystal clock on the mantelpiece above the marble fireplace, a recent present from Charlie, chimed ten o'clock. Adding two artificial sweeteners and a large dollop of whipped cream to her cup, Nina stirred twice, scooped a large frothy spoonful into her mouth and sucked it clean. Sighing happily she then dipped a small piece of toast into her cup and fed it to the fluffy white poodle lying panting eagerly beside her on the king-sized bed.

'There you go, Suzie Wong, Mummy's little darling. Doesn't Jackie look after us well?' she smiled, fondling the little dog, fiddling a moment with the pink satin ribbon in its curls. At forty-one Nina Kingsford was still beautiful, even in her tousled unmade-up state her skin had a youthful glow. Seductive brown eyes peeped from under darkened eyelashes, her high cheekbones delicately tanned. Casually strewn on the table beside her was an assortment of jewellery, including a heavy sapphire and diamond ring, a solid gold chain and two gold bracelets.

'Jackie, shut that curtain just a touch, there's a dear. The sun's a bit bright for us both this morning,' Nina said to the housekeeper, a short dark woman in her late forties who, having pulled back the bright floral curtains, was busy hooking the heavy twisted green cord around the gilt ring in the wall. 'Oh, and find me the social pages, will you. They make these papers so awkward to manage.' Nina buttered another piece of toast and bit off a tiny morsel.

Cheerfully Jackie obliged. She enjoyed working for the Kingsfords. Always concerned for his wife's welfare, Mr Kingsford paid handsomely for Jackie's services and she had the run of the beautiful mansion at Coogee, one of Sydney's smart eastern suburbs. Jackie also loved meeting the rich and famous who over the years had walked through the Kingsfords' doors.

'Just give me a call, Mrs Kingsford, if there is anything else you want. Your hair appointment is at eleven-fifteen and your outfit's all pressed and ready to go. You just have to decide on the hat,' she smiled, going through her regular morning routine. 'Oh, and I've organised for Frank to wash and polish the Bentley.'

'You're so clever, Jackie, I don't have to think of a thing,' said Nina, licking the tip of one manicured finger, already engrossed in the *Sydney Morning Herald* social pages searching for her photo. 'There I am!' she exclaimed gleefully, stabbing at the picture with a bright red fingernail as the door closed softly behind Jackie. 'Damn, I should have worn a bigger hat. That dreadful Angela Bagot has practically squeezed me out.'

Pouting like a spoiled child, she lay back against the pillows and then brightened at the thought of lunch. At least today she didn't have to do the flowers and chocies bit at the hospital with Charlie's wretched jockeys. Amazingly there hadn't been a bad accident at the track for over two months.

The gilt and ivory telephone jangled angrily from the bedside table.

'Helloo,' Nina sang as she answered, visualising herself in her latest little creation from Paris. Hearing her husband's voice on the other end, her tone changed to petulance. 'I thought you were going to join me for breakfast, Charlie? Why aren't you home yet? It's awfully late and I thought we were going to have a bit of fun before I have to go out.'

From the other end Charlie kept his voice as calm as possible. 'Neene, I'm ringing from the hospital,' he said quietly.

Nina groaned. 'Please don't ask me to come and visit your jockeys. I've got a very big luncheon today. Everyone'll be there.' She sank back into the pillows, only half listening to what Charlie was saying. How utterly inconvenient. He would insist. Then she would have to leave early and miss out on the big jewellery display.

Charlie's reply was tight and controlled, his words carefully chosen as he braced himself for the inevitable hysterics. 'Neene, listen to me. I'm not talking about one of my jockeys. It's Jo and Rick. They've had a bit of a fall, but they're all right,' he said slowly, wishing he could be with his wife instead of having to tell her over the phone.

Nina's fingers gripped the handpiece, the colour draining from her face. 'You're joking ... This is one of your weird jokes,' she blurted, pushing away Suzie Wong who was trying to lick her face.

'Now just stay calm, Neene darling, and listen,' implored Charlie. 'The twins are fine. They were riding track work when one of the horses stumbled. They've both been seen by the doctor but he wants them to stay in here at the Prince of Wales under observation for a bit longer.'

Before he could explain further, Nina let out a howl of misery. Forgetting the tray, she pushed away the bedclothes and swung her legs over the side of the bed, sending her breakfast sliding down the blankets and crashing to the floor. The pink bedjacket slipped from her shoulders. Suzie Wong leapt in fright from the bed and cowered under a wicker chair.

'My babies, Joanna, my Ricky, my beautiful little babies! How did it happen? How could you let this happen? Oh my God, I have to get to them!'

Hearing the crash, Jackie burst into the room as Nina stood up, turned around in the debris of broken china and burst into floods of tears.

'Mrs Kingsford . . . ' Jackie cried, rushing over to the white-lipped Nina.

'My babies!' Nina choked, her dark eyes filling with tears, her slim shoulders trembling. The receiver lay limp in her hand, Charlie calling frantically down the phone.

Carefully sitting Nina back on the bed Jackie rescued the handpiece. 'Let me talk to your husband, Mrs Kingsford,' she said quickly. With one arm firmly round Nina she listened carefully as Charlie explained. 'I'll sort it all out, sir,' she replied, controlled. 'No, no, she'll be fine, I'll make sure Mrs Kingsford is fine. I'll explain everything and we'll wait for you to organise a car to collect her.'

Nina snatched the phone from her. 'I'm not an invalid. I can drive myself there,' she snapped, swiftly wiping away a tear. If there was one thing she loved, it was driving her Bentley. 'Charlie, tell me again, are they really fine? Why can't they come home straightaway?' she hiccupped.

Five minutes later, the colour returned to her cheeks, a slightly calmer Nina replaced the receiver on its cradle. Suzie Wong had come out from hiding and was busy licking the cream off the broken crockery. Gathering the little ball of fluff in her arms, Nina hugged her close, the tears springing again to her eyes.

'Mr Kingsford wouldn't tell you Miss Joanna and Mr Rick were fine if they weren't,' said Jackie, quickly sensing Nina's mounting hysteria. Sometimes she wondered if Nina really understood how much Mr Kingsford loved her, or how much he sheltered her from the harsher realities of life. 'Come on, we'll get you a nice warm shower.' Slipping an ivory satin bathrobe around Nina's shoulders, Jackie firmly propelled her towards the bathroom.

Forty-five minutes later, immaculate in a daffodil yellow wool suit over which she had casually thrown a three-quarter length, mock leopard-fur coat, Nina stepped out of the silver Bentley in the grounds of the Prince of Wales Hospital. A voluminous yellow and ivory silk scarf wrapped Princess Grace of Monaco-style around her soft brown hair and creamy neck added the final touch.

Charlie walked rapidly towards her from the casualty exit. Thank goodness they had Jackie. Knowing his wife's volatile nature he had been terrified she might get hysterical while driving to the hospital and have an accident, but Jackie's rational approach had obviously calmed her considerably. As always Nina looked enchanting, enchanting and vulnerable. Tucking his arm firmly under hers, he led Nina into the casualty waiting area and sat her down.

'We still have to wait for the doctor's report,' he explained, stroking her fingers gently and watching her closely, the weariness creeping into his voice. It had been a long and scary morning. 'Then we'll get them home. Jackie'll help you look after them once they're home but you'll be right. They'll just need rest.'

Now that she was close to Charlie all Nina's calm suddenly dissolved as shock and fear returned. Pressing at her eyes to stop the tears running down her cheeks and spoiling her make-up, she turned to her husband. 'Are they ... I mean, how badly were they ... ?' she ventured, her bottom lip trembling.

'They've got a few scratches and bruises and Jo's got a couple of stitches in her forehead but they'll mend.'

Nina let out an anguished cry. 'Not her face! She's going to be a model!' Suddenly her fear turned to anger. Shaking her head in disbelief, she grabbed at Charlie's sleeve. 'This need never have happened. You know how I hate either of them anywhere near that wretched track. Why did you let them ride? Why don't you listen to me?'

Charlie's expression hardened. 'We can talk about all this later,' he said quietly.

'Why later, why not now?' she demanded for all to hear, her fingers digging through the cloth of his jacket, chest heaving, the tears finally spilling down her cheeks.

A nurse stopped and asked, 'Can I get you anything?'

Charlie shook his head and waved her away. The interruption was the distraction Nina needed.

Abruptly she snatched her hand away, staring accusingly at her husband, mascara smeared black under her eyes.

'How could you?' she repeated. 'Don't you care about your children? Oh my God, what am I doing sitting here? Where are they? I have to go to them.' Without thinking, she leaped up and started running down the corridor, her high heels tapping against the grey linoleum.

Charlie caught up with her in two long strides and she crumpled against him. Gathering her into his arms, he stroked her soft brown hair, the silk scarf fallen loose around her neck, her reaction sending his own emotions perilously close to breaking point. From the moment of the accident he had gone over and over those very same questions. Nina's shoulders heaved uncontrollably, great rasping cries tearing from her throat, her beautifully toned body trembling like a trapped butterfly against his; the heavy, musky scent of Oscar de la Renta wafting from her skin jarringly out of place in the antiseptic hospital. Inappropriately he thought, 'You are a child in a magnificent, erotic body that has never ceased to entice me.' He had never really expected more from Nina. Though he loved her desperately, from the beginning he had known he would always be the grown-up in their marriage.

'They're both resting at the moment, Neene,' he said softly as her sobs gradually subsided into intermittent gulps. Releasing her gently, he reached for her hands. Clasping them tightly, he explained briefly the extent of the children's injuries. 'Rick's practically back to his usual cheeky self, except he's a bit sore, but Jo's still pretty drowsy. They had to sedate her fairly heavily to put her shoulder back. Once the stitches are removed you'll hardly know it even happened,' he finished confidently. He dared not share the full extent of his fears with Nina. Only when he had learned that the twins were out of immediate danger had he dared to contact her.

Considering his fall, Rick had made a remarkable recovery. To Charlie's overwhelming relief his son had come to in the ambulance, although his breathing was shallow and he was obviously in a lot of pain. As well as having broken his nose, he had a broken collarbone, had jarred his neck and cracked three ribs. Charlie was still amazed Rick had escaped being crushed by the falling horses.

But it was Jo the doctors were still concerned about. As well as having dislocated her shoulder and badly strained her right wrist, they were worried about possible internal haemorrhaging from the bump on her head. Despite the skullcap having protected her from most of the impact of the fall, the deep gash and severe bruising on her forehead showed she had come down pretty hard. When Charlie had left a very drowsy Jo to find Nina, one of the resident doctors had just checked for any deterioration in her condition but found none. However, both twins were still being very closely monitored and would be for the next few hours.

Nina withdrew her hands and blew her nose on a wisp of lace-edged linen, her dark eyes flashing dangerously at Charlie. 'I kept telling you not to let them ride those wretched horses of yours. That's why we have track workers,' she sniffed, wiping away the smudged mascara and pulling the scarf back over her head. Smoothing back her lustrous hair, she retied the knot at the nape of her neck. 'Haven't I seen enough of all this with your jockeys?' Nina glanced sideways at Charlie, picking at her long red nails, her fingers trembling uncontrollably. 'I knew something like this would happen. If they . . .' The words choked in her throat. Her eyes threatened to spill over again with tears. '. . . I will never forgive you.' Her voice was a husky whisper.

Stroking his wife's cheek, Charlie said softly, as though speaking to a child, 'Neene, my love, they are both fine. They'll be right, I promise, and so will you. We'll all be fine.' At least they had managed to avoid full-on hysterics. He glanced at his watch. He still had a while before his meeting. 'Now, powder your pretty little nose and we'll go and visit them. What Jo and Rick need most right now is their mother to be with them.'

Nina blew her nose again. 'Hospitals give me the creeps,' she sniffed. Quickly she pulled her compact from her tiny clutch bag and checked her face in the mirror. 'I look terrible.' Charlie waited, outwardly calm, as she dabbed soft peach to her rosebud lips, a dash of powder to her nose, finishing with a liberal spray of perfume. With a final shuddering hiccup she rearranged her coat and together they went to find the twins.

In a semidrugged haze Jo vaguely remembered people moving her along corridors smelling of antiseptic, cold metal against her skin, and being asked the same questions over and over as she wafted in and out of sleep. She remembered the sudden relief from the pain as she drifted off just before her shoulder was put back, and at one point she thought she smelled her mother's perfume. Now as she opened her eyes and looked around she wondered if it had been a dream. Covered by a blue cotton hospital blanket, she was lying on a vinyl-covered bed in a tiny cubicle, a pillow under her head, pale green curtains drawn around her. Her right wrist was tightly bandaged and her arm was in a sling. Her head and shoulder throbbed mercilessly. At the foot of her bed a young male nurse was reading her notes.

'Welcome back. How're you feeling?'

'Not great,' Jo mumbled. 'I think I'm going to be sick.' The nurse shoved a pale green kidney-shaped bowl under her chin and she retched before collapsing back against the pillow, waiting for the world to stop spinning. She felt as though someone had pierced her shoulder with red-hot irons. 'How's my brother?' she asked, looking up anxiously.

'Doctor will be in to see you shortly,' answered the nurse, removing the bowl and straightening her bed. The curtains parted and a white-coated doctor appeared.

'Well now, young lady, how are you feeling? We've been very worried about you.'

'My head hurts and I feel sick. How's Rick?' insisted Jo. The drowsiness was beginning to recede.

'He's doing fine,' replied the doctor, lifting her eyelids and checking her pupils. 'Now, can you tell me your name?'

'Joanna Kingsford.'

'And do you know what day of the week it is?'

'Wednesday?' she replied.

'Good, now could you just wiggle your toes for me on this foot.'

Jo obliged. 'What about my brother?' she demanded, her anxiety increasing. 'Why does everyone keep treating me like a child?

'Let's get you sorted out first,' replied the doctor smoothly. 'Can you feel this?' He ran his thumbnail along the outside of her foot. Jo's foot jerked away from his hand.

'Ouch! Where is Rick? Will he be able to ride again? My horse fell ... ' The words stuck in her throat. Unwanted tears sprang to her eyes as she vividly relived the accident. How could he possibly just be fine?

'Sorry.' The doctor repeated the process on Jo's other foot. 'Your brother's knocked himself about a bit, and it'll hurt for a while when he breathes, but I'd say he's on the road to recovery. He was even sitting up a short while ago demanding something to eat,' he continued, checking her other reflexes. 'I don't know what good fairy is looking after him but he is certainly a very lucky lad. Maybe it's having a sister like you to worry about him.' He smiled down at Jo as he felt her pulse. Jo smiled feebly back. 'We'll give you something for that headache.'

'I've got this really strange feeling at the back of my neck too,' said Jo.

'You've had a pretty good shaking up so you will be a bit sore for a while, but you're young and fit. How old are you?'

'Sixteen.'

He nodded to the male nurse hovering at the foot of the bed, his face a bland mask. The girl was certainly alert but the headache and neck pain concerned him. 'She can have some more painkillers now and I might just recheck those X-rays.' Handing the doctor the big ochre envelope, the nurse then vanished through the curtains. 'Nope. Everything looks good to me,' the doctor said confidently after examining the X-rays. 'Try to rest and we'll come and see you in another hour.' He replaced the envelope at the foot of the bed and left just as Nina swept through the curtains, closely followed by Charlie.

'Oh Joanna, my darling girl,' she cried, rushing over to the bed. 'You were asleep before. Daddy said not to disturb you.' About to envelop her daughter in a hug, she stopped when she saw Jo's arm in the sling. Tears filled her eyes as she got a clear view of the disfiguring bruise on Jo's right temple, the black stitches stark against the fake suntanlike antiseptic paint. 'Your face, darling! Oh heavens, it's far worse than Daddy said, you poor, poor love.' She leaned over and gave Jo a quick kiss in the air just above her left cheek. Turning to Charlie, she covered her trembling bottom lip with her handkerchief. 'Charlie, are you sure it won't leave a scar?'

'What are you on about, woman? It's only a small scratch,' replied Charlie cheerfully, seeing the effect of Nina's comment on Jo. He grinned down at his daughter, squeezing her unharmed hand. Not only was he relieved to see Jo so much brighter, he had just learned the skull X-rays had shown up no abnormalities in either twin. Jo smiled tentatively back at her father. 'But I tell you what, that's the last of track work for you, my girl,' Charlie continued with mock severity. 'You've both given us a pretty good scare.'

Jo's face fell. 'You don't really mean it, do you, Dad?' Her violet eyes stared anxiously up at her father out of her pale oval face.

'We'll see,' he said, suddenly sombre. He hadn't actually meant to sound so final. Everyone knew that the best thing possible after such a fall was to stick the person straight back on a horse, but after the fright of nearly losing them both today, Charlie wasn't so sure. Nor could he relax yet, they both looked pretty right but the doctor had said he wanted to keep them under observation for a bit longer just to be certain.

Seeing her father's serious expression Jo asked, 'Dad, is Rick really okay?'

'Except for a broken collarbone, a couple of

cracked ribs and broken nose, he's fine,' Charlie answered, thankful she had not pursued the issue of track work. 'In fact, why don't you ask him yourself?' he added, swinging around as Rick walked through the curtains, dark purple bruises under his eyes, plaster across his nose, his right arm, like his twin sister's, in a sling.

'Still pretending you're sick, eh, sis?' Rick joked, the pain in his eyes at odds with his cheeky grin. 'I was the one the doctors and ambos were getting all steamed up over, remember?'

Blinking back tears of relief, Jo gave him a lop-sided smile. 'You made more of a mess of your face than I did,' she retorted, suddenly feeling much better. If Rick was teasing her, he had to be doing fine. 'What about Bella?' Jo asked, her eyes on her father.

For a moment Charlie was silent. 'I'm afraid she had to be destroyed.' Jo felt a stab of misery. 'Jack took care of it. It was quick.'

'You won't need to be worrying with those wretched racehorses again, sweetie,' Nina broke in.

Suddenly Jo could no longer keep the tears at bay. How could her mother say such a thing? She just didn't understand. Quickly Jo turned her face away. Poor Bella. She was such a brave, clever horse, clever enough to miss trampling Rick as she fell herself. Brushing away her tears she turned back, pushed the blanket away and sat up, cautiously swinging her legs over the edge of the bed. 'No point in hanging around here. You ready to leave, Rick?' she asked, her voice slightly shaky.

'You bet. 'Cept this bloke won't let me,' he grinned back, indicating the male nurse behind him, his cheerful reply easing the tension.

'I'd tell the lot of you to shove off, only Matron

wouldn't be too happy,' retorted the nurse, handing Jo two white tablets and pushing back the curtains. He smiled apologetically to Nina and Charlie. 'No, you should be right to go later this afternoon. We always keep suspected head injuries in for at least four to six hours.'

'I'm not a head injury, thanks, mate. Look, real wood,' replied Rick, tapping his fist against his skull and grimacing. 'Thanks for the chat anyway,' he added, sitting down heavily on a vacant chair.

'No worries, mate,' the nurse said, and retreated.

Charlie glanced at his watch. It was almost one o'clock. He rubbed his hands together. 'Righty-o! Apart from looking like you've been in a major fight, I reckon the both of you've been very, very lucky. So now you've shown me you're well enough to create mayhem, I'm going to leave your mother to sort you out.' The twins laughed. Nina's eyebrows shot up. 'Now don't go getting upset, Neene. I already told you I've got this bloke coming down from Brisbane I arranged to meet ages ago.'

Nina opened her mouth to protest. Not only was she shaken by the whole event, she was still very angry at Charlie.

'No, Mum, really, we'll be right,' reassured Rick quickly, seeing the look that passed between his parents. 'I'm feeling much better. So's Jo, aren't you?' Jo nodded. 'The doc says there's nothing I can do about my ribs. They'll just mend and a broken nose'll add a bit of character to my face.' He started to laugh, the pain in his chest cutting it abruptly short. Nina was looking increasingly anxious at the idea of driving the two home by herself.

'We'll be fine, Mum,' Jo echoed.

'Anyway, Sam'll be wanting his breakfast,' went on Rick. 'Poor old fella'll be wondering what's keeping us. I suppose you didn't feed him, did you, Mum?' The thirteen-year-old golden retriever, a present for the twins' third birthday, had always been Rick's dog. Each morning, from his spot on the wide, tiled porch steps of their house at Coogee, nose between his paws, his sorrowful velvet brown eyes watched Rick's every move as the group left for track work. Nothing could shift Sam from the porch until Rick's return and his greeting was always the same—delirious excitement, Sam's tail and half his body wagging furiously as Rick patted him. The greeting over, Rick always fed him before doing anything else.

'You didn't really expect me to worry about dogs when I heard what had happened to you two, did you?' cried Nina.

Charlie gave Jo a final peck on the cheek. 'Look after your mother,' he whispered and started to walk away.

Abruptly Nina ran after him. 'You don't have to go, damn it, Charlie,' she spat, panting to keep up with his long strides.

'Yes, I do.' He increased his pace. 'The doc says they're both going to be fine and this Brisbane horse's blood line is worth getting serious about. Especially since I've just lost a potentially great brood mare.' Charlie was panting too. 'I'm late. Matron says you can take them home after the doc's next rounds. Then just see they rest. You've got Jackie. If you're worried, bring them straight back here, and here, just in case, take this.' He pulled a wad of banknotes from his pocket and pressed it into Nina's hand. Before she could reply he had vanished through the exit doors.

Nina stared angrily at the empty corridor. 'Horses, always bloody horses before anything else and this,

this'll fix anything,' she screeched, waving the wad of notes. She knew she was being unfair, horses were Charlie's livelihood, and in truth she loved the glamour that surrounded their life; the money was his way of trying to make her feel better, but none of this need have happened. Stuffing the notes into her purse, she walked back to the cubicle.

'You can say goodbye to that place,' said Rick from the back of the Bentley, flicking at his head injury card as they drove out of the hospital gates and turned in the direction of Coogee. Standard head injury cards were presented routinely to all discharged patients who had experienced a blow to the head, however mild. Rick scanned the printed advice trying to ignore his aching ribs. Headache, blurred vision, nausea . . . He tossed the card on the seat next to his mother's coat, turning his thoughts to Sam.

Jo lay back in the front seat, enjoying the warmth of the afternoon sun flooding through the car windows. 'Sam'll be happy,' she said over her shoulder, reading Rick's thoughts. While much of her drug-induced drowsiness had worn off and the painkillers were still deadening most of the pain in her shoulder and head, she suddenly felt exhausted. The back of her neck was bothering her again.

'You all right in the back, Rick?' inquired Nina brusquely, briefly glancing in the rear-vision mirror, her scarf back in place, her fingers gripping the steering wheel. Still furious at Charlie's abrupt departure, the full force of the responsibility of getting the twins home on her own suddenly hit her. The knowledge that Jackie would be there to take over as soon as they turned through the wrought-iron gates didn't help at all. Jo still looked far too pale and Matron's dire warnings and those dreadful head injury cards had done nothing to allay Nina's fears. For the first time in her life she drove frustratingly slowly, decreasing speed well before each traffic light so as not to jolt the twins, creeping round each curve, ignoring honking horns and abusive shouts from frustrated drivers behind wound-up windows, her own level of frustration rising.

'Stupid idiot!' snapped Nina, accelerating as a car tried to cut in front of her, wondering if they would ever get home at this pace. She allowed the speed to creep up. 'You do realise what your father said earlier goes, don't you, Joanna? No more of this silly track work rubbish for you.' Jo mumbled a reply, half asleep. 'Jo! Listen to what I'm saying. Your father may have been joking earlier but I am deadly serious. You're lucky you haven't wrecked your good looks in all of this. Model agencies don't accept just anyone, you know.'

She flicked her indicator angrily to turn off the main road, only to find the traffic had been diverted. 'A burst water main. That's all I need,' she exclaimed, tapping her nails against the steering wheel, her chatter an outlet for her frustration and anxiety. 'And though your father may think differently, I know you'll have a scar from those stitches for the rest of your life. It's a good job I know who I know. No, my girl. It's pony club and dressage if you have to ride, and you can start acting like a lady.'

'Yes Mum,' replied Jo, wishing her mother would stop talking. Trying to concentrate was making her headache worse and she didn't have the strength to argue. She watched the fluffy white clouds drifting across the cobalt sky. Nina started up again as the traffic in lane two slowed to a crawl.

'Come on, Mum, give her a break,' said Rick. 'It wasn't her fault the horse bolted.'

'Rick, you just stay out of this. You're the one who caused the accident in the first place,' she shot. 'If you'd been paying attention to what you were doing, you wouldn't have fallen off your horse and caused all this trouble.'

'Oh, Mum, that's not fair,' cried Jo, leaping to his defence. 'Rick was doing his best on a difficult horse.'

'Listen to the pair of you. If the horse was difficult, why were you riding it? Your dad's got no sense at all. I've told him time and time again, I don't want you near those horses and that goes for you too, Rick, I've had enough of all this nonsense. The only one with any sense is Bertie.' She braked suddenly, almost running into the car in front. 'Oops, sorry.' Oh God, this was all such a mess. How had they ended up back on Anzac Parade going north? And where had all this traffic come from? It shouldn't take more than ten minutes to get home. 'You seem very full of your own opinions, Rick, how about telling me how to get home quicker.' The cars were moving at a reasonable speed again. 'Rick! Answer me when I speak to you, and you can cut out those stupid grunting sounds.'

Panic hit both Nina and Jo simultaneously. Nina's eyes flew to the rear-view mirror. Jo whirled around in her seat, her pulse quickening in fear, her sudden movement sending a searing pain through her shoulder. Rick lay deathly pale, slumped against the window. Ignoring her own pain, Jo heaved herself over the seat into the back and shook Rick's knee hard.

'Rick! Wake up, talk to me!' Rick did not respond. She shook him again. Still he didn't react. His breathing was coming in noisy erratic gasps. 'Mum! Mum! Stop the car!' shrieked Jo. 'There's something wrong with Rick! We've got to get him back to hospital!' She started trembling. She had no idea what to do.

'I can't stop here,' shrieked Nina. Now halfway into the fast lane, she dared not take her eyes off the road.

'Rick, answer me. Please! Open your eyes,' pleaded Jo, shaking him again, her heart pounding against her ribs. Rick's eyes stayed closed, his breathing changed to frightening gurgling sounds.

'Mum! You've got to turn back. Get into the right-hand lane. Wait for a gap in the cars and then just turn across the traffic,' ordered Jo. 'There's one coming up now, after this green truck.'

Trembling violently, Nina swerved the car.

'Get over, you stupid bitch!' screamed a driver whom Nina, in her panic, hadn't seen coming up fast on the outside. Nina slewed the car sideways just in time to avoid a collision, her sweating hands slipping on the steering wheel.

'Ignore him, Mum!' shouted Jo. 'Okay, I'll tell you when to turn. After this white car. Now, Mum, now! Go!' As Jo held Rick steady in his seat, Nina, hand on the horn, swung the car around in a U-turn across the oncoming traffic and pressed her foot to the floor.

The next fifteen minutes were the worst in Jo's life. As Nina charged back towards the hospital, jumping lanes, dodging cars and shooting red lights, Jo tried to protect Rick from swaying all over the car. He had flopped back against the seat, his breathing progressively more unnerving and gargling.

Swinging through the Prince of Wales gates, Nina screeched the car to a halt outside the entrance to casualty, the smell of burning rubber filling the air. Jo was out of the car almost before it stopped. Shouting at her mother to stay with Rick but not to move him, she ran screaming through the doors. Within seconds she reappeared with two attendants pushing a rattling trolley and running towards the car behind her. It took Jo as well as the two men to lift the unconscious Rick, a dead weight, out of the Bentley and onto the trolley and to propel him through the big swing doors, Nina teetering behind in her high heels.

'Code zero to casualty, code zero to casualty,' called the nurse at reception over the public address system, the signal to all doctors and nurses in the area to get as fast as they could to the emergency. Three nurses, the senior registrar and a junior resident doctor raced down the corridor towards them. As the attendants swung the trolley into the resuscitation room, Jo gasped. Panic rose to her throat as Rick suddenly convulsed, his chest and pelvis arching up clear of the bed.

'Acute posturing!' said the younger doctor.

'He's stopped breathing!' cried one of the nurses.

'We need to tube him,' said the senior registrar, taking charge. 'Get me a number seven endotracheal tube. Dr Taylor, get a line in.' He shone a light into Rick's eyes. 'Damn! He's blown a pupil. Someone call neurosurgery.' The flustered resident started fumbling with the intravenous drip as Jo and Nina watched with increasing fear.

'It would be best if you come and wait in here,' said a nurse firmly, ushering them into the tea room as the breathing tube was inserted and Rick was hooked up to the heart monitor.

Once in the stuffy waiting room Nina started pacing up and down, picking at her long fingernails and chattering about abusive drivers and hopeless traffic bottlenecks. In an agony of terror Jo stared unseeing at the tatty magazines on the low table before her. Had they been fast enough getting back to the hospital? Why had he suddenly gone so strange in the car? She tried to talk to her mother, but Nina wasn't listening.

'I have to ring your father,' she interrupted, searching in her clutch bag for her little notebook. She had no idea where he was. Opening the door she nearly collided with a nurse's aide carrying a tray of tea and biscuits. 'I need to make a phone call,' Nina demanded, pulling out a fifty-dollar bill.

'There's a phone just next to reception, Mrs Kingsford,' replied the aide, ignoring the money.

As Nina marched out of the room, Jo clenched and unclenched her unsprained hand, staring into space. He couldn't die. He couldn't. He was so well an hour ago, joking and laughing. She shut her eyes and rested her head on the wall, a cold sensation in the pit of her stomach. Her shoulder ached intolerably. The silence of the empty room was oppressive, the strange pressure in the back of her neck worse than ever. Nina returned.

'Your father's on his way.' She had rung the stables. 'Thank goodness his secretary keeps track of his movements.'

Jo nodded, her face pinched. Nina sat down silently, knitting her fingers together as the seconds ticked by. For once Jo longed for her mother's ceaseless chatter to drown out the fears in her head. She yearned to feel her arms secure around her and the soothing voice she knew as a young child telling her Rick was going to be all right. But she knew she was being unrealistic. Nina was barely coping. If anyone could ease Jo's fears it was her father. Rick's convulsion on the trolley had terrified her. It was like one last desperate reaching out to life. Rick, the brother she loved so much; Rick who teased her and squabbled with her and thought like her. Her twin brother, a part of her, always a part of her. A shiver ran through her. The pain in the back of her neck vanished. A few minutes later the door opened and the senior registrar walked in. Looking at his face, Jo's heart went cold. Nina rushed forward, childlike, her eyes full of hope.

'He's going to be all right?'

'Mrs Kingsford, why don't we sit down.' The doctor pulled up a chair, his quiet manner serving to alarm Jo further. Nina sat down. 'Your son had what is called an extradural haemorrhage. It is when bleeding occurs between the brain and the skull. It is impossible to detect from an X-ray. In your son's case the bleeding probably started slowly after the blow to the head and then without warning developed into a massive haemorrhage.' He paused. Jo sat absolutely still, her eyes wide, the pupils dilated.

'But he's going to be all right?' repeated Nina, leaning forward.

The doctor continued. 'Your son was already unconscious when you arrived at casualty. He had stopped breathing before we got him to the resuscitation room.' He took a deep breath. Continuing, he purposely dragged out the explanation of the medical procedure they had gone through, to give Nina and Jo a chance to grasp the truth. 'There was nothing more you could have done,' he explained to Jo, his eyes full of compassion. 'The convulsing you saw indicated severe brain damage had already

occurred.' He paused. 'No-one could have anticipated this, Mrs Kingsford. You both did everything
you could. I assure you, we too did everything possible. When his heart stopped we kept trying, but we
couldn't restart it.' He paused again. 'I'm afraid your
son died a few moments ago.'

Jo stared at him in disbelief.

Nina let out a howl of grief. 'No! No! He's not
dead. He can't be dead. That's why you have hospitals,' she cried, flinging herself around the room.
Turning on her heel she came at the doctor. 'Like
hell he's dead! Now you get your boss down here
immediately and get him to fix things up properly,'
she screeched. Pulling out the wad of notes she
waved them in his face. 'You get every neurosurgeon
in the country down here. I don't care how much it
costs.' She was shaking all over.

Jo had gone deathly pale. Her legs felt weak.
'Mum,' she said quietly, 'it's too late. He's gone.'
Even as she said the words she denied them to
herself.

'Don't be ridiculous, Joanna,' snapped Nina. 'This
man's obviously totally incompetent.' Her voice cres-
cendoed towards hysteria. 'You! You, find me a real
doctor . . .'

The registrar reached out to Nina. 'Mrs
Kingsford . . .'

'Don't you touch me!' she shouted, her shoulders
shaking uncontrollably. Leaving her hysterical
mother to the doctor, Jo slipped from the room,
silent tears tumbling down her cheeks. She had
known. The moment the pain in her neck had
stopped, she had known. Yet she refused to accept.

Rick was lying covered by a white blanket, the
breathing tube still sticking out of his mouth, his lips
a dusky colour, the heart monitor silent beside him.

He looked as though he were asleep. For a moment Jo simply stared down at him, expecting him to open his eyes. Then very gently she leaned over and kissed his pale cheek, surprised at how warm it felt. A tear splashed onto his face and she wiped it away.

'Rick, I love you,' she whispered. Tears blinded her as she felt her father's strong arm around her shoulder.

'And I love you too, son,' Charlie whispered. His voice cracked. 'And you will always be with us.' Then Jo buried her head in her father's chest and sobbed.

Chapter Three

*T*HE FUNERAL WAS held the following Tuesday in St Mary's Church, Randwick. Brilliant sunshine flooded through the stained-glass windows, splashing rich reds and purples on the white gilt embossed coffin and new mosaic tiles. The congregation in the little stone church overflowed into the street, with people crammed near the entrance and spilling out through the arched doors. The Kingsford family was overwhelmed by the attendance. No-one had expected such a reaction. It seemed the whole of the racing world had come to bid farewell to Rick and to acknowledge the sorrow of Australia's leading horse trainer.

Dressed in black, her long ash-blonde plait concealed beneath a neat black hat, Jo stared unseeing at the words on the service sheet, determined not to cry. But when her father faltered in the middle of the eulogy, Jo was unable to stop the tears rolling down her cheeks. Next to her, lean, good-looking Bertie, her nineteen-year-old brother, sat stiff and uncomfortable in his dark suit, surreptitiously wiping his eyes from time to time, occasionally fidgeting with his program. Between her two children, Nina, elegant in a fitted classic black suit and big black hat and veil, sobbed throughout the service, enveloped in the inevitable musky perfume.

There was nothing anyone could say that could take away the pain of the tragedy that had struck the Kingsford family. After the burial service friends and relatives gathered at the house in Coogee, handing out food and sharing memories. Many had travelled long distances. Nina's younger sister, with her husband and two boys, had flown up from Lavender Lodge, their exclusive health farm in Tasmania; while Charlie's elder brother Wayne, breaking the silence that had existed between them for the last six years, had travelled down with their mother, Elaine Kingsford, from Dublin Park, the family stud property in the Hunter Valley.

Feeling claustrophobic amongst the crowd of well-meaning mourners, Jo escaped into the back garden and wandered over to the fish pond. Shoulders drooping, her good arm cradling the arm in the sling, she stared down at the flashes of orange darting beneath the waterlilies, and tried to block out the pain.

From the wide sunroom windows Elaine Kingsford stood watching the forlorn figure of her grand-daughter, wondering a moment whether to join her. Stepping decisively out onto the patio, Elaine crossed the neat springy lawn and walked quietly up to Jo. A diminutive silver-haired woman in her late sixties, her gentle face and hands brown from country living, Elaine was half a head taller than Jo, with eyes as startlingly violet. Her heart went out to the wan, silent figure, noting the dark circles ringing her eyes. How she loved the twins and how she had looked forward to every one of their visits. It had been nearly two years since Jo and Rick had come up to Dublin Park and now Rick would never charge through her door again. Surreptitiously she rubbed a tear away from under her glasses.

Thank the Lord, despite the bitterness between her own sons, Charlie had never stopped his children from visiting her after he had moved his family to Sydney. She loved Bertie too, but from a distance. She had never really got to know him as he had taken no interest in the horses or the running of the stud. Like his mother, who for years had tried unsuccessfully to disguise how much she loathed Dublin Park, Bertie preferred city life. So it had always been just Jo and Rick who visited during the school holidays. Inseparable, they created uproar, keeping everyone up at night, insisting on patting every horse and naming every newborn foal, calf or chicken, their endless childish chatter in some measure creating its own healing after Sid's death and with the growing tension between Charlie and Wayne. Then, as the twins had grown older, they had learned to help around the property, feeding and caring for the animals, riding some of the horses, checking the mares on the daily rounds with the vet nurse when they were coming into foal. In those days the place was big and teeming with helpers. Darling Rick, he had names for everyone and everything, even Daisy the old bomb of a car they had learned to drive on. She glanced at the silent young girl next to her, so like Charlie in so many ways, her usual vitality drained from her, and wished she could think of something to say that might help.

Jo felt her grandmother's gaze. 'Rick called the fat one Blondie,' she said, pointing to one of the goldfish, a catch in her voice. She turned red-rimmed eyes to Elaine. 'Oh Gran, how am I going to manage? Dad's so shut off and I can't talk to

Mum. I miss Rick so much.' Her voice sank to a whisper.

Gently Elaine drew Jo into her arms, hugging her close. 'You'll manage just like we all will,' she said softly into Jo's shoulder. 'We're Kingsford women and we have to be strong. Give them time, especially your mum. She has to learn to cope too.'

Jo gave a shuddering sigh and clung to her grandmother, her words and the warmth of her body giving Jo a brief sense of security.

Elaine stared at the nearby pink camellias blurred by her tears, the embrace as much a comfort to herself as to Jo, and saw once more the twins running excitedly towards the stallions' yard, their blond hair streaked gold against the fading sun. She heard their laughter echoing across the valley, and remembered.

Life had been good to Elaine, hard but good. Marrying young, she and Sid had been a team, growing and building, their love for one another and for the horses the driving force that kept them going through the hard times. When the children had been born, first Wayne, then Charlie and little Jeannie, Elaine felt her life was complete. Building Dublin Park back up to its original heights as a top thoroughbred stud had been the culmination of a dream for them both but most of all for Sid. Then without warning everything changed.

Elaine would never forget finding his lifeless body lying in the stable under the feet of his favourite stallion, the horse stock-still so as not to harm him. The years immediately following Sid's death were the worst years of her life. Charlie and Wayne fighting, Wayne's compulsive gambling growing out of control, Charlie furious at her weakness over Wayne, ordering her not to bail him out any more, not understanding the gambling was like an illness, nor the terrible loneliness she felt without Sid. The surge of hope and secret relief she felt when Wayne, who had never been interested in horses or training, married and moved away to run his own importing business in South Australia, was as vivid in her memory as if it had happened yesterday. So too was her dismay five years later when both Wayne's business and his marriage disintegrated under the strain of mounting debts and he returned home alone, his wife no longer able to bear the constant pressure of living beyond their means. The feuding between the brothers reignited. Yet as a mother Elaine could not bring herself to turn her back on her foolish elder son even though it meant mortgaging the house, selling off some of their best horses and ultimately a large part of Dublin Park. It was the sale of the land that had been part of Dublin Park since 1865 that had caused the final rift between the two brothers. It had also finally woken Elaine up to where all their lives were headed.

Bob Comely, the family solicitor, had saved her. If it weren't for him she would have nothing now. Of that she was convinced. Stroking Jo's long silky hair, Elaine smiled grimly as she remembered how he had taken her into Sid's study, sat her down and gently talked to her for hours. Finally she had heard what Charlie had been shouting at her for years. Taking Bob's advice, Elaine had stopped paying Wayne's debts. Instead she had put him on a salary with the proviso that he worked on the property until he had paid back the rest of his debts, that he would build up his finances to start another business and that there would be no more loans. But the damage was irreversible and the land had to be sold. After the sale was completed Charlie moved to Sydney with

Nina and the children, taking some of the top horses from Dublin Park, and refusing to have any further contact with his brother. How that had hurt, yet at least Wayne had not totally destroyed her relationship with Charlie. She had wept long hours in secret for them all. Oh, she knew she was weak where Wayne was concerned. With him she had always been weak, but he was as much her son as her loving, strong, successful Charlie and she would not give up on either. She understood her boys so well and yet she felt somehow she had let them down. Then Charlie had given her back the twins.

Elaine brushed away more tears from her cheeks as she remembered the day Jo and Rick had come running across the veranda of Dublin Park House, tumbling into her arms for the first time since moving away. It had been as though the sun had once more flooded into her life. Today tragedy had brought the family back together to some degree, at least for the moment. Now she had to help Jo. The girl was like the goldfish—bright flashes of colour darting in and out of the shadows, searching for the light. Releasing her hold she kissed Jo's cheek and smiled at her. 'The school holidays are coming up soon, Jo darling. How about coming and spending some time with your gran? I'd like that very much and I think right now we both need each other.'

'Oh Gran, I love you,' choked Jo, kissing Elaine back and then hugging her again. Slowly, arm in arm, the two walked back to the house.

After the final guests took their leave and relatives subsided into chairs or moved out onto the patio, Jo quickly changed into a T-shirt and jeans.

'I'm taking Sam for a walk down the beach, Mum,' she called, grabbing the lead from its hook in the wide hall and whistling to Rick's golden retriever.

'Take Suzie Wong too,' called back Nina, make-up reapplied, and fortified by several large rum and Cokes. Suzie Wong, freshly bathed, perked up her ears and immediately jumped onto Nina's lap, turned round twice and sat down, scratching at the tiny black bows tied into her fluffy white curls.

'Do I have to?' Jo stopped at the sitting room door, groaning inwardly. Taking Suzie Wong to the beach meant either carrying her most of the way so she didn't get dirty, or washing and grooming her all over again on their return, and she didn't feel like doing either.

'On second thoughts, don't bother, sweetie. Just take Sam,' replied Nina, retying a ribbon. 'It breaks my heart the way he keeps crying and searching for Rick. Maybe a run on the beach with you will help settle him down.' She pressed her nose to the pood-le's face to hide the sudden flood of emotion. 'Little Suzie doesn't want to get her tootsies wet either, does she?' Recovering, she patted the seat beside her and called to her eldest son. 'Bertie, come and tell your Auntie Dawn how your law studies are going.'

Heaving a sigh of relief, Jo waved quickly to her grandmother and escaped with Sam, setting off at a fast walk towards Coogee Beach, a short distance from their house. She needed some time on her own. Sam trotted beside her, ears down, every so often looking behind to see if his master was coming. Jo felt the familiar lump in her throat seeing the dog still pining for Rick. Each morning since the accident Sam had gone to his usual spot on the porch and waited, head between his paws, his soulful gaze never leaving the gate through which his master was supposed to walk. Crying through the day and off his food even when Jo tried to handfeed him, he had finally wagged his tail feebly when she gave him an old jumper that smelled of Rick. At night Jo crept Sam into her bedroom, letting him out again before her mother woke. Gradually, with Jo's attention, the dog's crying had reduced to whimpers. Today, almost as if he knew the final goodbye had been said, Sam had remained quiet.

Holding her sling steady with her good hand, Jo broke into a run as they reached the sand's edge. The afternoon sunlight glinted on the breaking waves, shimmering through the misty salt haze blowing off the sea. Tossing off her shoes and quickly rolling up her jeans, Jo ran towards the dark blue water, the golden sand surprisingly cool under her bare feet. Gasping at the cold as she splashed into the water, she ran along the edge of the waves, the white foam rising and falling around her, her glistening wet footprints vanishing as quickly as they appeared, the pain from her shoulder a merciful distraction to thought. Sam watched, barking from the dry sand.

'Come on in, Sam!' called Jo. Sam paused a second then, tail lifted, he bounded across to her and into the water. Jo shrieked as he soaked her jeans and then she playfully patted his dripping coat. Charging along with Sam beside her, for a few moments Jo was only aware of the wind in her face and the cries of the seagulls overhead. Finally, panting from the exertion, she ran up the beach and flopped down on the dry sand. Staring across at the brilliant golden sunset above the skyline to the west, the pain and loss of Rick's death flooded back with renewed force. Bowing her head she sobbed out the grief she had held back all day. Why, oh why did it have to happen? He had seemed so well. There was no answer, no sense in anything. She felt a wet nose nuzzling at her face and a warm tongue licking away her tears. Lifting her head Jo patted Sam, wiping at the tears that still coursed down her cheeks.

'Oh Sam, I miss him so much. I wish I could bring him back for us both.' Sam shook himself vigorously, showering sand and water over Jo.

'Sam!' Jo cried, her sobs turning momentarily into laughter as she shook the sand from her T-shirt. Pulling Sam to her with her uninjured arm, she hugged the soaking dog, his sudden bid for her affection making her cry the harder. Sam licked her face again. Wriggling free he flopped down beside her, tongue lolling, the tip of his tail wagging inter-mittently, occasionally turning to bite his fur. Staring out to sea as the shadows crept out over the horizon, one hand fondling Sam's ear, Jo felt Rick's presence. It was as though he were there watching them both.

'He wouldn't want us to be sad, Sam,' she whis-pered, her voice choked with emotion, ignoring the tears still spilling down her cheeks. 'He'd want us to do the things we'd planned together. To be the best like we'd always dreamed.' She wiped her eyes with the back of her hand and sniffed. Sam thumped his tail.

Together the two watched the darkening sea as the great golden orb finally disappeared beneath the horizon, its fiery rays tingeing the tops of the clouds deep pink and fading back to grey, shrouding the world in a soft mist, the remnants of heat evaporat-ing as the light rapidly faded. Still the two sat. Finally when the light was all but gone, Jo stood up and, shivering, shook the sand from her sodden jeans.

'C'mon, Sam. Gran's right, we have to be strong. We have to go back and face the world.' Sam leaped up and wagged his tail, sending sand showering in all directions. Jo threw a stick for him to fetch. Her heart was still heavy but somehow she felt stronger.

The pain of Rick's death would be with her forever, but she knew what she had to do. She knew Rick was still with her and that made her feel better. Walking up the beach she slipped her feet into her shoes and turned for home. Sam padded behind his new master, ears pricked, the retrieved stick firmly in his mouth.

As Jo's wrist and shoulder gradually healed, so did her spirit, buoyed up by Sam's unwavering loyalty. Her all-consuming passion now was to persuade her father to let her return to track work. While he still refused to discuss riding the racehorses, Charlie had made no mention of staying away from the stables, so Jo spent every moment she could at Kingsford Lodge. Still hampered by her stiff shoulder, she fed and mucked out where she could, helped walk the horses in the afternoons after school and chatted with Winks. The seventy-year-old retired foreman and ex-jockey had been with the Kingsfords since before Jo was born and was always to be found pottering around the stables. At weekends Jo was back again at the stables, watching and listening as Charlie discussed points with the foreman and examined the horses with the vet.

The other reason that kept Jo up at the stables was that, while the doctor had advised her to wait until her shoulder was fully mobile before she rode again, she still had to look after her own horse, Buck's Fizz, a big-hearted golden brown gelding whom Jo called Fizzy. Having found the horse to be useless coming out of the barrier at the racetrack, Charlie had given him to Jo on her twelfth birthday. A member of the Eastern Suburbs Pony Club from the age of nine, Jo regularly rode Fizzy in the various zone and club events. Content to work and ride the racehorses, Rick had never been interested in pony club, so although Jo missed Rick unbearably around the stables, exercising Fizzy was one activity that brought back fewer painful memories.

One afternoon as Jo was returning Fizzy to his stall Winks came hobbling towards her on legs crooked from his many injuries as a jockey, pulling at the dilapidated peaked cap that covered his scrappy grey hair, deep furrows etched in his craggy sunburned face.

'I seen you take the old fella out these last three weeks reg'lar'n clockwork.' He peered over the half door into the gloom, chewing on his false teeth. 'You walks 'im, you feeds 'im and you locks 'im in his stall. When you going to ride the darned horse?' he asked chattily.

Jo bristled. 'The doctor said I have to wait a bit longer,' she replied rather too sharply. Stepping out of the stall she locked the door then checked it was secure. 'Now don't you go fiddling with it,' she admonished Fizzy, giving him a final rub on the muzzle. Fizzy flicked his head up in reply and whinnied. Jo laughed. Turning, she slipped her hand through the bent old man's crooked arm. 'Tell me some more about what to look for in your horse before a big race.'

Wink's face creased in delight, his eyes twinkling. He adored Jo. She was like the granddaughter he had never had. Time spent with her was like reliving his youth. She was so young and exuberant, yet so quick to absorb everything he told her about handling horses. She showed the same deep, inexhaustible love of horses as he did. Yet his agile mind had not missed the way she had quickly changed the subject.

'Watch your dad,' he replied, his voice husky from too many cigarettes.

'Is that all?' replied Jo in mock surprise, starting to feel more comfortable again. Conversations with Winks often began like this.

Winks nodded, fishing in his pockets. 'Yup, that's the one! Jest keep watchin'. You can't go wrong if yer jest keep watchin'.' He pulled out the squashed remains of a rollie and stuck the cigarette in one corner of his mouth. 'I known yer dad when he was a scrawny brat of eight. Even then he was watchin'.' Then he elaborated.

Jo listened intently, filing away all the details. Each time they talked she learned something new. 'I'm watchin' you, mind, and I see you're learnin', that's good,' continued Winks, winking broadly at her from bloodshot eyes. But his earlier comment about riding had touched a nerve that went deeper than Jo wanted to acknowledge and she was unusually silent as she drove home with her father in the white Rolls Royce later that day.

'You having any problems looking after that horse of yours with your sore arm?' asked Charlie gently. But Jo only shook her head.

One of the deals Charlie had made with Jo was that she must be entirely responsible for her horse if she wanted to keep him at Kingsford Lodge and that she could not expect the other stable hands to do her work for her. Born in the bush near Wagga Wagga in southwest New South Wales, close to the Victorian border, Charlie knew what it was like to go without and he was determined that his children would not take their lavish lifestyle for granted.

His parents had started out poor as the proverbial church mice, Sidney Kingsford scratching around as a farm labourer to make enough money to keep clothes on their backs, Elaine working just as hard in their meagre home. Charlie still had a couple of faded old brown photos taken by one of Sid's employers of Wayne and himself dressed in old flour sacks lovingly turned into shirts and trousers by his gentle mother and of his sister Jeannie proudly parading her flour sack pinafore. But his clearest childhood memory was when his father bought two old nags about to be sent to the knacker's yard for dog meat. Charlie had just turned eight and anger bubbled up in his young heart at the snickers and jeers his father received from some of the other horse owners and trainers. He wanted to smash those smirking faces. It was at that moment that Charlie vowed to make his fortune with horses. As he grew he watched every minute detail of his father's training methods, how he would stand for hours just staring, how he walked and trotted the horses, talked to them, what he fed them to build them back to respectable animals. When the nags came good, the Kingsford family's life changed dramatically.

Twice Charlie had seen his father build an empire only to lose everything on a single bet. Then finally he bought and built up Dublin Park into the thriving family business, the pinnacle of his horse training and breeding career and a business Charlie was proud to be part of. Five years later Sid was dead.

It was from Sid that Charlie had inherited his great gift with horses and his passion to continue the Kingsford dynasty. He recognised Jo's ability but he had been more excited to see it develop in Rick. Heck but he missed the boy. Since his son's death he had been oscillating about Jo. Some days he felt he ought to give in and get her back riding the racehorses, that doing so might help her come to terms with Rick's death more easily. At other times he swung the other way, terrified he might lose her the same way he had lost Rick. Jo was good, there was no doubt about that. He had been amazed at her work with Magic Belle. When she was with the horses she was happy, he could see that. Charlie glanced at the pensive expression on Jo's face as they fought the rush-hour traffic, and allowed Nina's opinion to decide for him. There would be no more track work for Jo. That was what Nina wanted and he would stick by that decision. Loving them both as he did, Charlie was concerned that Nina couldn't take much more. Lately she had become increasingly nervy and argumentative, crying at the slightest thing. Maybe it was time he organised for her to have a holiday. He made a mental note to talk to Gloria, his secretary.

'I think we'll organise for your mum to have a bit of a break. She's finding things a bit tough at the moment and needs to get away. You could cope if I fix everything with Jackie?'

Jo nodded again, turning to look at her father who was casually manoeuvring the wheel with one hand. At forty-four he was still a striking man. He was dressed immaculately as always in a beautifully tailored European suit, his tie perfectly knotted, his silk handkerchief casually stuffed into his breast pocket. As though reading his thoughts Jo asked, 'Dad, do you miss Rick?'

'Of course I do, chicken, why?'

'It's just that no-one ever talks about him any more, not even you and Mum. It's as if he never existed,' she whispered.

Charlie gave Jo's hand a squeeze, his eyes slightly misty. 'He existed, chicken, it's just that we have to get on with the rest of our lives.' He steered the car smoothly round the corner, feeling the tension in

Jo. 'Now, what lies has old Winks been telling you today?' he joked, forcing his mind from Rick, his heart reaching out to his daughter.

Jo sank back into the seat. At least she had spoken her brother's name without feeling the embarrassment of others.

By mid-August Jo was becoming increasingly anxious. The stitches had been removed from her forehead and the scar was healing nicely. Her shoulder only gave her the occasional twinge and although the doctor had advised her to wait another month to be absolutely sure, in her opinion she was quite fit enough to ride again. But what was uppermost in Jo's mind was that the Martha Wellbourne Trophy was only two weeks away and she still hadn't got back on Fizzy.

The Martha Wellbourne Trophy was the most prestigious award in the zone. Presented for the highest individual scores attained in a one-day event, it was also recognised as one of the most demanding in the pony club calendar. Previous winners had ended up representing Australia in the Olympic equestrian team. Jo had missed out by two points last year because Fizzy had baulked twice at the water jump, losing her precious seconds. She kept trying to convince herself she'd be all right. Full of confidence at Fizzy's ability, each afternoon she steeled herself to mount him, telling herself that today was the day, only to find her courage fail her when she arrived at the stables. She mentioned her fear to her mother on the way back from the doctor's surgery.

'You'd better get used to the idea that you're not doing anything at pony club until Doctor Brunswick says that shoulder is completely healed,' snapped

Nina, unsympathetic having just broken a nail. She glided the Bentley into the carport. Reaching over to the back seat for her lizard-skin handbag, she automatically checked her lipstick in the rear-view mirror and then stepped out.

'But, Mum,' cried Jo, slamming the car door and running around to her, 'it's the Martha Wellbourne Trophy in two weeks.'

'Careful with that door,' shrieked Nina. 'I don't care if it's the Governor-General's trophy, you heard what the doctor said. You could put your shoulder out again if you start riding too soon and rebreak it all over again.'

'Mum, it was dislocated not broken,' replied Jo, exasperated, 'and I can move it fine.' She demonstrated and winced at a sudden twinge, which was not lost on Nina.

'There, see what I mean,' retorted Nina. 'You're not taking any unnecessary risks and jeopardising your modelling career. Doctor Brunswick is one of the top doctors in the country and you will do what he says. How can you expect to become a top model if one shoulder's a different shape from the other?'

'I don't want to be any sort of model,' Jo replied, her voice rising in frustration.

'I can't cope with all this!' cried Nina, throwing her hands in the air. Hurrying up the steps she turned the key in the lock and pushed open the front door. 'Jackie!' she called frantically. It was an ongoing argument she had suffered with Jo for the past nine months ever since she had agreed Jo could leave school at the end of year ten. She had it all worked out if only Jo would stop being so difficult. Those high cheekbones and wide mouth were perfect for the new look the talent scouts were searching for. The scar could be fixed up with a dab of make-up or covered by a wisp of hair. With those fabulous ash-blonde locks and deep violet eyes she was ideal for the face of Yardley or that American cosmetics company she had recently read about. Nina had already started dropping hints in the right quarters.

'Jackie,' said Nina as the housekeeper came running, 'ring and change my nail appointment back to tomorrow ... Vicky should still be at the salon if you're quick.' Dropping her purse and keys on the marble-top hall table, Nina subsided with a long sigh into an overstuffed chair in the sitting room, kicked off her shoes and shut her eyes. 'I'm totally exhausted. I'd kill for a cup of tea,' she called over her shoulder to the retreating Jackie.

'The kettle's on, Mrs Kingsford. I'll make the call straightaway,' Jackie called back, giving Jo a brief smile as she hurried away.

Jo refused to be sidetracked. 'If it were Rick you'd have let him ride,' she pleaded. 'He'd have bullied you into letting him ride track work again by now.'

Nina's eyes flew open, Jo's words snatching her back from her daydreams. 'Don't you dare speak like that about your brother's memory,' she choked, glaring at Jo.

'But you would let him, Mum, you know you would. You always let him do things because he was a boy and ...'

Nina was on her feet in a flash. Fists clenched, eyes glittering dangerously. 'Don't ever let me hear you talk like that again!' she shouted. 'Here I am, going nonstop all day looking after you and you behave like this.' Stabbing one finger against her chest bone she screamed, 'Your brother is gone. Haven't I gone through enough over your stubbornness? Don't you realise the pain I suffer every time I look at you?'

Quivering, Nina plumped the cushion beside her. 'You will never again mention your brother's name in this house.' Her voice shook. 'He will be remembered for the loving boy he was and for the fine things he achieved in his short life. You will not taint his memory with your petty little problems.'

Jo stared at her mother in shocked disbelief. 'He was my brother, Mum. My *twin* brother. I can't just forget him,' she spluttered, rage and frustration fighting the misery bottled up inside her.

'You heard what I said. That is the end of it. Oh, I just can't cope with any of this. I need a cigarette. No, I don't, I need a stiff drink.' She flopped back into the soft cushions and rubbed her temples with her slender fingers. 'Oh, Jackie you're a life saver,' she cried, looking up helplessly as Jackie appeared with a tray of tea and biscuits.

'It's not an end to it,' fumed Jo, ignoring Jackie. 'I miss Rick as much as you do. He was part of me. Daddy talks about him . . .' She was trembling as much as her mother.

Taking a deep breath Nina pointed a finger at Jo. 'If you wish to live in this house you will abide by what I say.' Then, struggling to pull a lace-edged handkerchief from her pocket, Nina burst into tears.

'Why don't you let me handle this, Jo?' whispered Jackie just as Charlie walked in, nearly bumping into her as she headed for the brandy decanter.

'Have you been upsetting your mother again?' Charlie demanded of Jo, dodging Jackie and giving Nina a quick peck on the cheek. He deposited a large wad of hundred-dollar bills in her lap. 'Ballyhoo came in five to one. I got Ned Kelly to put a couple of quid on for me.'

Nina lifted her reddened eyes to her husband. She

liked Ned who had earned his nickname because he had started out in scrap metal, he was a bookie Charlie had trusted for a long time. She liked the money even more. 'Oh, Charlie, talk to your daughter. It's all too much for me.' She burst into fresh tears and Jo felt as though a knife had turned in her stomach.

'I didn't mean to upset you, Mum,' she mumbled.

Resting his hands on Nina's heaving shoulders, Charlie glared steely-eyed across at his daughter. 'If this is about track work again, we've discussed it, the answer is no and the subject's closed. You can make that two brandies, Jackie,' he added.

Jo opened her mouth to defend herself and changed her mind. For a second she stared bleakly at her father and then ran from the room. Grinding her teeth with frustration she raced to her bedroom, slamming the door behind her so the windows rattled and hurling herself on the bed. 'I don't want to be a model. I won't be a model, I hate models and I will talk about Rick,' she shouted into her pillow, pummelling it with all her might. 'How can she do this to me?' She loved her mother, she was so beautiful, but why couldn't she hear what she said?

The phone broke into her rage. It was Dianne Gibbs, her closest friend at pony club. After pouring her heart out for over an hour, Jo felt better. Dianne then offered for Jo and Fizzy to travel in the float to the one-day event with her and Cuddles, Dianne's horse, if Jo couldn't persuade her parents to have a change of heart. In whispers they planned the whole escapade. Dianne's mother had little time for Nina and as Nina took almost no notice of Jo's pony club activities, the two women rarely met. Charlie, on the other hand, considered Mrs Gibbs a sensible, reliable woman and had gained a few tips from her husband Neil, a lawyer whom he had met a couple of times at the track.

'You'll definitely get placed but if you win the Martha Wellbourne your dad'll be so thrilled he'll forgive you everything, I'm sure,' consoled Dianne.

Jo replaced the receiver feeling less desolate. There was a chance she could, in a quiet moment, persuade her dad to let her compete. And if she couldn't, she'd damned well compete without her parents' permission.

Chapter Four

*T*HE TUESDAY AFTERNOON before the one-day event Jo stepped into Fizzy's stall feeling utterly despondent. Her mother had left the day before for a two-week holiday on the Gold Coast, and her father had flown out to New Zealand that morning to a yearling sale. Just as Jo had plucked up courage to mention the Martha Wellbourne Trophy to her father the phone had rung. Charlie had then rushed out of the house and she had not found another opportunity to discuss it. Winks's words from a few weeks earlier rang louder than ever in her ears. Boiling mad at her mother and determined to win the trophy for Rick, Jo still had to get back onto Fizzy.

'We'll be fine, you and me,' Jo sighed, stroking his strong shoulder as she slipped the halter around his neck and led him towards the stable exit, his hooves clattering against the flagstones. Their strongest point was the showjumping, as long as Fizzy didn't get overexcited. Jo waved at Pete, a young stable hand who had a crush on her. 'Fizzy loves his new saddle blanket,' she shouted. It was a thick cream blanket with the initials *BF* embroidered on one corner. Pete blushed bright red and disappeared.

'You got to ride the darned thing to win.' Jo jumped as Winks appeared clutching a scraper. Fizzy tossed his head and stepped back, whisking his tail, sensing how keyed up Jo was.

'Winks! I didn't hear you coming,' gasped Jo, her heart still racing.

'Well, I'm here and you're getting on this horse so turn 'im around and git 'im saddled up and git on.' Jo had never heard Winks sound so firm. This late in the day the other horses were back in their stalls and the stable yard deserted. Winks moved his face close to hers and dropped his voice. 'Word gits around, you know. If you're going to git yourself in a heap of trouble at least win the flamin' trophy.' Jo stared at Winks open mouthed. 'I was a young 'un once too. Mum's the word. Now do like I say.' Laughing, Jo let him take Fizzy's reins and went to fetch the saddle and bridle.

'You'll need the martingale to keep 'is head down, seeing as how you two haven't been working together for a while. He's a big-hearted 'orse but he can git silly,' Winks called after her, patting his golden flank.

Jo nodded as she dived into the tack room, then hurried across the yard with the equipment. While the other horses watched, Jo quickly saddled Fizzy up, tightening his girth and checking that the rings on the martingale could not slip over the stoppers and get caught in the bit.

'That's it, now hop on,' ordered Winks.

Jo put one foot in the stirrup and stopped, her heart racing like mad, her blood thundering in her ears.

'Well, come on, girl.' Jo had gone ashen and her

hands were trembling so much she couldn't get a grip on the saddle. 'Are you getting on by yerself or do I have to lift yer?'

Jo took her foot out of the stirrup and turned to Winks, her eyes tortured. 'I can't,' she mumbled and leaned against the horse's warm soft body, fighting back the tears. All she could hear was her own voice screaming to warn Rick, all she could see was him lying on the turf.

Winks put his arm around her shaking shoulders and waited. He smelled comfortingly of hay and stale tobacco. Finally Jo raised her face. 'I can't do it,' she repeated with resigned finality.

Winks closed one eye and reopened it slowly. 'No such word as can't,' he said, shaking his head. 'You young 'uns, no stamina. I dunno.' He let go and handed her the reins. 'Now get on the bleeder and stop yer whingeing.'

At first Jo didn't know whether to laugh or cry. Then rage bubbled up inside her at the old man's astounding lack of understanding. 'I can't do it, don't you understand?' she choked as, ignoring her, Winks grabbed one leg and, with the other hand on her buttocks, gave her a heave. 'Let go of me! I can't! I'm scared . . . !' Jo shrieked.

Between her yelling and struggling and him pushing, Winks propelled her into the saddle and then stood back panting. 'That's better, the old ticker's still pretty strong, lass,' he puffed, patting his chest. Jo was still shaking and spluttering, more with rage now than fear. At least she had managed to stave off the tears. 'Now let's get to work.' Leading Fizzy firmly by the reins, Winks walked horse and rider out of the stable yard towards the practice area in Centennial Park.

By the time they had reached the park Jo had

stopped shaking and was ready to hug Winks. Deep down she had known she was too scared to get back on a horse and as the days stretched from Rick's death, while outwardly confident, underneath she didn't really believe she would ever ride again. Under Winks's expert tuition she was soon trotting and cantering around the exercise area, her confidence increasing with every stride. Two hours later not only had she gone through all the movements for the dressage, she had jumped several poles as well and was once more working as a team with Fizzy.

Walking back to Kingsford Lodge her heart lifted for the first time since her brother's death. This weekend she would win the trophy for Rick. No, she would win the trophy for Rick and Winks. Stepping into the yard she slid off Fizzy and hugged the old man tight.

'I love you so much,' she cried, fire once more lighting the depths of her eyes.

'You'll be right now, lass,' Winks replied with a lump in his throat. She was a winner this one, like her dad, that was fer sure.

With typical crazy logic, unlike in other countries, Australian one-day events took place over two days. Events were divided into individual pony club or zone events where competitors from different clubs and zones competed, zones comprising groups of clubs within each State. The one-day event for the Martha Wellbourne Trophy was now well into its second day. Being a zone event it was always held on a private property, this year at Duffy's Forest where the course was hilly and challenging. Yesterday Jo had been ecstatic at Fizzy's performance in the dressage competition. Up at the crack of dawn, today her fingers had been aching by the time she had finished twisting his thick coarse mane into rosettes, groomed him and plaited the top of his tail, then helped Dianne plait an extra tailpiece to her bouncy gelding Cuddles, who didn't have such a long luxurious tail as Fizzy.

Martha Wellbourne, a horsy English woman who had moved out to Australia in the 1950s and died in 1961, was revered in pony club circles. She was always a stickler for correctness, so attire and presentation played an important role in winning her trophy. Dressed in the formal style demanded for dressage events—Eastern Suburbs Pony Club brown jumper over a pale blue shirt and pony club tie and squeezed into cream jodhpurs, her hair securely encased in a hairnet peeping out from under her riding hat—Jo knew she looked smart. As she had walked Fizzy down the centre line of the dressage ring to salute at the end of her routine, the morning sunlight gleaming on his pale chestnut coat and glinting on his Pelham bit, her heart had nearly burst with pride. In the afternoon she and Dianne had walked the cross-country course which was set in a separate paddock from the dressage and show-jumping area. As Jo strode through the rustling, dry, hip-high grass, checking out the jumps with the other riders and parents and listened to Mrs Gibbs's encouraging advice to her daughter, Jo had felt a sudden pang that her own mother never took any interest in her pony club activities and that her dad was mostly too busy.

Now, as she strapped the breastplate onto Fizzy's saddle to stop it slipping forward during the cross-country, she went over the jumps in her mind again. The water jump was still her greatest worry. Knowing how nervous Fizzy was of water jumps, she had checked it from every possible angle. There was a good run up to the fence and if she could just keep him calm enough and not give him too much time to think, they should be all right. Though she had sworn at Winks at the time, now her heart brimmed over with gratitude that the old man had made her and Fizzy train so hard together during the last four days. The only blot on the so far unmarred weekend was Selena McFarlan who had purposely let her mean chestnut mare Cassie get close to Fizzy and the mare had promptly tried to bite him. Jerking the startled Fizzy quickly away, Jo had jarred her injured shoulder. The pain had kept her awake for most of the night and she tried to ignore the persistent dull throb as she tightened Fizzy's girth.

Nervously she mounted, slipped her spurred boots into the stirrups and walked Fizzy alongside the other competitors lined up near the gate leading to the cross-country course. Sliding a quick sideways look at Selena who was munching on a Kit-Kat, Jo groaned inwardly. It was unfair that Selena should be such a good rider and stay so amazingly thin and clear complexioned no matter what she ate. This morning Jo had broken out in a nervous rash all down her neck. Wearing the pale blue club T-shirt allowed for cross-country work and her cream jodh-purs, the new cream saddle blanket from Pete under her polished saddle, Fizzy's blue boots strapped neatly around each of his legs, protective bellboots covering his hooves, Jo was blissfully unaware that she and Fizzy were by far the most striking horse and rider there.

There were six other competitors at Jo's level, including Selena McFarlan, who threw Jo a dark look, stuffed the remains of the Kit-Kat in her mouth and turned and walked Cassie around. Jo's stomach churned as the minutes ticked by. She could feel the sweat building up under her riding cap as she too circled her horse to keep him supple. For the fourth time she adjusted the cloth bearing the number fifty-nine across her back and chest. Looking around to take her mind off the course, Jo's heart suddenly missed a beat as she saw Doctor Brunswick striding towards the refreshments tent. He was the last person she expected, or wanted, to see here.

'What am I going to do?' Jo whispered frantically to Dianne, pointing out the doctor. 'If he sees me he's bound to tell Mum.' Fizzy whinnied nervously.

'He's too engrossed with his snotty little grand-daughter competing for the first time to bother about you. Anyway, it's too late now, you're on,' whispered Dianne who was in a different grade and not competing. 'What were you going to do when you won the trophy, hide it under the bed?'

'I haven't won it yet,' hissed Jo. As Doctor Bruns-wick glanced in her direction, to Jo's relief the steward in charge ordered the competitors through the gate into the next paddock away from the spec-tators. For the next five minutes everything else was blotted from Jo's mind as she concentrated on cir-cling an increasingly excitable Fizzy, holding him in check so he didn't bolt before the start. Finally it was her turn. As she was given the thirty-second countdown in front of the two tree stumps that passed for starting posts, Jo sent a quick prayer of thanks to Winks.

'Three! Two! One! Go!' yelled the steward.

Jo kicked Fizzy into a fast trot and they were past the start and had cleared the first jump. As she felt the rush of wind against her face and Fizzy's pow-erful strides lengthen, her tension eased. Flying over each jump, cantering along in a steady rhythm, Jo gradually started to relax and enjoy the ride. Racing down the hillside they were across the bridge and nearing the dreaded water jump. As they approached the jump the adrenalin surged through Jo's veins. She could do it. Fizzy could do it. Sitting deeper in the saddle Jo aimed him at the fence at just the right angle, her palms sweating inside her riding gloves, her heart thumping against her ribs, her mouth dry. She could sense Fizzy's fear.

'Easy, Fizzy,' she whispered, her hands tightening on the reins, the sweat trickling down inside her T-shirt. They were almost at the fence. They were going to make it. At the last second Fizzy baulked, almost sliding into the fence.

'Damn,' muttered Jo, turning the strong beast around, conscious that every second counted. Once again they faced the fence. 'Come on, Fizzy. You can do it. It's only a puddle,' Jo whispered into the horse's ear, urging him on with every fibre of her being, her heart hammering in her chest as she willed him to jump. The gap closed and they were at the fence. With one giant leap the horse took her over the jump and down into the pond, water splashing up and soaking her legs, the landing jolting her shoulder again. But Jo was laughing despite the pain. Leaning forward she hugged the brave horse, praising him over and over as she trotted him slowly through the water, knowing the courage it had taken for him to make that leap and loving him all the more for it. Then, gathering him up, she popped him over the small jump at the other side of the water.

Racing up the final hillock, the sun hot on her flushed cheeks, Jo's eyes shone in her mud-spattered face as they leaped the last two jumps and cantered the final few metres through the gum trees to the finish. Fizzy's chest was heaving, his flanks flecked with foam as Jo walked him back into the other paddock and dismounted, her legs shaking from the exertion, her hair grimy and hot under her hat, but nothing could wipe the look of exultation off her face. Leaning against Fizzy for support, she wiped her mud- and sweat-streaked forehead with one arm and then reached up a hand as he turned to nuzzle her. She wanted to cry with joy. Still shaking she loosened his girth, walked him to the Gibbs's float and gave him a small drink of water.

'You were great, you were really great,' yelled Dianne, trotting up on Cuddles and grinning broadly. Jo grinned back, her eyes bright violet jewels.

'It was Fizzy. He's so terrific,' she burst out. She quickly calculated that she couldn't have got too many penalty points and she knew she had done well in the dressage. Now there was only the showjumping to get through. Then her heart sank as Doctor Brunswick strode up.

'I would not have advised your riding so soon after the accident. I presume your mother knows the dangers,' he said. Jo's heart went cold. Then before she could reply a small child rushed between them, fell flat on her face and starting bawling her eyes out. Forgetting Jo, the doctor scooped the child up in his arms. By the time he stood up Jo had vanished. Shrugging, he dropped a kiss on the child's tear-stained cheek and went in search of a drink for his grandchild. After all, he wasn't officially on duty today and Jo was not his responsibility. But he'd keep an eye on her nevertheless.

Half an hour later, having wiped the mud off her face, groomed Fizzy and changed back into full formal attire, Jo was once more walking Fizzy around near the showjumping to keep him limbered up, the churning in her stomach worsened by her confrontation with Doctor Brunswick, and trying to ignore the increasing pain in her shoulder. This was the final part of the competition and she was the last competitor.

The wind had come up, blowing dust around and unsettling the horses. Blankets flapped against horse floats. Straps rattled. Jo reined Fizzy in, knowing his tendency to get overexcited and race at the jumps. Most of the competitors had knocked down the bogie, jump number eight; four riders had been eliminated for refusing jumps three times, the final triple jump had caused havoc, and the last horse had bolted out of the ring. Just behind Jo in the cross-country, Selena on Cassie had baulked once and knocked down one pole. To beat her Jo had to equal her performance.

Suddenly a big gust blew a plastic bag past Fizzy's nose, spooking him as they entered the ring. Grabbing him just before he bolted, a white-hot flame shot up through Jo's arm as she forced him back on course and towards what she hoped was the first jump. Dizzy with pain, she tried to focus on the blur of red and white poles as Fizzy's back hooves clipped the rail. Unable to do more than concentrate on staying on, she had no idea if she was even going in the right direction. Thankfully, by the time she raced towards jump number four the dizziness was subsiding. Then Fizzy baulked at number five and knocked a pole at number six, the easiest jump. Jo could have wept with frustration. Now she had to clear number eight and finish the triple perfectly. The throbbing in her shoulder was so intense she had to hold the reins with her left hand, giving her little control over the horse.

As she headed for the bogie jump the enormity of what she had done suddenly flashed through her mind. With her shoulder a mess her mother would realise she had blatantly disobeyed her. Even if she won the trophy she could lose Fizzy. Blinded by the low afternoon sun they raced towards the narrow-angled jump. Landing awkwardly Fizzy jolted Jo so much she dropped the reins. Miraculously they were over with the poles intact but the pain was so intense, for an instant Jo considered leaving the ring. Then through her agony she felt the powerful surge of the big horse beneath her and remembered the water jump. Now it was her turn to show courage. Half grabbing up the loose reins, she urged him on with her voice, bracing herself against the pain as he lifted her over the first jump of the triple. As red poles merged again with white she knew she had to leave the rest to Fizzy. With the canny under-standing developed between horse and rider Fizzy took charge. Two strides and he was over the second jump, a bounce stride and they were over the last jump and then home free. Like a true champion, Fizzy tossed his head in salute to the clapping onlookers and trotted Jo out of the ring.

Jo had never felt so elated nor so proud in her whole life. Tears of joy and pain tumbled down her face, the adrenalin still coursing through her. Fizzy had won the Martha Wellbourne Trophy for her, for Rick, for Winks. They had won! Surely Dad would be proud. Grey-faced she leaned forward and patted Fizzy, slid off his back and collapsed on the ground, cradling her arm, pain now her only reality. A mother came running up to her while another rushed off in search of medical help.

'Jo!' cried a male voice filled with emotion.

Jo's heart lurched. In amidst her agony she looked

straight into her father's eyes and saw the fear and love there.

'I won, Dad. I won the Martha Wellbourne Trophy,' she whispered. 'I won for Rick and Winks and you and . . . and . . . please don't take Fizzy from me.' She slumped back against his arm. Behind him stood Mr Gibbs and a white-faced Dianne, her expression a mixture of anxiety and excitement.

'Take it easy, girl, let's get that shoulder looked at,' said Charlie unsteadily, kneeling down beside her, supporting her with his arms. Doctor Brunswick came running up. With great presence of mind he said nothing, and in no time her arm was back in a sling, she had been given something for the pain and, still high from her success, was starting to feel better. Once it was confirmed Jo really had won the trophy, Dianne and Mrs Gibbs hugged her and then each other, and Jo hugged Charlie and Mr Gibbs, and everyone hugged Fizzy.

'My dad was over in New Zealand fixing some horse insurance thing and he met your dad on the plane home. Isn't that just the most amazing coincidence?' sang Dianne still buzzing with excitement as they packed up after the presentation ceremony.

'Let's hope it was a good omen,' said Jo darkly.

Normally she fell asleep almost as soon as she left a one-day event, but today, all the way back to Randwick, she worried about the outcome. As she finally shut the stall door behind Fizzy she felt completely shattered. The painkillers were starting to wear off.

'What's Mum going to say?' she asked as she stepped clumsily into the Rolls, clutching the trophy.

Charlie looked proudly across at her weary figure. Black shadows underlined her eyes, her blonde hair was escaping from the plait, and he was transported back to his own youth when he had ridden in a rodeo against his father's and the doctor's orders and won the junior contest. His crooked left arm was testament to that day. Jo had scared him today, but how could he be angry? She was her father's daughter and a true Kingsford.

'You really think your dad's an old fool, don't you?' He patted her leg, his laugh was deep and comforting and reminded Jo of when she was a very little girl. 'I knew what you were about, chicken. I knew how much this meant to you. You are determined, pig-headed and frustrating beyond endurance sometimes and . . .' He paused, tears glinting in the back of his eyes. '. . . I am so proud of you.' Clearing his throat, his eyes back on the road, he added softly, 'I'll sort your mum out, never you worry.'

Jo leaned back against the soft leather and sighed. Within seconds, head flopped sideways against the window, she was asleep, her fingers wrapped tightly around the Martha Wellbourne Trophy.

Chapter Five

FOR A WHOLE week Jo was elated at her success. Charlie was as good as his word. Calming Nina, he persuaded her it was better to have Jo's energies directed towards pony club than towards the track. He was also very aware that Jo's blatant disobedience was part of her way of coping with her brother's death. Despite her annoyance at Jo's behaviour, Nina accepted Charlie's logic. Apart from a couple of well-chosen phrases about the stupidity of Jo pulling her shoulder again, she made no more fuss. In fact, she went out of her way to try to cheer Jo up, encouraging her to spend more time with her riding friends and even shocked her by inviting Dianne to stay.

Leaning out of her bedroom window the Saturday morning after her win, longing to be down at Botany Bay helping take the racehorses for a swim, Jo's efforts to prove herself seemed suddenly pointless. She plunged into a black gloom. Seeing Sam patiently allowing Suzie Wong to chew at his ear as he lay basking in the morning sunshine only heightened her misery. Her shoulder ached and the thought of not riding for a whole month stretched before her like a life sentence. Despondently she picked a bloom from the yellow banksia rose bush growing up under her window that had burst into flower two days ago.

Picking each tiny petal out in turn and watching it float down on the gentle breeze, Jo chided herself for being such a misery. She should be feeling incredibly happy. She had achieved a goal she had wanted ever since joining pony club. Instead she felt tired and dejected. The illogicality of the last few weeks kept running through her mind. Both her parents had forgiven her for entering the one-day event recognised as one of the toughest in Australia, yet she still wasn't allowed to return to ride track work. And Nina had been on again about a modelling career. The last petal floated down. Jo clipped the flyscreen back in place and slumped unhappily on the bed. If Rick were here, he'd help her. Dad would have said he could keep an eye on her and work the easier horses, not that she couldn't manage the stronger ones. She picked at her sling, her sense of helplessness overwhelming her. Slipping out of her nightie she pulled on a jumper and jeans. Why did they have all these stupid rules based on whether you were a boy or a girl? She was good enough to train horses. She was strong enough to do track work. Most of all it was the only job she had ever wanted to do, and countless times she had listened to her father tell his children, 'It is your absolute passion about what you are doing that makes you the best.'

'I don't want to be a rotten model, I want to train horses and that's what I'm going to do,' Jo said angrily to her reflection in the mirror, brushing ferociously at the tangles in her hair.

The other niggle looming was the School Certificate examination. Dianne was coming over this morning so they could revise history and biology together. Nina and Charlie had agreed that, as long as Jo passed with reasonable results, she could leave school at the end of the year. But the way she was going, her results would be anything but reasonable. Suddenly everything seemed impossible. Tossing her hairbrush on her dressing table, she climbed fully dressed under the floral doona and pulled it over her head. Two seconds later she threw back the covers, leaped out of bed and slipped on her sneakers. If this whole argument was because she was a girl, she'd fight it. Other women had succeeded in the horseracing world, so why shouldn't she? And there was another way.

Grabbing an elastic band, she tied back her ash-blonde hair and dashed out of her room in search of her parents. Charlie and Nina were finishing their breakfast in the sunroom, the morning sunshine pouring in. The room had a homely smell of fresh toast and coffee. Twiddling a pen in one hand, the latest race list on his knee, Charlie was on the phone to Ned Kelly, briefing him on which horses to back for the afternoon's races.

'Morning, Mum,' said Jo, giving Nina a peck on the cheek and standing with her hands on her hips, her back to the wide floor-length windows.

Nina looked up from her magazine and her heart gave a lurch. Slim and pale, her hair pulled off her face, Joanna, at a quick glance, could have been Rick.

'Is your shoulder feeling any better today, darling?' Nina asked hurriedly to distract her thoughts from her son. She worried about Joanna. She had lost weight and still wasn't eating properly.

'It's fine now, thanks, Mum, hardly a twinge,'

replied Jo, her shoulders square, a determined glint in her violet eyes.

'You look as if you want to tell us something,' said Charlie, replacing the receiver and looking up.

Jo gave a half laugh. 'I wish you wouldn't always read my mind, Dad.'

'Well, spit it out then,' smiled Charlie. There was no denying she was very beautiful. Maybe Nina wasn't so foolish in pushing her towards a modelling career.

Jo took a deep breath. 'Gran asked if I'd like to go and stay at Dublin Park for the school holidays. Can I go, Dad, please?' If she couldn't do track work at least she could put her energies into learning more about breeding and caring for thoroughbreds instead. Then, if Gran thought she showed promise, maybe she could persuade her parents to allow her to work at Dublin Park.

'It's just before your School Certificate,' replied Charlie slowly, drawing his eyebrows together in a deep frown. He started twiddling his pen again, feeling the familiar twist in his gut at the thought of his children anywhere near Wayne.

When Sidney Kingsford had died, Dublin Park had been at the height of its glory, one of the most highly regarded stud properties in New South Wales. For five years Charlie had worked to keep it that way. Then Wayne had ruined everything, and Elaine had let it happen. Fighting both Wayne and Elaine, never able to understand his mother's apparent blind spot over his brother's gambling, it was only because of his mother's sweet, gentle disposition that Charlie did not force the sale of Dublin Park. Knowing how much she loved the property and how important it was to her both as her home and the final resting place of the man she had loved for over forty years, Charlie, when he had finally had enough, had agreed to take his cut in horses. He also arranged for the lawyers to build into the agreement a clause enabling him to stand any of his mares to stud at Dublin Park, and agist his horses for free, a clause that infuriated Wayne who, loaded with debt, was in no position to do anything about it. The animosity between the two brothers was still very close to the surface, despite the uneasy truce called at Rick's funeral.

Charlie replaced his pen in his breast pocket, patting his shirt impatiently. The past was gone. You had to let it go. Misinterpreting his actions Jo braced herself for an argument.

'The dryness and the sun up there will ruin your complexion!' cried Nina, horrified. 'After your exams, Joanna darling, I have organised for you to do some modelling for a friend, just a trial to get you some experience. Then we've got to get you organised for Switzerland.' She stared doe-eyed at Charlie. 'I thought it would be rather nice if we all went over at Christmas for a holiday in St Moritz, before Joanna starts at Pierrefeu.' Lifting her cup of coffee from the glass tabletop, she took a sip.

Jo wanted to scream with frustration. Two spots of pink appeared on her pale cheeks. 'Mum, when will you get it?' she burst out. 'I don't want to go to finishing school. I'm too short and fat to be a model. I want to be a horse trainer like Dad. It's all I've ever wanted to be.'

'Don't speak to your mother like that,' ordered Charlie, putting down his race book.

Nina's fingers trembled as she replaced the cup and saucer on the table, using both hands to steady it. Tears welled up in her eyes. 'You'll lose the weight, darling ... Please, Charlie, we've been through this so many times,' she gulped.

Charlie rested his hand on her shoulder. 'Leave this to me, Neene,' he said gently. 'Before we go any further, Joanna, you will apologise to your mother,' he said firmly. Daughter and father stared at one another. Jo was first to look away, swamped with dismay. Her dad never called her Joanna.

'Dad, please don't keep pushing it aside,' she begged, twisting her fingers together, fighting back tears. 'If I can't do track work, I can keep learning about the horses. It was Gran's idea to go and stay. I promise I'll study when I'm up there. Mum, I'm sorry, I'm not trying to upset you.' Her plan was out, yet the threat of being whisked away into a life far from the animals she loved terrified her so much she had to keep pushing.

Charlie felt he was being torn in two. His heart urged him to share the greatest passion of his life with his daughter, to teach her all the intricate secrets of training, yet his mind kept telling him to stick to the safe path he and Nina had chosen. Jo would do her School Certificate, go to finishing school and train as a model. But as he watched her tense face, the black smudges under her eyes more evident than ever, and looked back at what she had been through over the last few weeks, he decided a couple of weeks away from the constant reminder of Rick's death might do her good. The girl looked too fragile. His mother too had looked frail and tired. Maybe they'd be good for each other.

'Look, your mother and I have agreed that you can leave school at the end of the year, but you know as well as I, the racing world's no place for a woman.' Jo felt as though she were slowly shrivelling up inside. 'However,' continued Charlie, 'I can't see that a couple of weeks at Dublin Park would do you any harm. In fact, a bit of sun on those cheeks of yours and a good dose of country air might be just the ticket.' His face split into a grin. 'Mind you, I'll be checking with your grandmother to make sure you keep up your study.' Jo didn't react. 'What I mean is, yes, you can go and stay with your gran. It'll probably do her as much good as you.'

Jo's face lit up. Joyously she ran into his arms. 'Thank you, Dad, Mum, thank you. I love you both so much.' She hugged them both in turn.

Nina reached for her phone book, relieved that yet another argument had been averted. 'As long as we're all happy,' she said, her lips pursed. Then, seeing Charlie's warning look, she smiled briefly. 'Why don't I give Wendy and John van Haast a ring. I'm sure they'd be delighted if you dropped in to see them at Baerami Creek. Haven't they got a daughter the same age as you?'

'You can bring us back a couple of bottles of their new red. Didn't they get into grapes as well as horses?' said Charlie looking at his watch.

'What's that about Baerami Creek?' asked a voice. Everyone turned as Bertie sauntered into the sunroom, a cream Irish cable knit sweater slung casually over one shoulder.

'Bertie!' squealed Nina, leaping up and throwing her arms about his neck. 'How lovely! Why won't you ever let us know when you're going to drop in?' During term time Bertie lived in at St John's College at Sydney University, so Nina was always delighted whenever he phoned or showed up, which invariably was irregularly. Concerned at Bertie's overattentiveness to the betting side of the horseracing industry, it had been Charlie who had insisted Bertie live on campus and learn to survive on a monthly allowance which he then demanded Bertie account for on a three-monthly basis.

Jo eyed her brother carefully as he allowed his mother to kiss him on both cheeks. Normally the confident, teasing elder brother, today behind his brilliant smile he looked hung over, wary and surprisingly nervous. His fingers fidgeted in his pockets, his eyes never quite meeting anyone's gaze.

'Hi, Bertie. What's so special about Baerima Creek?' she asked cheerfully.

'Hi, little sis. Nothing really, just a few of the blokes in my faculty suggested going up there for swat week before we start the end of year exams.' He held up his hands. 'I know: "If you haven't started studying before the old jacaranda starts flowering, you're history," ' he recited in a singsong voice. Everyone knew the myth surrounding the ancient jacaranda tree in the main quad at Sydney University.

'So you've been hard at it and now you're ready to take on the ARA, are you, son?' nodded Charlie, watching Bertie closely, sensing this was not merely a social visit. Charlie's own legal battles over the years with the prestigious Australian Racing Association were legend, as were the distinguished people who were on the committee.

'Not quite, Dad, but I did have a big win at a mock trial one of our lecturers got us to organise. Shot the QC down in flames,' said Bertie with a nervous laugh. 'What's all the excitement about anyway?' he asked, hurriedly changing the subject, pushing back a lock of dark brown hair that kept falling across his brow. Tall and square-shouldered, his black eyes added an enigmatic intensity to his good looks.

'Your sister's going to stay with her grandmother

at Dublin Park,' replied Charlie coolly.

'Is that all?' said Bertie unenthusiastically, his casual disinterest irritating his father further. Charlie still found Bertie's lack of interest in the thoroughbred industry deeply disappointing. Contrarily he had, however, always felt relieved that his eldest son had been so completely bored by Dublin Park, because this meant he had little contact with his uncle. There were elements of Bertie's personality that reminded Charlie strongly of Wayne and which worried him considerably. Charlie also viewed Bertie's unannounced appearances with suspicion. Almost without fail they were to ask for something. Today, he would bet his last dollar, was no exception.

'Actually, Dad, I wanted to ask you a big favour,' Bertie began, slightly breathless. Jo noticed his top lip had gone stiff, his eyes slightly startled. 'I wondered if I could have an advance on my allowance.' He reddened to the roots of his hair, his heart racing. Always in awe of his father, he didn't know how to explain that he had got drunk and lost over three hundred dollars playing cards one night, nor how the next day, ignoring his empty bank account and his father's advice never to give out IOUs, had run up a debt for another two hundred bucks on the races at Warwick Farm.

'You're not going to buy that junkheap of a car you were talking about, are you?' butted in Jo, dancing around, chewing on an apple, refusing to let Bertie's disinterest overshadow her delight at scoring a trip to Dublin Park.

'Do stop jumping up and down in that maddening fashion, Jo,' interjected Nina. 'Of course Dad'll let you have a month's advance, won't you, Charlie? You look peaky, Bertie darling. They are feeding you properly at that college of yours, aren't they?'

'Heavens, yes,' replied Bertie, quickly plucking up courage at his mother's support. 'Actually, could you make it two months', Dad?' Tiny beads of sweat broke out on his top lip and he wiped them away with the back of his hand.

'D'you want to tell me the whole story, son?' asked Charlie sternly, indicating for Bertie to follow him to his office.

Suddenly Jo felt sorry for her big brother. His bravado had fizzled like a pricked balloon at his father's words and he looked like a small boy caught with someone else's peashooter. Even his ears had gone deep crimson.

Undemonstrative and secretive, Bertie's only emotional outlet was extravagant spending sprees. As a child he always managed to wangle the most expensive toy in the shop from Nina, until Charlie put a stop to it. Then two years ago, after one of his friends died, Bertie had gone on a wild drinking and spending binge, charging everything to his father's account and very nearly blowing his chances of attending university. Rick's death had affected him deeply, although he could not articulate that, and he bitterly regretted his behaviour over the card game and the horses. Yet in a tiny corner of his mind he hoped that somehow, with Rick gone, his father would now treat him as the favourite son. Bertie swallowed hard as the study door closed behind him. There would be no help from his indulgent mother here, he'd just have to face the music alone.

In the sunroom Jackie tripped out with the dirty breakfast dishes and then hurried to answer the front door.

'I bet that's Dianne,' cried Jo, hearing the front

door bell and rushing out after her, glad to escape the tension.

It seemed no time before Jo was on her way to Dublin Park, her suitcase dutifully stuffed with school books. Driven by her father's chauffeur, Jo was full of mixed emotions as the car carrying herself and Sam turned in through the impressive sandstone gates of Dublin Park in the early afternoon in the last week of August and swept up the long gravel and dirt road.

Forty kilometres south of Denman at the head of the Widden Valley, known locally as the Valley of the Champions, Dublin Park was set in some of the lushest pastures in the area. Passing through the big sandstone entrance Jo was surprised at how the road surface had deteriorated since her last visit, the car bouncing over large potholes and slithering in soft hillocks of mud left ungraded after the recent rains. Although the fences were intact, as were the shelter sheds in the paddocks, and the grass mown neatly along the roadside, the place had an air of dilapidation Jo did not recall. Seeing the peeling paint on the fence posts it was hard to believe this was a stud with a reputation for breeding Melbourne Cup winners right back as far as 1902. Yet, despite its unkemptness, Jo felt a keen sense of belonging as she peered eagerly from the half-open car window, one hand resting lightly on Sam's collar, scanning the paddocks for horses. As they neared the barn area Jo's eyes filled with tears as she caught sight of two foals suckling at their mothers. Last time she had visited it had been Rick who had spotted the foals first. Panting beside her, Sam stood up, wagging his tail against her and whining. Then Jo spied Elaine in front of the grand old house which, like the gates, was built from local sandstone. Quickly wiping away her tears, Jo yelled out; waving frantically, Elaine came hurrying over, one gloved hand clutching her big straw hat, a small garden trowel in the other. Almost before the car came to a stop, Jo and Sam tumbled out.

'I've been watching the road all day. I had to keep myself busy knowing you were coming,' panted Elaine. 'Oh! It's so good to see you again. We're going to have so much fun, you and I,' she exclaimed, her face wreathed in smiles, her bright eyes twinkling as Jo grabbed her in a bear hug while Sam danced around them barking, tail wagging ferociously.

Extracting herself from Jo's grip, Elaine pulled off her gloves and shoved them in the big pockets of her skirt and straightened her blouse. 'You get more lovely every day, child. But your gran is still taller than you,' she chuckled, hiding the nervousness she felt at the memories this place was bound to evoke for Jo.

'Only just,' laughed Jo, stretching herself up to her full height. She was all of a couple of centimetres shorter.

'Just is good enough. Now tell me everything you have been doing since I saw you last,' insisted Elaine, tucking her arm in Jo's and walking her towards the house.

'It's just as beautiful as ever,' exclaimed Jo, stopping and staring enchanted at the roses climbing rampant up the wall exactly as she remembered. Bobbing pink flowers spilled over and tapped against the window, while a multitude of colours ran riot in the beds along the veranda where Elaine had been working when they had arrived. Yet while the garden was lovingly tended, the woodwork was badly in need of a coat of paint. The front door flyscreen hung half off its hinges and a faded blue tarpaulin flapped from the roof where tiles were waiting to be replaced. But despite its disrepair, Dublin Park House still retained its majestic impact standing at the head of the valley. Gazing around at the rolling green paddocks that stretched away on either side, Jo felt a catch in her throat. Turning back to her grandmother she was surprised to see Elaine surreptitiously wiping away a tear.

'Gran,' she whispered, her own eyes pricking, not sure what to do next, their light-hearted mood evaporated. Elaine patted Jo's hand and gave a small sniff. Although neither said anything, Jo knew they were both thinking of Rick.

'You look quite pale, child. You need some good country air to brighten those cheeks and something to eat. You've had a long journey,' said Elaine briskly.

'I intend to get plenty of both,' replied Jo cheekily, jumping onto the veranda, swinging on a wooden support, her shoulder bag flying around with her, trying to recapture their earlier cheerfulness.

Her words were cut short as an overweight, greying blue cattle dog bounded from nowhere, barking ferociously at Sam. Sam immediately went berserk. Wagging his tail and barking in reply he leaped in and out of the flowerbeds after the other dog. Jo shouted at Sam who, to her embarrassment, ignored her completely. At a couple of short commands from Elaine the cattle dog slunk off to his bed on the veranda while Sam, after being severely reprimanded by Jo, lay down panting under a nearby tree, big eyes watching, his tail stirring up the dirt.

'Silly creatures. Rupert's getting old and a bit deaf,' said Elaine, unmoved by the performance. To Jo's relief the pandemonium created by the dogs had broken the atmosphere and once more the two chatted comfortably as they stepped inside the house.

After the chauffeur had brought Jo's bag inside and said goodbye, and Sam had been given a drink of water and told to stay at the opposite end of the veranda from Rupert, Elaine ushered Jo through the vast open area that acted as a combined kitchen and dining room.

'Let's get you settled in your room first. There's plenty of hot water if you'd like a shower, but be careful you don't scald yourself. We've been having a bit of trouble with water pressure,' said Elaine, leading the way along the long corridor to the big sparsely furnished bedroom where Jo always slept. A large double bed with a new white hand-quilted bedspread sprayed with tiny white roses dominated the room. At the head Elaine had laid one deep pink rose. Dropping her shoulder bag, Jo rushed over to the bed.

'You finished it. It's beautiful,' she cried in awe.

Elaine beamed. 'There's not a lot else to do in the evenings and it's soothing work. Look a bit closer, dear.'

Jo rubbed her hand on her jeans. Hardly daring to touch the pristine white she bent closer. Entwined at each corner amongst the roses was her name.

'There will always be a place for you at Dublin Park,' said Elaine softly. 'Now get yourself freshened up and after we've had afternoon tea we'll take a turn around the property and you can meet our new vet nurse Linda,' she ordered brightly. Rubbing her hands in satisfaction, she slipped away to sort out tea with Cook.

As the door closed behind her grandmother, Jo, for the first time since Rick's death, felt a bubble of excitement forming in the pit of her stomach. Her gran made her feel wanted and comfortable. Running to the window, she stared out in delight at the stables and the lush green fields beyond. The view was just as she remembered. A magpie screeched from a nearby tree and fresh country smells filtered through the windows. Tripping along to the old-fashioned bathroom, Jo quickly splashed water on her face and washed her hands. She changed into a clean shirt and gave her hair a cursory brush, then ran back through the house to the spacious kitchen. Yes, she was most definitely going to have a wonderful time here.

'Wayne's promised to paint the outside of the house this year,' announced Elaine happily as, refreshed from fresh baked scones and hot sweet tea, she and Jo set off in the Landrover for the promised inspection of Dublin Park. 'Sometimes I think we're all quite mad. D'you know our stallion has a better-kept house than us? But I love the great beasts just like your grandfather did,' she sighed, stopping the Landrover under the covered walkway that led to the yard where the stud stallion was kept.

Jumping out after her grandmother, a million questions burning in her head, Jo nearly ran into Linda who appeared from the nearby stall.

'Linda, I hoped I'd catch you. This is my grand-daughter Jo,' called Elaine proudly.

Several inches taller than Jo, Linda had a pert mouth and shoulder-length wavy brown hair pulled back off her face with a plain hair clip. She was also running behind with her checks on the horses. Giving Jo a brief smile, she made her excuses after a couple of clipped sentences and drove off in one of the stud utes. Jo thought she was a bit of a snooty cow. Determined not to be put off by anything or anyone on her first day, however, she gasped in delight as the rich dark brown stallion cantered across and peered at her between the wide newly painted brown railings.

'This is Sir Lawrence. He's all heart, aren't you, you sweet thing?' smiled Elaine, gently massaging his forehead. In answer Sir Lawrence let out a loud whinny. Then, curious, he pushed his nose next to Jo's chest, checking her out. Jo stayed quite still, enjoying the soft warmth of his breath on her hand as he smelled this stranger. As if to signal his approval of her, the stallion tried to chew the button off her shirt. Laughing, Jo drew back.

'You're accepted,' nodded Elaine as they moved away and drove towards the small tower overlooking the paddock to the left of the stallion's quarters. This was where the broodmares who were within three weeks of dropping their foals were watched, and at this time of the year it was manned night and day. Close by were the barn and the paddock housing the newborn foals and their mothers that Jo had seen on her arrival.

'Still the same old watchtower,' said Elaine coming up behind her. 'It's early in the season, but we had a foal born last night that needed a bit of help.' She pulled her jacket around her as the late afternoon breeze caught at her. 'Remember when I let you watch for the newborn foals on your fourth birthday? You were so excited, I thought I'd never get you to sleep that night. It wasn't much different when you started to grow up either.' Jo laughed in delight as they sauntered arm in arm back towards the house, her cheeks rosy from the rapidly cooling air. 'I'll ring Linda later,' suggested Elaine, 'and get her to show you the mares we've got in foal tomorrow. You might like to help her when she does her rounds.'

'I'd love that, and would you let me watch for the foals one night?' Jo asked, whirling round. Long shadows were stretching dark fingers across the paddocks, the setting sun adding a golden glow to the hills. It was such a beautiful place.

'I promised your Mum you'd get some study done while you were up here, but we'll see,' Elaine smiled.

That night at dinner Jo met her uncle for the first time since the funeral. Back from the timber yards, sitting at the polished cedar table, Wayne regaled Elaine with plans for renovating one of the big barns and handed her a rough sketch he had drawn up for the improvements, with the bill for materials.

'It's time we sorted out all the buildings on the property,' Elaine said quietly, nodding approvingly. Jo watched the two intently. It was clear to her that her uncle had no real interest in the horses or the property and was simply grudgingly following orders. She gave an involuntary shiver. Wayne's eyes were almost expressionless and when he smiled it was only with his almost womanish mouth. While he addressed a few gruff comments in her direction, there was a coldness about him that made her feel like an outsider and she was glad when the meal was over and he bade them both goodnight.

In the intimacy of the crackling log fire, Jo and Elaine talked and talked. Tentatively Jo started talking about Rick and, under Elaine's sympathetic gaze, gradually let down the shield she had surrounded herself with since her brother's death, confiding in her grandmother in a way she had so often longed to do with her mother. Just being able to speak Rick's name removed a great weight from her heart.

'He understood my absolute love of horses . . . We had it all worked out,' Jo confessed. 'I was going to train and he was going to ride and when we got married it would be to people who understood and loved racing and training and breeding.'

Elaine smiled indulgently at Jo's ingenuous view of the world, pleased that she could once more get close to her grand daughter. Intense and serious when she spoke about the things she loved, Jo reminded Elaine so much of Charlie; Bertie and Wayne, on the other hand, were peas in a pod, certainly in mannerisms if not in looks. Hopefully Bertie wasn't as silly with money as his uncle, nor as impulsively shortsighted in his business dealings.

After Wayne and his wife had moved away from Dublin Park, for a while the tension had dropped as Wayne set up a company importing rattan furniture from Sri Lanka. For two years it had flourished and both Charlie and Elaine had rejoiced. But after the birth of Wayne and Amy's second child, Wayne started getting into financial trouble, borrowing too heavily and taking too much money out of the business to support his gambling habit and extravagant lifestyle. Unable to cope any longer, Amy left him and took the children back to her home town. The failed business and broken marriage had added jealousy to the resentment Wayne felt towards his brother, making life extremely uncomfortable for Charlie and Nina and their own family when he returned to Dublin Park. So when the split came between her two sons, while it had torn Elaine's heart that Charlie rarely visited, she had always been grateful that he had never stopped his children from coming to visit. Jeannie, Elaine's youngest child, had married a cattle farmer and the two ran their property in far northwest Queensland. While mother and daughter still communicated, the distance was so great they rarely visited.

Then there had been the dreadful business when Charlie's best mate had started buying up the stock from the property. Having set himself up as a rival horse trainer and breeder, Kurt Stoltz seized the chance to capitalise on the Kingsfords' misfortune. The already dwindling friendship between the two men was completely stamped out as Charlie watched in helpless frustration while Kurt built up his own property, Rosefield Stud, buying not only the Kingsford stud sires and mares but two-thirds of the land that had belonged to Dublin Park since 1865. While the whole incident had devastated both Elaine and Charlie, it had actually brought mother and son closer together. Having successfully produced two Derby winners and a Melbourne Cup winner all bred from horses bought from Dublin Park, Kurt then set up his own winery, Rosefield Estate, cashing in on the growing lucrative overseas market. Elaine would never forget the murderous look in Charlie's eyes the day he vowed one day he and Kurt would be even.

'Poor Sidney. All that hard work gone to waste. He had such high hopes for Dublin Park and the Kingsford dynasty,' sighed Elaine to herself. Of her three children, Charlie had been the most successful, but it had divided the family instead of joining it. Yet as Elaine watched Jo's face sparkling, her violet eyes filled with excitement, energy emanating from her as she talked on of her love for the horses, it gave Elaine enormous hope.

'I'm not asking too many questions, am I?' exclaimed Jo, noting her grandmother's sigh.

'Not at all, not at all,' replied Elaine gently.

'Tell me about Dublin Park, Gran,' asked Jo, her eyes round as twin moons. 'I want to know everything. Absolutely everything. What stallions you've got here, what their names are, which are the best mares, how many foals have already been born, how many you're expecting, who is watching them, what I can do . . .' Just then a horse whinnied in the distance. Jumping up, Jo ran to the window and pushed aside the old brocade curtains, peering out into the darkness. Headlights moved swiftly along the hillside. It was magic here. She couldn't wait to get out and help tomorrow.

'Where do you want me to start?' replied Elaine, buoyed up by Jo's eagerness. Just having the child around made her feel years younger.

'Anywhere,' replied Jo, running back and wriggling into the fat cushions in the old wicker sofa.

'This calls for supper,' exclaimed Elaine. Bustling into the kitchen, she organised Cook, who was about to slip off to bed, to bring tea and cake and a hot chocolate for Jo. Then, returning to the sitting room, she pulled down three thick photo albums from the overcrowded bookshelf. Sitting down beside Jo, she opened the newest at photos of the latest mares installed on the property.

'I started taking photos soon after I married your grandfather. We had a few official ones, but I thought it would be fun to have a complete record of exactly which horses went through Dublin Park. It's a sort of potted history. You'll recognise some of the horses.' She flicked through to a well-thumbed page. 'Here we are. This is He's-a-Lad. He sired three Cox Plate winners,' she said proudly.

Jo leaned across admiring the big chestnut stallion. Her grandmother smelled faintly of rose petals and cinnamon.

'And this horse, here, that's Kingsford Gold,' continued Elaine. 'While he was racing he either won or was placed in almost every race he ever contested. He was our prize stallion before he was sold.' A dreamy look came into her eyes. 'He was a magic horse. Your dad really loved him. One day I'd love to buy him back if he's not too old.' Jo examined the sleek strong body, noting the carriage of his head, the strong neck and hindquarters, stories heard at Kingsford Lodge about great racing thoroughbreds drifting through her mind.

As the old lady and young girl talked late into the night, Jo learned the names of everyone who worked on the property, the stallions, mares in foal, dry mares, and younger horses being worked, and how, after Grandfather Kingsford had died and things were tough, little by little Elaine had raised the property to the level it was now.

'It's not as big or as smart as when your grandfather was alive. Things need painting and fixing, but Wayne does a lot of that and we get by. After we bought Sir Lawrence, people started looking seriously at Dublin Park again. It was a good feeling,' admitted Elaine.

'Dad and you know so much, Gran. D'you think I could ever learn all of this?' asked Jo in awe. 'Mum's been around horses half her life and she hardly knows anything about them. She doesn't even like them.'

'There's plenty going on between those two ears of yours, and don't you kid me,' replied Elaine, smothering a yawn. 'You're like your dad. Listening to you talk, once you get the bit between your teeth there'll be no stopping you, whatever you choose to do with your life. Now, if you're going to get some study done and cram in all the other activities you've promised yourself while you're up here, I think it's time we packed you off to bed.'

Jo was so excited sleep was impossible. Snug in the big double bed, the precious white quilt pulled up to her chin, she stared wide-eyed into the dark. At every new sound she leaped to the window, peering into the moonless world, shivering in the cold, the lights from the watchtower shining onto the foaling paddock, tantalising her imagination. Once she heard voices and wondered excitedly if a foal was being born. Climbing back into bed, teeth chattering, as she lay watching a thin line of light creep under her door she determined to ask Gran to persuade Nina to drop this wretched modelling idea. For Jo tomorrow couldn't come fast enough, but still she could not shake off the feeling that there was someone missing.

Shrugging, she turned on her side and buried her nose in the sheet. It was something she was going to have to learn to live with because part of her would be missing for the rest of her life. Despite this sobering thought when she finally drifted off to sleep she felt happier than she had in weeks.

Chapter Six

*J*O WOKE TO the sun streaming in through her window. Furious she had overslept, she leaped out of bed, pulled on her clothes and quickly brushed her teeth. Dragging her hair into a ponytail, she buttoned up her shirt as she ran into the kitchen. To her dismay the clock on the wall said eight-twenty. Linda would already be well into her rounds with the vet. In a big wooden chair next to the window Elaine was busy going through her notes for the day.

'Don't panic, Jo dear,' greeted her grandmother, seeing the look on Jo's face. 'While we don't have a lot of sick foals I'm glad to say, there's plenty to keep a vet nurse and two healthy grooms busy all day at this time of the year. They'll be glad of an extra pair of hands.'

'Why didn't you wake me, Gran?' groaned Jo, tucking her shirt into her jeans and reaching for the cereal packet.

'I didn't have the heart to, dear girl. I popped my head in around seven but you were absolutely sound asleep. We were very late to bed. Anyway, Linda rang me from the office a few moments ago. Hurry and eat your breakfast, and you'll catch her on her rounds with Phillip Gregg, the new vet. They'll be either with the farrier in barn one or down in the hospital barn. One of the new foals has a bad case of scouring. I'll go down later myself and see what's what.' She scribbled a note in her diary. These poor little foals. So many of them started their lives with shocking diarrhoea. There had only been a few cases so far this year, but once the weather heated up the numbers were bound to creep up. 'You'll need your jacket, dear, it's brisk outside today, despite the sunshine,' she added.

Gobbling down a bowl of cereal, Jo washed it down with a glass of orange juice and grabbed her jacket from the hook where she had hung it the night before.

'Thanks, Gran. I'll see you later,' she grinned, running out of the door. 'You can come with me later, old fella,' she said to Sam, giving him a quick pat before bounding across the veranda and setting off at a run towards the barns past the paddock where the broodmares with foals at foot were kept. The mares stood quietly letting their foals suck as Jo ran past, except for a couple of maiden mares, who, alarmed by the sudden movement, flattened their ears and bundled their foals off down the opposite end of the paddock.

Gran was right. Last night's breeze had strengthened considerably and the chill wind bit through Jo's shirt and whipped at her hair. She struggled into her jacket, zipping it up to her chin as she ran. Inquisitive horses poked their heads out of stalls as Jo reached barn one. A rooster strutting along the top of a stall crowed imperiously above the farrier and young stable hand who were working on a three-month-old foal. Jo looked round quickly. There was no sign of Linda or the vet. Shivering, she wished she recognised more faces. In the last two years there had been a considerable changeover of staff at Dublin Park.

'She's up with the sick foals,' the stable hand informed her in a broad Irish accent, nodding her head in the direction of the doorway. 'I'd mind what you say to her though, she's been up all night and she's in a shocking mood.'

'Thanks for the tip,' nodded Jo, hurrying out. She found Linda sitting in thick straw in the third stall of the hospital barn. Dressed in white protective overalls and surgical gloves, her back against the wall, she was nursing a dehydrated four-day-old foal that had been scouring badly, the foal's head resting against her thigh. To her right above her head a bag partially filled with clear liquid was hooked over a pitchfork, the tube running to a catheter in the foal's neck which had been bandaged to keep it in place. Nearby, the mare, a soft-eyed bay, continually licked and nuzzled at her sick foal.

'She's been off the suck now for the last twenty-four hours, Sue, so we've got to keep pumping the fluids in,' said Linda to the stocky, dark-haired girl, also wearing protective clothing over a thick jumper, who was busy writing in the daily record book. Smothering a yawn, Linda checked the foal's heart rate and respiration. 'I'll get Phillip to have a look at her again when he gets back, but I think we could finish this bag and then give her another two litres of Hartmans in a couple of hours.'

'Would you like me to do the feeds?' offered Jo, peering into the stall, noting Linda's drooping shoulders and the dark smudges under her eyes. Her own shoulder now only gave her the occasional twinge—so she wasn't concerned about doing heavy work. 'I know which ones to check and what to look for.' The foal's head jerked up nervously and it stared around, startled.

'Well, are you awake?' said Linda softly to the foal, shifting herself free and standing up. 'I have to check the mares,' she said sharply, stepping past Jo, peeling off the thin plastic gloves. After only two hours' sleep the last thing she needed was to have to entertain some overzealous city schoolgirl. Detailing Sue to check two more foals with minor ailments, she stripped off the overalls and hung them on a hook next to the stall. 'Get Nick if you need extra help, and if there is any change at all in that foal, get me on the two-way straightaway.' Dipping her boots in the footbath by the stall door, she glanced quickly at Jo. 'If you want something to do, get one of the boys to give you a hand to chuck the feed bags into the back of my van. I'll be with you in a tick. And dip your feet on the way out,' she ordered, disappearing into the vet's lock-up room where all the medical supplies were kept.

Biting back a rude retort, Jo dipped her boots in the disinfectant and went in search of the feed.

'I'll introduce you to one of our lovely nurse mares on the way back,' said Linda less abruptly on her return, seeing the good job Jo had done organising the feed.

'Will you?' exclaimed Jo, guessing she was referring to the big good-tempered draughthorses that acted as surrogates to orphan foals each year. Gran had mentioned they had invested in three more, bringing the total to six on the property this year. 'But it can wait. I gather last night was pretty heavy work,' she added quickly. Linda nodded. 'I wish I could have been there to help,' sighed Jo, a note of longing in her voice.

'We'd better get a move on. I don't like the look

of the weather,' said Linda, letting in the clutch.

Jo glanced to the west where dark clouds were building. The van bumped down the long gravel road to the paddocks where the wet and dry mares were kept. At each stop, as soon as the horses caught sight of the vehicle, they came racing over to greet them, manes flying, tails lifted, stirred up by the chill wind, whinnying in protest at the lateness of their feed.

'How long have you been at Dublin Park?' asked Jo politely as they drove to the next paddock.

Linda relaxed a little. 'Six months. I love it here. Mrs Kingsford is a great boss. Look, I'm sorry I was a bit short earlier. It's just that I haven't had much sleep in the last few days—' The radio cut in. It was Sue. The foal was doing fine but one of the maiden mares had taken fright, run into the fence and cut herself badly, and the vet had left twenty minutes ago. 'Get them both into a yard, Sue, and keep trying to contact Phillip. I'm on my way,' ordered Linda into the radio mike. Her lips set in a thin line as she swung the van back towards the stables. Damn it, today was turning out to be a nightmare.

'I'll finish off for you,' offered Jo as they raced back. 'There's only the far paddock with that last lot of wet mares and then I can do the dries and the yearling up in the western corner.' Linda nodded gratefully.

Leaving Linda to tend the injured mare, Jo drove back along the gravel road, singing happily. Day two of her visit and she was feeding the mares. Not that there was any need for concern. None of these mares were ready to foal down for another three or four weeks, Linda had informed her, and she had assured Jo she had personally checked this group yesterday. Cheeks flushed from the cold, Jo was halfway through filling up the individual feed troughs made from old tyres cut in half, when six mares in foal galloped towards her, tails and manes flying, the wind ruffling their shiny fat bodies. As they approached, Jo watched them closely for any lameness or cuts. Delighted, she quickly finished distributing the feed, laughing at the leader of the herd as she roughly pushed the others aside to establish her superiority, watching them all jostle for their spot in the feed.

'If there is a heaven, it has to be near horses,' Jo said, walking around the herd and checking them all again. Scanning the paddock, she noticed one mare still standing in the shade of the trees. Concerned, she fetched the little bag from Linda's van and walked towards the big brown mare, a handful of lucerne in one hand. A broodmare off her food was not a good sign. As she moved closer, Jo recognised the horse. There was no mistaking the dazzling white blaze or the one white sock. This had to be Bountiful Lass, the mare her grandmother had talked about so proudly as they pored over the photos, the most valuable stud mare at Dublin Park.

Jo's heart was galloping in her chest as she held out the hay but Bountiful Lass still showed no interest. Instead she started moving around searching and turning, smelling the ground as though looking for a place to roll. Perhaps that was all she wanted, thought Jo hopefully. Walking right up to her, Jo stroked her gently, again looking for cuts or signs of lameness. Finding nothing she peered up under the mare's hindquarters to check the size of the milk bags. They were swollen but not dripping milk. As Jo stepped back she noticed Bountiful Lass was very loose around the vulva. This horse was looking for a place to foal.

'But you can't be ready!' Jo gasped in disbelief. She waited, her heart pumping with excitement as the beautiful mare went down in a sitting position. This mare was going to foal right in front of her eyes. Thirty seconds later Bountiful Lass had hopped up again, another twenty-five and she was back lying down. Jo's excitement changed to alarm. Something definitely wasn't right. She had watched too many mares in labour not to know a distressed birth when she saw one. Dry mouthed she raced back to the car and radioed the medical barn. She was answered by a young strapper.

'Linda says there's no way that mare can be foaling,' he drawled after an agonising wait.

'I have to talk to Linda now,' insisted Jo, biting her fingernails, her heart thumping against her ribs. If the mare broke her waters now, she would be in urgent need of veterinary attention, and if the foal wasn't on the ground within half an hour after that, there'd be little hope of saving it. It was worth risking Linda's bad temper. The mare was still straining and groaning. Finally Linda came to the radio.

'Bountiful Lass isn't due for at least three weeks. She's probably got a touch of colic,' the vet nurse snapped. 'It's a windy day, they're all stirred up and I've got an injured horse to deal with here. I'll get her brought down to the foaling paddock as soon as I can find someone who's free.'

Jo felt the panic rise to her throat. 'No! No! Linda, listen. You can't waste time. This mare's in trouble,' she shouted into the radio mouthpiece. 'Linda, please. I've seen enough mares in labour to know she's distressed. You have to get the vet up here now—'

There was a scuffling sound and the radio went

dead. Mouth open, Jo stared at the transmitter in disbelief. Didn't the stupid woman understand anything about horses? If they didn't act immediately they could lose both the mare and the foal. Gran would never forgive Jo. She radioed the medical barn again but got no reply. Neither could she raise anyone from the house.

'Please God, let her send someone,' she cried as she ran back to Bountiful Lass.

Talking quietly to reassure the mare, she examined her again. Her waters broken, Bountiful Lass kept straining, but there was still no sign of the foal. It must be lying wrong. Remembering her father's advice to keep a mare with a poor presentation moving until help arrived, Jo coaxed Bountiful Lass to her feet and started walking her around. Maybe there had been no reply because Linda was on her way. 'Please, please let her send the vet,' Jo repeated, stroking Bountiful Lass.

Hope lifted her as a cloud of dust appeared at the top of the hill. Jo wanted to shout with relief. Linda had understood the urgency. In seconds the dust had turned into a battered Holden sedan which sped across the paddock, carefully avoiding the other horses who had come bounding across to find out what was going on. Stopping just clear of the trees, a young man in his twenties wearing overalls leaped out and hurried over.

'I'm Phillip Gregg. I'm the vet. Let's take a look at this mare,' he announced, rolling up his sleeves.

'Thank heavens,' cried Jo, steadying Bountiful Lass, her own legs trembling with relief.

'My God, Linda was right in saying we should take you seriously,' he exclaimed with a quick intake of breath at Bountiful Lass's condition. 'You do know what you're talking about.'

Jo reddened at the compliment. 'Her waters broke about seven minutes ago,' she gasped. 'She keeps straining but nothing happens.'

The vet nodded. Quickly he leaned into the back of the car, reappearing with a bucket and medical bag.

'I'll get some water,' offered Jo, grabbing the bucket and dashing off to the water trough.

'Thanks,' replied the vet into thin air. He emptied his pockets onto the passenger's seat, relieved Jo seemed so at home in this emergency.

Jo ran back panting, the water slopping over the sides.

Adding disinfectant, the vet scrubbed his hands and arms. 'Hold her steady while I examine her, can you,' he ordered, liberally smearing on a lubricant. Then as Jo soothed Bountiful Lass, the vet plunged his hand up to his elbow into the horse. 'Let's have a feel, old girl. Whoa, steady there,' he encouraged softly as the mare backed away at the intrusion. 'The head's twisted to the side,' he said, withdrawing his arm and looking across at Jo. 'I'm going to need your help. Are you up to this?' The question was more a courtesy. Jo nodded tensely. 'There's some rope on the back seat. Put it in the disinfectant in case I need it. Then hold her head once I get her lying down again.'

For the next ten minutes, working as fast as he could between crippling contractions, Phillip carefully manoeuvred the foal's head around inside the straining mare while Jo gently stroked her. Softly Jo reassured the big horse as, mouth closed, she pushed and groaned against each new contraction, sometimes twisting her head up in an attempt to see what the vet was doing. When one foot appeared outside the mare, Phillip ordered Jo to move down and tie the rope round the leg so it didn't disappear back inside the mare's body.

Wishing there was more she could do, Jo kept comforting the horse, willing the foal to be born, grimacing in sympathy as yet another punishing contraction crushed the vet's arm. Gradually he eased the other leg up. Flies buzzed around the sweat on his forehead and neck as he finally succeeded in turning the foal until the head and legs were in the correct position. Panting with the effort, he removed his arm, stiff and bruised from pressing against the contractions, and ran his other arm across his brow. Jo's heart pounded with anxiety. The foal was now ready to be born but had it all taken too long? Then, with one final shuddering contraction, Bountiful Lass pushed while Jo pulled gently on the rope, easing the foal out onto the ground, its small dark brown body showing blue through the protective membrane. Through a blur of tears Jo saw its fragile chest slowly moving up and down. It was alive. Eyes shining, she looked over at Phillip, not knowing whether to laugh or cry as mare and foal, both exhausted from the birth, lay on the ground. Leaving the hind legs still in the mare's vulva to prevent the umbilical cord from breaking immediately, the vet carefully cleared the membrane from the foal's face and stood up.

'It's a colt and they're both going to be fine,' he grinned wearily. Roughly he wiped his bruised and aching arms clean with the cloth Jo handed to him. 'Boy, that was tough. I don't enjoy wrong presentations. You did well, Jo, thanks.'

Jo looked up at him with admiration, wiping the back of her hand quickly across her eyes. After a few moments the mare sat up and nickered at her foal, its dark brown coat and head damp with blood and mucus, a copy of its mother's famous blaze shining from head to nose.

Jo stretched and fetched some fresh water for the vet to clean up, helping him tidy away his equipment, feeling the tension gradually drain from her body. Mother and foal were so beautiful. After another ten minutes the mare stood up, naturally breaking the umbilical cord, and Phillip swabbed the foal's fresh navel stub with iodine. In their desperation to save the mare and the excitement of their success, neither had noticed the dark menacing clouds rolling in from the south. As the afterbirth came away, the temperature dropped rapidly and the wind started to build, tugging at their clothes.

'I don't like the chances of the little one if this weather gets any worse,' shouted Phillip. 'We could lose him after all. We'd better take him with us.' Jo nodded in agreement. At his words the heavens opened, drenching them both in seconds, the winds quickly building in strength.

Buffeted by wind and rain the two struggled towards Bountiful Lass who was doing her best to shelter the little creature. Scooping the sodden bewildered animal up in his arms, Phillip carried him back to the car. Sliding into the back seat, teeth chattering, Jo dried the shivering foal off as best she could with an old blanket, hugging it to her to try and warm it, watched with increasing anxiety by Bountiful Lass. Gathering the afterbirth into the bucket to be checked for abnormalities later, Phillip tossed it with his bag into the boot of the car, then tumbled into the driver's seat and slammed the door. As the wind tore at the gum trees and whipped the rain almost horizontally across the windscreen, the little procession slowly made its way back to the stables, Bountiful Lass, head bent against the weather, trotting close behind the car.

'I was going to suggest we called him Bright Morning, but Crazy Storm would be more like it,' said Jo, now warm and dry in Phillip's big multicoloured sweater and a pair of Linda's jeans back at the stables. Leaning on the stall door, she turned from watching the new foal who lay sound asleep in thick cosy straw. Bountiful Lass munched contentedly close by on fresh lucerne. Having been given a belly full of colostrum, the essential first milk for foals, taken from the store of frozen colostrum kept at Dublin Park for just such emergencies, the foal, who had struggled so valiantly to be born, was now sure of a good start to life.

'Crazy Storm? Not bad. And you the drowning mermaid?' smiled Phillip, lifting up a long damp strand of platinum hair. 'You saved his life, Jo. You know that.' His eyes were suddenly serious. Jo thought she had never seen such amazingly soft grey in all her life. Her insides suddenly felt as though they had turned to water. Embarrassed, she pushed her hair behind her ears.

'How about Kick Up A Storm, a bit like one of his rescuers?' chipped in Linda, looking straight at Jo, a new respect in her eyes. 'But it would have been touch and go for them both if you hadn't.'

'I like that . . . Kick Up A Storm, welcome to the world!' Jo grinned back, the antagonism between the two girls gone.

'I'll be back first thing tomorrow to check them out, Linda,' said Phillip cheerfully, 'and to collect my sweater,' he laughed as an afterthought. That girl was something else.

*

The day before she was due to return to Sydney, Jo sauntered across one of the large paddocks where several broodmares were grazing with foals at foot. Beside her Sam panted contentedly, stopping every now and then to sniff something and then bounding off, tail lifted, to catch up with his mistress. Utterly trustworthy around horses, Jo had no concerns at Sam accompanying her, besides most of the horses here knew him now. Bees hummed busily in the white carpet of clover and tiny white moths and bugs fluttered upwards as the two wandered along. Mares grazed peacefully, their foals resting half hidden in the fresh rye-grass that had shot up after the storm. Along the road the bright orange flowers of the silky oaks shouted their existence against the greens and greys of the gums and pepper trees. Shading her eyes, Jo drank in the beauty of the valley, trying to imprint the scene on her memory, filled with a mixture of elation at having been a part of Dublin Park and sadness that her visit was nearly over. Lush green fields shimmered in the sunlight; on either side of the valley ancient, majestic craggy outcrops stood guard. Chewing on a piece of grass, Jo wandered along, thinking about everything that had happened in the past two weeks, the sun warm on her back.

Dear Kick Up A Storm. He was such a gutsy little fella. Jo had visited him every day and had watched with satisfaction as he gained weight and nursed happily at Bountiful Lass. Having been held immediately after he was born, he was not afraid of people like many other foals so he let Jo rub and scratch at his neck and shoulders and hunt for the sweet spots. When she found them, breathing in his soft warmth, Jo watched in delight as the tiny beast stretched and twisted his neck in blissful contortions, his top lip curling in ecstasy. And then there had been the long talks with Elaine. It had been so wonderful just to share with her grandmother each day her excitement at being allowed to help Linda with the horses. Even silly old Rupert had calmed down and only occasionally growled at Sam.

'How I'm going to miss this place,' murmured Jo, tossing away the piece of grass and reaching for another. As she straightened she leaped back in alarm as a mare charged past her, whinnying and snorting. Then she spied the foal hidden in the long grass only a few feet away from Sam.

'Heel, Sam!' she yelled too late as the mare lashed out with her hooves, kicking Sam in the chest.

Sam yelped in pain and surprise. Then, as the mare bustled her foal off to the other side of the paddock, he flopped to the ground.

'Sam!' cried Jo, the blood draining from her face as she charged over to where the dog lay in the long grass, struggling for breath, his suffering obvious in his big brown eyes. Jo started trembling. Looking wildly around, she tried to collect her thoughts, her heart thumping with fear. There was no-one in sight. Sam was obviously badly injured but he was too heavy for her to carry. She had to make a decision.

'You'll be okay, Sam. I'll be right back,' she gasped, terrified to leave him yet having no alternative. Then she turned and ran as far as she could across the paddock to the road, praying the other mares would stay away from him while she was gone. 'Don't let him die, please don't let him die,' she kept repeating, her heart hammering against her ribs as she raced up the dirt road towards the stables, dragging in great rasping gulps of air, the pain in her chest increasing as she willed herself to run faster.

Her grandmother's Landrover was the first vehicle

she spotted. Knowing Elaine always left the keys in the ignition, Jo almost fell inside, starting the engine with shaking fingers as Nick, the young Irish groom, sauntered out of one of the stables.

'Hey, whoa there! Where are you off to in a mighty rush?' he called cheerfully.

'Nick!' Jo screamed. 'It's Sam, he's been kicked by one of the mares. I need some help.'

Immediately serious, Nick leaped in beside Jo as she swung the big vehicle around, slithering through mud still soft from rain, and charged back to Sam.

'I've got to get him to the vet,' panted Jo as the two lifted the now limp and wheezing Sam into the back of the Landrover. Sam looked up at Jo, his eyes filled with fear. 'It's okay, Sam old boy, we'll get you better,' she whispered, fighting back the tears. 'I'll go to Denman, Nick. Ring through and tell them Sam's been kicked by a horse and is having a hard time breathing,' she ordered, jumping into the Landrover and heading back to the stables.

As Nick disappeared into the office in search of the phone, Jo pressed her foot to the floor. When she raced across the ford three kilometres out from Dublin Park, water spurting in all directions, her eyes flicked down to the petrol gauge. It was almost on empty. Her heart in her mouth she listened to Sam wheezing in the back. If she ran out of petrol now, it would be too late for him. Then she remembered the gauge always read low. Eating up the kilometres to the veterinary surgery, she turned carefully into the driveway of the tiny weatherboard cottage to see the local vet nurse come running towards her, followed behind by Phillip Gregg. A great surge of relief hit Jo and she almost burst into tears. By now Sam's gums were blue, his breath shallow and rasping.

'Get him inside and straight onto the oxygen,' ordered Phillip, throwing Jo a compassionate glance. 'We'll do the best we can, but he's not young.'

A tight knot in her stomach, Jo insisted on helping lift Sam from the car and carrying him into the surgery. The vet nurse had the oxygen mask ready as they lifted him onto the operating table.

'We'll be right now. It's best you stay in the waiting room. Vet'll come and talk to you in a while,' the vet nurse said firmly, ushering Jo out once the oxygen mask was in place.

Jo had no choice but to obey. She glared angrily at the girl's back as she disappeared back into the operating room then, suddenly exhausted, slumped down on the hard wooden seat.

'You have to live, Sam. You have to,' she cried silently. She couldn't lose him. Not Sam who had shared her grief and her joy, who had become her constant companion, lovable, affectionate, silly old Sam who always knew when she needed his comfort and who gave it so willingly and adoringly.

The minutes dragged by interminably as Jo alternately sat and then paced the hot stuffy little room, chewing her fingernails, the silence broken by the intermittent buzzing of a solitary fly. She should have realised one of the mares might take fright, but she hadn't seen the foal nor expected the scared mother to come at them. Neither had Sam. Those horses were his friends.

'Not Sam, please not Sam. Not the last tiny piece of Rick,' she whispered, staring at a dark stain on the floor, reliving the bewilderment she had seen in the dog's eyes. She clutched her fist against her mouth, biting down on her knuckles, struggling against the misery that churned inside her. He'd be all right. Phillip would see he was all right. She started pacing again, twisting and untwisting the band in her hair.

Finally, after what seemed like hours, the door opened and Phillip walked in. Jo's heart gave a lurch. It was like some dreadful macabre replay of the waiting room in the Prince of Wales Hospital.

'Is he . . . ? Is he . . . ?' she whispered

'He had us worried there for a while, I admit,' said Phillip. Jo's sigh was audible. She sat down shakily, her hair falling loose around her face, her lips trembling. 'One lung was punctured by the force of the kick and I'd say he's got a couple of broken ribs, but we won't know exactly until the X-ray comes through,' continued Phillip. 'He's also got what we call a pneumothorax, that is air that's escaped into the chest, which I've managed to drain, so he's breathing much easier now and he's more comfortable. He'll need to stay here for the next two or three days, but with rest and quiet he should be good as new in a few weeks.'

Jo stared at Phillip as the information slowly sunk in. 'You mean he's going to be all right? My Sam—' The words choked in her throat. Overcome with relief she flung her arms around Phillip and kissed him on the cheek.

Gazing down at the young girl, tears streaming down her cheeks, feeling her trembling body next to his, Phillip completely forgot he was a vet saving a dog and kissed her back full on her mouth. For five glorious seconds he tasted the sweetness of her soft full lips, his hands naturally weaving through her silk hair, the heady perfume of her warm body making his head swim. Then Jo pulled away shyly, breaking the spell. Phillip dropped his hands in horror at his inappropriate behaviour and stepped back, colour flooding his face.

He cleared his throat. 'You can come and see him if you like,' he stammered. He turned and led the way into the operating room, still stunned by the effect of the kiss and his own unprofessional behaviour.

Sam was lying on the floor breathing normally, his eyes closed, the vet nurse sitting near him, the oxygen mask ready in case he showed any breathing distress. Jo's eyes blurred with tears. Wiping her hand across her eyes, she kneeled down beside him. He opened his big brown eyes briefly and feebly wagged his tail. For a few moments Jo stayed beside him talking quietly, then slowly she stood up.

'It might be best just to let him rest now,' said Phillip quietly, his emotions under control. He walked Jo out to the car.

'I'll be back to see him tomorrow,' she said, leaning out of the Landrover, one hand on the gear-stick. 'I'll never be able to thank you for saving him. He was my brother's dog. You never met Rick, did you?'

Her smile tinged with sadness tore at Phillip's heart. 'No, but your grandmother spoke of him,' he replied, trying to keep his voice steady. Her eyes were utterly bewitching. His words seemed to have no connection with reality. All he could think of was that he had fallen madly in love with this schoolgirl and that she was going to drive away in about thirty seconds.

'Then I'll see you tomorrow morning around seven,' smiled Jo as she started the engine.

'For sure,' said Phillip, completely forgetting to tell her that he was only acting as a locum at the surgery and tomorrow he wouldn't be here or doing the rounds at Dublin Park as he had to visit a property which would take him away from the Hunter

Valley for the next four days, by which time she and Sam would be back in Sydney and today only a memory. 'Which is probably just as well,' he thought soberly as the Landrover vanished into the distance. If word got out that he went around kissing some of his patients' owners, especially one so young, he'd better start looking for a new job and a different place to live. But still he couldn't shake the memory of Jo's lips against his.

The shadows were lengthening as Jo arrived back at Dublin Park immensely relieved that Sam was going to be all right, the car strangely empty without him. Gently she ran her fingers over her lips. Had Phillip really meant to kiss her like that or was it just an accident? She felt a shiver of excitement ripple through her. He had to be at least twenty-six and he was very good looking. She had liked it that he'd kissed her on the lips, even if it was an accident.

As Elaine came running out to greet the car, Jo tucked her hair back behind her ears, hoping Gran would understand her driving all the way to Denman in the family Landrover without a licence.

'Nick told me about Sam, darling,' Elaine cried, her voice filled with concern.

Jo stepped slowly out of the car and shut the door. The euphoria of knowing Sam was going to live had subsided and she felt incredibly tired. 'He's going to be all right, Gran,' she answered, then burst into tears. Elaine put her arm around her and led her into the house as Jo spilled out the whole story. 'I was so frightened, Gran, I really thought I had lost him,' she said, sitting down and watching her grandmother put on the kettle.

'You were lucky Phillip was at the surgery. He's an excellent vet,' said Elaine.

Dressed in an old shirt and working trousers, Wayne walked into the kitchen and helped himself to a beer from the fridge, twisting off the top and taking a long swig.

'You've got more spunk than I'd have given credit to one of me brother's brats,' he said unsmiling, his cold grey eyes staring straight at Jo.

'I think we've all had far too much drama and excitement this week,' said Elaine seeing Jo bristle. 'Now, Jo dear, you had better go and do some serious studying as you'll be staying a while longer. As it is we'll all be in strife keeping you here over the week. I'd better ring your dad and explain what's happened. By the way,' said Elaine bustling towards the phone, 'I don't think we'll mention the business of you driving the Landrover outside the property to anyone, will we?'

Jo grinned sheepishly. 'I love you, Gran.'

Chapter Seven

DESPITE ITS TRAUMAS, the break at Dublin Park had, as Charlie had hoped, done much to restore Jo's health and wellbeing. Within two weeks of her return to Sydney, with Sam almost back to his former self, although still slightly sore from his fractured ribs, Jo was once more singing around the house, much to her parents' relief.

Patting Sam happily, Jo returned from exercising Fizzy one afternoon after school to find her father and his foreman Mick Steiner in the yard. They were both intently watching Arctic Gold, one of the stable's top thoroughbreds, who was being examined by Sydney's leading equine vet, Frederick Zinman. After leading Fizzy back into his stall, having fed him and bedded him down for the night, Jo walked quietly over and stood beside the two men.

Owned by Charlie and three leading Australian businessmen, and having won a number of country races and been placed in last year's Caulfield Cup, Arctic Gold had been heavily tipped to win the Cup this year. The Caulfield Cup was considered the toughest 2400-metre event in the turf world and an important race in the lead-up to the most famous

Australian race of all, the Melbourne Cup. With only two weeks to go before the race, Charlie had been forced to pull Arctic Gold off track work today because of back problems. Arms folded, Charlie's face was grim as he watched the horse grunt and flinch under the vet's expert fingers.

Jo was dying to ask her father about the new stallion that had recently joined the stables, but now was clearly not the moment. Instead she moved over to a stall in the far corner near the undercover exercising arena and cautiously poked her head over the securely padlocked stable door. Seventeen hands high and pitch black, the stallion occupying the stall had a mean look and a clumsy gait that was clearly visible as he circled the stall. Yet for all his ugliness Jo found something engaging about the way he glared at her, head sideways, pawing the ground.

'He's something else that one, can open anything with his teeth.'

Jo jumped as Winks materialised from the shadows. 'I wish you wouldn't do that,' she complained light-heartedly. She never quite got used to the way Winks seemed to appear from nowhere.

'He's ugly as he's mean but he's a goer. Give your dad time to knock some sense into him and he could do very well,' said Winks, ignoring her complaint. 'The bloke as sold that bugger to yer dad, 'scusing my French, said if 'e wanted to try and make some-fink of him 'e was welcome. The crazy Kiwi bastard practically give him away.'

'I wish Dad'd give me a go. I'd teach you a few manners, you cheeky cuss,' she said, longingly, to the three-year-old.

'Don't you go trying any funny tricks with this one, lass,' admonished Winks soberly, his birdlike eyes suddenly clouded with concern. The stallion responded by giving a shrill yell.

Charlie turned his head abruptly in their direction. 'Get away from there, Jo,' he barked. 'What the flamin' heck d'you think you're doing, Winks?'

'Just taking a look, boss, no harm done,' replied Winks calmly. He grabbed Jo's elbow and propelled her round the corner. Immediately three heads popped out of separate stalls. Walking across to a doe-eyed chestnut mare, Jo rubbed her soft nose, still thinking about the stallion. What she would give to prove she could ride a horse like that.

'There's more'n just Chilly Charlie worryin' your dad,' prodded Winks, shaking his head, calling Arctic Gold by his stable name. 'He's tired all the time and snappy. Not like hisself at all.' He pulled out a battered tobacco swatch and a squashed packet of papers and started to roll a cigarette. 'I've known your dad for a good few years and I never seen him like this. Never.' He stuck the cigarette unlit between his lips.

'Mum's not very happy at the moment and it's upsetting Dad. I think it's mostly because of me,' Jo sighed, wanting to confide in Winks, but her loyalty to her father holding her back. How she missed her grandmother and the intimacy they had built up together in those two short weeks at Dublin Park. She had heard her parents again last night, voices raised, portions of their conversation drifting up into her room as she tried to concentrate on her revision.

Nina had done most of the talking, in that helpless little girl voice that grated against Jo and so easily escalated to hysteria, accusing Charlie of encouraging Jo to spend too much time with Fizzy instead of studying, complaining about the extra hours he was putting in at the stables.

'Why can't Mum just accept that both me and Dad

adore horses and stop trying to force us both to change?' Jo thought wistfully, her mother's words about models and finishing schools surfacing again. She scratched the chestnut mare, running her hand down her long silky neck, gaining comfort from the contact. Next week exams were starting and beyond that Jo didn't want to think any further. The mare started to nibble at her shoulder, reciprocating her caresses as though she understood Jo's thoughts.

'Do you believe horses have ESP?' Jo asked Winks as they wandered back to the main part of the stables.

'Of course they do. And what was it that made you ask a question like that?' inquired Winks.

'Nothing really,' replied Jo. She wasn't sure if she believed in ESP herself but she always felt better when she had been down to the stables. She felt as though she shared her innermost thoughts with some of these magnificent beasts without needing to voice them.

By now the vet had gone and Mick was leading Arctic Gold back into his stall. Her father called her over.

'Hold it a sec, Mick. Jo, you may as well learn a thing or two while you're here. What's your opinion of Chilly Charlie running in the Caulfield?'

Jo was slightly taken aback. She could feel Mick Steiner's curious eyes burning into her. Pride that her father had asked her opinion fighting uncertainty, she asked for Arctic Gold to be walked around so she could watch his gait. It appeared perfectly normal. However, remembering how the horse had reacted earlier when the vet had manipulated his back she replied, 'He was pretty uncomfortable when Mr Zinman examined him.' She paused. 'If the race were in Sydney I'd feel more certain, Dad, but having to travel down to Melbourne and being such a tough race, I don't think I'd risk it,' she said blushing furiously, feeling foolish as the men stared at her.

'And why's that?' asked Charlie.

Jo gave her reasons and Charlie nodded in approval. 'You're learning, girl. But I hope you're wrong,' he said, smiling down at her as Mick led Arctic Gold away. 'Now, we'd better get you home before your mother starts worrying. Tell her not to fuss about me. I've got some paperwork to catch up with in the office so I'll be here for a while longer. Run up and see Gloria. She'll organise someone to run you home.' He gave Jo a quick pat, his eyes clouding as he watched her disappear through the big green wooden gates, his mind returning to last night's conversation. Were they really doing the right thing forcing their daughter to follow a career she kept saying she had no interest in? But Nina had escalated the whole argument when he suggested they reconsider, accusing him of ruining Jo's chances in life by encouraging her with the horses. She had also accused him of not caring about her or wanting to spend time with her any more. How wrong she was. Illogical as it seemed, it was because he loved Nina so much that he worked so hard at Kingsford Lodge.

'He's a thousand times better than he was a week ago,' remarked Mick, breaking into Charlie's thoughts.

'He'd have to be,' nodded Charlie. 'I'm putting my money on Freddy's wizardry.' He shoved his hands in his pockets, swaying back and forth, frowning.'What d'you reckon with the new stallion, Mick?' he asked finally.

'You're going to need tough riders. But look at

some of the greats that started off mean and scrawny, practically given away.'

Charlie scratched his head. He hoped Mick was right, but he had too many other things worrying him at the moment to give it any more thought.

Her exams finally over, Jo sat contentedly on the sitting room floor in her pyjamas in one of those rare moments in life when she felt close to her mother. As Nina brushed her long blonde hair she felt more relaxed than she had for weeks.

'If we're all going skiing in St Moritz this Christmas, you and I need to go shopping,' announced Nina, running her hands down her daughter's silken locks, refusing to allow Charlie's repeated lateness to annoy her tonight. She had spent all day planning. 'That outfit I brought you back from Paris is fine for skiing, but I want you to look the part, darling, off the slopes as well as on. You never know who we might meet there. After all, they are always snapping royalty at these exclusive resorts.'

'New ski boots, Mum?' Jo smiled hopefully up at her mother. Having enjoyed several seasons in the snow both in Australia and overseas, Jo was an athletic if not brilliant skier. She had to admit she enjoyed wearing the latest gear, particularly the latest snap-in boots and step-in bindings.

'Of course, darling . . . Keep your head straight, I want to try something. More importantly, we have to get you a special outfit for the do in October,' continued Nina. The muscles in Jo's stomach tightened. Not wanting to shatter the fragility of the moment, she waited as Nina twisted her blonde hair around itself, clipping it into an enormous gilt-edged tortoise shell hair comb and grimacing at the effect. 'No, I don't think so,' she said, shaking her head and letting the hair tumble free. Fiddling around in the small basket beside her, Nina finally pulled out a simple gold clasp. 'That's better. Something slightly less obtrusive that doesn't take away from your eyes.'

'What do in October?' asked Jo cautiously.

'Oh, Jo, don't be like that. I told you about the Capricorn luncheon ages ago,' pouted her mother, dropping the brush into the basket, suddenly bored with fiddling with Jo's hair, the intimacy between them destroyed.

'Oh golly! Oh, I'm sorry, Mum, I'd forgotten,' exclaimed Jo, her words only making matters worse. Now she remembered—the fashion lunch in aid of the Prince of Wales Hospital, her mother had insisted they attend together. Her heart sank. Caught up in her father's disappointment of Arctic Gold not competing in the Caulfield Cup, she had mercifully managed to push the function clean out of her head.

'You forgot! How could you forget the biggest opportunity of your life?' squealed Nina, infuriated. 'I've had the editors of *Vogue* and *She* and half the glossy magazines in Australia phoning me shrieking about you, not to mention the money this family's donated, and you forgot! Jo, how could you?' An angry flush spread from Nina's cheeks down her neck. Pushing Jo away she stood up, winding herself up into one of her tirades.

It was on the tip of Jo's tongue to fight back when she suddenly realised the money and the function was as much about grieving for Rick as helping the hospital.

'Mum, Mum, please, no wait. What do you think I should wear?' she blurted out, scrabbling up and grabbing her mother's arm.

Nina's jaw dropped. Hurriedly shutting her

mouth, she snatched up the latest fashion magazine from the pile on the table. Sitting down again she skipped through the pages, chewing on her lip, then finally she stabbed her finger at a deceptively simple dress from Le Louvre, a leading fashion salon in Melbourne.

'There!' Nina exclaimed, her eyes once more sparkling with excitement. 'One of Lil's designs would be perfect. Simple, chic and it will give you height. We'll pop down for a fitting.'

Jo sat down cautiously on the sofa and peered over Nina's shoulder, her mother's soft fragrance making her long to recapture their closeness. A far cry from her comfy old shirts and jeans, the dress wasn't bad, except the model was three sizes smaller than Jo and about five foot eight. Why not get into the whole game and dress up for a day? After all it was only a luncheon, she thought. If it would recapture the warmth between her and her mother, it would be worth it.

'I think we should go for something quite different for your other two outfits. One a bit saucy,' continued Nina, pointing to a very revealing blouse, 'and then there's the casual sophisticated look,' she finished triumphantly. Jo's stomach gave another lurch.

'What d'you mean, other outfits? It's only a lunch, Mum. I'm not going to rush out and change between courses.'

'Jo, why do you always have to be so impossible?' complained Nina, tossing the magazine on the table.

'I'm sorry, Mum. Go on,' said Jo struggling to control her impulse to laugh at the pointlessness of it all.

Appeased, Nina dropped her voice to a conspiratorial whisper. 'There is this fashion editor a friend told me about who is looking for a new face for the launch of her magazine in the new year, I just thought it might be a good idea to have a couple of surprise outfits up our sleeve.' Jo stared in outrage at her mother. Nina held up her hand. 'Now don't look at me like that, Jo.'

'Mum, I don't have the looks for it,' cried Jo desperately.

Nina reached up and patted her daughter's cheek. 'We'll see, darling, we'll see. I don't think you have any idea how beautiful you are.'

Jo bit back a retort. She had discussed the whole problem of modelling and finishing school with her grandmother and was determined to try and stay calm. 'You're not there till you're there,' Elaine had said. 'You could do a lot worse than spend a year in Switzerland. The horses will still be here when you return.' It had comforted Jo at the time, but as she listened to her mother's endless prattle about editors, designers and catwalks, the fear that her life was closing in once again crept over her. Trying to express her worries to her father a couple of days later gave her little comfort.

'I bailed you out over the Martha Wellbourne Trophy, kiddo, now it's your turn to please your mother.'

Jo knew she had no choice.

The day of the fundraising lunch dawned. Dressed in an elegantly cut, flowing cream creation offset by a thick gold snake necklace and matching earrings, Nina slid into the back seat of the silver Bentley clutching her cream and gold hat. Feeling awkward and overdressed in the pale turquoise dress and jacket Nina had chosen from the Melbourne designer, Jo was completely unaware of the stunning effect she made. Getting into the car she shuddered at the thought of the other two outfits her mother had bought, and which she had sworn to herself she would never wear; one the top cut so low she blushed just thinking about it, the other so drab and ordinary she was amazed that anyone could so willingly part with over fifteen hundred dollars to buy it.

Checking her lipstick in the reflection from the tinted windows, Nina told the chauffeur to drive on.

'You look absolutely wonderful, darling,' cooed Nina, straightening Jo's collar and scrutinising her make-up as the great silver beast slid its way through the traffic into the city. Jo could easily pass for nineteen. 'Have you got your little purse? You must remember to touch up your lipstick after we've eaten and make sure you don't get any on your teeth,' she fussed. Today was the beginning of something really special. She rummaged in her own cream satin purse, trying to remember the name of the fashion editor, as Jo sat stiff and tense, wondering why on earth she had let her mother talk her into this.

The hotel foyer thronged with elegantly dressed, coiffured and perfumed women, some wearing hats, some obviously models. Accepting the fluted glass of champagne thrust into her hand, Nina wove through the crowd, introducing Jo to committee members and others who flocked around her, her eyes roving across the crowd to see who was present. Jo stared wide-eyed at four-inch heels and amazingly audacious outfits. Swooping down from the other side of the room Beryl Mawson, the president of the Capricorn committee, wearing a very large orange and yellow hat, placed a kiss in the air six inches from Nina's cheeks.

'Nina my dear, you look ravishing as always,' she smiled. 'And, Jo, you look more grown up every year. Come and I'll show you your table.' Tucking her hand under Jo's arm, she ushered them to their seats amongst the other hundred and fifty guests, flowers spilling over in the centre of each table, gilt names on white place cards marking their seats.

Once the State Premier's wife had been welcomed as the guest of honour and the president had explained the proceedings, luncheon was served. As they feasted on grilled salmon and light garden salad accompanied by a dry white wine, the fashion show began.

'See, she doesn't have your high cheekbones and perfect mouth,' whispered Nina to Jo, shaking her head as a tall dark-haired model paraded the length of the stage in a figure-hugging pant suit. 'You'd be perfect in that, darling, when you've lost a bit of weight. Jo's training to be a model,' she explained in a stage whisper to her table.

Jo felt the blush spread from her cheeks down over her neck. Never in her whole life had she felt so uncomfortable. As the parade continued, Nina insisted on making more embarrassing little asides that seemed to Jo to echo round the entire room, despite the accompanying blare of music. As polite applause petered out with the last model disappearing from the stage, Jo felt a hand on her shoulder.

'So this is the special young lady. I see what you mean,' gushed a large, overpainted woman in her late forties wearing an overpowering perfume. 'You're absolutely lovely, darling.' She placed her hand under Jo's chin. Turning Jo's head, she examined her from all angles. Biting the insides of her cheeks to stop herself from leaping up and running out, Jo somehow managed a frozen smile.

'You need to relax more. Part your lips when you smile, darling. Lovely, lovely.' The woman dropped her hand and whispered to Nina, 'She's divine, darling. I'll have a word in Irene's ear after the presentations.' Nina beamed as the other woman scuttled back to her seat at the next table.

'Irene who?' asked Jo suspiciously. 'And who was that?'

'Irene Sarrenson-Hicks runs Irene's, the top model agency in Sydney,' bubbled Nina, beside herself with excitement. 'And that, my darling, was Audrey Bishop. She writes the social column for the *Sydney Morning Herald*. Smile at her. I can't believe what she just said. She *never* hands out favours,' Nina whispered, waving and smiling to Audrey as the president introduced the Premier's wife.

Having given a charming and brief speech thanking everyone for their generosity in supporting the Prince of Wales Hospital charity luncheon, explained some of the immediate needs of the hospital, and accepted a large bouquet of flowers, the Premier's wife sat down.

'And now it is my delightful duty to invite one of our very special guests to the platform,' announced the president, resuming her place at the microphone. 'This lady doesn't consider herself a special guest but she honours our charity every year in a very special way. She is our very own and very dear Nina Kingsford.'

Smiling confidently, Nina stepped onto the platform amidst loud applause. Waiting for the clapping to subside, the president turned to Nina. 'On behalf of the Capricorn committee and of everyone here, I would like to thank you once again, Nina, for your very, very generous donation to the Prince of Wales Hospital. Last year we were overwhelmed by your generosity but this year . . . well, words fail me. Nina has donated a hundred thousand dollars to the hospital.' She was forced to wait until the clapping once again subsided. 'Nina dear, your generosity knows no bounds. Our hearts go out to you at your recent personal loss and we value you as our friend. Please accept this little token of our appreciation.' She handed Nina a vast bouquet of flowers.

'Beryl, you and I go back a long way,' began Nina, gathering the bouquet into her arms. 'I know you and your committee have worked tirelessly to organise today's luncheon and I can only admire you all. Functions like these really do make a difference and I'd like to say thank you to each and every one of you for your donations today. As you know my youngest son died earlier this year in the Prince of Wales Hospital, despite everything the doctors—' She stopped, her lips shaking, suddenly overcome. Jo felt tears prick the back of her eyes as her mother paused to regain her composure.

'My donation is for equipment and research,' continued Nina. 'It is also for all you mothers. This year I lost a child. If my contribution can help save you the heartache I and my family have gone through, then I will have done something that counts. I offer you all my sincere congratulations for supporting this luncheon today.' She put her hands together round the bouquet, leading more applause.

Blinking back the tears, Jo clapped with the others, watching her mother with pride. She could see she felt at home with all these ladies in their fancy gear, and it was true, she was generous. She didn't have to give the money. This was part of the healing process her mother needed, maybe they all needed. Now Rick would always be remembered. She glanced around at the upturned faces, then started at the sound of her own name.

'Come on, Joanna darling, stand up and let me introduce you to everyone.' Shrinking back into her seat, Jo blushed furiously as heads turned in her direction. Everyone was waiting. Reluctantly she stood up, waves of embarrassment sweeping over her, sweat trickling down her back and between her breasts as she felt everyone's eyes burning into her. Nina beamed with pride.

'Now don't you agree she looks quite lovely. I am trying to talk Joanna into becoming a model but she doesn't believe she can do it,' explained Nina, ignoring both Beryl Mawson hovering by her elbow and Jo's obvious discomfort. 'I hope one day she will be up here modelling wonderful dresses like some of the ones we've seen today. Wouldn't you agree she has what it takes?' She blew Joanna a kiss.

Jo gave her mother a stiff smile and the room erupted in spontaneous applause. Many had been moved to tears by Nina's short speech and were grateful for the opportunity to acknowledge this woman and her generosity once more. Jo sat back down in her chair, hideously aware of the models politely applauding in the far corner, a slow burning anger building within her.

As people crowded round Jo and Nina at the end of the luncheon, behind her stiff courtesy, Jo's fury grew. Without warning, her mother had first stirred up her emotions over Rick's death and then profoundly embarrassed her. Jo could have forgiven her all that but never the way she had publicly ignored Jo's own feelings about modelling. When Irene Sarrenson-Hicks swooped down on them as they were about to leave Jo could barely part her lips in a caricature of a smile at the woman who made it quite clear she had scrutinised every single awkward second Jo had been under the spotlight.

'You may not have it all yet, my dear, but you obviously have natural style and your mother is quite right, you will make a wonderful model. Ring me next week,' she said to Nina from under her ivory and black hat, pressing her card into her hand as she continued to look Jo up and down. 'Give me six months to get the clothes and the walk right and fix up the skin and hair . . .' Jo could see two gold fillings as she gave a wide smile. 'Learn to relax, child, and I'll make you an international star in no time.'

Ecstatic at having caught the attention of the top model agent in Australia, Nina gushed her enthusiasm, making Jo even more embarrassed.

'How could you speak to that woman?' spat Jo as they finally climbed into the Bentley. 'She criticised everything about me. What's wrong with my skin?'

'Calm down, Joanna. You have no idea what you are talking about,' ordered Nina, slamming the door and tapping the dividing panel, Irene Sarrenson-Hicks's words still ringing in her ears. Six months . . . an international star . . . Nina hadn't liked the criticism of the hair and clothes either, but what did it matter? Jo had been noticed.

'I hated every minute—' Jo began.

'I've had enough of your complaining, Jo,' snapped Nina, refusing to let her destroy the glory of the moment. 'One more word and Fizzy goes. There won't be anyone to look after him when you are in Switzerland anyway.'

She might as well have slapped Jo's face. Ghostly pale, Jo slumped back in her seat, staring unseeing at the passing cars. Fizzy! She wouldn't. Would she? Once home she raced upstairs, tore off her designer clothes, clambered into her jeans and an old shirt and fled the house. Racing down the street, she was just in time to catch the bus to the stables.

'I'm not there till I'm there. Oh Fizzy!' she kept repeating over and over. Just seeing him in his stall was enough to make her feel better again. Quickly saddling him up she led him to Centennial Park and rode him furiously around the circuit. On her return she found Pete, the stable hand, feeding the horses. 'Sorry you don't get to track work these days,' he said, blushing to his ears.

'Me too,' replied Jo grimly. For a few moments they talked about horses and riding as Pete struggled to keep the conversation going. Then, declining an offer to go and have coffee, she led Fizzy to his stall. When she emerged she was relieved to see Pete had vanished and the place was deserted.

Slumping down on an empty feed drum, Jo stared ahead, her violet eyes blazing in her pale face, the anger she had felt after her humiliation resurfacing, the memory of the afternoon washing over her in hot waves of embarrassment, the mention of Rick painfully sharp. How could Mum have done it to her? Why did she have to keep pushing when she knew how much Jo hated the idea of being a model? A sudden screech from the corner stall made her jump. Jo leaped to her feet. Damn it, two could play at this game. She'd show them all what she was made off. That way Dad'd have to let her be part of Kingsford Lodge and Fizzy'd be safe and Irene what's-her-name could go to hell. Jo was so fuelled up with anger and frustration, she failed to realise the illogicality of her thoughts as she dived into the tack room. Emerging with a saddle and bridle, she walked purposefully towards the new stallion's box and peered into the dimness, her heart thudding in her chest.

'Listen, you mean ugly brute, you can stop yelling at me right now,' she ordered, dropping the saddle on the ground, unlocking the padlock on the door and sliding the bolt. Slipping inside she stopped, bridle in hand, as the stallion, ears lying right back, raced round the stall, trumpeting imperiously, his hooves beating a muted tattoo on the sawdust. After a few more turns, when she still hadn't moved, the stallion stopped too, eyeing her in his strange crooked way.

Pulling a piece of carrot she had grabbed from the tack room from her pocket, Jo held out her hand. Inquisitively the horse edged over to Jo, sniffing her out. Arm still outstretched, Jo waited, bridle at the ready. Greedily the horse nuzzled at her closed palm with his lip. As he opened his mouth she quickly slipped the bit between his teeth, gave him the carrot and pushed the bridle over his head, fastening the two straps while he chewed.

Sniffing Jo for more food and finding none, the stallion gave her a sharp nip on the shoulder and received an equally sharp slap which set him racing around the stall again. But this time Jo had a loose hold on the reins. He tossed his head in defiance but Jo finally had him under control. She could see that to saddle him up would be too much, so instead, knowing the gates were closed and there was no way he could bolt except into the enclosed exercising arena, she led him out into the main stable yard, one hand gripping the reins firmly under his mouth.

Horses' heads popped out of stalls as Jo clambered up onto his back and nudged him forwards. Gripping on with her knees as he skittled and shied in all directions, her one goal was to prove to herself she could ride the beast. The rush of adrenalin as she realised she was astride him almost cost her a leg as the stallion tried to swipe her against the side of a stall. Using the reins to force his head down and sideways, her legs pressing insistently against his flanks, she eventually succeeded in urging him forwards. Glorying in her triumph she failed to see Winks step forward from the shadows, nor was she ready for the sudden clatter that spooked the stallion who reared up, front hooves fighting the air. Losing her balance as the reins suddenly went slack, Jo jerked sideways. Grabbing the horse's thick black mane she clung to the coarse strands with fingers that kept slipping. Her legs unable to grip at this angle, she could feel herself sliding backwards . . .

Charlie strode into the house and straight into the room he had converted into an office, intent on ringing Frederick Zinman to find out the results of a culture from one of the horse's lungs. He dialled the first three numbers then stopped as Nina appeared at the door.

'Aren't you going to ask how our fabulous lunch went?' she giggled, clutching a glass of champagne in one hand, the bottle in the other.

Charlie dropped the receiver back onto its cradle. 'I'm sorry, darling. Were they happy with the donation?' he asked, thinking quickly.

'Ecstatic,' replied Nina swaying slightly.

'And Jo?'

'Oh, Jo. She was not ecstatic. She hated it. They all loved her. Irene Sarrenson-Hicks said she'd make her into a star. Didn't she come home with you? I'm surprised she bothered to change she was in such a rush to get to her wretched horse,' she finished, unable to keep the bitterness out of her voice.

Charlie walked over to her. 'Neene, are you sure we're doing the right thing forcing her to go into modelling when she really doesn't want to?' He took a step towards her, her heavy perfume wafting enticingly around him. His eyes wandered over her full luscious curves, his mind no longer on Jo. It seemed forever since he had held his wife in his arms.

'You're not going to dredge up that old argument again, are you?' Nina said tartly, disappointment at his lacklustre reaction to her revelation about Irene turning to anger.

'But what if she did learn to be a horse trainer, would it be such a sin?'

'So you want to kill all my children, do you?' shouted Nina. 'The next step is Bertie gives up law and runs Kingsford Lodge with you.' She started to cry.

'The thought had crossed my mind.'

Nina was openly sobbing now. 'Why don't you just toss me away too and shack up with that Gloria woman who runs your life anyway? Do you know, I have to be the only woman in the racing industry who has to ring up her husband's secretary to find out where he is.' She was laughing and sobbing at the same time, the champagne spilling across the thick-pile carpet.

'Neene darling,' started Charlie, wresting the champagne bottle from her.

'Don't you Neene darling me. Spend some time at home. Make me feel wanted. Show you love me!' she screamed, trying to snatch the bottle back and falling against him. 'Charlie, what's happening between us?' The phone shrilled across the room. Nina beat him to it. 'Don't answer it, Charlie darling. Leave it just this once. Let what's-his-name fix the horses. You don't have to do it all.' Mascara was running down her face, her bottom lip trembled, her low-cut camisole revealed plump inviting breasts. 'Come to bed, Charlie,' she implored.

The phone still shrilled. Gently lifting Nina's hand from the receiver, Charlie pressed her fingers to his lips, his eyes filled with longing.

'Give me five seconds, Neene.' Her hand was still in his as he answered the phone.

'The horses! Always those bloody horses. I can never come before those bloody horses,' Nina shrieked at him, snatching her hand away and running from the room. Charlie could hear her sobbing into the sofa as he listened to Zinman's instructions. It seemed he had no choice, he had to check this horse.

'Neene, I love you,' he said to the back of her head, trying one last time, but she shook him away.

All the way to the stables Charlie kept thinking about Nina. He would get back early to her tonight. He would make it up to her. His love for her had never wavered, it was just that the stables were so demanding of his time. Maybe he should let Mick take over more but somehow he couldn't. He was terrified of losing the edge.

He turned the key in the big green door, already tense, and his heart started to race as he heard the shrill yell of a horse, followed by the clatter of hooves on the concrete. Flinging the door wide so it banged against its hinges, Charlie stared in alarm, first at Winks's scrawny back and then at the stallion rearing up, front hooves angrily pawing the air. As though stepping into his worst nightmare, he saw Jo sliding backwards along the stallion's back towards the ground.

'Jesus! Jo!' he screamed as the horse's hooves hit the concrete and the beast kicked out with his hind legs. Scrabbling back into the saddle position, struggling to retrieve the reins, Jo was immediately thrown forwards as the stallion bucked, determined to get her off his back. Charlie made a grab for the reins and missed. Trumpeting his disdain, the stallion once more kicked up his hooves and cantered off into the exercising arena. Jo's legs ached. Dark patches showed under her arms. Rivulets of sweat ran down her cheeks and into her mouth, sharp and salty as she ran her tongue across dry lips. Gripping the stallion's sides, she tussled with the great grunting beast, every nerve ready for another buck or rear. Finally, after the third unsuccessful buck, realising he was not going to dislodge Jo, the horse stopped, flanks heaving and damp with sweat, head hanging, blowing heavily from his nostrils. Jo's chest was heaving as hard as his yet she dared not relax. Shaking his head, the stallion scattered flecks of white froth from his mouth. Then, with one last defiant jerk on the reins he stood still.

'Thank you, you ugly bugger,' cried Jo triumphantly, leaning forward and patting him, chest still heaving as Winks and Charlie both leaped to take the horse from her. 'I'm fine, thanks. Now he knows who's boss.' Then she realised she was staring straight into her father's eyes.

'What the bloody hell d'you think you're up to, you stupid little girl? Don't you know you could have been killed?' shouted Charlie. Reacting to the sudden noise, the stallion jerked his head and skittered sideways. Charlie grabbed the reins and controlled the horse, pulling Jo to the ground. His face was like a thundercloud and he was shaking from head to toe. Wordlessly he led the horse back into the stall while Jo stormed off to the tack room with the saddle. Reappearing, the bridle over one shoulder, he locked the door and clicked the padlock into place, then came face to face with Winks.

'I told her she had to watch that big blighter. She

certainly showed 'im who was in charge, but. No doubts there,' he chuckled, more from relief than anything else.

Charlie cut across him. 'You bloody fool old man, how could you let her do it?' he exploded. 'You're fired. You can collect your pay and move out tomorrow.' Winks turned grey.

Stepping back into the yard, Jo blanched, unable to believe her ears. 'Dad, it had nothing to do with Winks. He didn't know anything about it. Don't take it out on him.'

Charlie turned on her. 'And you, my girl. I've had it up to here with you. Straight after you get home you can start packing. Your mother's right, the further away from horses you are, the better for all of us.' His eyes were hard and cold as he glared at his daughter, his stomach still churning. For a few minutes he had been convinced he would lose Jo too. Jo stared at him, stunned. 'Not another word,' warned Charlie, holding up his finger.

'Don't worry, lass,' said Winks softly, his eyes too bright. 'I've not been much use around here for a good many years now. Your dad's right, I'm a silly old fool. Time to move on, lass, time to move on.'

Jo's eyes filled with tears. Because of some stubborn, foolish need in herself she had lost not only the respect of her father and any chance of being part of Kingsford Lodge, she had also managed to wreck the life of one of the people she loved most dearly.

Charlie grabbed her arm as she tried to run to hug Winks. 'You're coming with me while I do what I came out to do, and then we're going home,' he ordered. Miserably Jo turned back to Winks but he had disappeared. In the emptiness that suddenly enveloped her, she could not stop the tears from rolling down her cheeks. Brushing them disdainfully away she ran beside her father as he strode towards the sick horse.

'Dad, please don't make Winks go because of what I did,' stuttered Jo.

'The subject is closed,' replied Charlie with finality.

'Dad, that is so unfair!' she cried, her violet eyes full of misery.

'I'm unfair, you're unreasonable,' snapped Charlie. 'You consistently ignore my advice and refuse to do what I say. You are a danger to have around the stables.'

Jo gasped. Sticking her chin in the air, she fought back the tears as she was marched down the stable aisle.

Three weeks later, as the jacarandas scattered their purple flowers across the countryside, a chastened, silent Jo slid into the airplane seat next to Nina on the flight bound for Switzerland.

'You do what your mother says,' was all the goodbye she had got from her father.

Bleakly Jo stared out of the tiny window, watching Sydney vanish from sight, furious at her father for refusing to listen to her side of the story and even more furious at herself. She had lost her father's trust and respect. What had bitten deepest was that he no longer trusted her around horses. Surreptitiously she wiped a tear from her cheek. If Rick were still alive, it would all have been so different.

Part Two

Chapter Eight

JO RETURNED THE volley, slamming the tennis ball viciously back across the hard court towards her opponent, seventeen-year-old Emma Bamford, her face red with exertion, her mind not on the game. It was a mild afternoon at the exclusive girls' finishing school Institut Villa Pierrefeu near Montreux, two weeks before the Easter break and Jo was livid.

'Game, set and match!' yelled the umpire as Jo shot the ball into the net.

'Darn!' muttered Jo, wiping her face with her T-shirt, oblivious of the breathtaking mountain scenery around her as she ran towards the tall, smiling brunette who came running up to the net from the opposite end. Beyond the tennis courts sunshine caught the snow-tipped mountain peaks against which the school nestled, and sparkled on the great Lake Leman that stretched out from the town of Montreux way down in the valley below.

'Whatever happened to you, Jo, you let me walk all over you?' asked Emma, puzzled, as the two shook hands and walked off the court. The girls were well matched in their sporting skills and normally enjoyed a good tussle, regularly going to three sets.

Today Jo's serves had been a disaster and she had repeatedly missed easy balls.

'Don't ask, Emma. That was really awful. I didn't know I could play that badly,' replied Jo frowning up at Emma who, in her opinion, looked far too cool for the match they had just played. Picking up her towel, Jo rubbed her face and then quickly struggled into her jacket, shivering as the sweat began to dry. Tossing the towel over her shoulder, she sucked greedily at the orange quarter handed to her from a plate by one of the other girls who was acting as ball boy. She felt really cross. Despite it being merely a friendly match, she should not have allowed her anger to detract from her playing. The lanky tennis coach employed by the college having proved totally useless, if it hadn't been for Emma's coaching, Jo would have almost certainly given up learning tennis before she discovered how good she really was. 'I got a letter from Mum,' she explained, pulling the band from her hair and shaking her long blonde hair loose.

'Oh,' said Emma as she replaced her chewed orange quarter on the plate. Letters from her mum always unsettled Jo.

'Hurry along, girls!' cried a high-pitched voice in French. 'You know we at Pierrefeu are always punctual for afternoon tea.' Jo and Emma quickly stuffed their raquets in their covers, whispering in English. 'Remember your posture, ladies . . . and speak French,' continued the voice in frustration.

Both girls stuck out their tongues at the receding back of Mademoiselle Viaud, teacher of savoir-vivre, always on the prowl to check the girls' behaviour. Giggling, they hurried towards the beautiful old brown and white chalet-style country mansion, Villa

Pierrefeu, that had been Jo's home for the last five months.

'How about we go for a ride before dinner?' suggested Jo, swiping at an imaginary ball with her raquet, trying to sound less angry than she felt. 'The horses might be a bit frisky because of the cold, but it's the last chance we'll have this term.' Emma nodded her approval. Riding, tennis and Emma were the three things that made Institut Pierrefeu bearable for Jo. The letter from Nina today had made her so mad because it once more confronted her with the fact that her life was going in entirely the wrong direction. As they headed for hot showers, Jo wondered how she would ever have managed had she not met Emma.

Still smouldering over the way she had been unceremoniously dumped the previous November at Institut Pierrefeu and having endured a miserable Christmas in St Moritz with her parents in which, to add insult to injury, she had been forced to stay in her ski class while Charlie spent time at the horseracing on ice, when Emma Bamford bounced into the three-bed room on the first freezing day of the January term Jo's life had finally started to pick up. Back for her second term Emma Bamford had tossed her Gucci handbag on her bed, dropped her hand luggage on the floor and slipped off her thick ankle-length coat. Unwrapping her long mohair scarf and sending a shower of melting snowflakes in all directions, she shook out her waist-length chestnut hair and announced at the top of her voice that she intended to become the first girl ever to go through the school without speaking a word of French.

As though on cue, the door opened and a

shocked voice exclaimed, 'Mademoiselle! *Non! Non! Non!* You must try *parler français*!'

Turning her brown doe eyes on the tiny Swiss housemother's assistant, Emma ran over and clasped her in a tight hug.

'Oh, Madame Fleuri, it's so good to see you again. Don't tell me—"Ve speak here only Franche."' Extracting herself from Emma's arms, blushing furiously, Madame Fleuri shook her finger at the girl, half smiling half scowling, and vanished in a flurry of 'tuts'. Emma collapsed in laughter. 'Poor Madame Fleuri. She falls for it every time. She's such a sweetie. You can cry on her shoulder any time.'

Jo stared in amazed envy at this bold beauty whose long legs and luscious curves beckoned to a thousand glossy magazines.

'But you must speak French, this why we come to L'Institut,' cried a buxom, olive-skinned Italian who had been allotted the third bed.

Emma rolled her eyes. 'Relax, Rossita. It was a joke. Anyway, top models are booked for their looks, not their conversation, and that's what I intend to be once I've finished being "finished" here.' Stepping round her two enormous suitcases, she took a quick turn across the room in a caricature of a model on the catwalk. With an enormous sigh she then heaved the largest suitcase on the bed, emptied out its entire contents and flopped down beside the pile, half of which immediately slid onto the floor. 'God! I hate unpacking!'

'So do I. That's why I only brought one case,' admitted Jo already almost entirely unpacked.

'Only one case? You're not serious?' Emma gasped in astonishment. She stared up at the ceiling for a few seconds and then she sat up abruptly. 'You're Joanna the new girl, aren't you? Tell you what! Let's swap. I'll finish putting your stuff away and you can sort out this mess.'

'No thanks, I'm nearly finished, and it's Jo,' laughed Jo. 'But I don't mind giving you a hand.'

'You don't? I must have died and gone to heaven!' exclaimed Emma. She threw her hands in the air and flopped back onto the bed. Laughing, Jo caught a washbag just before it hit the ground. Quickly she placed her last items in her chest of drawers. Then together they tackled Emma's bags.

Over the next weeks, as Jo and Emma wrestled with flowers that refused to be arranged, giggled their way through deportment classes and struggled to speak French, Jo discovered that behind Emma's glamorous exterior and apparent confidence lay a girl lacking in self-esteem, longing for love and struggling, like Jo, for acceptance. With her father, a high-ranking officer in the Royal Air Force, constantly posted to different air bases around the world, Emma had never really known a home. Two terms at Pierrefeu was stability to Emma. Holidays were mostly spent in camps or with her aunt in England. To make up for it, her parents gave her a huge allowance and sent her a series of expensive presents, but not once had there been any mention of them coming to visit.

'Daddy's work keeps him busy and he needs Mummy to be with him,' Emma explained defensively whenever anyone questioned her. Jo let it be, yet the sadness behind Emma's bright smile was not lost on her.

Escaping on Saturdays to ski the local slopes, the bond between the two girls grew and as the weeks passed they became inseparable. There was a maturity about Emma that belied her dramatic behaviour. Listening to her enthuse about modelling, Jo could almost believe she might even enjoy being a part of the glamorous, catty world for a while herself. It had also forced her to the reluctant decision that the only way to win back her father's trust and respect was to throw herself into the modelling career her mother wanted so badly for her. It need not be forever, she consoled herself. Yet deep down she wondered how long she could keep to her decision.

Tennis proved to be one of Jo's greatest releases. As the weather improved and they could play outside, Jo learned fast under Emma's practised eye, venting her pent-up frustration and disappointment on the little yellow balls. In return for the tennis coaching Jo helped Emma overcome her fear of horses and taught her to ride. Riding lessons were optional and could be with or without instruction at Pierrefeu. Once most of the snow had melted, Jo and Emma grabbed every chance they could to meander through the lush green countryside on their gentle steeds. Weaving through tall grasses alongside bubbling streams, the edges still lined with snow, inhaling the soft perfume of the ancient fir trees, the country's beauty stabbed at Jo's heart, reminding her of days at Dublin Park.

The only subject Jo could not talk to Emma about was Rick. Recently she had been having terrible nightmares, grisly hospital scenes, horses turned to monsters trampling her underfoot, men shouting violently at her, which unnerved her so much she woke sweating and crying in the night. Lying awake in the murky predawn, she would feel so homesick she'd wonder how she could live another second away from Kingsford Lodge and Dad and Winks and all those wonderful valiant horses. But Dad was still angry and Winks was gone and there were cooking classes to attend. Then today she had received another letter from her mother. The fiasco on the tennis court had been because Jo was so eaten up with frustration and misery she simply hadn't been able to concentrate.

'You're mad, Jo! Your mother wants to take you to the best photographers in Italy to put together the kind of portfolio other people couldn't pay to have, and you want to throw it all away to come and stay with me at Aunt Sarah's in her damp crumbling old house all because of some crummy old stables I mentioned down the road!' cried Emma as Jo, her freshly washed hair twisted up in a towel, tossed her mother's letter on the bed. 'I thought you'd decided to give it a go. Photos in Milan! Catwalk classes in Paris! Golly, Jo, grab it. Oh, for those sorts of contacts!' Letting out a sigh of exasperation, Emma fell back on the bed in her usual dramatic way, then quickly rolled over and stared at her friend, chin cupped in her hands.

'Of course I'm going to give it a go,' snapped Jo, fighting back the tears. Damn it, Emma was right. She should be feeling grateful not resentful. It was a chance of a lifetime and her mother was handing it all to her on a plate. In twelve months she'd look back on today and laugh, the sinking feeling in her stomach forgotten. In her own mind she had already geared herself up for all of this. But it was supposed to start at the end of finishing school, not now, not when she had been so looking forward to spending the Easter break in England with Emma. They had planned outings, picnics, long rides in the countryside . . .

'The crummy old stables down the road only happen to belong to Guy Compton and is only one of the largest racing stables in England,' Jo thought angrily, tossing the towel on the floor. It wasn't as if she was going to throw everything away. All she wanted was to visit the horses, watch them striding out, stroke their long powerful necks, feel their soft mouths nibbling at her fingers, be amongst the familiar sounds and smells she missed so much. That was all. The horses at Pierrefeu just didn't compare with the thoroughbreds she was used to. She didn't even know if she wanted to train horses any longer if it meant constantly fighting everyone. She could feel tears pricking the backs of her eyes again. God, she was such a cry-baby! Jerking open a drawer she pulled out a lace-edged silk slip and wriggled into it, shoving the drawer shut with her thigh, her eyes haunted. A Christmas present from Nina, the material clung invitingly to her young figure. Over the last few months, through the combination of vigorous sports and unhappiness, most of her puppy fat had fallen away and her body was now trim and firm.

'I can't believe you don't want to be a model,' exclaimed Emma.

'Give it a rest, Emma.' Jo slumped down on the bed, avoiding her friend's gaze, fingering the lace, anger slowly turning to resignation. At least her parents cared. Suddenly Emma's words about contacts registered with Jo. Straightening up, she turned to her friend, the life back in her eyes. 'Why don't we go together? I'm sure Mum wouldn't mind.'

Emma's face lit up. 'Are you sure she wouldn't?' she asked eagerly.

'Heavens no. In fact, she'd love you because you really want to be a model, and you've got to get your pictures taken too anyway.' Jo was getting more excited as she talked. 'You're so good at all this, Emma. You know all the right things to do and say and you don't make stupid mistakes about designer labels and . . . and we'd both end up with great portfolios. Oh Emma! I wouldn't feel nearly so bad doing it all with you. We could have such fun together.' She lay back staring at the ceiling feeling immensely relieved.

Just then the old church clock clanged the hour in the distance, reminding them it was almost time for afternoon tea.

'Oh heck! If we're late, there'll be hell to pay,' yelped Emma, leaping up and pulling a blouse from the cupboard.

'Oh jeepers, I'd forgotten—I'm supposed to be serving!' cried Jo, jumping off the bed and scrabbling into her clothes, her plan giving her new energy. 'I'll ring Mum tonight,' she said over her shoulder as she dragged a brush through her hair.

They were still discussing the idea as they scrambled down the stairs buttoning up their clothes and straightening their collars. Scuttling into the room, Emma almost fell into the vacant chair next to the other students already seated at the table and immediately assumed a look of total decorum while Jo, panting, grabbed a plate of home-made cakes and received a dark look from Mademoiselle Viaud just as the housemother entered.

Jo hated to admit it but she was actually enjoying the photo session. At first completely unnerved by the string of photos of the world's top models that lined the walls of the light, airy studio in Milan, as Julio Fellice, wearing jeans and a casual shirt, worked with her, Jo gradually lost some of her gaucheness and started to relax. In the full glare of the hot studio lights, she tossed back her head, smiled, twisted, played with her hair and changed poses to command under the world-famous photographer's skilful direction. Outside, the sun struggled through the yellow haze that hung over the city's crowded mass of rooftops, domes and turrets. Glancing fleetingly towards Nina, who was reclining in one of the big white settees, Jo marvelled at the difference Emma's presence had made to them all.

From the first moment they had met, Nina and Emma had got on famously and from then on everything had flowed smoothly. Emma's bubbly enthusiasm was catching, yet her down-to-earth approach impressed Nina. For Emma, having a proxy family was magic, and the cheery atmosphere between them all was a welcome relief for Nina. Life had been very difficult at home lately. On the increasingly rare occasions when she and Charlie were together they bickered, and she hadn't been looking forward to fighting Jo as well. It seemed every time either she or Charlie mentioned Jo's name, an argument followed, which in Nina's view was certainly not of her making. Hearing the enthusiasm in her daughter's voice for the first time since she had started at Pierrefeu further endeared Emma to Nina. Each day she marvelled that not only was this Emma Bamford stunningly beautiful but she had somehow engendered an interest about modelling in Jo where everyone else had failed.

'Joanna, *carina*, the smile . . . the eyes . . . We have to see more *passione* . . . more . . .' cried Julio, thumping one hand against his chest. He peered quickly into the camera lens. 'Head a leetle . . .' Stepping forwards he turned Jo's face a fraction to one side, repositioned her arm and stood back. Jo smiled once more into the lens, lips slightly parted, remembering how Emma had told her to 'make the lens your friend'. '*Si, si*! *Bene, bene,* very good ...' cried Julio. 'Now I see into your heart ... *e ancora* ... again,' he ordered, tilting the camera, clicking constantly, flashlight following flashlight, darting towards Jo then backing away.

Hurriedly changing films while the two assistants hovering in the background touched up Jo's make-up and hair between takes, Julio shot three more rolls of film. Pausing only to allow a third assistant to help Jo in and out of an amazing array of clothes, the photographer continued his filming for another twenty minutes, his instructions coming in a staccato mix of Italian and broken English. Finally the blinding flashes stopped.

'Bravo, bravo Joanna *bambina, eccellente,* is good.' Julio looked towards Nina. 'We stop now, *signora.* Tomorrow we film outside,' he grinned, his white teeth like one of his flashlights in his olive complexion.

Jo was surprised how exhausted she felt as she stepped off the set and disappeared to change into her street clothes. Then it was Emma's turn.

'You know, it was the best thing that could have possibly happened, you two girls meeting up,' Nina whispered to Jo, patting her hand as mother and daughter watched Julio flash away at Emma. 'Emma's so comfortable with modelling and she seems to know so much about it. What was it she said about the photos ... Wait a minute ... "The portfolio is a model's pulse, their life force." I like that. Emma's very mature for her age. Learn as much as you can from her, darling ...' She reached past the freshly made cappuccino at her elbow and helped herself to a piece of Lombardy coffee cake from the graceful Italian china.

'Mum,' groaned Jo, picking out a lump of candied

151

fruit from her slice of cake, the joy at her own attempts evaporating, Nina's words making her feeling hopelessly inadequate.

'Now don't be so touchy, Jo. I don't mean you're immature but Australia's so far away . . . Girls seem to grow up quicker in Europe.' She patted Jo's hand again. 'You can help her too. You speak much better French, and you're just as lovely.' While she was becoming very fond of Emma, Nina could also see a strong advantage for Jo in the two working closely together. Given the initial contacts, Emma's drive and beauty would open plenty of doors, yet Jo had the advantage of having the fresh-faced look sought after by magazine editors.

Jo was trying not to sink into despair as her mother chattered on. Had Jo really expected some metamorphosis just because she had decided to cooperate? Watching Emma further increased her own feeling of inadequacy. Emma looked so at home being photographed. She seemed to mature before her eyes. Like a dazzling butterfly emerging from its chrysalis, her actions became more confident, her eyes more luscious, her whole being exuding a glow Jo had never seen before. Yet Jo didn't feel jealous, she felt afraid that she would lose her friend and confidante for this glamorous stranger.

Over the next few days, while the two girls smiled and posed against the fabulous old buildings and statues in Milan, Jo's spirits plummeted further. But as they all pored over the results of Julio's work, gasping with delight at his skill, and she and Emma laughed and groaned over some of their strange grimaces caught by the camera, Jo's earlier fears receded and her heart lifted once more. Her friend was still the girl who had chased her down the ski slopes and ridden with her beside the mountain streams, the same person with whom she had shared her deepest secrets and one day they really would get to England together.

Deciding to celebrate in the Piazza del Duomo a few streets away, they stepped out into the cool April afternoon and set off at a gentle stroll down the narrow cobbled street, their heels echoing between the tall grey stone buildings, the lilting Italian shouts of housewives and shopkeepers carrying across from neighbouring streets. Young men on motor scooters wove past them up on the pavement, the screech of tyres heard long after they had vanished; others leaned up against the damp walls smoking and chatting, some whistling at them as they passed. The pungent aroma of freshly cooked food mixed with cigarillos filtered out from tiny restaurant doors, reminding Jo she was starving. Happy that everything was back to normal, she made the mistake of grinning at everyone they passed and soon a small gathering of young Italian men were tailing them. When one walked right up and pinched Emma's bottom, she let out a yelp followed by the only Italian swear word she knew and their stroll turned to a fast walk. Cutting across a park they almost ran towards the square, Nina teetering along behind on her new Italian high heels, collapsing in relief at a table outside a restaurant. Directly opposite, Milan cathedral towered above them in all its overdressed glory, a white marble wedding cake of intricate Gothic arches and soaring pinnacles.

'These dreadful Latin types,' gasped Nina, touching up her make-up, forgetting one of her best friends at home came from Italy.

'Golly, I'm starved,' laughed Emma poring over the menu, struggling to pronounce the dishes.

Nina's command of Italian was only marginally

better than the girls' and it took much pointing, shouting and gesticulating before the meal was finally ordered. Ten minutes later Jo and Emma gratefully sank their teeth into piping hot, freshly made pizzas piled high with thick tomato sauce, anchovies and garlic-flavoured salami, the mouth-watering cheese running down their chins and falling in thick threads down the side of the springy baked dough. Happily the girls twisted the delicious strands around their tongues and wound them round their fingers while Nina more sedately cut into *costoletta alla milanese*, the succulent morsel of crumbed veal parting easily from the cutlet bone. Mum was right, thought Jo stuffing the last piece of pizza into her mouth and wiping her mouth on the crisp white napkin. She and Emma did complement each other. They needed each other. She reached for her drink and stopped, her hand in midair as a strident Australian voice broke the silence that had fallen as they ate.

'Well I'll be darned. It can't be! I don't believe it—Nina Kingsford, what in the heck are you doing in the middle of Milan?'

Nina's head jerked up in surprise, her fork clattering onto the paving stones. Dropping her knife on the plate Nina pushed back her chair and leaped up. 'Jenny Cooper!' she shrieked in delight, darting across and hugging close the slim, tanned woman in her early forties. Elegant in casual white blouse and tailored trousers and wearing bright red lipstick, her ears were covered by oversize gold earrings. Enormous white-rimmed sunglasses were pushed back from her square face into her thick brown hair. 'You'll never believe this, Jenny, but I was going to ring you tonight. You're supposed to be in Paris. Sit down, sit down,' cried Nina, pulling up a chair from a nearby table and introducing Jo and Emma. 'Garçon—oops wrong country.' She waved at the waiter and ordered more drinks. 'Remember my little baby? Well she's grown up and now she and Emma ...' she leaned towards Jenny and dropped her voice to a stage whisper, '... are going to be models. Julio Fellice has just finished putting together their portfolios, and I was wondering ... Joanna darling, where's the book?' She flapped her hands at Jo, her cheeks flushed with excitement.

'Julio!' said Jenny, impressed.

Jo blushed as the other woman ran her eyes quickly over her and Emma before turning back to Nina, leaving Jo feeling a bit like a horse that had been inspected for sale. She pushed back a strand of blonde hair and twirled it in her fingers, watching the pigeons strut around the piazza.

'You know, you haven't changed one bit. How long is it?' asked Jenny, her bright face alight with pleasure.

'Too long to bother with,' Nina replied swiftly. 'We were at high school together. Then you got this idea to sell swimwear across the world,' she explained, half to Jenny, half to the girls. 'We all thought you were crazy but here you are. Australia's so proud of you, and I don't think we've missed one Christmas card in all those years.'

'Not Jenny Cooper of Paradise Swimwear?' Jo said in a hushed whisper, wondering if there was anyone in the fashion world her mother didn't know. Nina had pointed out the swimwear to Emma in one of the glossy magazines lying around at Pierrefeu.

'That's me,' Jenny grinned, stirring the ice with the straw in the Cinzano and lemonade the waiter had just placed in front of her, then taking a sip. 'It's a pity we didn't bump into each other a week ago. I've just finished a big showing of this year's Milan collection. The Italians go mad over the bright colours.' She pulled out some glossy brochures and handed one to each of them. Unclipping one of her enormous earrings, she rubbed her ear and clipped the earring back in place. 'If the girls are really serious about modelling, we'd better see what some of my new cozzies look like on them. I'm always looking for fresh faces.'

'I wasn't thinking of asking you to employ the girls,' interrupted Nina quickly.

'Look, I know you never would, Nina, and I'm probably jumping the gun. Tell me all your news. But first, what were you going to phone me about?'

Nina went slightly pink. She had everything she wanted to say all worked out in her mind but somehow asking a favour of a friend you hadn't seen for over fourteen years would have been much easier over the phone. 'Well, I might as well jump straight in. I was going to ask if the girls could stay with you in Paris for a few weeks, just until they get established. I mean we could find an apartment but—'

'Of course, darling!' Jenny replied quickly, waving away any further apologies. 'We need some fresh energy about our place. The only thing, Nina, I do go away a lot. But Claudette will look after you when I'm away—she's my housekeeper and like a second mum to us all. I don't know what my husband'd do without her. He's so vague when it comes to family matters. It'd be good for my son Jacques to have some younger people around. Maybe one of you'll be able to persuade him to get up before lunchtime. He's nineteen,' she finished with an impish grin, seeing the sudden interest in the girls' faces.

Nina squeezed her friend's arm in delight. 'Jenny,

you are such a dear friend. I knew I could rely on you. I'm sure the girls will manage.'

After the third Cinzano, and gelato for the girls, everything was settled. After term finished, Nina would fly with Jo and Emma to the Côte d'Azur for a three-week vacation and then on to Paris. Once she had settled them in with Jenny and her family, where they would live for the next six to twelve months, she would return to Australia. By the time they parted, Jenny had also given Nina the names of several modelling agencies and designers she could approach in Italy, France and Greece.

'Fancy running into Jenny like that. Isn't life amazing,' said Nina back at the hotel with a contented sigh.

Even Jo had to agree they had got off to a good start. Staring out over the rooftops of Milan, she toyed fleetingly with the idea of suggesting they stay with Aunt Sarah in England instead of going to France, but decided against it. Nina was set on giving them an expensive holiday in the sun and, knowing how much she disliked horses, there seemed no point in antagonising her when they were all getting on so well.

'You know, Emma, I'm actually starting to look forward to Paris,' Jo admitted, linking arms with her friend as they waved Nina goodbye and walked back up the steps of Villa Pierrefeu. Stopping at the top she turned around and gazed across the valley. 'What I am going to hate is leaving these beautiful mountains.'

The next three months left little time to wonder about the future as they crammed studies for their French and Swiss diplomas in between trips arranged by the school, only indulging their day-dreams in what little time they had free when riding or playing tennis. Before they knew it, their life at Pierrefeu was almost over.

'After tomorrow our life starts,' whispered Emma in perfect French as the two girls waited in line to receive their diplomas at the graduation ceremony.

Stepping up onto the tiny platform that had been erected in the main dining room for the occasion, Jo searched the sea of faces for her mother who, having flown out from Australia especially for the occasion, was dabbing at her eyes. How Jo wished that her dad could have been there too, but things were still cool between them, although she had spoken to Charlie on the phone a couple of times in the last two months. Seeing the pride on her mother's face, Jo resolved even harder to make the next year work.

Seated next to Nina, Emma's Aunt Sarah adjusted her gloves and wished her sister would take more notice of her daughter. Emma Bamford was destined for great things, Sarah had always been convinced of that. If a perfect stranger and an Australian to boot could recognise it, surely it should be evident to the girl's own parents. Emma had the drive and energy, as well as the looks, to do exceptionally well and now, thanks to the Australian girl, she had a place to stay and the prospect of some work during the summer break. Sarah had been looking forward to Emma and Jo visiting but it looked like once again it would have to wait.

Applauding restrainedly as each girl accepted her diploma and smiled for the camera, Sarah decided she would slip over to France for a weekend just to check out this swimwear designer. There was a look in Joanna Kingsford's eyes that disturbed her—as though she were permanently acting. She'd have to talk to Emma. Maybe the girl could come and stay at their place for Christmas, unless of course she was flying home to Australia. The mother seemed to flit about the world as though she were catching a number eighty-two bus. Still, with her own sister doing much the same, Sarah could hardly be too critical. However, she wasn't sure she approved of the racing connection. She would have to keep a careful eye on her niece and this Australian friend of hers.

Beaming, Jo linked arms with her mother and walked out into the sunshine, the school director's words ringing in her ears. 'We have done the best we can to prepare you for the world. Now it is your turn.' She hunted over the heads for Emma, and they smiled at one another through the crowd. They had made it through finishing school. She was glad the two of them were facing the next step together.

Chapter Nine

STILL TANNED FROM the holiday on the Côte d'Azur, and slightly out of breath, Jo dropped the armful of groceries gratefully onto the table in the middle of Jenny Cooper's kitchen in her apartment near the Bois de Boulogne in Paris. It was early September and the trees were starting to take on their glorious autumn colours. Nina had returned to Australia at the end of August; Emma was in Florence on a photographic assignment, and it was a long way up the four flights of stairs with the lift out of action. Wriggling out of her thick, ankle-length, navy coat and long, red scarf, Jo hung them on one of the many hand-carved wooden hooks Jenny had collected from flea markets across the world and began unpacking the long French bread sticks, cheese, vegetables and *vin de maison*. The smell of ripe roquefort cheese invaded the room.

Although a highly successful fashion designer, at home Jenny was the exact opposite of the chic businesswoman Jo had met in Milan, and her home reflected that. Furnished with a mixture of rare antiques and paintings and trashy collectables it had a definite bohemian flavour that appealed to Jo but did not always sit comfortably with Jenny's French husband Louis Bercy. The kitchen in particular, with its wide window overlooking the busy street, strings of onions and bulbs of garlic hanging in a corner and bundles of pots and ladles strung from giant meat hooks, had become a haven in the strange new world Jo had moved into.

'You're looking particularly long-faced this morning, *chérie*,' said Jenny, breezing in from her studio opposite the kitchen, carrying several pieces of material, a box of pins and a paper pattern of her latest swimwear design. Having lived in Paris for nearly ten years, and with much of her work in Italy, she was more accustomed to speaking French and Italian than English. Snippets of coloured thread clung to her loose smock and gipsy skirt, a pen stuck through her hair. She flicked the switch on the coffee percolator.

'I dropped into the agency again and they didn't have anything,' said Jo, trying to sound bright. She placed the lettuces on the draining board next to the unwashed breakfast dishes. 'Actually, Jean François was extremely rude, which didn't help, and I miss Emma like crazy,' she admitted in a rush. Jean François, who while her mother was still in Paris had fawned all over her, this morning had given Jo a dressing down when she asked about a job he had promised to follow up on, telling her to lose weight and grow four centimetres taller and that the favours were all used up. Spitting mad by the time she left, Jo had struggled to contain her tears as she jostled her way through the local food market.

'Jean François, pah!' exclaimed Jenny, scattering pins everywhere. 'Jean François is a tiny *escargot* who should crawl back under his leaf. He only got that job because I talked to Veronique,' she explained, lifting her skirt above her knees and crawling under the table.

'He wiggles his hips,' Jo giggled, bending down to help retrieve the pins and starting to feel better. From now on she would think of him as a snail whenever she had to talk to him.

When she and Emma had arrived in Paris with Nina, Jenny had warned them it would not be easy. While the girls had been given a few small jobs organised by the two older women who called on favours from friends, ultimately, as Jenny had pointed out, it was their own beauty and persistence that would get them good careers in modelling. Because she was shorter than the standard model, Jo had only managed one assignment in four weeks. Emma, on the other hand, being a good deal taller, had walked straight into a string of small jobs and last week had landed herself a two-week shoot in Florence with more work to follow.

'These people only want to work with successes,' explained Jenny, sitting back on her heels. 'It's like the chicken and the egg—once you are a success everyone wants you, but until then no-one will talk to you. Personally I think you can make it, that's why I want you to be in my next showing. Unfortunately, that horrid little Jean François is right, your height is your biggest drawback. Emma got the job in Florence because of her height as much as her looks.'

Jo went bright red. 'I'm not jealous of Emma or anything. I just miss her,' she said, kneeling up quickly and banging her head on the underside of the table. Swearing loudly in French, she then apologised profusely and stormed across to the sink where she started washing up ferociously, wishing she was anywhere but in Paris.

Dropping her pattern scraps on the unpolished wood table, Jenny spread them out and examined them carefully. 'I know you miss her, *chérie*,' she said gently, pouring herself a cup of coffee. Pulling the pen out from her hair she made a few notes on the brown paper bag that had held the bread, stuck the pen back in her hair and started pinning. 'What you want is some cosmetics company to use you, then your height won't matter.'

'That's what Mum was hoping for,' said Jo glumly. 'But how am I going to be the face of the latest wonder cream? You have to be a film star or a successful model before they'll look at you, and we're back to me being too short.'

'Nothing's worth getting that miserable about,' said Jenny cheerfully. 'Why not attack from a different angle? Give a couple of magazines a ring and see if you can get a job as ... a ... a dresser's assistant,' she suggested brightly, waving her hand in the air, almost knocking the pins off the table again as she searched for the word in English. 'God, it's so long since I talked English this much ... Or try the make-up department, or just offer to be a general girl Friday while you are waiting for modelling work. Pay's pretty terrible but you'd get to know the people in the industry, let them get to know you. Most of them love Aussies because we work so damn hard.' She looked over at Jo. 'Leave all that to Claudette. Get on the phone now while you're feeling brave,' she ordered.

'Oh, Jenny, you're so encouraging,' said Jo, relaxing her shoulders and quickly drying her hands. Above all things she hated failure and, having committed herself to modelling, she was determined to make it work. She disappeared into the hallway. After the third call she put down the receiver feeling slightly stunned. Searching for Jenny she found her back in her studio.

'I got the fashion editor for *Elegance Internationale*! Her assistant is off sick and she's desperate for someone to help for the next two weeks,' exclaimed Jo. 'They want me to go for an interview straightaway!'

'Well, there you go, *chérie*,' replied Jenny cheerily, pausing her scissors mid snip. 'It'll give you something to do. Never know, you might be offered a permanent position.'

Two hours later Jo returned, grinning like a Cheshire cat. 'Guess what! I got the job and it's permanent! The other girl rang in to say she was resigning, while I was being interviewed!'

Jo spent her first day as assistant to Jutta Utz, *Elegance Internationale*'s superefficient, extremely excitable fashion editor, bagging up clothes used in Jutta's latest fashion shoot and organising for them to be returned to the various designers. Working in the spacious area assigned to the fashion editor, surrounded by clothes on moveable racks, Jo folded and packed while Jutta talked nonstop on the phone, only pausing to demand fresh cups of coffee. Huge posters of models on the books of the various Paris agencies stared down at her from the walls, several she recognised from Jean François's office, but hers was not amongst them.

'You must be Jutta's new assistant,' said a short dumpy young woman with frizzy mousy hair that struggled to escape from a battered hairband. They were in the tiny kitchenette, Jo on one of her frequent trips for coffee. The woman opened a packet of biscuits and offered one to Jo. 'Thank goodness they hired someone short this time and who doesn't look anorexic. At least you might stay a bit longer than the last two. They were hopeless. They only took the job to try and get modelling work through Jutta. I could have told them they were wasting their time,' the woman blurted out, picking up two mugs of coffee and a handful of biscuits. 'Jutta only uses certain models. She's very fussy.' Jo reddened, feeling caught out. 'Have fun, she'll keep you on your toes.'

It didn't take Jo long to discover that almost everyone in the office was terrified of Jutta, or why she had difficulty keeping assistants. Short-tempered, chain-smoking, in and out of the office chasing after designers, attending fashion luncheons and racing to photo shoots, Jutta made decisions in seconds, ignored her assistant unless she was issuing orders and shouted at anyone who got in her way. Used to Nina's volatile ways, Jo only occasionally became rattled when Jutta sent her in several directions at once, and mostly managed to concentrate on the job in hand. Her life became almost as hectic as Jutta's as she raced around the warehouses of Paris in the company van, collecting clothes Jutta had ordered for her latest fashion story, as the four- or eight-page spreads were called, and helped her lay them out on the floor of the fashion area. Mixing skirts and jackets from designers with tops and scarves from the vast array of clothes that surrounded them on the racks, Jo fished out handbags and costume jewellery from the storeroom until Jutta was satisfied she had the look she required. Then Jo rang up all the designers to find out prices and details to print in the magazine.

'I need you to find me a pair of russet suede shoes,' demanded Jutta, jabbing at a particular shade in the scarf she had selected. 'Try Henri; if he hasn't got them, ring round all the other designers. Take my car. It's easier to park.' She stood up and lit a cigarette, surveying her handiwork.

Jo hurried back to her desk and started wading through Jutta's scribbled telephone numbers. After several phone calls she had a list of possibles. Dashing out of the office she sped across Paris in Jutta's tiny Fiat to Henri's warehouse, returning two hours later with the precious shoes.

Sticking tape to the soles to protect them so they could eventually be sold, watching the stream of hopefuls sent from the model agencies as Jutta looked them over like heifers at market, Jo's frustration grew. While she quite enjoyed seeing this side of the fashion world and earning a regular salary, playing the assistant was getting her modelling career nowhere. She would have to talk to the despicable Jean François again. To add insult to injury, Brigitte, an arrogant willowy brunette, whom Jutta finally chose, handed Jo her half-smoked cigarette while she slipped into one of the costumes. Jo had no choice but to take it.

The shoot was in a studio a short drive from the magazine's offices. Having safely organised the chaise longues, a ladder and numerous other little props, hot and sweating, Jo spent the rest of the day trundling racks of clothes up lifts, making sandwiches and coffee and running out for last-minute items and extra packets of cigarettes for Jutta and the photographer.

'Help Brigitte more with her clothes next time and make a bit of extra fuss over her. She's starting to get choosy over her work and I want to keep using her,' Jutta told Jo, flopping down in the studio at the end of another exhausting day. 'Get me a glass of that *vin ordinaire*. Mon Dieu, what a day!' She lit the last cigarette in her pack and downed the red wine Jo handed her, going over her notes. 'Well, that's all that sorted out. I'll see you bright and early in the morning.' She shut her book with a resounding snap. Standing up a few moments later, she pulled on her coat. Then, leaving Jo to wash up and tidy the studio, she was gone.

Jo sat down, her chin in her hands, staring at the coffee cups and overflowing cigarette butts. Out the back, the photographer clattered around fixing up equipment and checking film with his assistant. It had been one of Jutta's bad days. Snapping at everyone, she had reduced three of the girls to tears, the hairstylist had thrown a tantrum when his comb had gone missing, and Jo was still no closer to getting any modelling work herself. She daren't take the odd badly paid assignment Jean François threw at her and risk losing her job at *Elegance Internationale*, which was her only source of income. Her back and legs ached from heaving the racks; she was sick of supercilious bitches who looked through her, and she longed for a hot shower. Stretching, she stood up stiffly and started to clean up, wondering if it wasn't time to quit this whole charade.

'Stick it out a bit longer, *chérie*. You knew it would be tough,' said Jenny encouragingly over supper after Jo, feeling less murderous towards the world having had a long hot bath, finished pouring out her woes. 'It's all facade. Most of the models are so worried about their next job or if they've put on weight, they don't have time to worry about anyone else except themselves. You've got more get up and go than the lot of them. Eventually the right break will come. Just stay in the industry.'

Staring at a family photo she kept by her bed, Jo

had to agree Jenny's advice was sound. She also had to accept her own pride wouldn't let her give up until she had at least done one good shoot.

A few days later, chatting with Simone, one of the models Jutta often used for the smaller shoots, Jo let slip that she was looking for modelling work herself.

'Move on if Jean François is treating you like that. Everyone knows he has his pets,' advised Simone after she had wheedled out of Jo the name of her agent. Jutta was calling for the girls to come and be tried out. Quickly she shoved a card in Jo's hand. 'Give my agent a ring. Tell her you're a friend of mine. She talent scouts all over the world so she's in and out of the country, but she's lovely and her agency's going places.' Smiling at Jo she headed across the room towards the male model Jutta had picked out.

Jo looked at the name—Jean Curie, Model Management. It didn't sound as chic as some of the others and her card wasn't as flamboyant but it could be the opening Jo had been waiting for.

Phoning Jean Curie the next day while Jutta was out of the office, Jo made an appointment to see her. Impressed with Jo's portfolio and even more so with Jo in the flesh, Jean Curie started sending her on small assignments. The bookings were modest and mostly what the other more established models turned down, but Jo wasn't proud and she was excited that finally she had started getting work for herself. When Jean booked her as one of the models for the launch of a small cosmetic company, Jo's spirits lifted. What encouraged her most was the attitude of her agent. Jean Curie was excited by Jo's fresh Australian complexion and her haunting violet eyes and seemed far less upset about her lack of height than the others. The work was still too erratic for Jo to feel confident enough to leave *Elegance Internationale*, but the spark was back in her eye and she attacked her work with Jutta with renewed vigour.

Shortly before sunrise one chilly morning at the beginning of October, blinking the sleep from her eyes, Jo clutched her seat in *Elegance Internationale*'s wardrobe van as Jutta manoeuvred her way across the city with typical Parisian lack of interest in human life, at the same time issuing a stream of instructions to Jo. Tearing through the still sleeping streets, the clothes swaying dangerously in their racks, Jo was finally shaken fully awake as they lurched round the corner onto Le Pont Alexander III. Driving the van straight up onto the pavement, Jutta stopped abruptly under one of the ornate wrought-iron lamps that ran the length of the bridge and lit a cigarette with shaking fingers. She inhaled deeply then reached for her notes, her face haggard from pressure and lack of sleep. Stepping out into the chill autumn air Jo pulled her thick coat around her and peered across at the shadowy shapes on the banks of the Seine, the wind biting into her cheeks and rattling the dead leaves along the bridge.

The deadline for the next edition of *Elegance Internationale* was only a few days away and this morning they were doing a frantic last-minute shoot on Jutta's fashion story 'Elegant Evenings' using Brigitte who, because of her increasing modelling commitments, had only been able to fit Jutta in today. Jo wasn't sure which was worse: listening to everyone at the office gabbling at the top of their voices in French, the phones ringing non-stop and designers screaming for their clothes to be returned when she had only managed three hours sleep because of her moonlighting jobs, or standing in the freezing cold with Jutta in a complete panic over a shoot that should have been completed three weeks ago. Looking around, Jo wondered if somewhere in Florence Emma was also tramping through the dark. Jutta, standing by the bonnet, was lighting another cigarette from the glowing butt and talking to André the make-up artist who, having just arrived, stood stamping his feet in the cold. Wrinkling her nose in displeasure at the smell of cigarette smoke that constantly permeated her clothes these days, Jo dived into the back of the van and started organising coffee for everyone. Brigitte was a pain but she got on with André and Fifi, the hairstylist, so the day, while long, would at least be bearable. A short way along the bridge the photographer was erecting his light reflectors while his assistant marked out the working area with gaffer tape.

'Coffee, Jo. Then help André get ready for Brigitte,' ordered Jutta as Jo emerged with steaming coffee in disposable cups. 'Gaston!' she screeched, suddenly noticing the two figures in the murky half-light. Snatching a cup from Jo she hurried over to the photographer, waving her notepad in her free hand, her thick beige wool coat flowing out behind her.

'Let me. There's plenty of time,' offered André, calmly helping himself to a biscuit. Relieving Jo of three cups, he sauntered along the bridge. He was used to Jutta's feverish overefficiency and the girl was looking cold and flustered. On his return Jo smiled gratefully. Having checked all the outfits were still on their hangers and the accessories sorted, Jo walked over to where André was leaning on the bridge.

'It's beautiful at this time of day, isn't it,' he murmured. Cupping her frozen fingers around her drink, Jo nodded, sipping the hot liquid and feeling it warm her insides. Together they watched as the light crept up over Paris, the soft mist on the water gradually evaporating to reveal barges and houses and a waking city.

Having sorted out the shots with Gaston, Jutta came hurrying back. 'Is Brigitte here yet?' she asked, trying to sound calm, thrusting her empty cup at Jo.

Sales always went up when Jutta used Brigitte and she needed the sales, which was why, regardless of printing deadlines, Jutta had insisted on using the model for this shoot. She also happened to like the girl. But Jutta always got nervous on big shoots and today was for a full eight-page spread. They had a lot to get through. She was also terrified of upsetting Gaston. Jutta had been trying to get the internationally acclaimed photographer interested in the magazine for months. It had taken hard work, persistence and a lot of cajoling to book him, and tomorrow he was flying out to New York.

Jutta glanced at her watch and then across at the sky. 'Where is the girl? Gaston wants to use the early morning light,' she said irritably.

Half an hour, three cups of coffee and half a packet of cigarettes later there was still no sign of Brigitte. The traffic on the bridge was building, cars spilling out their fumes, pedestrians hurrying by, staring at the forlorn little group. Lighting yet another cigarette with shaking fingers, Jutta ordered Jo to go and ring the agency. 'Maybe she's ill, in which case I'll have to get someone else,' she said, wondering which of her regulars she could get at this late date. She frowned anxiously across at Gaston who, shoulders hunched against his spare frame, hands thrust deep in his coat pocket, was staring out across the river.

Jo set off at a run towards a nearby phone box, the light on the scurrying clouds tantalisingly effective as the minutes ticked by. It would take a good two hours to get Brigitte ready even when she got here, and rain had been forecast for later in the day. The agency confirmed Brigitte had rung in to say she would be at the shoot and reassured Jo the model should be there any moment. Gaston was looking decidedly unhappy and Jutta increasingly nervous.

'This is ridiculous!' exclaimed Jutta tearing open her third pack of cigarettes, her temper rising.

Just as she was thinking they would have to ring and organise another model, Jo spied a taxi pulling up. Running forwards quickly she opened the door and gasped at the smell of bourbon and men's after-shave. Clad in a crumpled white evening dress, over which was casually flung a man's dinner jacket, Brigitte stepped barefoot onto the cobblestones. Swaying dangerously she took a step forward, grabbed at the door, missed and instead got Jo's out-stretched hand.

'Ah! The good little assistant,' she said, turning her arrogant unfocused gaze on Jo. The remnants of smudged mascara accentuated her puffy blood-shot eyes, her brown lacklustre hair a tousled mess caught back in an oversize silver clip. It was clear she had been crying.

Jutta came running up behind with André and Fifi hard on her heels. 'Brigitte,' she squealed, in relief, then her hands flew to her mouth, the colour draining from her cheeks. 'Oh, *mon Dieu! Mon Dieu!*' Then shock turned to panic. 'André, get her into the van and fix her up. Fifi . . .' She pushed the hair-stylist towards the van.

'Hello, Jutta,' Brigitte smiled sweetly. Then, ignoring everyone else, she carefully wove her way towards the photographer. 'Gaston, dear darling adorable Gaston . . .' She stretched out her arms to clasp him round the neck, tripped and fell against one of the reflectors, sending it toppling sideways. The silver clip clattered to the ground, freeing her tangled mass of curls. Dashing forwards, Jo almost collided with Gaston's assistant in her efforts to save the reflector. Disgusted, Gaston stepped back from the girl and turned on Jutta.

'Is this some kind of a joke?' he stormed. 'Who is this girl that she thinks she can come here like this? You waste my valuable time. I, Gaston Manoir, who am wanted all over the world . . . It will take two hours to sober her up and another two—more—to make her look like anything, if we can do anything with this face.' He waved his hands in disgust and rolled his eyes heavenward.

'Do you think this is my doing?' shrieked Jutta humiliated, the strain clearly showing in her face. Furious, she turned on Brigitte. 'How dare you come here in this state, girl! You're fired. Don't think you will ever model again in Paris. Someone get her out of my sight.' Then, realising her whole shoot was in danger of being aborted as Gaston started giving orders to pack up the equipment, Jutta cried frantically, 'Stop! No! Gaston, please! We're both creative, we can come up with something. You know what it means to *Elegance* to have you do our shots, this is the first time anything like this . . . I've got a deadline,' she pleaded, nearly in tears. 'I'll get another girl.' She proffered the shaking cigarette packet.

'Ha! And we start shooting after sunset? If you cannot organise your girls, this is not my problem,' he snapped.

Quietly Jo picked up the clip and helped Brigitte back to the main thoroughfare, shocked that someone as successful as this girl could so mindlessly ruin her career.

'He's married. Married! How stupid can one be?' announced Brigitte, pulling abruptly away from Jo. She started to giggle and then burst into tears.

Hailing a taxi, Jo firmly bundled the sobbing girl inside, paid the driver and directed him to the agency. Slowly she walked back towards Jutta, who was still pleading with Gaston. The early morning light long gone, it was obvious there was no point in arranging for another girl.

Pulling hard on his cigarette, Gaston glared angrily at Jo as she approached and then noticed her eyes, which were luminous with disappointment. Quickly looking away, Jo felt a wave of heat sweep over her as Gaston's eyes burned across her face and down her body, his expression changing to one of excitement as Jutta burbled frantically in his ear.

'Look at me like that again, girl,' he ordered, tilting Jo's face up to him, ignoring Jutta. Blushing deeper, Jo lifted her dark violet eyes to his once more, her heart fluttering against her ribs, her wool jumper suddenly too hot.

'*Formidable!*' he cried, turning to Jutta, his eyes alight with excitement. 'Why do you not give me a face and body like this little one to work with in the beginning?' he demanded. 'With this I can do something.'

'What?' exclaimed Jutta in disbelief. The whole day was now a complete waste of time. 'No, Gaston darling, she's just my assistant. Give me one more day and I promise I'll get you a superb model. I'm really sorry to have messed you about like this,' she gabbled, lighting yet another cigarette, fingers shaking.

Gaston glared at her. 'I do not 'ave another day,' he said, looking down his nose at the fashion editor. 'You wish my photographs, I wish to work with this face, we make something.'

Jo listened in open-mouthed disbelief. Then, as he pulled the band from her hair and piled the silken platinum strands on her head, one finger on his chin, she realised he was in earnest. The fluttering against her ribs changed to a pounding and her legs threatened to buckle under her. *Elegance Internationale*—an eight-page spread of *her* in *Elegance Internationale*—she must be dreaming.

Jutta started biting her nails. This was madness. She would have to go along with the whole fatuous idea using a girl who was too short and too fat, wasting her own time and using up her precious budget, but she dare not upset Gaston if she wanted to use him again.

'What am I going to do, André?' she whispered huskily, her mind working overtime. 'I won't be able to use the photos, all the colours will be wrong, but if I don't, he'll never work for me again.'

'Just go along with it, Jutta darling,' replied André, enjoying her discomfort. 'After all, if he's so good he's got to come up with something, and if he doesn't, bury them in the back pages of the January issue.'

Jutta looked up at the make-up artist and for the first time that day she smiled. 'André, you're marvellous.' She pulled Jo to one side. 'Humour him. I need to use him again for the magazine when he gets back from New York,' she whispered. 'We've still got one day to get the shoot done.'

Jo felt suddenly deflated. For a few moments she

had honestly believed she was to be the stand-in for Brigitte. Of course it was an absurd notion, she realised now, thudding back to earth. Smiling bravely at Jutta, she clambered into the van.

Jutta shook her head. She had made all this fuss about using Brigitte and now it had all blown up in her face. As André started smoothing foundation cream onto Jo's face, she had to admit the girl wasn't bad looking. She was quite a bit shorter and slightly fatter than Brigitte, but all that could be fixed with Gaston's gaffer tape and butterfly paperclips ... No, the whole notion was ludicrous unless ... unless Gaston's name could give her the sales she needed. She'd have to talk to Rachelle the editor around noon, otherwise tomorrow could prove even more frantic than today. If only there was more time.

For the next two hours everyone worked frantically, lifting hems and cuffs, pinning and tucking, sticking and manipulating the luxuriant fabrics. While André demonstrated his skills as a make-up artist, changing Jo from simple office girl to alluring woman, Fifi created magic with Jo's hair, brushing it until it glistened, twisting it and pinning it so it clung elegant and sophisticated to her head, perfect for the first outfit. Climbing into the designer creation Jo suppressed an excited sigh as, complete with gaffer tape and butterfly clips, she walked towards Gaston as he directed.

'*Non! Non!* You look too happy,' cried Gaston after a moment. 'Look at me how you look before,' he ordered, camera clicking; but no matter what Gaston said, Jo could not reproduce the emotion he was after. Even the wind cutting through the thin satin and stinging her bare shoulders could not dissolve her sense of elation. Her eyes shone, her whole

176

being glowed, all her previous disappointment evaporated as, caught up in the moment, she let herself enjoy the experience.

Finally Gaston stopped. 'You have family?' he asked. Jo nodded. 'You love them very much?' He paused, his eye pressed to the camera. 'Now, imagine someone close to you has just been killed.' He might as well have punched her in the stomach. All Jo's effervescence drained from her. Tears welled up in her eyes and she forced them back, fearful of smudging her make-up. '*Oui*, that is it! Now run to me,' he ordered. Jo ran towards him the satin cape billowing out behind, her eyes swimming with tears which spilled over down her cheeks. '*Oui! Oui!* Now we make music!' cried Gaston excited. 'Next shot we look happy, *chérie*. André, we need a touch-up.'

Jo finished the shoot in a ferment of emotions. Somehow outwardly managing to recreate the emotions Gaston demanded with each new change of clothes, inwardly she boiled with misery and rage. Gaston the photographer all of France wanted, talented, arrogant, uncaring, to him she was just a face, a body. Yet he couldn't have known about Rick, she kept telling herself. She hadn't told anyone since leaving Australia ... And the pain was for nothing. She was just a means to an end. The photos weren't even going to be published.

The November edition of *Elegance Internationale* hit the stores in the last week in October. Even Jutta had been stunned at Gaston's results.

'Run with it!' Rachelle had cried on seeing the transparencies. 'And I'd say you'd better start looking for a new assistant.' She was right. Suddenly everyone wanted to hire Jo. Jean Curie was ecstatic.

177

Whilst Jo had by no means reached front cover status, her eight-page spread had made her the face of the moment and magazines latched onto her image.

For the next few months Jo hopped from one side of Europe to the other like a mad thing, wishing she could share some of her life with Emma who had been taken under the wing of an agent in Florence. Having met many designers while working at *Elegance Internationale*, Jo received offers of further engagements as she travelled. Freezing in Rome for *Vogue* in skimpy swimwear in front of the Colosseum, sweltering for designers in overheated fashion houses, jostling and shoving her way on huge cork platform heels through the warlike zone of backstage catwalks in Milan, waiting around endlessly on photo shoots in Athens, somehow Jo managed to survive her baptism of fire.

Her list of engagements was endless. As well as the shoots and fashion shows, she was expected to attend gala dinners, charity events and parties for every conceivable excuse, accompanied by men of all colours and ages. Hardly given time to draw breath, finally, on Christmas Eve, Jo dumped her overnight bag on the bedroom floor in Jenny's apartment with a sigh of relief, stripped off her thick, grey, wool jumper and knee-length, black leather boots and collapsed on the bed.

'They're fantastic!' cried a familiar voice.

Jo leaped up. 'Emma!' she screamed and rushed to greet her friend for the first time in months.

'You're absolutely stunning,' effervesced Emma. 'When I saw that first shot in *Elegance* with you running . . . Wow! The expression in your face tears you apart. I don't think anyone noticed the clothes!'

Jo's violet eyes blazed with anger. Last night she

had run into Gaston at a party in Barcelona, reminding her of the pain his comments had caused. He
had even had the gall to ask her out. Her head
throbbed from the bad air conditioning in the
planes, and her clothes reeked as usual of cigarette
smoke. 'I hate that man and I hate modelling. I've
been running around like a chook without a head
for the last two months. God, what am I doing with
my life?' she cried, utterly exhausted. Then she
buried her head in her jumper and burst into tears.

Taken aback, Emma stared down at her friend.
Then gradually Emma drew the story out of Jo,
Rick's death, Jo's disappointment that her father
never wrote to her, her mother's constant pushing,
fears that she would never work with horses again,
and the disgust she had felt at the way Gaston had
tried to force himself on her using the fact that he
had launched her modelling career.

' "Use them and lose them" is their motto, Jo. You
have to learn to do the same. That's what Carlos tells
me when I get down in the dumps. I had no
idea . . . You've got to develop a harder shell. Here,
open your mail. There's got to be something in here
that'll cheer you up.' Emma handed over a pile of
envelopes.

Jo sat up and blew her nose.

'Who's Carlos?' she asked as she rustled through
the pile. There were two letters from her mother
and one from her agent. Putting her mother's letters
aside, she tore open the elegant printed envelope,
expecting an update on her itinerary. Instead she
pulled out a cheque for what she considered a quite
ridiculously large sum of money with a cheery note
from Jean Curie. Having already received a modest
sum of money from the agency, Jo gasped. Then she
looked across at Emma and started to laugh. 'Is this

for real?' she cried, showing Emma the amount.

'That's peanuts compared with what you are about to start earning,' Emma replied, hugging her friend, relieved Jo was sounding happier. 'I just met Claudette in the hall and she's been going crazy ever since you left. Your agent hasn't stopped calling; they've been getting calls from agencies all over Europe wanting to book you.' She stood up, excitedly pulling Jo up with her. Thrusting a towel in her arms, she propelled her towards the bathroom. 'You're going to have to get a move on, I've organised for us to be at the hairdressers' in half an hour. You haven't forgotten it's Jenny's annual Christmas Eve party? She's asked half of Paris so we'd better look like something ... and I still have to tell you about Carlos. He's the most divine photographer I met in Florence and he knows everyone ... The other news,' she shouted through the bathroom door, 'is that you and I are going to stay with Aunt Sarah in England for New Year. I've got three weeks before I fly out to New York, so what about it?'

'And does that mean I get to visit the crummy old stables as well?' gasped Jo, poking her head round the door, dripping wet, suddenly feeling incredibly happy.

'I guess so ... Oh, Jo, I've missed you so much and I've got so much to tell you.'

'And I've missed you too. You have to tell me everything that's happened to you since I saw you last. Don't leave out one single tiny little bit,' she insisted as she disappeared back into the bathroom. It was so good to see Emma again. As she quickly lathered her body with scented soap, her old determination returned. A two-week break would be heaven, enough to replenish her flagging energy. Then she would give this whole chaotic exhausting career a bit longer so there was no way her father could accuse her of giving up without trying. The money certainly made a difference. If only Dad would write or phone or do something . . . but she wouldn't think of that now.

Happy to be back with Emma and Jenny, wearing a stunningly simple black dress she had been given in Italy, Jo squeezed through the throng that had managed to squash into the Bercy apartment, handing out canapes, laughing and chatting, quickly caught up in the festive mood. Then just as she dodged Jacques' fifth attempt to kiss her under the mistletoe, the phone rang—it was long distance from Australia.

'Dad!' shouted Jo, struggling to hear above the noise. 'How's everything at Kingsford Lodge? I miss you all so much.' Having given Jo a quick update on events at home and which horses were doing what in the stables and assuring her that Fizzy was well looked after, he finished, 'I love you, Jo. Both your mother and I are very proud of you. Everyone here is very proud of you. Well done.'

It was the best Christmas present Jo could have asked for.

Chapter Ten

AUNT SARAH WAS waiting on the platform of Worcester Station as Jo and Emma piled out onto the platform with their luggage the day before New Year's Eve. A solitary figure wrapped in a heavy tweed coat, her wiry grey hair escaping from her paisley wool scarf, Aunt Sarah hugged Emma and then clasped Jo's gloved hand strongly in hers. Gathering up Emma's largest suitcase, she strode smartly out towards the car park. Following behind, snowflakes swirling around her in the midafternoon gloom, Jo was reminded of the sort of person Martha Wellbourne might have been. With her brusque manner and deep voice, there was an authority about Aunt Sarah that Jo found both daunting and at the same time comforting.

'Hot baths and early bed by the looks of both of you,' said Aunt Sarah, heaving the suitcase into the boot of the ancient gleaming black Daimler, taking in the dark shadows under Jo's eyes and Emma's pinched cheeks. 'What have they been feeding you on over there? You both look half starved.'

'You say that every time you see me, Aunt Sarah. If you had your way I'd be a roly-poly dumpling,' laughed Emma, kissing her aunt on the cheek, blinking away the snowflakes from her eyelashes. Shivering, she and Jo piled the rest of the luggage into the boot.

'Well, it mightn't do either of you any harm to put on a pound or two,' replied Sarah firmly, slamming the boot shut and getting into the driver's seat. Happily Emma clambered in next to her, while Jo, after first pushing away the pile of leaflets from the local Red Cross society, slid gratefully into the back of the car, rubbing her freezing fingertips, her ears burning from the cold. In no time their body heat had steamed up the windows.

The journey to Aunt Sarah's house took thirty minutes. Wiping her sleeve across the window Jo peered out and gasped in delight as the car sped through a magic white world of winding lanes and tall trees, their branches bowed with frozen snow. Sometimes they drove under whole frosted arches then broke out into misty light, travelling past stretches of undulating snow-covered fields, the clusters of farms grey in the distance, the clouds heavy with snow. Rattling across a narrow wooden bridge, Aunt Sarah turned sharp left past a magnificent old village church into the tiny village of Shelsley Walsh. Squeezing past old stone buildings they turned down a narrow lane, the clipped hedges on either side just missing the car, and finally swung into a wide, well-tended driveway, stopping in front of a rambling old moss-covered brick house, the lights behind the drawn curtains invitingly warm.

'Welcome to The Rookery, Jo,' said Aunt Sarah, pulling on the handbrake rather too hard. Jo's immediate impression was how well the house's austerity fitted in with Sarah's character. Almost immediately the white front door with its gleaming brass knocker opened and a tall man with a slight stoop and thin greying hair stepped out to greet them.

'This is my brother Charles. He comes down for the pheasant shooting,' explained Sarah, introducing Jo as they heaved the bags out of the car and tramped across the freshly fallen snow. Dodging the bare Virginia creeper branch that had fallen down from above the door, Jo was nearly knocked flying by a large black shape that hurled itself at her.

'Get back inside, Winston, Churchill!' commanded Sarah as another shape joined the first. Dropping her bags Jo knelt down, grinning from ear to ear, hugging the two black retrievers as they frantically licked first her and then Emma, tails circling like windmills in their excitement. Jo was reminded of Sam whom Nina, in her last letter, had said was fine. 'Inside!' repeated Sarah. With one final lick the dogs obeyed. 'We trained them as gun dogs, but I'm afraid they've got very spoilt, what with the nephews and nieces coming to stay,' she added, looking pointedly at Emma.

Inside, the smell of fresh polish mixed with cooking aromas wafted through from the kitchen to the neat hallway, making Jo realise she was exceedingly hungry. Family portraits hung from the walls next to original prints of pheasants, partridges and other local wildlife. In little niches on the staircase and along the corridor to their bedrooms Jo noticed treasures ranging from French provincial pottery to oriental pots and jugs, all carefully arranged. Finally reaching the third floor, Jo stopped to catch her breath.

'This is known as the children's wing. You're in here and I'm next-door,' cried Emma, flinging open the door to Jo's room.

Jo nodded excitedly. She stepped into the large bedroom with its sloping ceiling and tiny windows and looked around. In one corner stood a wash stand and big china jug, next to which was a cluster of fir cones in a little basket and a piece of soap in a china dish, a bed and a long mirror on a stand. The walls were papered in tiny pink rosebuds. Jo dropped her bags on the floor and ran to the window. Snow had settled in one corner of the windowsill. Peering out into the gathering dusk, she could just make out a vegetable garden, and the grey shadows of a copse behind. The snow was still gently falling.

'Aunt Sarah's mad about growing her own vegetables, won't touch bought ones,' explained Emma. She pointed to dark, snow-laden lumps standing in straight rows like soldiers. 'See those? They're Aunt Sarah's prize brussel sprouts. What's the betting we have some for dinner tonight. The bathroom's down the corridor. I'm going to get out of these clothes. They stink of British Rail. See you in a mo.'

Jo smiled contentedly. Already she felt refreshed and she had only been here twenty minutes.

Dinner in the formal dining room with the long polished mahogany table was quiet but pleasant. Aunt Sarah caught up with news of Emma's activities while Charles explained the intricacies of hanging pheasants to Jo. Afterwards, relaxing over coffee around the big open fire, the pine logs spitting and sparking, Jo, to her intense embarrassment, drifted off to sleep. Next thing she knew, Emma was shaking her and helping her off to bed.

Waking the next morning to the sound of rooks calling in the nearby copse, Jo admitted she hadn't slept so well in months.

'You can't fall asleep tonight. We've been invited to celebrate the New Year at the Hiscott-Halls',' grinned Emma bouncing in half dressed, clutching her socks and a thick sweater. Shivering, she pulled her polo-neck jumper over her head and tucked it into her black velvet slacks.

Yawning, Jo sat up, pulling the eiderdown up with her and tucking it under her chin. 'Who are the Hiscott-Halls?' she asked, the tip of her nose tingling in the cold, reluctant to leave the cosy warmth of her bed.

'They're family friends. Aunt Frances is a friend of Aunt Sarah's. She's not my real aunt. She's got three sons in their mid-twenties by her first marriage who are *so* goodlooking and Lelia from her second marriage to Sir William. Mum always reckoned he married her for her money and she married him for the title. Aunt Frances's father was something to do with Rolls Royce engine parts. Made an absolute pile. The locals used to stick their noses in the air and talk about "new money" until Aunt Frances donated a huge sum to renovate the local church. That shut them up for a while.

'I never actually met Sir William.' Emma's voice became muffled as she dived into her sweater. 'He was quite weird, a sort of shadowy person; he always skulked off whenever I went to visit with Aunt Sarah. Once I sort of met him when he waved to me from the far end of the conservatory. Then when Lelia was twelve he cleared off with a twenty-five-year-old. Poor Aunt Frances was devastated. I don't think Lelia even noticed. She just flounced around in frilly dresses. She's four years older than me and we never really got on. She had this whiny little voice and used to try to lord it over me when we were little. I thought she was the biggest wet in Worcestershire. I haven't seen her for years. Don't even know why I'm chuntering on about her now. Just thought I'd give you a little local background. Look, the sun's trying to come out.' She smoothed her hair off her face and retrieved a sock from under the bed.

'Sounds just my type. As long as she isn't a fashion editor screeching in my ear, I don't care how awful she is,' Jo grinned back, finally braving the cold. Padding across the threadbare rug in her brushed cotton nightie, she thrust open the window and leaned out, breathing in deep, cold lungfuls of air. 'Mmm! It smells so clean up here.' Fresh snow had fallen during the night and there were tiny bird foot-prints everywhere, the watery sunlight catching on the snow so it sparkled like diamonds. A chill breeze fanned Jo's face, bringing the colour to her cheeks and making her shiver. Hastily she withdrew her head and shut the window. 'Brrr, don't the British believe in central heating?' she exclaimed, rubbing her arms.

'Not Aunt Sarah, she'd be the last person on earth to have heating. Why spoil good healthy nature? Makes you tough.' Emma grinned as she pulled the errant thick knee-length sock on over her tights. 'Mind you, one thing she does have is masses of hot water.'

'Great,' said Jo grabbing her towel and disappearing. Twenty minutes later, wearing a thick green jumper over a white polo-neck sweater and black corduroy jeans, Jo joined Emma in the big breakfast room overlooking the fields surrounding The Rookery, and together they tucked into steaming bowls of porridge followed by hot toast and home-made marmalade, the oil-burning radiator turned so low it barely took the chill off the room.

Aunt Sarah strode in, dressed in a thick overcoat thrown over a tweed skirt and Fair Isle jumper, her face free of make-up, her nose pink from the cold, her paisley scarf in one hand.

'We'll be leaving at seven-fifteen tonight for the Hiscott-Halls', Emma,' she announced, removing the car keys from their hook beside the bookshelf. 'I hope you slept well, Jo. You were very tired. I'm going into town to pick up some wine and bits and pieces for Frances. Why don't you show Jo around, Emma? There's some cold pheasant in the fridge and fresh eggs and soup in the larder. A brisk walk would do you both good. Take Winston and Churchill, they need a good run.' Retying her paisley scarf, she swept out of the room.

'That means standing in the hall ready to go at seven-fifteen on the dot,' explained Emma as the Daimler drove off. 'I love Aunt Sarah, she's wonderful, but in this house you keep everything in its rightful place and do everything to the second. It should have been her not her father who was in the army. Come on and I'll introduce you to our next-door neighbours. It's only a couple of miles down the lane.'

Whistling up the dogs, the two girls set off down the windy lane next to the property, the ruts in the road hard under the soft layer of snow, their feet crunching through the frozen puddles.

'You know, I hoped it might be as beautiful as this,' sighed Jo happily, feeling more light-hearted than she had since leaving Australia. Shaking a branch, she watched the shower of snow float down sparkling in the morning sunlight. Running along she shook another branch and tried to catch the snow in her hands.

'You've seen snow before,' laughed Emma.

'So?' cried Jo, running with the dogs. Scooping up a handful of snow Emma chased after Jo and threw it at her and hit her square on the shoulder. Churchill started barking. Winston tore off in the opposite direction.

'Hey, that went straight down my neck!' exclaimed Jo and quickly retaliated.

Soon the girls were in a full-blown snowball fight, laughing and tripping over the dogs, who ran in circles underfoot, trying to catch the flying snowballs, barking and jumping. Twice Jo nearly slipped and twice she felt cold snow seep in down between her jacket and her neck which only renewed her endeavours to shower Emma; finally, laughing helplessly and gasping for breath, they stopped, their cheeks flushed, eyes sparkling.

'It's so good to be just me!' exclaimed Jo, throwing a handful of snow in the air and fishing a lump from out of her collar. 'Oh, Emma, thank you for inviting me to stay.'

'It's great to have a friend here,' Emma said, suddenly shy. 'So often, with Mummy and Daddy on the other side of the world, I have to brazen life out on my own. Aunt Sarah's a dear but it's not the same . . . I really missed them over Christmas.' She threw a snowball for Churchill. 'Tonight's going to be fun,' she went on quickly, regaining her usual cheerful mood. Digging deep into her coat pocket, she retrieved several pieces of stale biscuit and fed them to the panting dogs.

As Jo watched her friend she thought, not for the first time, that maybe her own life really was the easier of the two. 'Tell me again who you think'll be at this party tonight so at least I can get some of the names right,' she demanded as Winston bounded off into a pile of virgin snow.

As the big grandfather clock chimed seven-fifteen, Jo, wrapping her maxi coat around the black dress she had worn to Jenny's party and looking closer to nineteen than seventeen, slid into the back seat of the Daimler alongside Emma who was wearing crushed green velvet. With an approving nod from Aunt Sarah and a cheerful comment from Charles, the four set off towards Shelsley Manor, the Hiscott-Halls' beautiful old country home. Because of Sarah's strict notions of propriety and punctuality, they were almost the first to arrive. Having been formally introduced and presented with a glass of orange juice, Jo stood in an agony of embarrassment struggling to make conversation with Frances Hiscott-Hall's elderly very deaf father and a giggly little woman spilling out of a low-cut floral dress who went to great pains to inform Jo that she worked for the local barrister who advised the owner of the local TV station, who she was sure would be coming to the party. Purposely splitting the girls, Frances had whisked Emma across to talk to another group of early arrivals. Sarah had vanished to inspect the hors d'oeuvres.

Despite Frances's wealth having been pronounced 'new money', her house quietly proclaimed her good taste and love of beautiful objects. Antiques and elegant pieces were scattered through the large entrance hall and around the vast drawing room, the heavy red velvet curtains complementing the thick Persian carpet. To Jo the room felt hideously open and silent, her own voice too loud in her ears as she struggled with the flagging conversation. Searching around for some topic of conversation, her eye was drawn to the magnificent ornate gilt and torquoise antique French clock set on the mantelpiece above an enormous marble fireplace. Beneath, flanked by two magnificent andirons in the shape of eagles about to take flight, a roaring fire hurled out heat into the room, adding a red glow to the solid blackened shapes. Mentally Jo willed the hands to whirl round to midnight as guests dribbled in.

Just as she was trying to explain for the third time that she had taken two dogs, not one of Britain's ex-prime ministers, for a walk, there was a loud commotion in the hall and all eyes turned to the doorway. Laughing uproariously at one of Frances's jokes, a bright-faced, slightly overweight man in his mid-forties strode across the Persian carpet, stroking the snowflakes from his thick, light brown hair. Accompanied by an elegantly dressed woman about ten years his junior, his presence suddenly made the place seem overcrowded. Jo was convinced she knew them both but couldn't place them.

'And this is our Australian visitor, Joanna Kingsford. She is staying with Sarah and Emma over at The Rookery,' explained Frances, ushering the two towards Jo, her severely tailored suit rustling as she moved. 'Both Jo and Emma are building successful careers as models. You know how much Emma always talked about being a model.' Gratefully Jo shook hands with the newcomers. 'Jo dear, Mr and Mrs Compton have the most beautiful stables not far from here,' explained Frances. 'I tell you, Guy, those horses of yours have a better life than most of us. Sally, come with me, I want you to meet a friend of mine,' she finished, whisking Mrs Compton away.

Suddenly Jo understood her feeling of familiarity. Her pulse started to race and a flush spread upwards from her neck to her hairline. There was no need for any introduction, she had seen the man's face often enough and heard his name bandied about at home. She was staring into the eyes of Guy Compton, leading British horse trainer, winner of three Epsom Derbys, several races at Royal Ascot, placed second in last year's Prix de l'Arc de Triomphe at Longchamps in Paris, and the owner of the famous Stockenham Park—the crummy old stables down the road Emma had joked about. Speechless, Jo struggled to think of something intelligent to say.

'Kingsford? No relation to Charles Kingsford the Australian trainer?' asked Guy, his eyes gimlet sharp despite his bluff friendly manner.

'I'm his daughter,' stammered Jo.

'What? You're Charlie's girl? Well I'll be damned. How is the old rascal . . . I mean, your father? Now there's a man who knows his job. You'll have to pay us a visit sometime, tell us some of your father's secrets,' he joked. 'We're only up the road from here.'

Jo's heart lifted. Talking about her father and Kingsford Lodge, her awkwardness gradually vanished. The thrill she always felt around racing people returned as she and Guy Compton swapped stories, oblivious to the room filling up, the noise level rising and Frances determinedly circulating her guests.

'It's lovely to see you two so engrossed but I'm going to have to steal Joanna from you,' Frances interrupted finally, beaming at Guy.

Firmly clasping Jo by the elbow, she propelled the girl towards a group of young accountants up from London. Politely Jo joined in with their trivial banter. With their extremely snooty girlfriends, Jo found them boring in the extreme, particularly when the conversation inevitably turned to modelling and Jo's features in the glossy magazines. Jo glanced back longingly at Guy Compton. She had been just about to ask when it would be convenient to visit Stockenham Park when Frances had whisked her away from Guy.

The crush in the room was extraordinary, the noise escalating so that to have any sort of conversation you had to shout at the top of your lungs. Hoping she would get another opportunity to talk to Guy, Jo searched for Emma and caught a glimpse of her engrossed in conversation with a dark-haired man Jo guessed from the giggly woman's description must be the owner of the local television station. Excusing herself from the group, Jo squeezed through the crowd to the table by the French windows and picked up a glass to help herself to a drink. Making a face at her grotesque image in the gleaming silver tureen, she scooped up a ladleful of punch and was about to pour it into a glass when she was almost sent flying by a young man clutching five empty glasses above his head, who careered into her sideways, shouting at his friends across the room.

'Hey! Watch out!' she cried in frustration, bumping her hip on the table, her voice lost in the clammer. The ladle shot out of her hand, pink liquid splashing across several dozen upturned glasses.

'God, it's crowded in here! Here, let me help,' shouted the young man, rescuing the ladle. Incensed, Jo reached for a paper serviette, one hand pressed to her throbbing hip. 'Hiscott punch! Wonderful! Just the kick you need on a cold winter's night and it's bloody cold out there tonight, I might add,' the young man continued. Turning to Jo he handed her a brimming glass, a piece of apple floating on the surface, and suddenly stopped, his smile fading. 'I say, I'm most awfully sorry. Did I hurt you?' he inquired anxiously.

'It's fine, don't worry,' mouthed Jo, giving her hip a final rub and accepting the proffered drink. 'Cheers!' Wondering how much of the stuff he had already drunk, she looked up at her assailant and her heart missed a beat as she stared into beguiling sea-green eyes, laughter lurking in their shadowy depths. Several years older than her brother Bertie, rugged, tanned and with luscious dark brown hair, he was the most heart-stoppingly gorgeous man she had ever laid eyes on. For the second time that evening she was completely tongue-tied. Blushing furiously, she gulped down half the glass of punch.

'Hardly the best way to introduce oneself but Frances's bashes are always hopelessly overcrowded. I don't know where she finds all the people,' gabbled the young man, running his fingers through his hair. He held out his hand. 'I'm Simon Gordon and you? ... You? ... I know you,' he said more slowly. 'Why do I know you? No, don't tell me.' He lifted one finger to Jo. '*Vogue* ... This month's *Vogue*! Of course, that's it. You're staying at The Rookery with Emma. God! You're just as beautiful in real life.' Then he blushed at his own foolishness. 'I'm sorry, that was incredibly rude. I'm not scoring too many points here so far.' People were moving into the buffet dinner next-door so the noise had dropped enough to have a conversation.

'The punch is good,' replied Jo, finally finding her tongue. Shakily she took another sip, her heart sinking, seeing the inevitable conversation about modelling and magazines coming. 'What do you do?' she asked politely, wishing with all her heart that he would see her as a person not a magazine cut-out.

'Actually, I work in a bank in London. Tell me, how do you stop getting goosebumps when you're doing all those gorgeous shots on the beach in mid-winter?' grinned Simon.

Jo's eyes opened wide at the unexpected question. She paused a moment, watching him over the rim of her glass. Then she started to giggle. 'You think warm, something you Brits must know a lot about if Emma's aunt's house is anything to go by. She's a lovely lady but . . .' Her voice petered out, the laughter frozen on her lips as she stared again into those sea-green eyes, a thin trickle of fire pulsating through her body. For an eternity she drowned in their laughing depths, convinced he must hear the wild hammering of her heart against her ribs. Neither of them spoke. Finally Jo looked away, twiddling the stem of her glass, her palms sweaty, legs trembling, not knowing what to do next.

'Yes, well, um, Sarah's attitudes towards warmth do tend to vary somewhat from the rest of humanity,' remarked Simon finally, slightly breathless, his eyes still lingering on her face. Hurriedly knocking back the rest of his drink he reached for Jo's glass. 'I think I need some more Hiscott punch.' Refilling the glasses with rather unsteady hands he carefully handed Jo's drink back to her. 'How long are you up here for?'

'Just over the New Year then we're back to Paris,' replied Jo equally breathless, avoiding his gaze. The brandy in the punch was spreading through her veins like liquid gold. Noticing his strong square hands, the way one eyebrow lifted when he took a sip of his drink, she wanted to tell him that he was the sexiest man she had ever laid eyes on, that of all the well-tanned, beautiful men she had met in the last year, he was the first who turned her legs to jelly. Instead she said, 'I was hoping to visit Stockenham Park before we leave, and by the way, you're about to lose your cufflink.'

'Oh!' cried Simon, quickly glancing at his cuff peeping out from the sleeve of his dinner jacket, the cufflink ready to drop. 'How embarrassing. I must have grabbed the wrong pair. These are too small. I was running late. I'm always running late.' He rolled his eyes.

'Don't worry. You don't have to explain to me,' said Jo, relieved they were back on safe territory. 'Here, let me take it off so you don't lose it completely. Is the other one falling out too?' She reached out to remove the cufflink and handed it to him. As their fingers touched, Jo smothered a gasp at the sudden current that rippled though her body.

'Thanks,' said Simon, quickly placing the cufflinks in his jacket pocket. 'Promise you won't tell anyone,' he pleaded, leaning towards her, tucking his shirt cuffs back up into his sleeve. 'It's not the done thing to come to one of Frances's dos only half dressed, you know,' he grinned, his eyes dancing wickedly.

Jo grinned back conspiratorially, the sharp tang of his aftershave setting her heart flapping again. 'Only if you promise not to tell anyone I've drunk half a gallon of Hiscott punch.'

'Not a murmur shall pass these lips,' he whispered into her ear.

'There you are, Si! I've been looking everywhere for you!' shrieked a female voice.

Like guilty children the two quickly drew apart. Looking round, Jo blinked at a tall goddess shimmering in metallic grey, the fabric clinging to her willowy almost too thin figure as she glided towards them, the short skirt revealing long shapely legs. It was the dress Jo had recently modelled for *Harpers Bazaar*. Jo put her in her early twenties. A halo of soft blonde hair surrounded a delicate heart-shaped face with a classic creamy English complexion, her ruby red lips a perfect bow. Jo could not help admiring her exceptional poise and beauty. Heads turned to follow her as, ignoring Jo entirely, the young woman walked up to Simon and slipped her hand through his arm.

'Well, are you going to tell me where you've been, Si darling? I've been frantic with worry,' she pouted, clinging to him, her cool grey eyes misty with mascara, enveloping them all in a cloud of Chanel No. 5.

'Caught in icy fog on the A40. At one point I thought I'd never make it but it cleared just after Cheltenham,' explained Simon, looking slightly uncomfortable. Gently he removed the young woman's hand, patting it rather as you would an errant puppy. 'This is Jo Kingsford, the model friend of Emma's your mother was talking about. She's staying over at The Rookery.' His smile illuminated their corner of the room as he spread his arm out to include Jo.

The goddess gave Jo a winning smile. 'I've always been fascinated by models, but don't you think it's rather cheap selling your looks for money? I mean, it's really only one step from prostitution,' she remarked casually.

'Excuse me?' replied Jo, her eyes bright with anger at this unexpected attack.

Immediately the young woman's hands flew to her mouth. 'Oops, have I said something wrong,' she tittered, her grey eyes appealing to Simon. 'Oh golly, *you're* the model friend. I'm terribly sorry. That must have sounded so rude. I didn't mean you personally. Actually I do admire you. It must take such dedication, all those celery sticks and lettuce leaves.'

Jo shifted uncomfortably, still shaky from the effect of meeting Simon.

'Jo hardly looks as if she lives off lettuce leaves,'

said Simon quickly with a half laugh, a hint of irritation in his voice. 'I'll get us all some champagne.'

'Oh dear, there I go again, foot in mouth,' laughed the girl, swaying seductively in Simon's direction as he moved away in search of a waiter. 'It must be the punch. I don't know what they put in it. Si says if my foot was any bigger it wouldn't even fit in my mouth.' Dropping her voice in cosy conspiracy, she aimed another barb at Jo. 'Tell me, do they really airbrush all your photos to make you look thinner?'

'No,' replied Jo enraged, hanging onto every shred of self-control she could muster. With each word the young woman uttered, Jo disliked her more. Every part of her wanted to reach out and slap that perfect, smiling arrogant face.

'I love your little black dress. I expect you go to lots of parties with celebrities. It must be so exciting.' The young woman flicked back her long flowing locks, smiling disarmingly, playing with the single large ruby in the centre of her diamond and pearl necklace. 'How long are you staying?'

'Until the fourteenth of January,' said Jo, wondering if she was simply misreading everything this person uttered. In the last six months she had learned to handle plenty of bitchy women, but nothing matched the performance of this one who alternately fascinated and repulsed her. Like a mouse caught in a snake's hypnotic gaze, Jo watched in fascination as the girl continued to fiddle with the jewel, her eyes roving around the room as she chatted on.

'Did Jo tell you Sarah's still as frugal as ever with the heating?' asked Simon, reappearing and handing out the champagne, apparently oblivious to the predatory subplot being played out before him.

The young woman shook her head, accepting her drink. Peeping adoringly up at Simon through her thick eyelashes, she stroked his cheek. 'Simon, you naughty boy, you still haven't introduced me properly,' she complained with a knowing smile.

'Haven't I? Oh golly, I'm terribly sorry, Jo!' cried Simon, turning the full brilliance of his smile on Jo so her heart once more lurched uncontrollably. 'I have absolutely no manners at all. May I introduce my fiancée, Lelia Hiscott-Hall.'

'It's being officially announced in the *Tatler* next month,' crowed Lelia, her eyes shining.

Jo couldn't stop her jaw from dropping. Quickly shutting her mouth, she stared dumbfounded, first at Lelia and then at Simon, unable to keep the disappointment from her face.

'Congratulations,' she replied, her lips dry. Then, to Jo's immense relief, Emma materialised, clutching a large plate of chicken vol-au-vents with the owner of the local TV station still in tow.

'Martin! What a lovely surprise,' exclaimed Lelia whirling round and throwing her arms around the TV tycoon, kissing him on either cheek.

'Up to your old tricks again, eh, Tiddles?' grinned Martin in a broad Yorkshire accent. His expression softened as he kissed her hair and disengaged himself from her clutches. 'You're a lucky man, Simon.'

Ignoring Lelia, Emma introduced Jo to Martin.

'Poor Martin. There stands a broken-hearted man,' flirted Lelia. Glancing pointedly at Emma, she asked loudly, 'How's Milan and all those luscious dark-eyed Italians? Which one is it this time? Nico, Mario? Sarah told me about the wonderful Carlos.'

'Shut up, Lelia. You can be such a bitch when you want,' snapped Emma.

'Ooh, ooh! Temper, temper,' cried Lelia gleefully.

'Time to move on, I think, Lelia,' said Simon firmly, nudging her away from the group. Letting her arm slide seductively down Martin's arm, Lelia smiled triumphantly at Emma and Jo.

'Come on, Si darling, let's leave these two little adolescents to their chatter with the great TV wizard and go and find the others.' She pulled Simon's hand tightly around her waist. 'I hope you survive, Martin,' she said as her parting shot. Batting her eyelids, she allowed him to kiss her hand. Briefly, Simon and Jo's eyes met. If she had known him better she would have sworn he was appealing for forgiveness. Jo looked away to hide the anger and humiliation at Lelia's final jibe.

'That's the lovely Lelia,' whispered Emma smoothly. 'The only good thing she's done in the last five years is to spend a fortune on elocution lessons to lose that awful whine. Here, eat some of this.' Hurriedly she stuffed the plate of food under Jo's nose, convinced her friend was about to explode.

Jo let out an enormous sigh. 'I've just made the biggest fool of myself,' she confided, helping herself to a vol-au-vent. 'Why didn't he tell me he was engaged? Oh, how embarrassing!'

'Don't give it another thought. She won't,' said Emma and patted her friend's arm encouragingly. She offered Martin a vol-au-vent.

Biting into the crumbling pastry, Jo watched in reluctant admiration as Lelia worked the room like royalty, smiling with one guest, shaking hands with another, sharing a joke with a third before she moved on, the crowd naturally parting for her as she walked around, her hand always close to Simon. What amazed Jo most of all was that everyone looked happier after this willowy, calculating beauty had spoken with them. For a few seconds she had even made Jo feel good.

'She's fabulously beautiful, safely engaged to the most handsome man in the room, and after tonight I'll probably never see either of them ever again, so why do I feel as if I have just looked into the eyes of a rattlesnake?' sighed Jo, knocking back her fifth glass of champagne, her words only very slightly slurred.

But Emma, totally engrossed with Martin, hadn't heard a word she'd said. Jo decided the only solution was to get roaring drunk . . .

Jo woke the next morning while it was still dark to Emma shaking her violently. She sat up, slowly clutching her forehead, the throbbing like ten thousand hammers beating inside her scull.

'Was I actually conscious to see the New Year in?' Jo asked, carefully squinting out of one eye.

'You were. You were singing and dancing and except when you insisted on dancing the charleston with Simon and then rushed out and threw up very neatly in Aunt Frances's lav, you were quite amazingly charming to everyone. How do you do it, Jo?'

'I've no idea,' groaned Jo, flopping back on the pillow, eyes closed. 'I've never been drunk before. And if this is the result, never again.'

'Good. Now get up,' insisted Emma unsympathetically. 'We're meeting the hunt at the Hiscott-Halls' in forty minutes.'

'I think I'm going to die,' moaned Jo without budging.

'No, you're not. And even if you were, you still have to come. Aunt Sarah disapproves entirely of hunting,' explained Emma, 'but once a year she's willing to waive her principles to charge ten pounds a bowl for her home-made soup. In the subarctic temperatures she's never known anyone to refuse. She and Frances concocted the idea about six years ago and now the Hiscott meet has become a tradition around here. Sarah makes a packet each year for the Red Cross.'

'Are you going to ride, Emma?' asked Jo, gingerly clambering out of bed, trying to ignoring her throbbing head.

'I don't know. I said I'd meet Martin at Shelsley Manor, but we may just help serve soup and then gallop off on our own, so to speak.' She gave Jo a wicked grin.

'Be careful,' advised Jo.

'You be careful too. I saw the way Lelia looked at you last night. She's not a good person to have as an enemy and she didn't like you dancing with her precious Si.'

'Don't be ridiculous, Emma. They're engaged. What notice is he going to take of some silly teenager who drank too much punch on New Year's Eve?'

'That's not the impression I got,' replied Emma.

'Well, you've got an overactive imagination,' said Jo staggering out to the bathroom.

The combination of black coffee, painkillers and subzero temperatures did much to alleviate Jo's misery. She insisted Aunt Sarah accept her ten pounds even though she refused the soup, and watched blearily as everyone milled around in the half-light in the forecourt of Shelsley Manor. As the hounds began barking excitedly and the horses clattered on the cobblestones, Jo gradually started to feel better. Like Aunt Sarah, Jo detested hunting, but when the stable hand bought over her hack she couldn't resist the temptation to go for a ride. Climbing carefully into the saddle, she fastened the strap of her riding hat under her chin, her queasiness replaced by a wonderful sense of elation. Patting the horse she urged him forwards, wincing slightly at the hunting horn blast announcing the start of the hunt.

Then she was flying through the snow-covered fields, the hounds tiny brown and white dots pelting ahead. Soaring over fences and galloping across ditches, she revelled in the ride, her cheeks tingling in the wind, her spirits once more soaring. Halfway across a ditch she caught sight of Simon who had come off his mount. Reining in her horse to check he wasn't hurt, she watched him quickly remount and gallop off into the misty morning. To Jo's relief there was no sign of Lelia. Then Sally Compton rode up beside her. For the next few miles the two women cantered gently along, chatting about horses and modelling and fashion days at the races, letting the others fly past, Jo enjoying the view and the rhythm of the horse beneath her. By the time they all met up for lunch, her headache had gone and she was starving. Because of the short winter days the afternoon passed in a flash. Deciding to miss out on further partying at Shelsley Manor, tired but happy, Jo returned to The Rookery with Aunt Sarah and several enormous empty saucepans and soup ladles. As they turned into the driveway Emma came flying out to greet them, excitedly flapping a piece of paper.

'Guy Compton's stable manager rang inviting you to visit Stockenham Park tomorrow and asked could you ring back as soon as you get in. His name's Kurt

Stoltz. Here's the number. I'll help Aunt Sarah. Go and ring him straightaway.'

Squealing with delight, Jo grabbed the scrap of paper from Emma and dived indoors, promising faithfully to return to help with the pots.

'Well?' asked Emma as Jo walked into the kitchen, grinning from ear to ear.

'He's sending over a car to collect me at eight o'clock tomorrow morning, would you believe!' she cried, hugging Emma, her eyes shining.

Kurt Stoltz was a small wiry Australian with sharp dark eyes that managed to be everywhere at the same time. Once a handsome man, his years of hard living had taken their toll. Greeting Jo warmly as she stepped out of the chauffeur-driven car, he lit a cigarette. Cupping it in his hand against the breeze, he immediately started chatting as he showed Jo around the immaculate Stockenham stables. Feeling as though she had come home, Jo thought how out of place Emma's description of the crummy old stables had been. Money oozed from the place. Brass name-plates gleamed on freshly painted stable doors, every piece of leather and metal in the tackroom gleamed from hours of polishing. Not a straw was out of place.

'We run a clean ship here,' explained Kurt, nodding to a couple of strappers busily sweeping away the remains of yesterday's small snowfall. He took a drag of his cigarette, letting the smoke trail out of his nostrils. 'You know, I started out at this game the same time as your father. We were partners for a short while all those years ago,' he confided, introducing Jo to one of their top thoroughbreds. Sniffing in the familiar warm horse smell, Jo listened entranced as the man talked. 'Yes, your dad and I started off with four old nags between us, two your father had been given that were the joke of the town, and two that had cost me my last cent. After working on them for six months we put them in the local races and you can guess which ones came in first—your father's old nags. Be blowed if I knew how he did it, but he turned those two old bags of bones into respectable horses that got placed in more races than not.'

'Dad never mentioned it,' said Jo, watching a horse rolling in a sandbox, her eyes filled with pride.

'He was never one to boast about his successes, your dad,' replied Kurt, his smile more like a grimace. 'We were only about eighteen at the time, with big dreams and big egos. I even dated your mum once before things got serious with her and your dad.' A look Jo couldn't quite fathom flitted across his face.

Stamping the stub out on his shoe, Kurt flicked it into a sand bucket and fished another cigarette from his pocket. 'Yep, those were the good old days,' he sighed. 'Then life moves on and you move on and now I'm over here and me mate's model daughter's visiting.' He stuck the cigarette unlit in his mouth. 'Come on and I'll show you some of our yearlings. I gather you had quite a good old yarn with Mr Compton.'

Jo nodded, smiling. Surrounded by the familiar smells and sounds, she relaxed, so when Kurt asked her how her modelling career was going, instead of clamming up, Jo recounted some of the funnier moments in Europe and finally admitted her longing to return to working with horses. Talking about Kingsford Lodge and her family, the ache in Jo's heart grew. When it came time to leave, unable to come up with an excuse to return, she plucked up courage and looked straight into Kurt's hard, worn face. 'Can I come again tomorrow?' she asked, slightly breathless. 'If you let me, I'll help muck out the stalls or do odd jobs or anything . . .'

'Sure you can. Come as often as you like. I don't mind a beautiful sheila brightening up this old yard,' he replied.

Taking Kurt at his word, Jo borrowed Uncle Charlie's old bomb of a car and the next morning drove the hour journey leaving in pitch darkness, and arriving at Stockenham Park in time to help with the horses returning from track work.

Over the next week she managed to get over to the stables two more times. Happily she helped muck out the stalls, clean the tack and did an assortment of little jobs around the place, wondering how she could ward off her return to Paris. Kurt was less visible but a couple of times she caught him glancing in her direction as he hurried past while she led a horse back to its stall or groomed another after his playtime in the big round sandbox. The low winter sun had sunk beneath the trees and the puddles were starting to ice over again on the third visit as Jo finally wrenched herself away from the horses and hurried in search of Kurt to thank him for allowing her to work at the stables. She found him going through some notes in his office.

'I've been watching you. You're a good solid worker, and you obviously love working with horses,' he said slowly, walking her to the car. 'We could do with a young keen person like yourself. As a matter of fact, one of the girls resigned two weeks ago and I've been looking for someone reliable to train up in her place. I don't suppose you'd be interested in giving up all this modelling stuff and coming to work at Stockenham Park? I'll be honest with you—pay's not as good as tramping up and down a catwalk, but from the look in your eye I'll bet you'd be happier.' He gave a short laugh.

Jo blushed and started to open the car door. A moment later she whirled around.

'Did I hear right? Did you just offer me a job?' she exclaimed squeakily.

Kurt nodded. 'You'd start as a junior stable hand, but with your experience there'd be room to move up pretty quick,' offered Kurt gruffly, the strange look back in his eyes.

Jo gulped. 'Can I give you my answer in the morning?' she asked hesitantly.

'Not a problem. It's been nice getting to know you. Remember me to your dad,' Kurt said smoothly, the muscles in his jaw working ever so slightly.

'You've been busting to tell me something all evening. Are you finally going to let me in on the secret?' exploded Emma as they sat on her bed huddled up in eiderdowns, the moonlight flooding across them through the tiny window.

'I'm not going back to Paris. I've been offered a job working at Stockenham Park and I'm going to take it,' announced Jo, her violet eyes huge in her oval face.

'What?' exclaimed Emma.

'I've gone over and over it all evening. I could hardly eat at dinner, my stomach was churning so much, but now I've made my decision,' she said confidently. 'I'll ring him first thing tomorrow. I just hope I haven't blown it by not saying yes straightaway.'

'You're not serious, are you? Tell me you're not

serious,' cried Emma 'Your career's taken off like a rocket and you're talking about shovelling horse manure?'

'We've had this conversation before and last time you were right, Emma. But I can't do this any more,' replied Jo. 'I'm going to be eighteen in just over a week. When I was over at Stockenham Park I kept asking myself when I was going to get my life going in the right direction. Then Kurt offered me a job and suddenly I had my answer—now! You just don't get that sort of opportunity handed to you twice, not to work in stables like that. I really think Kurt wants me to work there too.' She looked up at her friend, her eyes brimming with emotion. 'You're such a great friend, the way you've encouraged me to keep going with the modelling, but you've always been the one who was passionate about it. I only tolerated it.' She fiddled with a strand of platinum hair, winding it round her finger. 'I know I've made the right decision. I don't care if I have to muck out stables for the next five years.'

'I guess I'm not all that surprised,' admitted Emma taking a deep breath, running her fingers over the eiderdown. 'But what are you going to say to your parents? They're hardly going to support this crazy change of plans. What about all your bookings in the new year? What about money? What am I going to say to Jenny when I rock up without you?'

Jo leaned forwards, the moonlight dancing on her hair and turning it to silver. 'I've thought it all through, except the bit with Dad. That's the tricky part,' Jo replied quickly. 'I feel bad about letting Jean down, but she said herself I'd captured a niche market which was probably a bit of a flash in the pan. I'm sure if I explain she'll understand. I'll ring her tomorrow. I've got twenty grand saved up in the bank, so I won't starve, and when I ring Mum for our Sunday night chat I'll tell her I've decided to stay over for a bit longer visiting friends. That'll give me a bit of breathing space.' She paused. 'Would you tell Jenny I'm staying here until the end of January? By then I'll have figured out how I'm going to break it to Mum and Dad.' She pulled a face.

'This doesn't have anything to do with Simon, does it?' asked Emma, watching Jo carefully.

Jo shook her head vehemently, her eyes sparked with fire. 'I'm not that stupid, Emma.'

'Well, that's a relief. Because there's no future there. Our lovely Lelia's got her hooks embedded far too deep into him.' She wriggled her toes under the bedclothes. 'So how are we going to manage it? I'll tell Jenny you've decided to celebrate your birthday in England and stay on a couple of weeks. That takes us up to the beginning of February. Then what? What about Aunt Sarah and Uncle Charlie?'

Jo's eyes were huge dark pools in the moonlit room. Hugging the eiderdown close she explained her plan. Emma and she would leave The Rookery as arranged, but then Jo would change trains and go on to Stockenham Park while Emma returned to London and Paris. Because Jenny was due to leave for a two-month trip around Europe the day after the girls were scheduled to arrive back in Paris, she would be far too busy to question Emma's explanation as to Jo's whereabouts. Emma herself was flying out to New York the following week.

'So when will you tell them?' asked Emma.

'I don't know,' said Jo candidly. 'I just know I'll have to face the music soon if I want to get on with my life.' Having finally admitted all this aloud, Jo felt as if a cloud had lifted from her. She looked cheerfully across at her friend.

'If this is really what you want, I'll help,' said Emma with a yawn. Watching the happiness in Jo's face she realised of the two she was going to miss Jo more. There was an air of optimism about Jo she had never seen before.

Two days later, having hugged Aunt Sarah one more time and promised not to leave the next visit so long, they boarded the train for London. One station down the line, Jo leaped onto the freezing platform, her heart banging against her ribs, thankful she only had one suitcase.

'Promise you'll write,' choked Emma, giving Jo one last hug.

The guard blew his whistle and the train started to move.

'I'll read about you in magazines,' shouted Jo, running along the platform, her eyes swimming with tears.

As the last carriage was swallowed up in the murky fog she blew her nose, picked up her suitcase and hurried across the platform to catch the next train to Stockenham Park and her new life.

Chapter Eleven

*C*HARLIE GLANCED ACROSS at his wife who, despite the January heatwave, was looking remarkably cool in a big cream and black hat and cream outfit as she chatted happily to Archie, Charlie's leading jockey, astride the horse that had just won him a fat prize at Sydney's Rosehill Gardens. Wiping the sweat from his brow, Charlie wondered how he was going to stop her giving it all away without causing yet another screaming match between them. Sighing, he patted the two-year-old filly owned by him and his best mate and top client, Jack Ellis. It was ludicrous to be standing here worried about money, but he had good cause. Squaring his shoulders he produced a smile for the media and shook hands with two Japanese owners, part of the syndicate his horse had just beaten. He felt tired. There seemed no time to rest. Just before Christmas he'd had a health scare but the pains in his chest had proved to be stress related. His heart was as healthy as ever and his schedule as frantic. In two days he was flying out to Hong Kong, stopping over for two nights to discuss details with a new syndicate, then on to Ireland to check out the stallions and broodmares at Airlie Stud, and then straight back to Australia in time to race some promising horses at a couple of big country meetings. But before all that he had to stop Nina's crazy spending sprees.

Jack Ellis came up behind him. 'Things not as good as they might be, despite our little win?' inquired the stocky blue-eyed man.

Charlie looked him up and down, wondering whether to confide some of his concerns but decided against it. 'Not a worry in the world, mate,' he lied more cheerfully than he felt. 'If that horse can keep performing like she did today, we're in the pink, mate.' He slapped his friend on the back. 'Some of these Irish mares have got the potential to produce major players. Could set us up very nicely for the next year or two, thank you very much. You interested at all?'

'Could be.'

Their conversation was cut short as the horse was led away and they were ushered towards the platform for the presentation.

'Can't satisfy all your fillies at the one time, eh?' joked Jack quietly, reading between the lines. He had known Nina and Charlie long enough to understand that life was not always as smooth between them as outward appearances would have the world believe.

'She'll be jake,' muttered Charlie, stepping up to receive the trophy amidst the flash of camera bulbs and a feeble clapping from the members' stand. Then the crowd swarmed around congratulating Charlie and Jack as they stood with Nina and Archie for more photographs. Charlie might be tired but his heart felt slightly lighter. Jack was a good friend, now all he had to do was talk some sense into Nina.

The confrontation wasn't as bad as Charlie had

anticipated. Once Nina had stopped crying and hurling cushions and abuse at him, he had managed to persuade her they simply couldn't hold up all the charities in Australia at once and that donating a large sum of money once, or at the most twice, a year was the absolute maximum. Then, taking her in his arms, he kissed her softly on the lips. Nina clung to him, her tongue seeking his. Breathless, like young lovers, she undid his shirt and trousers while he unzipped her dress and slipped her bra straps from her shoulders. Burying his face in her breasts he felt her shudder against him. Leading her up to the big wide bed, they made love gently until late into the night.

'Oh, Charlie, if it could always be like this,' sighed Nina, stroking his forehead as they lay cocooned in the sensual aftermath of their lovemaking, the muted streetlight from the open curtains the only illumination, the overhead fan purring softly.

'Shh,' murmured Charlie, kissing her silent again.

'How long are you planning to stay in Hong Kong this time?' asked Nina.

'Not long,' replied Charlie on the verge of sleep.

'You know it's Jo's birthday next *Friday*,' continued Nina, lying on her back, watching the shadows from the branches outside flicker across the ceiling. 'She'll be eighteen, Charlie, and that's special. Why don't we fly out and surprise her?' She rolled over and kissed him on the nose. He was breathing heavily. 'Charlie!' she shook him gently. Charlie murmured an endearment and pulled Nina to him. 'No, Charlie, wake up.'

'I am awake,' he said defensively. 'Sounds a great idea.'

Nina shook him again. 'No, listen to me. We can stay with the Lims in Hong Kong and while you're busy doing your horse stuff I can get some outfits made. Yen Ho never minds if I ring at the last minute.' The Lims were a delightful Chinese couple whom Nina and Charlie had known for several years and Nina could happily fill in two days with Yen Ho. 'Then we fly on to England, surprise Jo and then you go to Ireland.'

'Whatever you like, my love,' murmured Charlie and rolled over.

Nina lay back, suddenly wide awake as the trip formed in her mind.

'We won't even give a hint of our arrival,' bubbled Nina the next day at breakfast on Charlie's return from track work. 'We'll just arrive on Emma's Aunt Sarah's doorstep laden with presents. If we ring Sarah first she's bound to let something slip. I want it to be a complete surprise for my darling gorgeous model daughter. We don't have to stay there, so we won't be putting Sarah to any trouble. I'll take Jo to a couple of shows in London and we'll get some more photos done to update her portfolio and bring back to show all our friends here. We'll fly back to Paris while you go on to Ireland. I'll give Eve at the travel agency a ring straightaway. She'll be able to tell me what's on in London and organise tickets. Bertie will be fine now he's got this summer job organised in that law firm. Between them he and Jackie can keep an eye on the house and look after Sam,' she finished happily.

Miraculously Nina organised herself quickly and two days later they flew out of Sydney into the stifling Hong Kong heat.

Charlie found he was just as excited as Nina at the prospect of seeing Jo again. As he discussed business with his Hong Kong associates, his mind kept wandering uncharacteristically and he was as eager as his wife when they stepped onto the plane to London. Jo had shown herself capable of giving this modelling a go and succeeding. He had always thought she was beautiful, but the way she was sticking at a career she hadn't chosen filled him with pride. And he couldn't wait to tell her that to her face.

The biting cold of England was almost a relief after the exhausting humidity of Hong Kong, except that Nina caught a cold. After a quick detour to Knightsbridge, London's elite shopping grounds, the Kingsfords headed out of London. Charlie's heart was full as he looked across at Nina's bright face while she chatted away excitedly, trying to ignore her worsening cold, the hired car piled high with presents as it flew along the motorway. Booking into a pretty little Tudor pub outside Worcester overnight, they set out for Shelsley Walsh after an early breakfast, Nina sneezing and blowing her increasingly red nose.

Sarah was out walking the dogs when the Kingsfords arrived and Cook answered the door. Refusing her offer to come into the warm for fear of spoiling the surprise, they sat in the car for the next twenty minutes, the heater turned up full blast and fogging up the windows, until they saw a tall figure wearing a mud-spattered duffle coat and gumboots striding down the lane beside the house accompanied by two black retrievers, tails wagging, tongues lolling, sniffing at everything in sight, their panting breath billowing from their mouths in great white clouds. Hurrying across, Sarah peered at the early morning visitors and then exclaimed in surprise as she recognised them.

'Nina, and you must be Mr Kingsford! What a lovely surprise. You should have warned me you were planning to visit and I would have made myself more presentable.' She pushed back a strand of wiry grey hair that had escaped from her paisley scarf, and called the dogs to heel. 'Come into the warm. I'm sure Cook can rustle up coffee and cake.'

'We wanted to surprise Jo on her birthday,' beamed Nina, leaping out of the car and patting each dog in turn as they milled around her, ignoring Sarah's command and sniffing at Nina. 'Is my darling girl about, or are we too early?' she asked, unable to curb her excitement any longer.

Sarah looked at Nina in surprise. 'Jo's not here She's gone back to Paris. I put her on the train to London with Emma a week ago.'

'Paris!' cried Nina, blanching under her heavy make-up, shivering in her thick wool coat. Her head felt as though it was stuffed with cottonwool from the cold and she was sure she was getting a temperature. 'She can't be. I spoke to her last Sunday and she told me she was staying on in England till the end of the month.' Her eyes flew to Charlie's face in concern.

'No, no, you must be mistaken. She is definitely in Paris,' replied Sarah firmly. 'Emma rang to say she had arrived safely . . .' Her voice trailed off as a horrible suspicion crept into her mind.

'Can we go inside first and then talk about it?' suggested Charlie, his shoulders hunched against the cold, noting the set of Nina's mouth. He felt extremely foolish. He should never have let Nina's enthusiasm persuade him to leave everything to chance like this, but he had wanted to surprise Jo as much as Nina. Quickly he slipped a hand under his wife's arm but she pulled away. Angrily scrunching her way through the muddy snow, she stamped her boots viciously on the mat and followed Sarah into the house. Frowning, Charlie wiped his shoes rather less violently before stepping inside after the two women.

'Oh dear, this is simply dreadful. Have you any idea who she might be staying with?' asked Sarah after Nina, between sneezes, had explained again that Jo had said she was staying in England visiting friends.

'We just assumed she was staying with you and that you knew what was going on,' replied Nina tartly, swiftly pulling off her leather gloves and tucking them in her new leather handbag. Tears pricked the backs of her eyes. This was so disappointing. How could Jo have been so irritating as not to let them know where she was, and this house was like an igloo. She shivered again.

'I wish I could say that was true,' replied Sarah worriedly.

'Well, have you any idea where she might be? Can you call anyone?' asked Charlie, as disappointed and annoyed as Nina, but also concerned for his wife. Her cheeks were becoming noticeably flushed. Sarah shook her head. Emma was in New York, Jenny was in Greece, and the last she had seen of Jo was waving her goodbye at Worcester Station. She racked her brains. '. . . Wait a moment—there is one person who might know something . . .' She picked up the phone and dialled, hoping her suspicions were unfounded.

Leaning across the farrier's workbench amongst discarded horse shoes, Jo blew out the eighteen candles on the birthday cake amidst raucous applause from her new stable mates. Delighted at the surprise birth-day celebration organised by Faith, her room mate, Jo sank the long knife into the cake, shut her eyes and made a wish.

'Let Daddy understand my need to work with horses,' she whispered in her heart.

'Tell the horses to answer back,' yelled John, a tall, gangly nineteen-year-old who had quickly made friends with Jo. He had not stopped ribbing her since he had caught her whispering to one of the horses on her second day at Stockenham Park. As a result, everyone else teased her about it too.

'They already do,' laughed Jo, blushing happily and giving John a shove before cutting up the rest of the cake. Having handed everyone a slice, she sank her teeth into the fluffy yellow sponge cake, marvelling that she was actually an employee of Stockenham Park.

For the next few moments the only sounds above the munching were sparrows twittering in the rafters and occasional noises of horses moving around in their stalls. From where she stood Jo could see clouds scurrying across a wintry sky. A shaft of watery sunlight caught on a brass plaque on a stable door. Finishing her cake she thanked her new friends shyly for the wonderful surprise and they all drifted back to work.

It was almost ten o'clock in the morning. Piles of snow turned to grey slush needed to be cleared and the wind tossed strands of stale straw waiting to be removed. Having established that England was about ten hours behind Australia, Jo had earlier decided to ring her parents in the late afternoon. That way she would not only give herself a few more hours, but she'd be pretty sure of catching her father at home after track work. It would be easier to talk to Dad first. Raking the dank hay out of one of the stalls and tossing it onto the pile in the main courtyard, she went over and over in her mind what she was going to say to her father, a hard knot forming in the pit of her stomach.

She was so absorbed she nearly jumped out of her skin when Kurt tapped her on the shoulder. There was a sly expression in his eyes that sent a shiver down her spine.

'You've got a visitor,' he said sharply.

Jo's heart leaped. Emma! She'd said she'd drop in when she was least expected. She was back from New York and it would be just like Emma to turn up unannounced on Jo's birthday. Planting the pitchfork in the hay, Jo dashed out of the stall, an expectant grin on her face, Kurt following her slowly.

'Hello, Jo,' said Charlie.

'Dad!' Jo stopped dead in her tracks, the colour rushing to her face, the smile evaporating. Recovering, she ran to him and flung her arms around him but quickly dropped them and stepped back when he made no move to return her embrace. 'I was going to ring you tonight, Dad. I can explain everything,' she gabbled, twisting her hands together. 'Kurt has been so good to me, and Mr and Mrs Compton too, and I've learned so much, Dad. You'll be really proud of me when you've got over being cross. I just wanted to show you I could manage working with horses so you'd really believe I could do it . . . I couldn't think of another way . . .' It all came tumbling out. When she finally stopped, Jo was shaking from head to toe. Charlie hadn't moved a muscle.

'Your mother's in the car. She's so angry she wouldn't get out,' he said grimly.

Jo's eyes flew to his. 'Mum's here too?' she echoed, her cheeks burning.

'We were going to surprise you on your birthday. It was her idea. Well, it's certainly been a surprise for us. We have to talk in private, my girl,' he said with finality.

Quickly Kurt stepped forwards. 'She's employed in my stables and she's got work to do. Get on with it, Jo. You can talk in your lunch break,' he ordered.

'Not so flash now, since you got into the "funny money",' taunted Charlie, rage boiling inside him at Kurt's attitude. He had been shocked to the core when he had been confronted by his long-time enemy on entering the stables and he was furious beyond words at Jo.

'Jo,' repeated Kurt ominously.

'You bastard. How dare you order me about over my own daughter,' exploded Charlie, all his previous calm evaporating, 'And as for you . . .' he grabbed Jo by the arm.

'Daddy please,' pleaded Jo, pulled sideways, her violet eyes filled with misery.

'Leave my staff alone or I'll have you forcibly removed,' said Kurt coolly, ignoring Charlie's reference to his disastrous investments which had forced him back to working for others. 'Just like old times, fighting over a sheila, eh?' he added with a smirk. He jerked his head in the direction of the stall. 'Go on, Jo, if you want to keep working here.'

'Yes, let her go,' said a husky voice.

Jo and Kurt whirled round to see Nina picking her way carefully across the slush and dirt which hadn't yet been swept away, an angry red spot on either cheek, a handkerchief to her nose.

'Nina. Well I'll be darned. As beautiful as ever,' greeted Kurt.

'Mum!' cried Jo.

'Hello, Kurt,' said Nina, tight-lipped. Her mouth was quivering at the corners. Her eyes swept across Jo and back to Kurt. 'You're welcome to her if you can get the selfish little bitch to do any work and not simply take your money.' She stepped towards Jo, anger spilling out of her watering eyes, her head throbbing. Her words hit Jo like a physical blow. 'If this is what she wants, let her have it. Let her slop around in all this muck and filth.' Her eyes darted to Jo's face. 'You ungrateful little bitch. How dare you do this to me? How dare you insult me and my friends? You're quite happy to have me spend all my money and time on you to set you up, to make you something, and then you do this to me. How dare you?'

Jo watched unable to speak as the tears spilled down over her mother's flushed cheeks.

Charlie strode across to Nina and put his arm around her shaking body. He could feel she was burning up. 'Neene, darling, you're not well. We'll come back later and talk about this calmly,' he said gently, trying to stem the hysteria, but Nina for once swept him aside.

'No, Charlie, no,' she cried between sobs and coughs. 'We've spent the last two years going to endless expense to give her the best and she just throws it back in our face and then lies and sneaks around behind our backs. You may be happy to just sit by and let her continue to accept our handouts but I'm not! She's told us what she wants. Let her have it.' Once more she turned on Jo. 'You won't last five minutes here after playing the princess across all of Europe. This is just a game to you. A game where you don't care who you insult or who you hurt. When are you going to grow up? Let her learn her lesson, Charlie. Leave her in all this dirt and slush and when she's ready she'll come crying home.' Her eyes glittered with fever. 'I'll give you six months at the most.' She broke into a fit of coughing.

'Mum, please Mum, it's not like that . . . Listen to me . . . Don't do this to me,' cried Jo, shaking uncontrollably at her mother's vicious attack. Tears spilled unchecked down her cheeks but Nina refused to look at her. Turning on her heel, Nina picked her way blindly back across the stables and out to the car.

'Never could control your sheilas, could you, mate. Now, I've got a stables to run here, so could you keep your family squabbles for later,' jibed Kurt.

His words were the last straw for Charlie. Torn between supporting Nina and seeing the devastation in Jo's face, he gripped his daughter's arm tightly and dragged her with him as he stepped to within millimetres of Kurt's face, his other hand bunched in a fist.

'You've made one clever move too many, you mongrel, one you'll regret for the rest of your life.' It took all Charlie's self-control not to smash his fist into that mean, leering face.

'Are you threatening me?'

'Too damn right I am! We're going, Jo,' barked Charlie, propelling Jo towards the stable exit.

Breaking away, Jo's eyes darted first to Kurt and then to her father, her whole being tortured with misery. 'I can't, Dad. I work here. This is my job,' she choked and then fled back to the stall, leaving Charlie standing in the centre of the courtyard, and started stabbing blindly at the hay, the tears still coursing down her cheeks. It had all gone horribly wrong. Her mother hated her and now her father would never understand. She'd probably lost her job as well. She shook away the tears that continued to blind her as she heaved a pile of stale hay on the fork. She could hear Kurt and Charlie yelling at one another in the courtyard. Then suddenly everything went quiet. Tossing the last load of manure on the heap, Jo banged the fork against the wall and dragged out the hose. The fork clattered to the ground but for once Jo let it lie. Hosing down the stall, she swept it out and laid fresh hay in record time. Hurrying out in search of fresh lucerne, she nearly bumped into John coming out of the tackroom, carrying a couple of saddles.

'Bloody look where you're going, can't you!' she swore, head down. She pulled out a hanky, blew her nose and dived into the storeroom. The morning seemed interminable.

'You can take an early lunch if you want. Your father's waiting for you in the office,' Kurt called kindly, peering into a stall where Jo was changing a bandage on a horse's fetlock.

Jo mumbled her thanks without looking up. When she had finished bandaging the leg, she washed her hands and splashed some water on her face. Red-eyed and blotchy-faced she hurried across to the office, the frost-covered flowerbeds as empty and bleak as her heart.

Charlie was sitting reading a magazine. He stood up as she entered, his mouth set in a grim line. 'Right! Get in the car! I'm taking you to lunch,' ordered Charlie.

Meekly Jo obeyed, knowing there was no way she would be able to swallow a morsel. There was no sign of Nina.

'Daddy, if you'll just give me a chance to

explain . . .' Jo started once they were settled in a corner of the George and Dragon, determined not to start crying again.

'No. You listen to me, Jo. You have no idea what you're doing. That man is evil. You're only there as a means to ruin me and wreck Kingsford Lodge. So get any of those silly romantic ideas out of your head. Why d'you think he hired you when he could have had his pick of dozens of more experienced girls?'

'Because I've got experience, Dad, he told me . . . experience working with you,' Jo fired back. 'Where's Mum?'

'She's got a fever. Do you really believe that? Jo, you are so innocent.' He stretched out his hand to touch her but she quickly withdrew her arm and picked at her nails in her lap.

'Don't patronise me, Dad, I'm eighteen and I know what I'm doing.'

Charlie's eyes hardened. 'You're only just eighteen and you have no idea what you are doing or who you are dealing with. Kurt Stoltz is an evil man. He has never forgiven me for marrying your mother and for being more successful than him. He hired you because you are my daughter and he will grill you until he learns my methods. Get out of there before you ruin us all.' Jo squirmed at the memory of some of Kurt's more persistent questions. 'I'm right, aren't I? He's had a go at you already, hasn't he?' continued Charlie.

'You're wrong, Dad. He's not like that,' retorted Jo defensively and pushed away the steaming dish of steak and kidney pie Charlie had insisted on ordering. She flicked a strand of hair back off her shoulders. 'He told me all about you and Mum and him.' She couldn't stop her eyes filling with tears as she mentioned her mother, but doggedly she continued.

'He said he really admired you when you were starting out. He used to be a lot handsomer. He told me
you were mates and that he liked Mum but he knew
she always loved you. He said you were one big
happy family. Why should he make all that up?'

Charlie sucked in a large breath. 'Is that what the
bastard told you? Well, you listen to me—'

But Jo wasn't interested in hearing more. 'I like
him, Dad, I like what I'm doing.' She stood up and
pulled on the jumper she had earlier discarded.
'The Comptons are proud of me working at their
stables, Mrs Compton told me so. I've got friends.
Kurt respects me. I know I'm right and I'm staying.
Now, could we go back?'

'You're wrong, Jo, absolutely wrong,' said Charlie
standing up as well, his fury escalating at Jo's inability to see Kurt for what he was. Yet the man was a
brilliant con artist.

Charlie freely admitted he was the first to snap up
a good opportunity when he saw one, but he could
never forgive the triumphant way in which Kurt had
seized the Dublin Park land when the family were at
their lowest ebb. If it had only been the land that
he had wanted, Charlie could have almost understood, but he had wanted more. He had and still
wanted everything that Charlie had but most of all
he wanted Nina. Good looking, smooth talking he
had nearly won. Entranced by Kurt's romantic
advances and seeming gallantry, only some uex-
pected antennae deep in Nina had held her back at
the last minute from waltzing up the aisle. Relieved
more than he could ever express, this time the
triumph had been in Charlie's eyes. Yet the romance
Nina had woven around Kurt as her first boyfriend
had taken a long time to fade. Charlie shuddered at
the memory of Nina in Kurt's arms before they were

married, when he thought he had lost her for ever. The memories only served to feed Charlie's rage and frustration against Jo.

'You've broken your mother's heart, offended our friends and wasted I don't know how much time and money we've spent on you. Enough is enough, Jo. You will go back to Paris and get on with being a model or else fly home with me.'

'And work with you at the stables?' Jo's eyes lit up for a second.

'Don't go through all that again, Jo,' snapped Charlie, pulling out his wallet.

Jo's heart sank. Her father was unreachable. Her mother wouldn't even talk to her. She had never felt more alone or more riddled with guilt, but she refused to give in. 'Dad, I'm sorry. I never meant to hurt you or Mum. I love you both so much, but why can't you understand this is what I have always wanted to do? You love horses. You taught me to love horses. Why can't you accept that I do too?' Her voice cracked. 'If you won't let me come back and work with you, then I'm staying at Stockenham Park until you decide otherwise. Now, I have to get back, my lunch break is over.' Jo's legs were trembling so much she wondered if she would be able to walk out of the door. Wiping away the tears she could no longer stop, her agitation increased as she watched her father meticulously pulling the pound notes out of his wallet. 'Dad, please.'

Unbending, Charlie stared back at his daughter, refusing to let go of his own anger and hurt, yet recognising the same tenacity in Jo that was in him.

'Well, if that's the way you want it ... But from now on, until you come to your senses, like your mother says, you're on your own. Don't come crying to me when it all falls to custard.' Tossing the money on the table, he strode past Jo into the fresh air.

Smiling bleakly at the landlord, Jo hurried after her father. Outside the cheery sun had vanished behind threatening clouds and an icy wind cut across her face. Neither of them spoke as they travelled the windy narrow lanes back to Stockenham Park.

Charlie stopped the car and Jo stepped out, her throat tight with misery. 'I'm sorry, Dad. I love you both so much, please believe me,' she whispered, her face level with the window. 'Please tell Mum . . .'

Charlie looked back unsmiling. 'Sorry? You're sorry? You have no idea what you have done,' he said and drove off.

Blindly Jo walked into the storeroom, sat down on the stone floor and burst into tears.

Chapter Twelve

ROCKING BACK AND forth, impervious to the freezing stone floor, her arms clutched tightly around her knees, Jo cried her heart out, huge shuddering sobs racking her body. After a long time the waves of crying gradually lessened and the shaking subsided, the soft smell of fresh oats and chaff filtering into her numbed brain and reminding her where she was. It was a smell Jo normally associated with happiness but there was no happiness in her heart right now, just an unbearable heaviness. Her eyes stung and her chest felt tight. Then she felt something soft and warm slink along her leg. Listlessly Jo raised her head and watched Puss the stable cat with lacklustre eyes. Mewing, Puss arched her back and rubbed her soft grey fur back and forth against Jo's jeans, her white chest and belly gleaming in the dimness. Jo continued her rocking. Undeterred by her lack of interest, Puss jumped up on to Jo's knees. Balanced precariously, the cat attempted to rub herself against Jo's chest, her mewing more insistent, her huge topaz eyes staring appealingly at Jo.

Hiccupping, Jo stopped rocking and smiled wanly. 'You're a persistent puss,' she said, stroking the cat.

She straightened her legs. Immediately the mewing stopped. Turning round three times Puss settled in Jo's lap. Within seconds she was purring loudly, her claws kneading Jo's thighs through her jeans, the contented rumbling reverberating through Jo's body. Comforted by the warmth and sound of the cat, Jo went back over the whole ghastly episode with her parents, her fingers rhythmically stroking the soft fur, another shuddering sigh occasionally overtaking her. She wasn't sure which hurt most, the coldness in her father's eyes or her mother's absence. She would rather have been subjected to another tirade than just be shut out, and Jo simply couldn't accept her mother's fever had been that bad.

'I got what I wanted, didn't I, Puss?' she sighed at last. 'Freedom. Freedom to work with the horses I love, but why couldn't Daddy understand, Puss, why couldn't they understand?' Her throat tightened and fresh tears pricked at the back of her eyes, but for the moment she had no answers. Leaning back against the wall she stared out at the brightness through the half-open door, too emotionally wrung out to think any more. Puss continued to knead and purr. After a while, trying not to disturb the contented animal, Jo wriggled. Her buttocks were starting to go to sleep and the cold stone was freezing her whole body.

'Well, there's no use crying over spilt milk, you'd understand that, wouldn't you, Puss? Now I'm on my own I'd better get on with it,' she said resolutely, gently lifting the cat in her arms. Holding the soft warm body to her cheek for an instant, she placed Puss carefully on the floor and stood up. Stretching her legs she brushed off most of the chaff and dust from her jeans and shivered while the cat, satisfied with her short rest, stretched, yawned widely and wandered off.

Rubbing her numb buttocks Jo checked her face in a broken piece of mirror on the nearby bench and retied the band in her ponytail. Deciding she didn't look too much of a disaster, she poked her head cautiously out into the stable courtyard. There was no sign of Kurt or of anyone else, only a black horse with a large white blaze chewing at the bottom door of his stall across the other side of the paving stones and a bay staring curiously around. Assuming by some miracle she still had a job, Jo headed for the clattering sounds down the other end of the stables.

The following Monday, to her astonishment, Guy let her start riding track work.

Neither she nor Kurt referred to her parents' visit or abrupt departure, but while he was still outwardly friendly to her, Jo felt a change in him. Much as she tried to fight her own reaction she felt uneasy when he was about. Questions she had found harmless before now seemed more intrusive, his presence more sinister. With her father's words ringing in her ears, while she forced herself to appear open and chatty, inwardly she was far more cautious when Kurt was about, mindful to keep the secrets she had learned as a child strictly to herself. Yet she knew she had to get past the unease she felt about Kurt and the black despair that threatened to swamp her. Working herself as hard as she could was the only way she knew to numb the pain. The first to arrive at the stables in the pitch-black predawn and last to leave after the horses had been bedded down for the night, Jo found the next few weeks hopelessly bleak. Only her own stubborn pride kept her going.

As winter gave way to spring and the mornings lost

their biting chill, the black cloud surrounding Jo began to lift. Tiny yellow aconites pushed through the frozen ground, the first flowers to show their faces to the sun. Soon snowdrops and hyacinths filled the air with their heady perfume and Jo's heart began to sing again. Her mind also started working sensibly once more. On her days off Jo scoured the local area for powerful, age-old natural remedies she had learned to use at Kingsford Lodge and Dublin Park. Ignoring the strange looks and comments about witches' broomsticks, black cats and horn-of-unicorn, she finally gathered together a small collection of herbal oils, extracts and powders from assorted plants which she kept in a first-aid box tucked safely under her bed.

Clattering through the tiny village of Stockenham for the early morning rides, its medieval square and quaint little houses shrouded in mist, she started returning Guy's cheery greetings. Then, as she put the horses through their paces on the heath, her spirits lifted for the first time in weeks. The rush of wind stung her cheeks rosy red; the pounding of the powerful beasts beneath her, their breath billowing white clouds through flared nostrils, their grunts echoing across the heath, reawakened the thrill she had felt when she was riding back home in Australia.

Kurt, on the other hand, was less buoyed by the onset of spring, his triumph at having the Kingsford girl working at the stables having turned to anger and frustration.

'She'll have to go. We're not going to get much more out of her now her father's bloody got to her,' muttered Kurt to his leading jockey Willie Carstairs at track work one day, watching Jo thundering along the heath. 'Damn Charlie to hell.'

'Mmm, I dunno,' replied Carstairs picking his

teeth, heavy lines etched down each leathery cheek. Five foot nothing and thin to the point of emaciation, Willie had been riding Compton horses now for five years. 'If I was you I'd keep watchin'. Women and horses, they're all the same. Treat 'em nice long enough but show 'em the whip now and then and you'll find out what yer need ter know.'

Kurt grunted ungraciously but for the moment he decided to take Willie's advice and bide his time.

In mid-April Jo received a letter from Emma with a newsclipping enclosed featuring a photo of Emma grasping another model's hair on the steps of an expensive hotel in Paris, the caption blazoned across the top CATFIGHT FROM PARIS CATWALK.

'Talk about any publicity being good publicity,' wrote Emma. 'I've had more highly paid jobs since they ran that story on me and Meloney than I've ever had before. My agent's gone crazy. Mind you, Meloney was being a perfect cow and deserved having her hair pulled, although maybe on the steps of one of Paris's top hotels was not the best place to do it!'

Her letter cheered Jo immensely. Finally plucking up courage to ring Jenny that evening, Jo asked to speak to Emma. Jenny sounded exactly the same, which made Jo feel even more guilty and she apologised six times during the phone call.

'She thinks your mum and dad went a bit over the top,' confided Emma after the two had caught up with each other's activities. 'I miss you heaps. Write to me, you lazy cow.'

'You can talk!' laughed Jo before the beeps went for the third time and she had to hang up.

How she missed Emma's cheerful good humour

and lack of respect for conservative attitudes, Jo thought as she helped unload the horses returning from a midweek race at Cheltenham. Yet she didn't miss the glamorous life Emma led one jot. No, here was her glamour; her happiness was right here amongst what her mother had so succinctly described as 'muck and filth' and Jo had every intention of staying in it for far longer than the prescribed six months. There was a lilt in her step as she walked towards Outsider, a promising brown three-year-old gelding still secured in one of the horse floats. A recent addition to the stables, he threw back his head and screamed at Jo as she approached. Hastily she stepped back.

'Keep away from that one!' yelled a strapper as Kurt stormed over to the horse with an extremely concerned Guy Compton and the vet. 'Pulled his shoulder in the last race. He was bad enough when he came here. Now he's got really vicious with the pain.'

Quickly Jo went in search of other work. Hosing out another float she could hear the noisy struggle above the jet of water as two burly stable hands held the horse down so the vet could get close enough to examine him. Seventeen hands high and powerfully built, Outsider was a handful at the best of times; now the terrified horse was fighting and screaming like a wild thing. Taking longer than usual to settle a timid filly, Jo peeped through the bars and watched the men continue to tighten the restraining ropes, her heart going out to the huge horse who, ears flat against his head, whites of his eyes clearly visible, fought the vet off as he tried to give him an injection.

'Keep still, you bugger,' yelled Kurt, adding his wiry strength to control the horse while Willie

Carstairs, who had been riding the horse when he had sustained the injury, looked on. Hopeful of a big win in two weeks' time, Kurt continued to struggle, scowling ferociously until finally between them they managed to control the horse long enough for the vet to administer a painkiller. Watching Kurt walk away from the group Jo got the distinct impression he had just received a severe dressing down from Guy. Later when the stables were quiet, carrying her first-aid box, Jo went over to Outsider's stall and peered inside. Immediately, ears flattened, nostrils flared, Outsider shouted at her, kicking out.

Ignoring the horse's threatening behaviour Jo stood still and whispered to him. After a while he stopped darting about the box and stood eyeing Jo off. When she was sure he was more settled, she rubbed some aromatic herbal oil from her box on her hands, carefully unbolted the door and slipped inside. Immediately Outsider started darting about again. Continuing to whisper, Jo stood quite still to one side of the stall, apparently fascinated by a pile of manure. Gradually the horse settled down and for the next ten minutes continued to eye Jo off while she picked at imaginary bits on the wall. Finally, unable to resist, he walked over and sniffed her. Slowly raising her hands Jo showed the horse her palms. Curious, Outsider sniffed at the oil, his warm breath tickling her skin. Then, whinnying loudly, he turned his head away. Satisfied she had made enough progress for the moment Jo backed slowly towards the door, still whispering, and slid out of the stall.

The next day the burly men were fighting Outsider again in preparation for the vet.

'Why can't they be gentle with him? Can't they see they're just making him worse? He's absolutely terrified,' cried Jo from the tack room almost in tears, what progress she had made with the horse now completely undone. About to rush out, she was grabbed from behind by John.

'D'you want to lose your job, you idiot? Have you seen the look on Kurt's face this morning? That horse's costing the stables a fortune, the guv's already laid into him for careless track work. Kurt wants the horse back on the track. This is the only way.'

'No, it's not!' cried Jo, snatching her arm away. 'I could fix that shoulder in no time if Kurt'd let me near him.'

'Oh, you could, could you, Miss Kingsford? So tell me, just how are you going to manage a miracle like that?'

Whirling round, Jo was confronted by Guy Compton. 'Mr Compton, will you let me have a go? I know how to fix him, truly,' she blurted out.

'And land yourself in hospital? No, Jo, you keep away from that horse, young lady,' Guy said sternly. Then his face softened. 'Out of interest, how were you planning to fix him?'

'Talking and herbs, the way my dad showed me when I was eight years old,' replied Jo matter-of-factly. 'We had this great filly that was favourite to win the Oaks but she trod in a hole and wrecked her shoulder, the same as Outsider. No-one thought she would run, but she did.'

Guy Compton threw back his head and roared with laughter.

'Talking and herbs!' he spluttered, his eyes almost disappearing into his chubby cheeks. 'D'you know how much that horse's worth? ... Talking and ... Oh, the marvellous arrogance of youth!' Finally he subsided. Pulling out a silk handkerchief, he wiped his eyes, blew his nose and replaced the hand-kerchief in his breeches pocket. Kurt strode up, inquiring what all the commotion was about. 'She wants to fix up Outsider by talking to him,' Guy explained, starting to laugh all over again.

Jo reddened as Kurt joined in the joke with equally uproarious mirth.

'No, really it works. I'll show you,' pleaded Jo.

Kurt stopped laughing, his eyes narrowing.

'Why not give her a go, guv? A bit of talking never did anyone any harm,' he grinned, his eyes shifty. 'But only talking, mind.'

'Don't be a damned fool, Stoltz,' snapped Guy. 'The girl could get badly hurt. Or if not, she could make Outsider worse. There's no way I'll allow—'

Kurt pulled at his peaked cap. 'No harm can come if she's this side of the door and Outsider's the other, guv,' he interrupted.

Guy looked at him sharply and then relaxed slightly. 'Well, if you put it like that, I'd have to agree—but the bolt stays put,' he replied sternly.

'Well Jo, shall we give it a go? Thought of every-thing you need to say?' grinned Kurt, nodding at Jo.

'Give me two seconds,' cried Jo jubilantly, ignor-ing the jibe. Dashing across the yard she dived into the tack room and emerged with a small plastic bucket containing a number of herbal oils and some scraps of cloth. 'If he settles, will you let me into the stall?'

'Sure, sure,' said Kurt, giving Guy a knowing look.

Outsider shouted in outrage as the three approached his stall. Ears flat, he bared his teeth as he had before with Jo, darting back and forth in the box, poking his head out in fury trying to bite her and the two men. Nothing Jo could do or say made any difference. Filled with humiliation, Jo asked Guy and Kurt to step back, but Guy drew the line.

'We can stop this nonsense now,' he said firmly. 'That horse is not to be approached by anyone without my or Kurt's supervision.'

Kurt nodded and walked away smirking. The girl, in his opinion, was far too pally with the Comptons.

Seeing Jo's dejection, Guy looked kindly at her. He liked the lass and she was a good worker. 'It was a lovely idea, Jo, but I'm afraid that sort of airy-fairy stuff doesn't work in the real world. Why don't you come up to tea with Sally tomorrow? She'd enjoy your company, what with our own girl overseas at the moment.'

Jo smiled weakly, her cheeks burning with embarrassment. 'Thank you very much. I'd like that,' she replied, bitterly disappointed. Returning to the tack room she replaced her plastic bucket in her locker and picked up a hay fork. 'They can laugh and sneer all they like but I'll show them I can fix your shoulder, Outsider,' she muttered under her breath, jabbing at a pile of hay.

Sneaking back to the stables after work was finished for the day, she rubbed some aromatic oil on her hands and stuffed the bottle in her pocket. Cautiously approaching Outsider's stall, she froze as he let out a scream of terror when she opened the top door. Looking nervously around to see if anyone had been alerted she caught sight of John.

'Don't you ever give up?' he cried.

Jo put her finger to her mouth. 'Watch this,' she whispered. 'Don't move a muscle.'

Outsider was once more circling fearfully around the stall. Standing stock-still, Jo waited. As before, seeing Jo apparently uninterested in him, the horse came over to her and sniffed at her jacket. Sensing the time was right, she slipped into the stall and waited again. After a moment she slid her hand up onto the horse's back and almost jumped out of her skin as he turned and gave her a sharp nip. Biting her lip, she nearly laughed out loud as she realised her mistake.

'I'm sorry, Outsider. It's the same as before—lavender oil,' she whispered, holding up the palms of her hands for the horse to sniff. Satisfied, Outsider nibbled at Jo's jumper and let her stroke her hand along his back, as she had often done before he hurt himself. 'You poor old thing, you really did it this time,' she whispered soothingly.

Gradually she worked her hand across his back, stopping if he showed any agitation, slowly building the horse's confidence in her, all the while picturing in her mind how she wanted him to react, until she reached the sore spot. Flinching, Outsider turned to nip her. Immediately Jo stopped, leaving her warm hands resting gently against his gleaming coat. Stamping one foot, Outsider shook his head but this time did not attempt to bite her. Taking her cue from the horse, Jo cautiously started to work the sore muscle, whispering as she worked, her touch getting gradually stronger. From time to time she added more oil to her hands, always allowing Outsider to check the perfume before she returned to her massage, the picture in her mind staying clear and vibrant. Gradually a transformation came over the horse. As Jo worked, the pain lessened and the muscle relaxed, just as she had seen it in her mind.

'There you go, old fella,' she whispered, finally stopping. 'I'll give you some more tomorrow.' She fished in her pocket for a piece of carrot. Outsider nuzzled into her shoulder, blowing warm breath onto her shirt while Jo talked quietly. With one last stroke Jo slipped out of the stall and slid the bolt carefully back in place. Collecting up her oils and cloths, she started as she saw John, whom she had completely forgotten about, staring at her goggle-eyed.

'Are you still here?' she exclaimed.

'Are you a white witch or something?' John whispered huskily, his eyes wide with amazement. 'I wouldn't have gone in there in a month of Sundays.'

'No, stupid,' laughed Jo picking up her bucket. She eyed the young man. 'My dad taught me a thing or two,' she said sweetly then hurried towards the tack room.

'Amazing. Fancy a gingerbeer down the George and Dragon to celebrate?' asked John, following after her.

'Yeah, I would, thanks. Promise you won't mention this to anyone, though.'

The next day when the vet came, Outsider didn't need such rough handling. In the late afternoon Jo was back working on him again. Unseen, Kurt watched her from the other side of the stables.

'I'm buggered if I know how she does it,' he muttered to Willie who was standing next to him. 'Two days ago the vet couldn't bloody get near the animal, let alone a slip of a girl. Now she's got him eating out of her hand. Makes him smell like a bloody florist's shop but that horse is mending quicker'n I've ever seen.' He scowled, frustrated and angry at his inability to extract information from the girl.

'If you ask me, it's just nature taking its course,' replied Willie curtly. He didn't approve of Jo messing with the horse but had earlier received a sharp rebuke when he had voiced his disapproval to Kurt.

'Probably,' nodded Kurt unconvinced, his scowl deepening as Jo emerged from the stall, wiping her hands and shooting the bolt home. Then, swinging her bucket, she walked jauntily towards the tack room. 'She's like her father,' Kurt continued, digging his hands deeper into his overcoat pockets. 'He'd do all this stuff and more, but you could never actually see what he was doing. It was more a sort of ESP—like he was telling the horse something without telling him. Now I'm going nuts. I tell you what though, I'm bloody finding out this time.'

But he didn't. However, neither did he stop Jo working on Outsider and he was temporarily appeased when the horse was able to compete at Doncaster and came in second, picking up a sizeable cheque for the stables. Jo, whom Kurt had insisted look after Outsider while they were away, was delighted too. Tears rolled down her cheeks as the crowed roared and she watched him, ridden by Willie Carstairs, streak home a nose behind Lester Piggott on Blood Royal.

A week later at Newmarket, while searching for a clean pair of socks under her bunk in the enormous Compton horse bus, she couldn't avoid overhearing Kurt order Willie Carstairs to slow his mount down in the third race. Convinced she must have heard wrong, she kept her eyes glued to number sixteen as the horses leaped from the starting gates for race three. Willie, who had been expected to get a placing, came in fifth.

On her return to Stockenham Park Jo mentioned the incident to John.

'I'm not surprised. It wouldn't be the first time. The odds were pretty good on the winner,' shrugged John. 'But I never told you a thing,' he added quickly.

'Are you sure . . . I mean, not Kurt, surely? I know

it goes on but . . . ' Jo couldn't disguise her shock.

'For someone who has been around racing stables for most of her life, Jo, you are so naive,' replied John.

Unable to get any further comment from him, Jo walked off, still unconvinced. Racehorses had off days too. It wasn't necessary to do that sort of thing out of this stables. The horses were too good. Anyway, why would anyone want to lose? The next day she forgot about the incident entirely when Kurt announced Outsider was the stable's elect for Ascot and she would be in charge of him making sure he was safe and comfortable travelling to and from the racecourse and looking after him before and after the races.

As June got closer Jo's excitement mounted. Completely recovered from his injury Outsider was performing brilliantly. She loved the great valiant horse and spent as much time as she could working with him. The second reason she was excited was this was her first ever attendance at Royal Ascot, the pinnacle of British racing, and just going there was enough for Jo.

Finally the great day arrived. Wide-eyed, Jo listened from the stalls to the cheers as the royal procession entered the winners' enclosure. Brilliant in bright yellow with a matching broad-brimmed flowered hat, the Queen smiled and waved to the cheering crowd as she travelled the course to the royal box in her open carriage drawn by the famous Windsor greys, Prince Philip by her side. The grounds were packed, the women decked out in the latest fashions and wearing an astonishing array of hats, the men adding their own dash of elegance in morning suits and top hats. Flowers spilled over neatly manicured flowerbeds. The sky was a perfect pastel blue. Jo's heart fluttered with excitement as she finished grooming the horse Willie was riding on day one, and then held him steady for Guy to saddle up.

The next day Jo was so taken aback when the Queen stopped and spoke to her on her way to inspect her own horses before the start of the races, she forgot to curtsy, and when she led Outsider out onto the field with the other contestants on the final day, Guy Compton's brilliant red and orange jockey's colours glistening on Willie's back, the loudspeakers blaring out his history, Jo's heart nearly burst with pride. The only thing she would have changed, had she been able, was the jockey. From the first she disliked and distrusted Willie; he had small eyes and a mean mouth, but she had to admit he was a good consistent rider and Outsider needed that stability.

Squinting against the sun from her position in the grandstand with the other Compton strappers, Jo's heart was in her mouth as the barrier gates shot open and the eight thoroughbreds pounded down the straight mile. A strong favourite, Outsider quickly settled into second place with the Queen's horse, wearing blinkers, hard on his tail. As they rounded the second bend Outsider was still in position, gaining on the leader but still behind. Stretching out his stride he gradually pulled level until they were neck and neck. As the horses turned into the final stretch the crowd in the grandstand rose to their feet as one, their cheers a wall of noise. Jumping up with them, bending to one side to see past a vast orange hat, Jo shouted herself hoarse urging Outsider on as he thundered towards the winning post, struggling to gain the lead. Willie's whip arm was thrashing like a windmill, his tiny body a blob high above the horse's back, the commentator's voice blaring out above the roar of the crowd.

Tears streamed down Jo's face as the gallant three-year-old lifted himself up a gear and in the final seconds shot past the leader, streaking home to win by a head. The crowd went mad, shouting and hugging one another, throwing their hats and programmes in the air. Crying and laughing all at once, Jo dived through the crowd down to the enclosure where a sweating but triumphant Willie, perched on top of Outsider whose dark coat glistened with sweat, panted out his elation to the media. Leading Outsider back to the stalls while Guy and Willie stepped up to receive their trophy from the Queen, Jo overflowed with love for the big-hearted horse.

Chatting away to Outsider as she hosed him down and gave him a rub, Jo longed to be able to share this magic moment with her dad. Throwing a light rug over the gelding's back to stop him catching a chill, she walked him round a small paddock area behind the grandstand away from the main races to let him gradually cool down and pick at some grass. There had been no word from Charlie since the fateful day in January, although Jo had written a couple of short stilted letters both to him and to her mother in the hope that they had got over their anger. She had received curt replies from her mother as if she were a distant relative. As she walked round with Outsider, Jo made a pact with herself that if they could not put the hurt and anger behind them, she would. She would write and pour out the love she had for these great beasts and the thrill she found in her work, not expecting a reply but at least then knowing her father understood how she felt.

Jo was so lost in her reverie she didn't hear the voice calling her name. Jumping at the tap on her shoulder she looked round and stared in amazement at Simon Gordon, dashingly handsome in his grey morning suit, his top hat in one hand, his members' badge dangling from one lapel.

'Jo Kingsford. It is you! I wasn't sure when I saw you with Guy at the stalls. You look so different dressed like that.'

'Simon!' exclaimed Jo. Flinging her arms around him, she kissed him lustily on the cheek, the reins still securely in her grasp. 'Isn't he just the best horse you've ever come across?' She flushed with excitement and laughed as Outsider leaned over in a proprietoral manner and shoved his nose between them. 'It's all right, you gorgeous beast, he's taken. You're still the only man in my life.' She leaned into Outsider's shoulder and scratched his neck, then blushed scarlet as she realised how her words must have sounded. 'I didn't know you were interested in racing,' she stammered pushing back a strand of hair, wishing he wasn't having exactly the same effect on her now as he'd had at Shelsley Manor.

'It's only a hobby but I have thought from time to time it'd be fun to own a racehorse,' Simon replied, his eyes burning into her.

Jo's blush deepened. 'Where's Lelia?' she asked, snatching for something to say, quickly walking Outsider again. Her legs felt like jelly. And she must look a total mess.

'She's with some friends,' replied Simon, falling into step beside Jo, his own heartbeat quickening.

'You look great. How's Emma?' He glanced across at Jo, thinking how dazzlingly beautiful she looked, her cheeks flushed, the sunlight warm on her face. 'I've been to Ascot a few times, but today's been sensational. In those final seconds the crowd got so excited, everyone quite forgot about the old British stiff upper lip.' He gave a short laugh at the irony of making polite conversation when in reality he ached to take her in his arms and cover her face with kisses. Blushing at his utterly disloyal thoughts, he dragged his eyes from Jo's tantalising lips, made more inviting by their lack of any trace of lipstick. He beat his race book against the palm of his hand. 'What happened to the modelling? I heard you were working for Guy and Sally, but I didn't believe it.'

Having reminded herself that Simon was not in the least interested in her and that he was engaged to another woman, Jo managed to settle down enough to make sensible conversation. Soon they were engrossed in the finer points of racing, arguing as though they had known each other for years. Guiltily she found herself enjoying the warmth that flooded through her as his eyes wandered casually over her, and praying that Lelia wouldn't show up. Only when she looked into his eyes for an instant and caught a glimpse of something deeper in their sea-green depths did her superficial chatter fade and her heart give a violent lurch.

'I've only ever considered racing a hobby, but I do enjoy it and it gets me out of the office,' admitted Simon, watching Outsider drop his head and start pulling contentedly at the grass. 'Which reminds me, do you ever get any time off?'

'Not much,' replied Jo, her heart leaping guiltily again, 'but I don't mind. I'd rather work hard at something I love than have heaps of time off and hate my job. Why?'

Simon paused for a moment, fiddling with his programme. 'I wondered if you'd like to join a house party I've organised next month in Norfolk. My aunt has a cottage near Fakenham. We thought we'd go to the Newmarket races on the Saturday and then spend Sunday exploring the countryside. There are some great little pubs you can stop at for lunch. D'you think you'd be able to persuade Guy to let you escape for a weekend?'

'It sounds wonderful,' gasped Jo, her heart beating against her ribs. She was finding it hard to breathe.

'Escape from what, Si darling?' squealed Lelia, teetering towards them on high heels that kept sinking into the grass.

Jo's heart sank, her enthusiasm quickly replaced by a polite blankness. Dressed from head to toe in figure-hugging baby pink, one hand clutching an enormous pink hat, the clouds of chiffon topped by a massive satin bow, Lelia practically fell into Simon's arms. What on someone less attractive could have been disastrous only served to make Lelia look even more stunningly beautiful and softly feminine. A wave of disappointment swept over Jo. Any tiny niggling thought that Simon might possibly not be serious about Lelia vanished completely. How could any man not be mesmerised by her beauty or bewitched by her beguiling helplessness? Beside her Jo felt utterly shabby and dull.

'Mixing with the stable hands, are we now, darling? Hello. Is that the horse that just won?' Lelia nodded briefly in Jo's direction and then peered at her again. 'Do I know you?'

Jo stared blankly back.

'Christ, Lelia, don't start another one of your little games. You met Jo at your mother's house. You couldn't stop talking about her for three days,' snapped Simon. Jo blinked at his unexpected retort.

For a few more seconds Lelia looked perplexed, then her hand flew to her mouth and she giggled prettily. 'Oh heavens, you don't mean Emma's little model friend?' she said, fanning her face with her programme. 'Well how on earth was I supposed to recognise her like this? I mean . . .' she asked accusingly, her voice high-pitched. She looked straight at Jo. 'You do look a bit different dressed like that, you know.' Sighing, she controlled her irritation at having seen the two in a cosy tête-à-tête. 'It's a tough world, modelling, but you were doing so well, so I heard. Only the very best survive of course, but I'm sure if you'd kept at it . . .' She gave Jo a winning smile.

'I've invited Jo to come to our weekend in Norfolk,' explained Simon.

'Oh.' Lelia paused. 'How nice. That will make our numbers work out,' she rushed on, noting the brief frown that flitted across Simon's face. 'I hate to sound rude breaking up your little chat, but I'm going to have to whisk Si away.' She placed one hand with its fingernails painted deep coral possessively on Simon's arm, ostentatiously displaying her vast solitaire diamond engagement ring. 'Lord and Lady Cleaver want us to join them and the royal party for more champagne. Well, I suppose we'll meet again in Norfolk.' She smiled brilliantly at Jo. 'You can tell us all what it's like working in a stables.'

'Here, give me a call when you know if you can get the time off,' said Simon rather too briskly, handing her his card. 'I hope you can make it.' A shiver ran through Jo as his fingers brushed against hers. Her eyes flew to his face and for an instant the world and Lelia vanished as Jo felt the full power of his beguiling eyes on her and she almost believed he cared about her. Then reality cut back in.

'Yes, we'll enjoy seeing you there. Cheerio,' squeaked Lelia, dragging Simon off towards the members' enclosure.

'Yes, we'll enjoy seeing you there,' mimicked Jo, leading Outsider back to the horse bus. 'Like hell. Go and get some more elocution lessons, you stupid cow. That's one lovely weekend I won't be going to.' She tore the card up angrily and stuffed the bits in her pocket, wondering who she was trying to fool. 'Come on, Outsider, let's get you sorted out and settled for the journey home.' Nearby, other strappers were busy packing up their gear to truck the racehorses out from the course.

It was such a heart-rending waste. 'Still, it would never have worked even if he hadn't been engaged,' Jo thought resignedly as she threw a rug over Outsider and fastened it in front of his chest and between his back legs, her fingers still tingling from Simon's touch. They were so different. They moved in completely different circles. She would always be the square peg, while he appeared to be unquestioningly happy with his lot.

Outsider whinnied impatiently, turning his head towards Jo and stamping his hind leg. 'Cheeky thing! Just because you're such a champ, I haven't forgotten you,' she laughed, her thoughts back with the horse. Smoothing the rug along his back, Jo secured Outsider in his area of the horse bus, filled up his feed tin and started tidying away bridles and halters from the mess of junk on the floor. Contentedly Outsider buried his nose in the chaff, occasionally shaking his head and shuffling around in the box, while Jo worked away and other Compton horses were led into the bus for the journey home. Finally grabbing a bulging brown paper bag from the front of the vehicle, Jo sat down on the steps that divided the horse area from the place where the workers slept. Staring into space she pulled out a stale sandwich and slowly ate it, thinking about Simon.

'God, what an idiot I am,' she muttered in disgust, stuffing the last mouthful of sandwich in her mouth. Suddenly she felt overpoweringly exhausted. How could she have been so stupid as to fall for a man about to get married? But she could not forget the aching longing she had felt watching Lelia laughing up at Simon, nor the hopelessness inside her as they had walked away.

'There are other fish to fry,' she told herself firmly as the last horse was secured. Squashed between two male stable hands she accepted a Coke and determinedly joined in with the raucous singing as the big bus wove its way across England back to Stockenham Park.

By the time Jo finally crawled up to her room, buoyed up by the euphoria of the others, not to mention the large quantities of champagne they had all consumed after all the horses were safely bedded down, she had convinced herself that Simon would somehow suddenly come to his senses. Realising the terrible mistake he was about to make, he would rush over to Stockenham Park, sweep her into his arms and declare undying love. With that thought securely in mind she snuggled up in bed and fell fast asleep.

Chapter Thirteen

THE PARTYING AFTER Outsider's success continued back at Stockenham Park as though it
would last forever. Every evening someone
bought another round of drinks up at the George
and Dragon or threw a party at someone's house
which everyone was expected to attend, until Jo
began to wonder if it was worth going to bed at all.
Tempers became frayed and track work grew tenser.

Waking dog-tired on Tuesday morning three
weeks after the race, her temples throbbing despite
having switched to Coke after the first two rounds
of black velvet, her lungs dry from all the cigarette
smoke, Jo lay for a moment with her eyes shut.
Vowing she would never again touch the Guinness
and champagne mix, she also swore that regardless
of any attempts to persuade her otherwise, tonight
she would go to bed early. There was a big race
coming up in York at the weekend and they were
preparing to take a number of two-year-olds over to
France at the end of the month. Reluctantly pushing
back the bedclothes, she sat up, rubbing the sleep
from her eyes. The room felt stuffy. It was going to
be one of those hot July days when the horses tired
easily and were difficult to handle. Then she realised

the sunlight was streaming in through the half-open curtains.

Glancing over at her room-mate Faith's neatly made bed, her eyes flew in horror to her alarm clock on the dressing table. She had to look twice to believe her own eyes. She had overslept by two hours. Leaping out of bed she checked the alarm switch. As she feared, she had forgotten to turn it on. Hurling on her clothes, she scrambled into her riding boots, grabbed her jacket and riding hat and tore out of the building towards the stables. Kurt would eat her alive. She was supposed to be working John's horses today as well as her own as he had gone home for his grandmother's funeral. Jo's breath came in short sharp gasps as she ran. She might just make the tail end of track work. Then her heart sank as she saw the procession of track workers on their mounts filing back into the stable yard. Sidling into the stables with the last horse, she quickly started helping unsaddle the horses in the futile hope that no one had missed her. But Kurt had seen her try to sneak in and immediately charged across, his expression thunderous.

'I'm terribly sorry,' Jo mumbled, avoiding his eye. 'My alarm didn't go off.' The horses were milling around edgily, everyone was bad tempered.

'You want to work here, you turn up for track work. We're not running a Sunday picnic,' snapped Kurt. Track work had been disastrous. The mud from recent rain had made the going tough and messy, the stiff warm breeze unsettling everyone. 'Someone get that horse!' he barked as one of the horses broke loose.

Jo leaped to the gelding too late to stop him bumping himself against a stall door and scraping his skin, at which Kurt let loose a tirade of abuse on the girl. Outraged at being blamed for something that was not her fault, yet fearing Kurt might sack her on the spot, Jo led the horse back to his stall and removed his saddle, her heart pounding with rage as she dabbed ointment on the graze. Later, still smouldering at Kurt's insults, Jo went in to check a filly that had caught a chill at the weekend and noticed she hadn't touched her breakfast. Normally a horse to give Jo plenty of cheek, today she stood dull-eyed, head down. Jo stroked the horse gently, worried at her obvious depression. Kurt chose that moment to peer over the stall door. Seeing her apparently doing nothing and suspicious that he might be on to one of her secrets, Kurt charged into the stall, startling the horse and demanding to know exactly what Jo was doing.

'I don't think this horse should race tomorrow,' Jo replied, looking up sharply. She had been watching this filly for several days but with John away the vet, reliant on the stable hands to check the horses for minor ailments, must have missed her.

'If the vet's happy, so am I,' retorted Kurt abruptly.

'I don't think she should travel in this condition,' persisted Jo. She had seen a similar scenario at Dublin Park when she was thirteen years old. This filly was obviously unwell, so why put her under more stress, which in Jo's opinion was entirely unnecessary. They were collecting plenty of other winners.

'Don't you bloody tell me how to run these stables or I'll see you don't work here much longer,' threatened Kurt, glancing briefly at the horse.

'Could you ask the vet to have one more look at her just to make sure?' Jo pleaded.

Kurt's face turned several shades darker, his fury

escalating at Jo daring to question his authority. He shoved his face close to hers, his narrowed eyes glinting dangerously. 'Let me tell you something, girl. I run these stables and I say that horse races tomorrow,' he snapped. Then he turned and stormed off.

'I don't trust that Kingsford girl, not one little bit,' Kurt confided to Willie in the pub over lunch. 'She's very cleverly turned the tables on us, if you ask me. We're getting nothing out of her, but what's she learning from us to take to the next stables she works at or, worse still, back to Australia and Charlie bloody Kingsford? She's got to go, Willie, but I can't sack her after one mistake.'

'She'll make another, they always do,' said Willie calmly, gazing steadily at Kurt.

'Or I'll make one for her,' growled Kurt maliciously. What was it about these Kingsfords that got under your skin, made you lose all sense of reason? It'd been exactly the same with Charlie all those years ago. Damn and blast the whole lousy Kingsford family. He'd get them yet ...

'Why didn't you wake me? I thought we'd agreed to wake each other so we didn't sleep in?' demanded Jo in a quiet moment when she and Faith were exercising some horses in the river beyond Stockenham village.

'I thought you were awake,' replied the other girl sourly, leading her horse out of the water.

'Have I done something to upset you?' asked Jo, surprised at Faith's unfriendly tone.

Avoiding a direct answer, Faith tied the horses to a fence rail. She had been fighting a growing jealousy at all the attention Jo had been receiving since she'd fixed Outsider's shoulder, but even Faith had to agree that Kurt had been a bit rough on her today.

'I'll make it up to you,' she said, furiously rubbing down one of the horses. 'We're planning to take John out to dinner when he gets back from his grandmother's funeral. There's a great little pub in Tenbury Wells that serves the most scrumptious Italian food. I'll shout you.'

'Oh, thanks,' said Jo surprised. Feeling more cheerful, she clicked her tongue to the horses and the two ambled back across the meadow, the long grass brushing against their legs. Reaching the gate, Jo followed Faith as she led the little group into the lane. Wild roses and frothy white old-man's-beard tumbled over the hedgerows, the horses' hooves clip-clopping on the bitumen. Above a lark sang. It was difficult to remain upset for long in surroundings like these.

John returned to Stockenham Park the following week and all the regular stable hands tumbled into their battered old cars and headed off for the Horse and Groom in Tenbury Wells. Ordering noisily, they tucked into mountains of spaghetti and ravioli accompanied by the house red. Feeling adventurous, Jo chose octopus in a delicious herb and garlic sauce. The evening succeeded in its purpose of cheering John up and everyone fell into bed shortly before midnight.

In the early hours of the morning Jo woke with agonising stomach cramps. Crawling out of bed she stumbled to the bathroom, threw up and passed out. Coming round to find herself lying on the cold linoleum, she vomited her heart out for the next hour, the cramps doubling her up in pain. Staggering back into the bedroom, she lay down on the bed, ghostly grey.

'God, you look terrible,' said Faith half dressed for track work. 'Do you want me to get the doctor?'

Jo shook her head and disappeared back into the bathroom, clutching her middle. 'Tell them I won't make it to track work but I'll be down at the stables as soon as this stops,' she groaned, the acrid taste of bile stinging the back of her throat.

'Don't worry, I'll explain everything,' called Faith through the half-open door, pulling on her sweater and tying back her hair. 'Must have been the octopus. You were the only one who had it.' She disappeared, leaving Jo slumped miserably on the bathroom floor.

After a while Jo struggled to her feet and fumbled in the cupboard in search of something to stop the vomiting. She swallowed a tablet which stayed down for the best part of one minute, then crawled back into bed and dozed fitfully. Waking at ten she slowly sat up. Her muscles ached from all the retching and she felt completely exhausted. Finding she could move without throwing up, she dressed very carefully and made her way to work.

The normally welcoming stable smells hit her like a truck. Stomach heaving, she gingerly started to muck out one of the stalls, wondering how long she could stand the stench of horse manure. Kurt saw her from his office. When Faith had delivered her message, he'd almost laughed out loud. It was just as Willie had said. Triumphantly he marched across the yard, chin thrust out belligerently, heels clicking loudly on the paving stones. Flinging open the stall door he stood in the doorway, the sunlight outlining his small frame like some evil goblin. Leaning heavily on the hay fork, Jo stuttered out her apology.

'I don't have time for any of this. You had your warning last week,' declared Kurt glaring at her.

'We're looking after valuable horses here. If you can't act responsibly and keep your social life under control, I don't want you around. You can ask the office to make up your pay.'

'But didn't Faith explain—I've got food poisoning. The seafood was off,' protested Jo, frantically searching her jeans pockets for a handkerchief, the cramps returning.

'I'm sure it was. Now collect your pay and go. I want you out of here in an hour. You are no longer an employee of this stables,' ordered Kurt, ignoring her obvious misery.

'I'm telling the truth, I swear ...' pleaded Jo, pressing the hanky to her mouth. 'I'm sorry,' she gasped. Diving past Kurt she rushed into the toilet.

Smirking, Kurt strode back to his office. Who was he to diagnose food poisoning? Quite clearly the girl had a hang-over—or that was what he would say to anyone who dared to question his decision—and good riddance to her.

In tears Jo emerged from the toilet and headed up towards the office. Faith, checking that Kurt was safely down the other end of the stables, tore up behind Jo and stuffed a small packet in Jo's hand.

'The vet gave me this to give to you,' she whispered, glancing anxiously over her shoulder. 'Take two straightaway. He told me to tell you it should settle your tummy down and stop the pains.' Still the colour of green-tinted parchment, Jo swallowed the tablets with a shudder. Faith gave a half-hearted laugh. 'He said not to be concerned if you start whinnying in the middle of the night, the effect wears off after two days.' Jo grinned feebly, a flickering of life in her dull eyes. 'Actually, what he really said was, "It'll glue her up for a month and she won't feel a thing"!' finished Faith.

'Thanks.' Jo's laugh ended in a sob.

'I've got to get back before Kurt sees me, but are you going to be all right?' whispered Faith anxiously.

'Sure, I'll be fine,' said Jo, feeling anything but.

'I feel so awful. If I hadn't suggested we go out for the meal, none of this would have happened,' gabbled Faith. 'I'm sure you'll easily find work, though. There are heaps of stables round here and everyone knows how good you are with the horses.' She gave Jo a quick embarrassed hug. 'Good luck. I'm sure we'll catch up again on the track.' Then she bolted back to the stables.

Fighting back tears, Jo collected her pay and returned to her bedroom. Even the girl in the office had been shocked at her state. Mercifully the tablets the vet had given her started to work quickly, so after two more bouts of dry-retching Jo managed to drink a glass of water and miraculously keep it down. Burping, she stared at her chest of drawers, wondering through her fogged mind what to do next. Her whole body ached and she had no idea where to go or how to get there. Her first thought was to ring Aunt Sarah and ask if she could stay with her. Then she remembered how livid Emma had said Aunt Sarah had been when she had learned about their deception, and right now Jo didn't think she could cope with the recriminations that were bound to surface even though Sarah had since forgiven them both. Wearily Jo pulled her suitcase from the back of the wardrobe and slowly started folding her clothes. She was well over the hour Kurt had given her to pack and go, but she was past caring. Finally she was finished. Clutching a Coke bottle full of water, she slung her purse over her shoulder and picked up her suitcase. With one last glance around the room, Jo trudged down the stairs and out of the gates of Stockenham Park.

Catching the last bus into Stockenham village she stayed her first night in a poky little bed and breakfast that smelled of damp and mildew and looked out over a rubbish dump. Deciding it wasn't worth moving as she was convinced she would soon have a job at another local stables, Jo paid the dumpy, wiry-haired landlady a week's rent in advance, hired a car using some of her savings and started searching for work. While she quickly recovered from the bout of food poisoning, what she couldn't recover from so easily was the impact of Kurt's viciousness and the speed with which his ugly rumours had been passed along the grapevine. Travelling to one stables after another Jo soon discovered that far from being the saviour of the top Compton horse, she had now sunk to the lowest of the low in the eyes of the local racing fraternity.

'Nope, we've got all the workers we want,' said the owner of a medium-sized stables whom she had met a couple of times at the track. 'I don't hire female strappers,' said another, avoiding her eye. 'I'm not hiring lazy, unreliable hands who upset the horses,' snapped a third. Downhearted but determined not to give up, Jo kept trying, but by the end of the week she realised it was pointless hunting for work anywhere near Stockenham Park. Kurt had done his work superbly. 'Give up and go back to modelling,' advised a kindly owner, leading his pony to a water trough. 'You were good at that. Leave all this stuff to the men.' Jo boiled with rage. Returning to the dingy bed and breakfast, shoulders sagging, blisters on both heels, she made herself a cup of tea, heaping in the sugar, and slumped down on one of the rickety old chairs.

'Never mind, luv, something's bound to come up,' said the landlady encouragingly, wiping her hands on a grubby apron and serving up three-day-old soup and grey scrambled egg. Jo was so hungry she ate the lot, plus the two currant buns she'd bought earlier at the local bakery in a fit of depression.

'But what?' thought Jo gloomily, stuffing the last corner of bun in her mouth. 'First Mum and Dad, then the sack and now all this.' Searching in her jacket pocket for the packet of Polo mints she had bought earlier that day, her fingers touched a piece of card. Pulling it out she stared at it curiously. It was part of Simon's business card that she had torn up at Ascot. She flicked it back and forth between her fingers, as if by holding it she might once more feel the vibrant happiness she had experienced when he was near. Perhaps Dad was right, this was a man's world and it was time to face up to the reality that she was trying to compete in a profession where the odds were stacked impossibly against her.

'No, damn it, I won't let this beat me,' she cried, glaring at the card, angry that she should be reminded, now of all times, of Simon. 'And I won't waste any more time torturing myself over something that never was.' Pulling out the remaining bits of card, she turned out her pocket to make sure she had removed every last scrap. Carefully piling the pieces into a tiny heap in the grate, she grabbed the box of matches from beside the gas stove and set the paper alight. Sitting back on her knees, Jo watched, a lump in her throat, as the flames licked round the card, flaring and dying, gobbling up the pieces until all that remained was blackened wafer-thin parchment that quickly crumbled and collapsed, severing her last remaining connection with Simon.

'You never had an inkling,' she whispered, her shoulders sagging. A draught from under the ill-fitting door scattered the ashes as though to make a further point. Brushing her hands together in an action of finality, Jo stood up and squared her shoulders. It was time to stop moping and get on with her life.

Chapter Fourteen

T HE NEXT DAY Jo hitched a lift to Newmarket with one of the local shopkeepers. Once there, to cheer herself up and because she quickly discovered life in these parts without a car was nigh impossible, Jo bought an old, beat-up, dark blue Morris Minor with her rapidly shrinking resources. Feeling somewhat more optimistic she set off in search of work. But Newmarket proved to be as fruitless as the Stockenham district, even without Kurt's malicious rumour-mongering. There was no work to be had, or if there was, they wanted a lad, their catchcry always that a girl track rider wasn't strong enough to take the horses to the gallops. Regardless of what Jo said, no-one would budge.

By the second week of her search she was getting desperate. Down to two stables on her list, she despondently put a large question mark against the first name, having heard some disturbing tales of the way they handled their horses, and set out in search of the Orion stables owned by Nicholas 'Neddy' Fox. The day was depressingly grey and wet. A sharp wind whistled through a hole beside the Morris's brake pedal where rust had fallen away two days after she had bought the car and whined between the badly fitting doors. Drips fell from the leaky driver's window and splashed onto Jo's jeans, the spreading wet patch darkening on her rapidly chilling thigh. Turning the car off the main road between Thetford and Norwich, she wove through the maze of narrow, badly signposted country lanes, thinking of Winks and wishing she was back in Australia and the sunshine.

Stopping at a T-junction to check the map, Jo wound down the window and peered out. The rain had lessened to a light drizzle but the signpost had almost completely rotted away and what was left of the moss-covered words was illegible. Staring dejectedly out across the flat soaking landscape, she realised she was completely lost. She had two choices. She could either go back the way she had come or continue on in the hope that she would eventually find a readable signpost. Just as she had decided to turn back, she caught sight of two horses racing across a field in the distance, their tails flying. Hoping she was where she thought she was on the map, she sped in the direction of the horses. Sure enough, not far down the lane, she found the Orion stables but her heart sank as she stared past the rickety gate and along the muddy track. Next to a ramshackle house with tiles missing from the roof stood some tumbledown buildings that passed for stables. Hinges were missing off the tops of two of the stable doors; a great pile of manure sat to one side of the yard and mud-sodden muck lay strewn everywhere. Jo wondered how the buildings had stood the bitter Norfolk gales for so long. The place appeared to be deserted. Parking the car beside the ditch next to the overgrown hedge, Jo picked her way across the mud. She peered into one of the stalls amazed how any real horse lover could let the place fall into such disrepair. A large bluebottle flew angrily past her.

'Who be you lookin' for?' Jo nearly jumped out of her skin. Turning, she watched as a surly fellow in his early sixties, wearing baggy old trousers and a dirty peaked cap, crossed the yard leading a moth-eaten looking nag, splashing through the dirt and puddles in his mud-caked gumboots. Stubble covered his chin; what teeth he had were badly nicotine stained; his cheeks were sunken into his weatherbeaten face and his nose was a blotchy purple.

'I was looking for Mr Fox but it doesn't matter. I was wondering if he needed a stable hand,' stuttered Jo beating a hasty retreat, deciding this was not a place where she wanted to work.

'You're not from these parts, are you? Do you know anything about 'orses?' the man growled.

'I'm Australian and, yes, I know about horses,' replied Jo, wondering whether to bolt now.

'Australian, eh? I'm Neddy Fox. When can you start?' he barked, stroking the horse gently on the muzzle. The horse chewed affectionately on the old man's cap.

'Well I ... straightaway, I s'pose,' Jo replied politely, taken aback by the offer after so little questioning. Nothing in the world would make her work in a place like this. Then curiosity got the better of her. How could a man who so obviously commanded the affection of this animal let his stables become such a dump? 'Do you have any living quarters?'

Leading the horse to a stall, Neddy showed her a dingy room above the stables, badly in need of a coat of paint. There was a blackened two-burner stove in one corner; the lavatory seat was broken, and dirty brown and green stains ran down the chipped enamel bath from where the gas water-heater leaked.

'How many horses do you run?' Jo asked casually as they descended the rickety wooden steps, watching the old man carefully. Despite his unkemptness and shabby dress, there was something touching about him, a sadness in his faded blue eyes.

'Ten between me and me mate Will. They're not yer nobs' 'orses but they goes. This place's got a bit run-down wot with me back going on me and 'im getting sick and everything. We woz looking good afore summer. You afraid of hard work?'

Jo shook her head, her attention distracted by the sound of a horse coughing. 'You got a sick horse?' she asked, deciding it really didn't matter if the old man thought she was prying, as she had absolutely no intention of staying.

'Come down poorly a couple of days ago. Ready for the knacker's yard if she don't pick up soon. Bloomin' shame. Good 'orse, her. Looked after me well, she 'as,' he said. Jo thought she detected tears in his eyes.

Squelching through the mud and manure, she poked her head over the stall door and her heart turned over. The filly was almost identical in colour to the one Kurt had refused to let her help and, if she knew anything at all about horses, in a very similar condition. Dull-eyed and depressed it stood head hanging in the stale straw, every so often giving a hacking cough that sent a shudder through Jo. Her eyes sparkled with tears as she turned to the old man.

'I could save her if you'd let me,' she announced, her words sounding precocious even to her.

'Hmph. You know summat I don't?' replied

Neddy abruptly, but Jo had seen a glimmer of hope in the old man's sunken gaze and suddenly more than anything in the world she wanted to save this horse.

'Yes,' replied Jo and then she was spilling out the story of the filly at Stockenham Park and how she could have saved it but she hadn't been allowed to and how it had died needlessly on the racetrack a few weeks ago and that she'd worked with racehorses all her life.

'Hmph,' Neddy said again. Then after a pause, 'You want the job or not?'

'I'll go and pick up my stuff and be back within the hour if you'll just show me how to find this place again,' she grinned, her eyes sparkling. There was a heap you could do with a pitchfork, a hose and a tin of paint. She'd pick up a new toilet seat and some disinfectant in town while she was about it. Running back to the car she pulled out the map. 'I must be mad,' she thought to herself but this was one horse that wasn't going to die.

Within a month Jo had transformed the place. Starting first with the stalls, she gradually worked through the whole stables, mucking out, hosing down and disinfecting every inch of the place, in amongst her regular duties. With the help of a local young lad she recruited from the nearby dairy farm, stale bedding was replaced by sweet-smelling straw, the flies banished and the manure heap spread where it was most useful. After a bumpy start with the track worker who often arrived late or not at all, grumbling that he never got paid, Jo managed to set up a schedule that suited them both. She worked the horses on weekends and when he was off racing midweek, and agreed to pay him cash on the day if he turned up punctually when he had agreed to work or let her know if he couldn't make it. Mostly it worked out.

All this time Jo was working on the filly with Neddy. It took her two days to persuade Neddy to allow her to get the vet in and that his grandfather's old folk remedies just weren't going to do the trick. Even then, as the horse didn't immediately respond, she thought she was too late, but as the antibiotics took hold and the drainage tubes relieved the fluid in the horse's lungs, gradually, with better feed and an old herbal treatment learned from her father, Jo watched the life return to the filly's eyes and her coat regain its shine.

The day the horse stuck her head over the door and loudly demanded her breakfast, a transformation came over Neddy. Sauntering happily over with her feed after exercising the other horses, Jo was rewarded by seeing the horse, still thin, impatiently butting the old plastic bottles Jo had hung up as playthings to stop her getting bored while she was confined to her stall.

'I don't believe it,' said Neddy, sitting down hard on an old wooden bench near one of the stalls, wiping the tears from his eyes and thanking Jo over and over again. 'That 'orse is the joy of my life,' he confessed. 'Winny's Pride I called her, after my wife Winifred. We was married forty-one years. She died of cancer three years ago. Used to have this place looking like a new pin. She weren't afraid of hard work neither. I couldn't bring myself even to use her name when I saw the way that 'orse was going down-hill.' He looked up at Jo, relief flooding his face. 'But don't you think you can go fetching that vet in every time them 'orses gives a whimper. Them vets're all alike. Charge too blinking much and for what? A packet of pills.'

Jo laughed and gave the old man a hug. 'We saved Winny's Pride,' she said, her eyes shining, 'does it really matter how?'

Jo's relationship with Neddy changed dramatically after Winny's recovery. First he put up her pay. It was the only way he could think of thanking her properly. Then he agreed to let her get someone in to fix up the roof tiles on the house. But more importantly they talked. Jo discovered while they were inspecting the stirrup leathers that, to add to the pain of his wife's death, Neddy's two sons, now married and with children of their own and living close by, refused to speak to him. Blaming him for their mother's death, they had accused Neddy of being too mean to get her proper medical help until it was too late, when, in truth, he had simply been trying to shelter his sons from the pain of their mother's incurable condition.

'Families are funny,' said Jo sadly, replacing the leathers on their hooks and lifting down a saddle to polish. Another night, shuffling out of the house shortly after ten o'clock to investigate a noise, Neddy found Jo screwing new hinges on the stable doors.

'Why d'you work so blinkin' hard? You nuts?' he demanded.

Jo shrugged. 'One day I'm going to be a top trainer with a top stables and I'm going to win the Melbourne Cup. You don't get there by sitting around and watching,' she replied, her face lighting up.

'From these stables?' replied Neddy.

Jo grinned at him and turned back to her job. 'You've got to start somewhere,' she laughed over her shoulder.

Neddy walked slowly back to the house, muttering under his breath, but Jo noticed the spring in his step the next afternoon as he led Winny's Pride down to the meadow with Jo perched on her back. Jo too felt exhilarated as she put the horse through her gentle routine, the wind catching at her hair under her hat and rippling through the ripening corn in the nearby fields. Out of the corner of her eye she could see Neddy watching proudly, one foot resting on the gate. Leaning forwards she patted the horse on the neck, praising her quietly, and then nudged her into a trot. That was one battle she had well and truly won.

August came and went and the leaves started turning. Tramping ankle deep through rust and yellow leaves towards the house one crisp morning in early September to join Neddy for their mid-morning cup of tea, now part of the day's regular routine, Jo hurried inside, put the kettle on in the old kitchen and shook out a packet of biscuits onto a plate.

'This is my next project,' she thought, running her eye over the scratched cupboards and the peeling paint on the walls.

Waiting for the kettle to boil she stared out across to the stables, now smart with a new coat of bright green paint, thinking with satisfaction of all she had accomplished since arriving on that soggy day in July. Colourful curtains flapped from Jo's tiny lodgings above the stables, the autumn sun shedding a soft glow across the fields. Winny, a rug thrown over her, grazed peacefully in a meadow close by, and Jo could hear Neddy clattering about upstairs. 'I'm happy here,' she thought. 'This is my little oasis.'

Filling the old brown teapot, she placed it next to the chipped milk jug on the table. Then she pulled up a chair and sat down. Resting her chin on her hands she stared into space, tossing around ideas for training the horses. The sound of a vehicle driving up into the yard interrupted her thoughts.

'That'll be Harry come to do the shoes,' she called to Neddy, jumping up and pulling out a notebook and pencil from her pocket. 'We've got four for you today, Harry. Northern Gypsy's worn his shoes out again,' she explained, head bent, running the pencil down her list as she opened the door. Wrinkling her nose at the pleasant whiff of aftershave, she looked up and stared in speechless disbelief into sea-green eyes.

'Simon!' she gasped, rooted to the spot, all her carefully buried emotions resurfacing like some gigantic tidalwave. Her heart started hammering in her chest, the pencil slipped from her fingers and clattered unnoticed on the stone steps. For what seemed an eternity neither spoke. Jo's brain seemed to have stopped functioning altogether and Simon couldn't stop staring at Jo.

'Jo! Is it really you? Have I found you at last?' he stammered. He had gone over in his mind a thousand times all the things he was going to say to Jo and how he was going to act when he finally found her, now it was all coming out wrong. What kept racing through his mind was how she had grown even more vibrantly beautiful and that he wanted to crush her to him right there and then and hold her forever. An immense wave of relief surged over him, followed by an aching longing as he stared into her enormous, startled eyes. Collecting his wits, he bent and retrieved the pencil and held it out to her with shaking fingers. 'Jo, I have to talk to you. Is there somewhere we can go?' he asked urgently.

The blood was pounding so hard in Jo's ears she could hardly make sense of what he had said. Like someone in a dream she accepted the pencil, staring stupidly at it. Her mouth had gone dry and she couldn't make her lips work.

'I didn't know yer had any nobs fer friends,' growled Neddy defensively, walking up behind her.

'He isn't a nob, Neddy,' Jo laughed unsteadily, running her tongue round her lips, but his interruption had broken the tension. 'This is Simon Gordon, an old friend of mine. This is Mr Fox who owns Orion stables.' She smiled at Simon, the corners of her mouth quivering. He was still hopelessly handsome in his light canvas slacks and open-neck shirt. His sea-green eyes against his tanned skin were as beguiling as ever, but he had lost weight and there were tiny lines at their corners she hadn't noticed before.

'Hmph. We're a busy stables here. The lass can't stand around natterin' all day. Say what yer have to say and be on yer way,' grumbled Neddy, glaring at Simon. 'And you, Jo, go and find out what's happened to that old coot Harry. Time we git them 'orses shod, not stand around entertainin' nobs.'

Jo blushed with embarrassment. Her heart wasn't clamouring so loud now and the drumming in her ears had lessened.

'I'm sorry, sir, I won't keep her,' interjected Simon quickly, a flicker of desperation in his eyes.

'I finish here around about five if you want to come back then,' said Jo agitatedly, glancing around for any sign of Harry.

'Could I take you out to dinner?'

'I'd like that,' she said shyly.

'Right,' said Simon decisively. 'I'll pick you up at

six-thirty. It's taken me three months to find you, I can wait another few hours.'

Confused and shaking, Jo watched Simon drive away, wondering how wise it was to have agreed to go out with him and churn up all those old feelings, yet she had been unable to let him just walk away. For the rest of the day she found it almost impossible to concentrate. She kept wondering what had made him come looking for her and what it was that he so urgently needed to discuss with her. By midafternoon her stomach was in a tight knot. Knocking off half an hour early, she sank into a deep hot bath in an effort to calm herself and then dressed in her prettiest blouse and slacks. Her fingers shook so much she could hardly do up the buttons and she smudged a large dollop of mascara below one eye and had to start all over again. It was the first time she had worn make-up since she had started at the stables, but when she had finally finished she was pleased with the effect. Sweeping her brush through her long blonde hair she left it loose around her shoulders. Then, hearing the car drive into the yard, she grabbed her coat and bag and scampered down the loft stairs.

'You look sensational,' greeted Simon. Jo blushed hotly. Helping her into the battered olive-green sports car, he shut the door and quickly slid into the driver's seat. 'I thought I'd take you to the Plough and Bell. It's not too far. Have you been there?' he asked, shoving the gear into reverse and looking over his shoulder, his hand resting along the back of her seat for an instant. Jo shook her head. Turning the wheel Simon spun out of the yard.

'Don't let Neddy catch you doing that,' Jo laughed, hoping the tension she felt wasn't apparent. Simon seemed much more in control than he had earlier. The desperation had gone from his eyes but Jo still sensed an air of suppressed urgency, which set her even more on edge.

'What was it you needed to talk to me about?' she asked casually, unable to bear the suspense a second longer as they bowled along the country lane, the last rays of the sun slipping beneath the horizon. Simon slowed down, pulled over against the hedgerow and stopped. He turned to Jo and gazed so intently at her that she felt herself blushing.

'I called off the wedding,' he said bluntly, watching her eyes grow round with astonishment.

Jo's heart gave a lurch. 'You did what?' she cried and immediately looked away, hoping he hadn't caught the sudden flash of hope in her eyes.

'Called it off. I never got married.' His eyes softened as he took one of Jo's hands in his and turned it over. It looked lost and small against his own tanned fingers. Lifting it to his lips he kissed the palm. He wasn't sure what he had seen in her eyes but now she was quivering like a captured bird. 'How could I marry Lelia when I was in love with you?' he whispered, his heart full.

Jo stared back in disbelief.

'You're not married?' She could hardly take it in and her heart was thumping wildly.

'No,' Simon whispered huskily. Gently he leaned over and brushed his lips against hers. When she didn't pull away, he kissed her again very tenderly.

Like someone waking from a deep sleep Jo slid her arms around his neck and returned his kisses, letting the waves of emotion course through her, the heat of his body searing into her. Enveloped in the heady scent of his aftershave, drowning in the insistent pressure of his lips, she wanted his kiss to go on forever. After a long time he lifted his mouth from hers.

'Oh, Jo, I have wanted to do that for so long,' he murmured, still holding her in his embrace.

Gazing up into his wonderful tanned face she hardly dared believe her own ears. She could feel his heart beating against her and her own heart rejoiced.

Simon traced a trail with one finger across her forehead, playing with her hair. 'I was never in love with Lelia but I wouldn't face it,' he admitted softly, his fingers sending tiny thrills through Jo's body. 'We'd been going out for two and a half years and we just sort of slipped into getting engaged and the wedding plans followed. Then I met you and you toppled my entire world. After Frances's party I couldn't think of anything or anyone except you.' He gave a huge sigh. 'I thought I was going crazy. I'd wake up in the middle of the night panic-stricken that I'd never find you again. I didn't know what to do. I kept making excuses to myself, putting it down to tiredness and prewedding nerves, trying to convince myself it would wear off, but it didn't.' He shifted in his seat, smiling at her. 'Seeing you glowing with happiness at Ascot wearing those baggy old jeans and T-shirt, mud on your face, talking to that horse, I realised that for the first time in my life I was hopelessly and completely in love—with you.' He paused.

'You don't know how hard it was to walk away from you that day.' He clasped Jo's hand tightly in his. 'The next day I told Lelia the whole thing was off. It was awful. Jo, you're so beautiful. I love you so much. Don't ever disappear on me like that again.' He kissed her again more passionately.

'And there was me, absolutely crazy about you,

and I didn't think you'd even noticed me, let alone cared,' she blurted out as soon as they broke free, her lips tingling from his kisses.

Simon's eyes lit up at her words. 'I hardly dared to hope . . . You mean, you feel the same about me?'

Jo nodded. Then she was once more in his arms, her lips against his, her tongue seeking his, luxuriating in his caresses as he ran his fingers through her hair, crushing her carefully ironed blouse, returning his kisses with all the passion and longing she had kept pent up for so long.

'I didn't think it was possible to be this happy,' laughed Jo as she straightened her blouse and smoothed her hair.

Still reeling from Jo's reaction, it took Simon a few seconds to respond. 'I'm sorry. I've crushed your blouse and messed up your hair,' he said, contrite.

'Who cares?' Jo cried and kissed him again. Breathless they finally drew apart.

'I'm starved,' said Simon happily. 'Let's go and get that dinner I promised you.'

Tucking her blouse back in her slacks, Jo peeped in the mirror on the sunshade. 'Fat lot of use wearing lipstick,' she cried, amazed at the dazzling reflection that looked back at her. Normally critical of her looks, she could not possibly miss the warmth that now flooded from her face.

'Don't bother to put any more on, I intend to kiss you a lot more before the evening's over,' ordered Simon, starting the car in the autumn twilight.

'How did you find out where I was?' asked Jo once they were ensconced in a cosy corner of the Plough and Bell, Jo with a lemonade and Simon with a pint of the local bitter. A pretty little Elizabethan pub, the interior was lit by antique paraffin lamps set on each carved oak table which lent a quaint cosiness to the low-ceilinged room. A large old-fashioned plough hung from one wall, and a yoke and other antique farming implements hung from ancient blackened beams alongside old swords and scythes.

'You don't make it easy for a chap,' Simon replied, taking a sip from his thick glass tankard and leaning back against the old wooden settle, watching the lamplight dance in her eyes. 'I must have searched every stables from here to York. I'd almost given up hope when I walked into Orion.' He put his arm around her and gave her a squeeze, marvelling that he had finally found her.

'You know, you think you know people and you don't really,' he said slowly. 'I knew it wouldn't be easy breaking up with Lelia but I naively thought she would agree it was better to break up before we got married than to find out afterwards I was really in love with you. But she didn't quite see it that way. After she had cried all over my shirt and told me I needed her more than she needed me, she threatened to kill herself if we didn't go through with it, saying she couldn't face the humiliation. I don't think she ever would have carried out her threats, but she terrified me. Mum was beside herself too. She had Lelia's mum on the phone to her every day and there were all the wedding arrangements to cancel and the presents to return. It was not a good time.' He paused, his expression grim as he remembered the endless exhausting scenes as Lelia alternately ranted, pleaded, flirted and cried as he tried to convince her cancelling the wedding was best for them both.

'I know I'm rambling on a bit but I don't want there to be any secrets between us,' he paused.

'Go on,' Jo said quietly, watching his face.

Some of the tension in Simon relaxed and he

continued. 'There seemed to be no way to end the relationship. I thought I'd go nuts. Then, having had her sobbing down the phone at work the whole of yet another day, I walked into our local pub that night to find her sitting on my exbestman's knee surrounded by a group of my pals. Marcus looked like the proverbial cat who had licked the cream and Lelia was back to her old flirting self. She said she'd invited everyone to celebrate . . . What did she call it? "Her new life's awakening." I tried to escape but my so-called friends wouldn't let me. Then, calm as you like, Lelia held out her hand to me and said, 'I hope you'll be very happy with your little stable hand friend,' as if there had never been a single scene between us. God, how to make a chap feel rotten! Then she slipped off Marcus's knee, threw her arms around me and whispered, "I love you." I was so angry, after I'd disentangled myself I left. I had no idea whether she was telling me to go to hell or playing another of her little games to win me back, but when she rang me saying maybe she'd gone a bit over the top and would I forgive her, I finally got through to her I wouldn't be blackmailed by her any more and it was over between us.'

Jo listened round-eyed, her heartbeat quickening. Feeling the tiny change in her demeanour Simon immediately tightened his arm around her and gazed anxiously into her lovely eyes. 'It really is over between us. You do believe me, don't you?' Jo nodded and relaxed. Simon brushed his lips gently against her cheek. 'Anyhow, to get to the point . . . after I'd broken off with Lelia, and Mum had calmed down, I drove up to Stockenham Park expecting to find you and discovered you'd gone so I asked for Kurt, only to find he'd gone too. Then I talked to John and he told me the whole story.

'Apparently Guy had been watching the rotten little bastard for a while, convinced Kurt had been race rigging. Guy couldn't prove anything, but the man had got under his skin and there were other little things about the way he ran the stables Guy wasn't happy with. He was also very fond of you and admired your pluck so Kurt sacking you was the final straw. Guy booted him out the next week with the threat that if he made any trouble he'd tell a few influential people a thing or two that'd knock him out of racing for good. The man's like a damp squib now, all bluster and no punch, but no-one had the faintest idea where you'd gone.'

Simon smiled and Jo thought the small crow's-feet around his eyes only made him sexier. He laid his arm casually along the back of the settle and played with her hair as he continued, sending ripples of excitement through Jo.

'Then, just as I thought the whole thing was useless, my aunt came to the rescue. She owns a cottage near Fakenham about three-quarters of an hour's drive from here and she'd heard about you. Out of the blue she rang and said she'd been talking to a vet friend of hers who was singing the praises of some young girl who had let him get near Neddy's horses after five years of fighting, and maybe it was worth a try. I never really expected it to be you but I would have flown to the moon if someone had suggested, I was so desperate.'

Laughing, Jo reached out and stroked his chin. It felt like fine sandpaper and sent a shiver of delight through her. In fact, every part of him, everything about him, sent her nerves humming. She had not felt so alive or so happy since Rick's death and with every second she stayed in Simon's company, her longing to be back in his arms increased. The intensity of her feelings was almost scary.

'From the moment you mashed my hip against that table at Frances's party my life has been hell,' Jo admitted after the waiter had set two plates of scampi, chips and locally grown peas before them.

'Oh God, did I do that?' groaned Simon.

Jo shook her head with a smile. 'The physical pain didn't matter. What was so unbearable was that I had fallen in love with a man who was completely out of reach. I didn't think you'd even noticed me. As the bruises faded it was like losing you inch by inch,' she said dramatically but with a catch in her voice.

Simon dropped a kiss on her head. 'And now I'm taken again,' he laughed. 'Eat up your dinner or it'll be cold. I've got to be allowed to get one thing right tonight.' Jo took her first mouthful and realised she was ravenous.

The evening flew by as they talked together tucked in the cosy little corner with the lamplight flickering, sharing their longing for each other and their lives for the last few months, holding hands and gazing into one another's eyes, each amazed that their feelings were reciprocated. Helping herself to a mint chocolate Simon had ordered with coffee, Jo noticed the old clock on the mantelpiece and her heart sank.

'Is that really the time?' she cried. 'Don't take this the wrong way but you're going to have to take me back. By the time you're falling into bed, I'll be having to get up and I'm useless at track work if I don't get enough sleep.' Reluctantly Simon looked at his watch and helped her into her anorak, sliding his arm around her and holding her close as they walked back to the car.

'Don't you go running off anywhere. I couldn't bear to lose you again,' he said, briefly turning his head and running a finger down her flushed cheek, his other hand on the steering wheel, as they sped back towards the stables.

'I'm not going anywhere. I'm staying right here,' laughed Jo sleepily. It had been a long emotional day. Driving in the pitch dark along the narrow lanes, snuggled close to Simon, feeling the warmth of his body against hers, Jo watched the headlights catching hares and foxes in their glare and wished tonight didn't have to end.

Simon stopped the car at the top of the lane leading to the stables and wrapped Jo in one last lingering kiss, the heat of his desire burning into her and leaving her breathless.

'When can I see you again?' he asked, the desperation back in his eyes.

'Sunday week's my next day off. Maybe we could go for a drive somewhere if the weather's nice,' suggested Jo, her pulse still racing.

'Wild horses wouldn't keep me away,' grinned Simon turning into the stables. 'I'll ring you through the week and I'll be here at ten o'clock sharp, you darling beautiful wonderful girl. I want to take you somewhere really special.' He walked her to the steps and watched her scamper up into her tiny loft. All the way back to his aunt's cottage he sang at the top of his voice, his clear baritone ringing out across the dark mysterious Fenlands.

Chapter Fifteen

*I*T POURED WITH rain all Sunday and it kept up all week, but Jo couldn't have cared less. Squelching around in her gumboots, raincoat and sou'wester, drenched after track work and freezing at night as the rain and wind whistled through the cracks in her loft despite her efforts to block them up, nothing could dampen Jo's spirits. As she bumped her way over to the Huggins's farm to collect a horse for Neddy that would otherwise have gone to the knacker's yard her spirits soared. Crawling her way home behind an enormous combine harvester that took up the entire road, her thoughts were filled with Simon. Ripples of excitement ran through her as she relived the pressure of his lips on hers, the salt taste of his mouth and the strength of his arms as he had held her. He rang her every night and just hearing his voice filled her with such intense happiness and aching longing that at times she wondered how she was going to survive the next few agonisingly long days and nights before she saw him again. Then on Friday night the rain stopped and the wind dropped and by Saturday the place was starting to dry out again.

All through Saturday Jo worried in case he

wouldn't turn up, that his car might break down, there'd be a family crisis or, worse still, something more important would crop up and he'd just forget. Telling herself she was a fool and no man was worth all this worry simply made her jitters worse. Tossing and turning through the night, waking every hour like a child on Christmas Eve, finally she could stand it no longer.

Impatiently she pushed aside the bedclothes well before dawn, despite Sunday being a rare chance for her to sleep in, dressed, spring-cleaned the loft, washed her hair and was ready to leave hours before Simon was due to arrive. The sun shone through the tiny window and there was a nip in the air as she stepped outside carrying her anorak and camera. The soft smell of wood fires wafted on the breeze. It was going to be one of those balmy autumn days.

'Don't you go runnin' off with no nobs, now. I need you here,' teased Neddy, plodding across the stables with a bag of feed, seeing the obvious happiness in Jo's face as she carefully placed her things on the old wooden bench.

'Oh, Neddy I'm not running anywhere. Simon's going to show me around the district,' cried Jo unable to contain her excitement. Not knowing what to do with herself, she followed Neddy around, chatting nonstop, offering to do half his chores, checking her watch and turning towards the gate every five seconds to see if there was any sign of Simon.

'I seen that look in me wife's eye just afore we was married. Now git out of me way and let me git on. You're like a flea in a bottle this morning. Won't make the time go no faster,' stated Neddy.

Jo blushed. Just then Simon's car roared up the lane and into the yard. Swerving to miss a puddle, he stopped and leaped out. Dressed in baggy old green cords, his dark brown hair ruffled by the breeze, his tanned face grinning at her above his open-necked shirt and much-loved thick wool sweater, Jo thought he looked more handsome and more desirable than ever.

'Morning, sir,' Simon nodded at Neddy. Quickly turning to Jo he stared at her in frank admiration. 'How can anyone make an ordinary old pair of jeans and a jumper look that good?' he exclaimed.

'They're not old!' cried Jo flushing with pleasure, gathering up her anorak and camera.

'You take good care of her, young 'un,' ordered Neddy, his beady eyes pinned on Simon who was holding the car door open for Jo. 'Larkin' around. I dunno. Some of us've got work to do.'

'I thought you said it was your day off,' murmured Simon anxiously to Jo as she slid into the passenger seat.

'It is. Don't take any notice of Neddy, he enjoys a good grumble,' laughed Jo, settling herself in while Simon got in the other side.

'Have you ever visited Burnham Overy Staithe?' asked Simon, glancing across at Jo as they sped towards Fakenham.

Jo shook her head. 'What's it like?' she asked excitedly. All she knew was that it was near the coast.

'I want you to see it first,' grinned Simon, openly delighted that he would be the first to show her his beloved Norfolk. As they flashed along the flat countryside past ancient churches Jo stared out at pretty flint stone cottages with their tiny gardens, the sun catching on the low grey and white stone walls. Inside the sports car there was little room to spare, so Jo kept accidentally knocking against Simon's arm, shockwaves rippling through her each time.

Slowing down they drove past a village green and turned onto one of the minor B roads where Simon stopped the car abruptly. Jo looked up at him in surprise. Taking her in his arms he kissed her thoroughly.

'That's better,' he said, slipping his arm around her and driving on.

'Mmm,' murmured Jo as she snuggled against him, peeping up at him between her lashes. His heart turned over for the umpteenth time and he forced himself to concentrate on the driving. Every time he glanced at her she made him want to stop the car and kiss her again.

For the next hour, still pinching herself occasionally to make sure this was all real, Jo listened as Simon chatted happily, pointing out landmarks and giving small snippets of local history, the fresh country smells invading the car. Some of the places dated back to the Stone Age. Detouring along another country road to get a closer look at the famous Burnham Windmill with its big flat sails that could be seen from miles around, they skirted Burnham Market and finally arrived at Burnham Overy Staithe. Parking on the hard shingle known as the staithe, which was still damp from the ebbing tide, Simon drew the car to a stop, switched off the engine and pulled on the handbrake. Immediately they were enveloped in a blissful peace.

'This is it. My special place. I fell in love with it when I was five and whenever anything really important happens in my life I come here.' Simon stepped out of the car and opened Jo's door.

Scrambling out, Jo gazed in pleasure at the vast flat marshlands, beyond which lay the North Sea, the fresh salt tang tickling her nose, the cries of the seabirds echoing across the stillness. Before her a creek wound out from the pretty little harbour, the shingly mudflats spattered with sailing dinghies rapidly being left high and dry, their masts tipped sideways, the salt lavender covering the marshlands a shimmering haze of mauve.

'There's such an isolated beauty about it,' sighed Jo. She shaded her eyes with her hand and pointed into the distance. 'What's that greenish mound over there?'

'Scolte Head. It's an everchanging island. Because the mud and sand is always shifting, it changes too. In summer there's a lovely little bay where I'll take you swimming.' Jo could just make out a little sandy beach at one end. 'If the tide's right you can walk out to the island along the causeway, otherwise there's an old fisherman called Jimmy who takes day-trippers out at high tide, but that's not for hours. We've got the whole day in front of us.' His voice was suddenly husky. Gently he pulled her into his arms and kissed her.

'Do we have time?' asked Jo when they finally drew apart, trying to sound far calmer than she felt.

'Time for what?' asked Simon, his head still spinning.

'To walk out to the island.'

'I'd say we could just make it before the tide turns,' cried Simon, quickly glancing at his watch. 'What a glorious day! I'll go and check the times.' He took off towards the large wooden signs by the little black and white boatshed close by.

Jo strolled to the water's edge, breathing in the fresh salty air. Simon was right, it was a glorious day. Slipping off her sandshoes, she held them in her hand while she gingerly poked a toe into a puddle of water. It was chilly but bearable. Taking a few more steps she gasped at the cold then relaxed, enjoying the sensation of the mud squelching up through her toes. Beside her, bunches of blue-green sea asparagus and marine thistles swayed with the salt lavender. At the edge of the creek an old wooden rowing boat lay rotting in the mud. She bent down and felt the tough paper-like mauve flowers.

'We can probably make it halfway there,' said Simon, returning from the boatshed. 'There's just this small creek to cross and then the causeway's slightly higher and dries out fairly well.' He rolled his trousers up above his knees. 'You'll need to wear your shoes once we're on the causeway. The stones are pretty sharp. Shall we give it a try?' Catching his enthusiasm, Jo quickly rolled up her jeans, grabbed her shoes and skipped toward the creek.

'Hang on a sec,' laughed Simon. Jo turned expectantly. Before she knew it he had swept her up in his arms and carried her giggling across the short stretch of water, setting her down lightly on the shingly causeway, his arms still holding her.

'Sea lavender, that's what your eyes remind me of. Of course! I've been racking my brains,' he announced, kissing her lightly on the tip of her nose.

Jo laughed, her straight white teeth emphasising her wide full mouth, her fresh pink cheeks and lips devoid of make-up. She let her hands linger on his chest a moment as he set her free. 'I'm not sure I know what to do with all this nurturing and comfort,' she said with a wide grin. 'I seem to have been battling uphill for so long, it feels kind of odd.'

What was meant as a throwaway comment ended as a serious statement. Before she could stop herself, Jo was pouring out everything that had happened in the last eighteen months, telling him about her

285

determination to become a trainer, her parents' opposition, their disastrous surprise visit, her mother's terrible accusations and her polite impersonal letters. Shocked, Simon listened.

'With you my world is complete,' Jo went on, her voice sharp with longing. 'But you have to understand, I can't give up my dream now. I've lost my family for it. I have to prove to myself I can do it, then maybe they'll accept it.' Tears sparkled in her eyes and spilled down over her cheeks. 'I love you so much, I couldn't bear to lose you too.' She was trembling again. 'At least Mum writes but Dad—' She couldn't finish the sentence. Accepting Simon's hanky, she blew her nose.

'They'll come round eventually, I'm sure,' said Simon gently, slipping his arm protectively around her, wishing he could magic away all her hurt.

'Just being with you makes me feel good,' Jo said with a small sniff. Leaning into him she turned her attention to the beauty around her. Strolling arm in arm along the causeway, following its winding course as it twisted and turned between the marshes, Jo's buoyant mood gradually returned. The sun glistened on the large wet stretches of mud and caught on the stones, the breeze caressing Jo's cheeks and ruffling the sea lavender. Birds wheeled overhead or scurried across the flat, their cries carrying across the mudflats.

'Look at those. Aren't they magnificent?' cried Simon, relieved to see the happiness back in Jo's face. He pointed as a flock of terns surged up from the sand.

Jo gasped in delight, caught up in the magic of the marshes. The vast openness reminded her in some strange way of home, the pale blue sky a great dome that seemed to swallow them both up.

'It amazes me these birds cover so many hundreds of miles back to the same place each year. Look at that one with the black and white chest and red legs. He's my favourite. He's an oystercatcher. He'll be migrating soon.' Simon pointed to a cheeky little bird running nimbly across the gleaming wet mud. Standing behind Jo, he twisted her in the direction of the bird, resting one hand lightly on her arm and pointing his other arm over her shoulder. Jo clasped her hands over his, her heart full as they stood and watched together. Then the oystercatcher swooped up from the mud and swirled overhead, its distinctive cry easily recognised above the others, and Jo understood why Simon called this his special place.

'It's awesome,' she whispered.

'This is what I wanted to share with you,' Simon murmured. 'I wanted you to see it and feel it. You can't put it into words. But I wanted it to become your special place too and for us to remember it all our lives.' He turned her around till she was facing him again. 'I love you, Jo. I love every tiny thing about you, your passion, your tears, the way you love all those horses. I'll never take your dreams from you, my darling.' His voice cracked. 'This is where I wanted us to be when I asked you, here in the middle of the marshes away from the rest of the world, just you and me and the birds crying around us. Marry me, Jo.'

She stared up into eyes filled with such longing and love that she thought she would drown in them.

Before she had a chance to reply, Simon pulled her to him and kissed her passionately, revelling in the softness of her lips as they parted beneath his, wrapping her in his embrace, unwilling to let her go for fear she might vanish any moment. His answer came in her response. Joyously she kissed him back, her senses reeling, her pulse racing and, as he covered her face and neck with kisses, awakening to a new and sweet yearning. Releasing her, Simon took a step back and felt a cold wetness seeping into his shoes. They had been so absorbed in one another, neither of them had noticed the tide had turned and was racing in. Clasping hands they ran back along the causeway, the wind catching in Jo's hair, tossing about the glorious stream of silver blonde that flowed out behind her and bringing a rosy glow to her cheeks.

Jo stopped suddenly, her expression serious. 'I have to ask you this,' she panted, her throat dry, suddenly imagining a whole disastrous scenario. 'You won't ask me to give up my work at Neddy's stables, will you?' she cried, her eyes deep amethyst pools.

Simon wanted to shout with relief. 'Is that all? I don't care if you work in a million stables as long as you say yes.'

'I love you so much, Simon, but how will it work with you in London and me in Norfolk?' asked Jo, her lips trembling.

'My dear, sweet, darling girl, that's easy. I'll move to Norfolk. I've been looking for a good excuse to get out of London,' he replied, kissing her again.

'You'd do that for me? Just like that?' gasped Jo, wrenching her mouth from his, her eyes wide with surprise.

'I'd walk to the edge of the world for you,' he laughed, 'but I've actually got a much easier solution. I happen to know there's a good opportunity coming up in a branch of another major bank in Norwich. I mentioned to my boss last week that I was interested in it.'

Jo's eyes opened wide with amazement. 'Of course the answer's yes, you silly ... Oh, Simon, I love you so much. I'm the luckiest girl alive.' She threw her arms around him and started kissing him all over again. They had returned to the tiny creek they had crossed earlier, the water now swirling in fast. Jo looked up adoringly at Simon, her whole being glowing with happiness as he once more swept her up into his arms and splashed through the water, his heart singing, completely forgetting to roll up his trousers, not even noticing the way they flapped soggy and cold against his legs after he stepped out of the creek and set her down gently on dry land.

'Time to celebrate, and I know just the place,' declared Simon as he opened the car door for Jo. 'The Lord Nelson. It's a great little pub in the next village from here—very atmospheric. We'll crack a bottle of bubbly. Did you know that Lord Nelson was born near here?' he added for no reason whatsoever other than he was ecstatically happy. He was seven years her senior, yet he felt by far the younger. He felt crazily, madly, fantastically in love with this beautiful girl and incredibly lucky.

Contentedly Jo snuggled against Simon as he started the engine, basking in the warmth and security of his love. He understood her passion and he loved her for who she was. With Simon beside her she could take on the world and win. The cries of the oystercatchers were still ringing in their ears as they drove slowly away from Burnham Overy Staithe.

Two weeks later Jo drove up to London to meet Simon's parents. Secretly dreading the meeting, knowing she was the reason for Simon calling off his wedding, Jo was relieved at how welcoming his parents were towards her. To ease the tension of the weekend they wandered around some of London's antique markets and jewellery shops inspecting rings, but Jo didn't really relax properly until she was back in Norfolk.

'I can't wait until we are married and I don't have to tear myself away from you and go back to London all the time,' confided Simon as they wandered arm in arm along the winding country lane behind the Orion stables one chilly October afternoon.

Jo kissed him lightly on the cheek. She was tired and she too hated the partings. Lately she had been very busy and it had been difficult for her to take time off. Today she had only been able to snatch a couple of hours, not wanting to be far from the stables or from Neddy, who had come down with a severe case of bronchitis.

'Dad'll be getting ready for the Melbourne Cup,' she said, stifling a yawn, watching a flock of sparrows quarrelling on a wall, a long fawn cashmere scarf Simon had bought her wrapped loosely around her head, the ends tossed over her shoulders. A sharp wind blew across her face, throwing up a flurry of dead leaves and dust. Beside them dark ploughed fields stretched away into the distance, the straight lines of trees dividing them now almost bare of leaves. Winter was on its way. Jo gave a sudden shiver.

'He's won the Cup twice. One day it'll be me,' she said, bending and picking up one of the leaves then crushing it in her hand and watching the wind carry off the fragments. 'Mum's letters are a little more friendly since I told her about you. Reading between the lines, I think she misses me.' She looked up at Simon for a second and then walked on, her face solemn for a while. Then, shaking her hair free of the scarf, she ran to a gate and leaped up, sitting on the top bar and grinning broadly. 'It's too nice a day to be gloomy and I'm too happy with you,' she cried, clapping her gloved hands. 'I demand a kiss.' She leaned forwards, pouting her lips invitingly, and tried to grab him by the shoulder of his overcoat.

'Well, you'll have to wait,' laughed Simon, fumbling in his pocket. Catching her left hand in his, he pulled off her glove.

'Hey, my fingers'll freeze off,' she cried and stopped, her eyes wide with surprise as he slipped a vast emerald ring encircled with tiny diamonds on her wedding-ring finger. Even in the misty afternoon light the stones sparkled brilliantly.

Clasping the tips of her fingers, Simon stared up into her face, holding her still. 'Joanna Kingsford, I adore you and I will love you to the end of time. I know you've already said yes but now I'm officially asking you to marry me.' As his voice cracked, Jo's eyes filled with tears.

'Simon Gordon, I adore you,' she whispered back. 'I will love you till the end of time and I very much want to be your wife.' She slid off the gate into his arms and lifted her face to his. Closing her eyes she let the tears of happiness seep out from under her eyelids and trickle down her cheeks as their lips met, their bodies moulding as one, the wintry chill forgotten. For a long time neither of them moved. Finally pulling away, Simon wiped the corner of one eye. He was shaking from head to toe.

'Men aren't supposed to cry, but I don't think you will ever really know how much I love you, my darling Jo,' he said huskily, thoroughly aroused. 'If we stay here much longer, you'll be a mother before you're a wife. You're too seductively beautiful.'

'Well, I'll be a mother with cold toes,' laughed Jo

unsteadily, her whole being throbbing with desire. They had been standing so long in the one spot, the cold had seeped up through her shoes and made her toes numb. Stamping her feet, she gazed enraptured at the magnificent engagement ring, twisting it back and forth, watching the light play on the diamonds, accentuating the deep richness of the emerald.

'It's so beautiful and it's just the one I wanted. When shall we tell everyone?' she cried, her fingertips reddening in the cold, refusing to think about her parents' reaction.

'Why don't we phone Mum and Dad straightaway before I leave?' suggested Simon.

'And I'll tell Neddy. He's been on at me for weeks now about the "nob" and then after I've fed the horses and bedded them down for the night, we'll ring my Mum and Dad as well.' She stretched out her fingers, twisting her hand this way and that again and then squeezed his arm. 'You're very naughty. I had no idea you'd gone and bought it and it fits perfectly.'

'There have to be a few things you don't know about.'

'No there don't,' retorted Jo happily, enjoying the strange new sensation of the ring on her finger as they strolled slowly back to the stables.

Smoke drifted up invitingly from Neddy's chimney as they walked the final few yards to the entrance to Orion stables; the fire Jo had lit in the living room was obviously still burning. Neddy should be waking. She'd take him a glass of milk with a shot of whisky before dinner. He always enjoyed that, she thought, as they walked through the gate. She could hear shuffling in the stalls and then she heard Winny whickering. Life was wonderful. She had so many exciting plans for this place and there was so much she could achieve here. Then she heard a clatter. Startled, they both looked towards the house to see Neddy shuffling out through the front door.

'Jo,' he hollered and was struck with a violent coughing spasm. Jo rushed over to him and tried to calm him down and get him back out of the cold, but he waved her away, purple in the face, his handkerchief pressed to his mouth.

'Phone! Australia!' he rasped furiously, pushing Jo inside. Helped in by Simon, he collapsed in a nearby chair, wheezing and coughing. 'Said she's yer mother.'

Jo's heart lurched. 'Take care of Neddy,' she called to Simon as she flew into the little office she had set up to run the stables. The old black receiver was lying on a pile of papers.

'Mum, is that you?' said Jo. 'I was going to ring you today. Oh, Mum, I miss you and Dad so much. I've got some wonderful news. Simon and I are engaged.' Then the colour drained from her face as she heard the panic in Nina's voice. Shocked, Jo tried to make some sense out of her mother's hysterical ramblings.

'I'll be there, Mum,' she said very gently. 'I love you. Tell Dad I love him too.' She heard the click of the phone at the other end and replaced the receiver carefully in its cradle, sitting down ashen-faced, staring unseeing in front of her.

Simon hurried into the room followed by Neddy who was still wheezing hard.

'What did she say, darling?' asked Simon protectively, then he saw the colour of Jo's face. Swiftly he crossed the room and knelt down beside her, anxiously placing one hand on her shoulder. Jo tried to speak but nothing came out.

'Take it easy,' Simon whispered.

'It's Dad . . .' Jo croaked finally. 'He's had an accident. He's in hospital and he may not make it . . . I've got to go home . . . Oh God!' With a shuddering sigh she buried her face in Simon's chest and wept.

Part Three

Chapter Sixteen

CRAMMED IN BETWEEN an overweight businessman and an excessively talkative New Zealander on the 747 bound for Sydney, Jo buried her head in the in-flight magazine and pretended to read, her mother's words going round and round in her head. She had rung home with her flight details just before she left and had been surprised at how lucid and calm Nina had sounded—almost emotionless. Dad was still in a coma in intensive care. He and his foreman Mick had been travelling home from Queensland on a back road when a truck had shot out from a track beside a property, slewing them off the road and crushing the car. Mick had been killed outright and they had had to cut Dad out of the wreckage. A local farmer had found them. Dad had sustained head injuries and suspected spinal injuries, but they couldn't tell the extent of the damage until he started to come out of the coma, if in fact he did come out of it. Jo lay back in her seat and shut her eyes. Tears pricked behind her closed eyelids, her throat tense with misery. He might already have gone while she was in the air. The air hostess was pulling down the shades and dimming the cabin lights. Jo brushed away a tear and pulled the rug up around her chin, the frustration of the long flight before her depressing her further. There was nothing she could do but sit and wait.

When she stepped wearily off the plane onto Australian soil she was momentarily comforted by the familiar sights and sounds of home, but this was far from the triumphant homecoming she had dreamed of. After another interminable wait she heaved her luggage off the conveyor belt onto a trolley and pushed her way through the arrivals gate into the Kingsford Smith Airport main foyer. Anxiously she scanned the crowd pressed up against the barrier. Catching sight of Bertie, she hurried impatiently past the other dawdling arrivals and squeezed her way through the crush.

'Hello, little sis,' said Bertie.

Ignoring the endearment she loathed, Jo gave Bertie a hug. 'Is Dad ... ?' she faltered into his broad shoulder.

'He's still in a coma in intensive care. Mum's with him,' said Bertie bluntly, speaking quickly to hide his emotions.

Convinced Bertie was going to tell her their father was dead, Jo couldn't stop the tears of relief coursing down her cheeks. 'Then there's a chance ... ?' she cried, stepping out of his arms. Quickly she wiped the tears away with the palms of her hands and rummaged for a tissue.

Bertie hunched his shoulders. 'The doctors say it's too soon. We just have to wait.'

'How's Mum coping?' asked Jo, blowing her nose then stuffing the tissue in her pocket with a sniff. Bertie looked shocking, his face pale and strained. Dark shadows outlined his eyes and his mouth turned uncharacteristically down at the corners.

'Not brilliantly. Joan Ellis has been with her since it happened,' he explained, his voice tightly controlled. The wife of Jack Ellis, Charlie's best mate, the couple had been close friends of Charlie's for the last ten years. 'D'you want to dump this stuff at home and get changed or go straight to the hospital?'

'Go straight to the hospital,' replied Jo quickly, pushing her trolley towards the exit, blinking away the tears, anxious to get to her father. There was so much she had to tell him. Why was it you only realised it at times like this? At least she would have some support in coping with Mum. Joan Ellis was one of the most down-to-earth people Jo knew and she was used to Nina's rapid mood swings.

Stepping through the hospital doors, Jo gave an involuntary shiver at the antiseptic smell and the hushed atmosphere. A cold emptiness enveloped her as they stepped into the lift, silently watched the floor numbers and then hurried out, following the yellow line on the floor towards the intensive care unit. At the smoky plastic double doors Bertie pressed the buzzer in the wall and waited, shifting agitatedly from foot to foot.

A nurse appeared through the doors. 'Mr Kingsford? Are you relatives?' inquired the nurse.

'I'm his daughter and this is my brother,' replied Jo, fingering her engagement ring, Simon and their happiness together somewhere in another dimension.

The nurse's face softened. 'If I can just explain,' she said gently, standing between Jo and the door. 'We find if we explain before you go in what to expect, it makes it a bit easier. It can be a bit of a shock seeing someone close to you in intensive care. Mr Kingsford is on a ventilator, which means he has a tube from his mouth down into his lungs to do his breathing for him. He also has a feed tube in his nose and another from his arm, and he is attached to a heart monitor. There are quite a lot of noises from the machines but that tells us that they are all working . . .'

Jo nodded, a sickening sensation in her stomach. 'Mum's sort of told me a bit,' she said unsteadily.

'Good girl.' The nurse patted Jo's arm. 'At this stage we advise you only stay a short while in the ward and that there are not too many people all at once. It's too tiring for the patient. Mr Kingsford still needs lots of care and rest. Mrs Kingsford is in with him at the moment. Maybe one of you would like to wait in the waiting room?'

'You go in. I'll wait out here,' said Bertie, extremely pale, giving Jo a gentle shove. He was finding it hard to cope with the whole ordeal. He had very nearly passed out the first time he had visited his father and seen him hooked up to all the machines. Listening to the nurse made him feel queasy again.

'Thanks,' said Jo sombrely. Memories of Rick flooded back as she followed the nurse through the double doors, the sickening sensation in her stomach increasing.

Charlie was lying in bed number six just as the nurse had described. Eyes closed, deathly pale, he lay against crisp white pillows, his right shoulder swathed in pristine white bandages, his hands lying on top of the covers. A drip from a bag hanging from a stand was attached to his left hand, and another clear plastic tube protruded from under the bedclothes into a bag hanging down one side of the bed. Suddenly light-headed despite the nurse's explanation, Jo stared down at her father, the shush-shush of the dull blue ventilator next to his bed forcing air in and out of his lungs too loud in her ears. A nurse sat to one side monitoring the venti-lator and making notes on a chart. A few paces away Nina, talking to the doctor, caught sight of Jo. Abruptly breaking off her conversation, she came hurrying over.

'Jo darling, Bertie found you all right,' she whis-pered distractedly, brushing her lips against Jo's cheek. 'I was just talking to the doctor.' She took a deep breath. 'You're going to have to be very brave, darling. We're all going to have to be very brave. Your dad is very, very sick.' She pressed her fingers to her trembling lips. Jo returned her mother's kiss, her throat constricting with misery, the dizziness receding. Absently Nina stroked Jo's arm. 'I'll talk to you in a minute, darling. I have to catch the sister in charge,' she said and walked off.

Jo sat down in the chair beside the bed and stared into the still grey face of the father she adored, her eyes filling with tears. 'Dad,' she whispered, her hand hovering over his. She longed to kiss his pallid cheeks yet she dared not touch him. She felt lost and useless in this world of machinery and imper-sonal efficiency. What if he didn't make it? What if she could never tell him again how much she loved him and wanted his respect? What if she could never explain to him why she had done what she had done? She bit hard on her bottom lip.

'You can squeeze his hand, dear,' said the nurse

monitoring the ventilator quietly, seeing the distress in Jo's face. Her heart went out to the girl. It was hardest for the young ones.

Jo glanced up briefly, nodding her thanks, and carefully closed her hand over her father's limp unresponsive fingers, the contact causing the tears to spill down her cheeks.

'I love you, Dad. You'll never know how much,' she choked. 'You have to get better.' Around her nurses bustled about dealing with the other critically ill patients. It was like being in another world with the big work station and its monitors in the centre of the room, the beds fanned out in a circle, a nurse to each ventilator.

Nina hurried back to Jo and sat down wearily beside her. 'These doctors, they're supposed to know everything, aren't they? That one I was talking to before couldn't answer a simple question and the sister's no better. All I want to know is how long he's likely to be like this,' Nina whispered petulantly, leaning towards Jo, twisting her handkerchief in her hand. 'All this equipment and everything, you'd have thought they could give me an answer . . . And they wrap everything up in all these medical terms . . . I don't know what they mean half the time. I wish the sister who was on yesterday was here. She was so much easier to talk to.' She wiped the corners of her eyes.

'What did the doctor say?' asked Jo. Letting go of her father she reached out and squeezed her mother's hand.

'The same as before: at this stage it's difficult to say. We just have to be patient and see how he progresses.' Nina choked. 'Patient, how can I be patient? The doctors are hiding something from me, I just know it.' Abruptly she stopped talking, her eyes wide with anxiety as a nurse bustled over, her starched uniform rustling, and checked Charlie's pupils lifting each eyelid in turn and shining a penlight into each eye, then replaced the almost empty bag on the drip stand with a full one.

'There's a nice healthy lunch for you, Mr Kingsford,' she said cheerfully, having checked the flow rate of the liquid into the tube. She smiled briefly at Nina and Jo and moved briskly away.

'I'm sure they're doing the best they can, Mum,' said Jo, trying to sound convincing. 'Anyway Dad's going to be okay. When have you ever known Dad to let anything beat him?' She gave a forced laugh. 'In a few days he'll be sitting up and we'll all be joking about this.' Her words had a horrible ring of familiarity to them. Nina's mouth tightened and she withdrew her hand. Jo saw the panic in her eyes.

'What am I going to do, Jo? I'm so frightened. He's been like this for three days. I can't manage without Charlie. He's my life. Your father's the only man I've ever known. He's always done everything in our marriage. I don't even know where to start.' Jo felt a stab of terror shoot through her as her mother spilled out all her fears since the accident, spiralling downwards, painting a picture of gloom and despair, confiding intimate details of her relationship with Charlie to Jo, arguments she had had with him, the guilt she felt at not understanding his love of horses. Jo had never seen her mother so scared nor so vulnerable, and it shook her to the core.

'Mum, Dad wouldn't want us to be talking like this,' she whispered, her chest tight with anxiety, trying to stop the flow, grasping at anything that would turn her mother's thoughts around, anything to get her back and coping. 'He'd be saying things like, "Pull yourselves together, girls. Be positive.

You're not getting rid of me that easily, and anyway there are all those trophies to keep shiny." He'd say, "Have you checked what's going on down at the stables?"' she rushed on, relieved to see her mother brighten slightly. 'Have you, Mum? Have you spoken to Gloria?' she finished.

'Don't you talk to me of stables or horses!' Nina cried, her voice crescendoing, her eyes wild, Jo's words touching a raw nerve. Exhausted after three sleepless nights, her rationality shot to pieces, Nina turned the full force of her grief and anger on her daughter. 'Wasn't it enough that I lost Rick because the two of you had to ride those wretched animals, and now Charlie. I tried to stop him but he wouldn't listen. I tried . . .' She gave a choking sob. 'How much more grief do I have to bear because of those damned stables? Sometimes I think you love them more than your own family. Didn't the misery you caused your father and me teach you anything? I don't care if they bloody burn to the ground.'

Tears started in Jo's eyes. She had no idea what to do to help or why her mother had suddenly turned on her. White-faced she bit back the words of anger that sprang to her lips.

A sister came hurrying over. 'Why don't you go and get some fresh air and something to eat, Mrs Kingsford,' she said firmly. 'It's been a very long and worrying night. Perhaps you can have your discussion a bit later.'

'I'll sit a bit longer with my husband, thank you, sister, but I think you should go home, Jo, and get some rest,' replied Nina curtly, noticing for the first time the dark purple shadows under her daughter's eyes too large in her pinched, drawn face. 'Joan's in the waiting room. She insisted on staying,' she added more gently. 'Have a hot shower and get some sleep.

Bertie'll be home soon. I'll ring you if there's any change in your dad.'

Relief spread through Jo at her mother's abrupt return to normality. 'I think I will, Mum. I'm not doing much good here.' She smiled wanly. 'I love you,' she said, kissing her on the cheek.

Nina nodded and patted Jo's hand again. Emotionally she had little more to give. She sank wearily back into the chair.

Jo walked out of the surreal atmosphere of intensive care, fighting off the fear that threatened to engulf her. She too felt emotionally drained. Her mother's volatility terrified her. What terrified Jo more, however, was the realisation that of the three she had to be the strong one. Her mother was lost and it was frightening to witness. Yes, she had to be the one to worry about the stables. There was no point in asking Bertie. He had always loathed anything to do with them, but it would break Dad's heart to see them go downhill. Far more importantly, they were the family's livelihood.

In the waiting room Joan put her arms around Jo and gave her a big hug. 'He'll pull through, never you mind. Your father was never one to give up without a fight. He'll be walking out of here in no time, you'll see. Now, let's get you home, give you a hot bath and pack you into bed. You look shattered.'

'No, I'm fine really. I've woken up now. What I do need is to get down to the stables and see what's happening there. You couldn't drive me there, could you?' replied Jo briskly.

'We're on our way,' said Joan wishing her husband Jack was not over in Hong Kong. 'I'll pick you up in an hour,' she said as they pulled up at the stable entrance. Gratefully, Jo smiled her thanks and turned and walked towards the big green doors. Turning the key in the ignition, Joan looked back with a jolt seeing the distinctive Kingsford stride. In fact, she thought as she drove away, except for the hair, from behind and at a glimpse, Jo could easily have been mistaken for her father.

The stable yard was empty, the horses settled down in their stalls after their early morning exercise. Deciding to check out the horses before going to see Gloria, Jo walked along peering in boxes, recognising old faces and seeing new, noticing a few empty stalls. At every step she kept expecting her father to appear around the corner. Familiar objects and smells jarred at her already frayed emotions. Arctic Gold shrieked at her as she ducked around the corner and slipped into Fizzy's box. Allowing herself a few seconds' escape from grim reality, she hugged the gentle beast, whispering to him, resting her head against him, comforted by his horsy smell and the soft warmth of his breath on her hand as he nuzzled against her, searching for pieces of apple. Stroking his soft golden coat she heard the clatter of horses' hooves in the yard. Quickly slipping out of the stall she looked around and saw Hawk, the blow-in who had become one of her father's regular track riders and whom Jo had always disliked and distrusted, leading a fit-looking bay from a stall with two other men she didn't recognise. Instinct told her to wait and she stood in the shadows, watching and listening, the men's voices clearly audible as they walked the horse down the yard. The conversation was general at first, about the condition of the horse and races they planned to enter the horse in, but then Hawk's unmistakable

Australian twang rose above the others.

'There's no point keeping the horse here no longer,' he said, glancing quickly around to check the yard was empty. 'Charlie's had it. If he pulls through, he'll be in a wheelchair for the rest of his life, silly as a goat from wot I heard. They say he's not moved a muscle since the accident. Nope, you're best over the fence and gone, that's my advice. Pity. He was a good trainer and it's a real shame but them's the breaks. Rosy'll look after you.' He was half turned in Jo's direction and she could see him tap the side of his nose.

At first she couldn't believe what she was hearing then, as the full extent of what Hawk was saying sank in, she felt a slow burning fury build inside her. Shifty, sarcastic, ready-to-put-you-down Hawk, the track rider who had never made it as a jockey, was actively encouraging owners to leave Kingsford Lodge. She had never understood why her dad had let him ride his horses in the first place, now she was determined he never would again. Realising she couldn't just rush out and vent her fury on the man while the owners were there, Jo waited until Hawk returned, her anger mounting. Whistling, he strutted down the yard, flicking away a bit of muck with the whip he was clutching in one hand. When he was almost parallel with Jo she stepped out of the shadows across his path.

'What the fuck . . .' he cried, leaping in the air but quickly recovering. 'Well, if it isn't the boss's little girl,' he leered, his shifty eyes not quite meeting her bold stare. 'Sorry to hear about your dad,' he added as an afterthought.

'That's the last time you are ever going to do anything like that to us again,' Jo said icy calm, her violet eyes almost black.

Hawk's eyes darted across her face. 'Us, who's us? I dunno what you're talking about,' he exclaimed smugly.

'You know damn well, Hawk,' Jo hissed. She took a step towards him. Hawk crossed his arms and stared insolently at her, the whip dangling idly in his hand, one knee jiggling agitatedly.

'Well, do remind me, cos I seem to have forgotten,' he replied, glad he had needled her. The girl had always needed taking down a peg or two in his opinion.

'You purposely got that man to take his horse away from this stables!' Jo exploded.

Hawk's expression changed to one of anger. 'Whoa! Whoa! Now you just hang on a moment before you go accusing me of things that serious. I was just advising the man. Giving him a few tips all in good faith. He wasn't very happy.'

'You lying, cheating creep! I heard every word you said and it certainly wasn't tips in good faith. You deliberately told him to take his horse away from here. I don't know why Dad ever let you near his horses!' she shouted.

'Is that a fact?' interrupted Hawk, leaning towards her. 'Well now, it doesn't matter, does it? Wake up to yourself, girlie! You don't really believe your dad's going to get up from his bed and come charging through those gates again good as new, do you? Face it, his days as a trainer are finished and so is this stables. No-one with any sense is going to keep their horses here now.' Jo could smell the stale sweat and cigarette smoke on his emaciated body; her fingers curled into tight fists. She wanted to smash them into his smug, leathery face. She was shaking from head to toe.

'You've made your last nasty little move around

here, Hawk. You're fired. I'll get Gloria to make up your pay. We won't be needing your services here again—ever.'

'That's funny, that is!' guffawed Hawk. 'You can't fire me. You sound more like your mother every day.'

They both froze at the sound of slow hand-clapping.

'More like her father,' exclaimed a deep voice.

Jo whirled round and stared up at Pete, the old stable lad who'd had a crush on her, now six foot two, broad shouldered, his face bronzed from the outdoor work. Hawk took a step back.

'Pete!' squealed Jo.

The office door banged open and Gloria came panting across the yard, her loose jacket flapping round her plump motherly figure.

'Hawk! Pete! Whatever's going on? Jo, what on earth are you doing here?' she cried, startled.

'Hawk's fired. Could you make up his pay,' Jo asked through gritted teeth, not sure whose side Pete was on.

Colour flooded Gloria's face, her eyes flew from Jo to Hawk and back to Jo, taking in her pinched face and glittering eyes. 'Now calm down, dear. You can't go around firing people for no reason,' she exclaimed, gathering her jacket around her. 'Hawk's been helping out for the last few days. What's happened?'

'No, Gloria, she's right. I've been wondering why we've had a sudden exodus of horses over the last few days,' interrupted Pete.

Gloria stopped and glared at Hawk. She too had never liked the man. 'Well, I—' she started but Hawk interrupted.

'Don't bother, Gloria, I'm not that strapped for

cash and Jo's right about one thing. I won't be working here again. Enjoy your gee-gees, little girl,' he smirked. Turning on his heel, he started towards the exit, slapping the whip angrily against his leg.

'I'll have that, thanks. It's one of ours,' said Pete striding after him and snatching the whip out of Hawk's fingers, returning triumphant. Swearing, Hawk hurried away. Gloria was looking decidedly flustered.

'I heard the lot,' announced Pete grimly to Gloria and Jo in the relative privacy of the stable office. 'I'd suspected something was going on before Mick and your father's accident, but today was so blatant. Up until today there wasn't anything I could really prove. It was his word against mine.' Then he explained the whole incident with Hawk to Gloria. 'Hawk's not a nice bloke to know but I don't think he can do us much more harm. But you, you're amazing, Jo. In fact, you gave me a real shock. For a few seconds back there I actually thought you were your dad. Are you feeling ill?' he asked anxiously as Jo sat down, suddenly fighting back tears.

Gloria, her own emotions a mess since the accident, burst into tears.

'I'll make us all a cup of tea,' said Jo leaping up. 'D'you still keep the sugar in the same place?'

Nodding, Gloria fished in her desk drawer for some paper tissues. 'What a silly fool I am, but these last few days have been dreadful,' she cried, wiping her eyes and blowing her nose loudly. 'Is there any more news about your father?' she sniffed, red-eyed, as Jo reappeared with mugs of tea and biscuits for the three of them.

'He's still fighting,' replied Jo soberly, handing Gloria her tea. 'And he'll make it. He's got the

Kingsford spirit,' Jo went on determinedly, although a frown flitted across her face as she thought of her mother.

'Not something you want to get on the receiving end of too often, I can tell you,' laughed Pete.

'Thanks, Pete,' grinned Jo, pretending to be offended. Then she asked Pete what had been going on in the stables over the last year and who had been Mick's assistant.

'No-one in particular. There've been quite a few changes in staff recently,' replied Pete. 'We all just pitch in when we're needed.'

Sadness and guilt swept over Jo as Pete talked. It should have been Winks she was asking, not Pete. If she hadn't got the old man sacked he'd be telling her all this. She kept hoping and half expecting Winks to materialise from the shadows behind Pete and tease her as he used to, that hideous day of his dismissal all too clear in her mind.

'Right. Well, the first thing I'll need to do is to get myself registered with the ARA as Dad's licensed foreman so I can run the stables till he gets better,' she said, her full attention back with Pete and Gloria. 'We'll do that straightaway, Gloria. It's only a phone call and a couple of forms. Then we can officially keep training. I'll be down at track work tomorrow morning. You will stay on as my assistant foreman, at least till I see what's going on, won't you?' Jo asked Pete anxiously. 'You know this place inside out.'

'Sure. You'd better expect a bit of stick from some of the older stable hands, though,' replied Pete, looking pleased.

'Let's worry about that if it happens. What d'you think, Gloria? Can you cope with that as long as I promise not to yell at people too often?'

'You betcha, my girl. You're your father's daughter,' replied Gloria admiringly, sipping her tea. Then she noticed Jo's engagement ring. 'No-one mentioned you were engaged!' she blurted out.

Jo stopped, her cup halfway to her mouth, her longing for Simon flooding over her. It had been a grim morning. 'Yes, I am,' she said quietly. 'His name's Simon and we're getting married as soon as Dad's well enough. I haven't even had a chance to tell Mum properly. It all got sort of lost in the rest of the crises.'

'Well, what d'you know! Sharon and I got engaged two weeks ago,' said Pete proudly.

'Congratulations!' cried Jo. For the first time that day everyone was smiling.

Chapter Seventeen

JO SLIPPED INTO working at the stables as though she had been in charge all her life, her nomination as licensed foreman accepted by the ARA. Without exception the staff at Kingsford Lodge were amazed at her quiet confidence and her involvement with everyone and everything, even those areas considered off-limits to women. Constantly exhausted, Jo juggled her time between the horses and their owners, visits to the hospital and long hours spent bolstering up her mother who clung to her like a frightened child, the brightest spot in the week always Simon's voice at the end of the telephone or letters waiting in the mailbox.

Off the critical list three weeks after Jo's return, Charlie, to everyone's intense relief, showed signs of coming out of the coma. At first the signs were so minor that no-one believed it was really happening but when the doctors weaned him off the ventilator and he was able to breathe by himself for the first time, Jo and Nina hugged one another in the hospital waiting room, the tears streaming down their faces. Less demonstrative, Bertie hugged them briefly and started teasing Jo to hide his emotion. For the first time since the accident Nina slept for a full eight hours.

However, a few days later, after a series of tests, the doctor dealt the next crushing blow. Charlie was paralysed from a stroke he had suffered during the accident and unable to speak. The doctors were still unsure of the extent of the brain damage or of the outcome. Once more Jo and Nina's spirits plummeted, whilst Bertie took himself off to the races and lost a lot of money.

Fighting off her depressing thoughts, Jo sat one sunny afternoon beside her father who was now propped up on pillows in the high-dependency ward, determinedly chatting to him while he stared blankly in front of him, unmoving. Encouraged by Jo, Nina had gone to one of her charity functions' meetings.

'I never told you about Outsider, Dad. He's the most gallant horse I have ever met,' said Jo, stroking Charlie's hand, cheered that at least his eyes were now open. She had no idea whether her father understood or could even hear what she was saying, but she kept talking as she had when he was in the coma, pouring out the love she had felt for the horse, explaining how she had helped fix his shoulder, telling Charlie how she had remembered all the little details she had learned from him as a child, and how excited she had been when she found she was in charge of Outsider at Ascot.

'It was just wonderful and when I heard the crowd roaring as Outsider thundered past the winning post, I thought I would burst with pride,' she said, her voice rising, as she relived the whole race in her mind. 'I kept thinking, "This is how Dad feels, this is what it's all about." You love them, you work them and then they turn on the performance of a lifetime.' She slumped back in her chair, feeling slightly foolish, wishing Charlie would react somehow, anyhow, but now his eyes were shut. Then as she watched, wondering if he would ever know how much she admired him, tears oozed out of the corners of his eyes and slowly trickled down his cheeks. Shocked, at first she didn't know how to react. Then, like a blinding flash of lightning, she realised he could hear her and he understood.

'Dad,' she whispered, a lump in her throat. Leaning over very gently, she wiped the tears from his cheeks. 'Dad, I love you, I love you so much. You're going to get better. Mum's fine and loves you too and you'll be walking out of this place before you know it.' Clutching his hand tightly, she told him about Simon and their plans to get married as soon as Charlie was better. The next day she bought her father a new designer hat and placed it on his lap and again he cried and this time Jo cried with him, but they were hot tears of joy that tumbled down her cheeks.

Life in the Kingsford household changed dramatically after that day. Buoyed up by the belief that her father could understand what she was saying even if he could not respond, Jo's visits lost their traumatic edge and became a time when she shared with him all the tiny daily details of running the stables. Each time she walked into the ward she noticed an improvement in her father; there was an expectancy in his eyes that had not been there before, and she always felt better when she left.

'Archie won three races at Rosehill on Saturday and he's riding Titian Girl in the Villiers Stakes next week—should go well. The track was as heavy as anything this morning yet she handled it really well,' she told Charlie jubilantly in the middle of December, arranging a large bunch of flowers in a hospital vase and placing them on the table by his bed together with the ribbons Archie had been presented with. 'I don't know what I'd do without Archie. He's such a great jockey. I've learned so much working with him.'

From the day Jo had walked back into the stables Archie, with his unmistakable Scottish accent, had supported her. Always at track work with her in the morning advising her, he also found other jockeys to ride for her, easing a lot of the initial load while she found her feet. His loyalty to Charlie astounded her. Unlike other jockeys always grabbing the best rides, Jo learned that since the accident, if there was a choice between riding a Kingsford Lodge horse and another, Archie always chose Kingsford Lodge, even if it was the inferior mount. Careless that it set tongues wagging about his ability as a jockey, Archie knew it kept confidence and interest in the stables alive and Jo was eternally grateful.

Jo's decision to invite Pete to become assistant foreman had also turned out extremely successfully. Despite being one of the younger members of the team, he was excellent at handling people and calming owners' concerns about how long it would be before Charlie was fit enough to get back to training again. While it galled Jo that he managed to get cooperation where she failed, simply because she was female, she refused to let it get her down, preferring to concentrate on running a smooth operation. Pete also had a lot of friends who kept him posted about what was going on in the racing world.

'I can't believe it's all going so well,' Jo told Simon excitedly on one of their regular weekly calls. 'But I miss you so much. I wish I could climb down this wire and into your arms.' Then she told him that Nina had extracted a cautious prognosis from Charlie's neurosurgeon. While Charlie was unlikely ever to retain the full strength down the right side of his body, with the proper physio and hard work on his part, he could very well regain much of his mobility. 'So I could be back in England by Easter if things go well,' she said optimistically. After chatting a while longer, and learning that Neddy had got over his bout of bronchitis, she hung up reluctantly, thinking how unsatisfactory long-distance calls were and wishing she didn't remember all the things she had wanted to tell Simon after the call was over.

Still very fragile, Charlie was allowed to spend Christmas and Boxing Day at home. It was both a joyous and sombre occasion. Jo missed Simon dreadfully but they all made a special effort with their celebrations, despite Charlie's inability to speak. Nina, in a total panic and struggling not to burst into tears, downed three glasses of wine in quick succession and was slightly tiddly by the time Charlie arrived. Helped into the house by a male nurse and Bertie, they sat him in the coolest part of the sitting room under one of the fans. Elaine, who had visited Charlie several times in hospital, had come down from Dublin Park with Wayne, and Jack and Joan Ellis joined them for Christmas lunch. They all pulled crackers and put on the paper hats and read out the silly jokes, trying to pretend that everything was normal.

Then, before the Christmas pudding, after Jo had recounted a particularly funny incident at the stables, Charlie banged the table with his spoon and waved it shakily in Jo's direction, mumbling what sounded like 'Got-to-go' at Jo. There was a shocked silence and Jo turned bright red. Surely after all this time her father had forgiven her. Leaping up, she

317

tried to get him to write down what he was trying to say, but all he could scribble were shaky vertical lines. Dropping the pencil, he stared intently at Jo, repeating the strange little phrase over and over. Patting her husband agitatedly on the hand, Nina removed the spoon and gave Jo a wobbly smile. Charlie relaxed back in his chair and everyone started talking again, but there was a tension for the rest of the meal that would not go away.

'Maybe the old man has lost his marbles,' murmured Bertie to Jo later on the veranda.

Vehemently she shook her head. 'I think he's just trying to speak and we should all be glad he's managed something, even if it was strange,' she said firmly, bending down to Sam who was lying panting in the heat. He had been so excited at her return, and now he banged his tail loudly on the floor as she rubbed his tummy. But a tiny niggling worry remained with her. Then the phone went and it was Simon.

'Happy Christmas, darling. Did you like my present?' He had sent her a beautiful book on Norfolk with the bookmark in the page on Burnham Overy Staithe.

'I loved it,' replied Jo, relaxing at the sound of his voice. 'Happy Christmas to you too, darling. I miss you like crazy. I know I said I'd be back in England by Easter, but I think I was being a bit optimistic, I'm afraid.'

'Don't worry so much, Jo. We've got the rest of our lives together. What's a few more months?' said Simon cheerfully and suddenly Jo felt as though a weight had rolled off her shoulders. With Simon chattering on about Christmas in England and his family, her heart lifted and she felt that there really could be a happy ending to this part of her life.

'I love you,' she whispered again. Replacing the receiver, she went in search of Elaine. 'You'd just love Simon, I know, Gran,' she bubbled. 'He's so understanding and patient. I miss him so much.'

Elaine put her arms around Jo and gave her a big hug. 'You deserve someone special,' she said brightly. 'You're such a special courageous girl, but you must give yourself time off or you'll wear yourself out.'

'Yes, Gran,' smiled Jo and wandered off.

Elaine bustled thoughtfully into the kitchen in search of a cup of tea. She worried about Jo. Bertie should be taking more responsibility for the stables instead of running around with all his rich friends. There was too much resting on the poor girl's shoulders and although Nina was a lot calmer these days, she still leaned heavily on Jo. Elaine frowned, wishing there was more she could do. Bertie seemed to be growing more and more like his Uncle Wayne but mentioning anything to Nina would simply set her off into one of her hysterical crying fits and certainly not help Jo.

One bright sunny afternoon early in March Jo strolled along the Manly esplanade with her friend Dianne Gibbs on one of her rare days off. The two friends from pony club had finally caught up a couple of weeks ago. Dianne was now working as a trainee manager in one of the big new hotels recently opened overlooking Manly Beach. Swapping stories about what they had been up to over the past three years, Jo found herself laughing like she hadn't laughed in months. It felt so good and she felt free from all the cares that usually weighed her down. The sun sparkled on the blue water and waves broke gently on the bleached yellow sand, leaving behind a soapy froth. Today marrying Simon and leaving Australia seemed almost possible. She pulled out a photo he had sent her of a dilapidated old rectory he had discovered outside Norwich. Built in the typical Norfolk red brick and flint and with a jungle of a garden, Jo could immediately see the potential that had attracted Simon to the house. With some careful renovation and lots of tender loving care, it would be a delight. Best of all, there was room for stables at the back of the rectory.

When the two young women reached the hotel where Dianne worked, they hugged and arranged to meet again early the next week. As Jo wandered back to the ferry wharf she thought about her friend. Dianne had always been very practical and ambitious and she had asked Jo a couple of searching questions about the future which Jo had been unable to answer. Refusing to let anything ruffle her day off, she decided on the spur of the moment to take a ferry ride to Circular Quay and back. Stepping jauntily across the gangplank of the *Mary Jane*, Jo walked up to the front of the boat and leaned over the side, watching the water churning beneath her, a cauldron of boiling sea. The sun blazed down on her head and the wind caught in her hair, the salt spray tingling in her nose, as they pulled away from the wharf. It was refreshingly different from her usual surroundings and relatively uncrowded. Resting her arms on the side of the ferry, she watched boats of different shapes and sizes sailing leisurely around the busy harbour. Two windsurfers streaked across the waves and in the distance a vast tanker led by its pilot ship slowly made its way towards the famous Heads and the open sea. It was good just to watch and gaze and think.

The stables had settled in to a comfortable routine. Pete and Archie were angels in disguise, Jo decided, her mood buoyant, and while they had fewer horses to train than usual due to the exodus caused by Hawk and rumours that Charlie was not quite right in the head, the horses they were training were winning and winning well. Sending rumours galloping round the racing industry as to the competence of Kingsford Lodge was not the only problem Hawk had caused. Finding he was getting fewer and fewer offers of rides, Hawk had accepted Charlie's offer before the accident to work as his clocker, timing the horses at track work. Having sacked him, Jo had to find someone to take his place. It had seemed to her a simple enough job, just be there, time the horses as she called them and record the times on the daily sheet. However, as Jo quickly discovered, finding a reliable clocker was not as easy as she had imagined. Having employed a number of people who had been both unreliable and inefficient, she had even in desperation asked Gloria to be the clocker on a couple of occasions.

'It'll sort itself out,' she told herself with more confidence than she felt, pushing her hair back from her face. Buffeted by a rowdy group of schoolkids on an excursion fighting to stand at the head of the boat, Jo turned round to move away and caught sight of a familiar-looking figure. Not sure, she walked up to the old man and her face split in an enormous grin.

'Winks!' she cried and hugged him before he had a chance to realise who she was. Startled, he dropped the brown paper bag containing his sandwiches. Quickly catching them before they were trampled underfoot by the schoolkids, Jo planted the sandwiches back in his lap. He looked older and more weather-beaten, and his hands were gnarled and unsteady, yet his eyes were as alert as ever.

'Jo! Well I'll be darned. Never thought to set eyes on you again,' he said, his face lighting up.

'Never know who you'll pick up on a ferry ride,' joked Jo. 'How have you been?' Her heart gave a jolt, reminding her again of the last time she had seen Winks and the guilt she felt at his dismissal, and how much she still missed his company.

'Good, real good,' replied Winks slowly. There was a sadness at the back of his pale blue eyes. 'Sorry about your father. He was a hard man but a top trainer. You're not doin' so bad yourself from what I hear, young 'un, even though you're a girl,' he added with a quirky smile. He lifted his peaked cap, stroked his bald head and replaced the cap firmly on his head.

'Getting there. Dad's on the mend and at least the horses don't mind I'm a girl,' Jo replied cheerfully, echoing words she had so often heard from the old man. As the ferry ploughed its way toward Circular Quay they chatted of this and that. Winks told her he'd been doing odd jobs here and there, gardening and fixing things, but today he was off to meet a mate who might have a job for him as a cleaner at one of the racecourses.

'Don't seem to be able to keep away,' he chuckled.

Knowing how proud Winks was, Jo turned away to hide the sympathy that sprang in her eyes, her mind racing madly as she wondered how she could make up for what she had done to him. Then it struck her. It was so blindingly obvious she wanted to laugh aloud.

'Winks, would you be my clocker?' she asked excitedly as the ferry slowed down near the jetty. Winks stood up to get off.

'You don't want a silly old duffer like me around the place again,' he said quietly.

Clutching his arm, Jo asked him again, this time with more urgency. 'I'm desperate, Winks. I've tried a dozen different people—blokes, girls, doesn't matter who. They either can't do it accurately or they don't turn up or they come late. I'd never need to worry about you. You'd just do it. I'd have asked you before but I had no idea where to look for you. Please, Winks, I need you.'

The ferry was drawing into the quay. The attendant hurled the rope onto the wharf and swung the gangplank out. Winks took one more step towards the exit and then sat down on the nearby seat. 'Well I'll be blowed. I might just at that.' He paused. 'What about your dad, though? D'you think he'd take an old fool like me back again?'

Jo clapped her hands in delight and hugged him. 'You bet he would. I'm not offering you any favours, mind. I need your help. Is it a deal?'

'It's a deal,' replied Winks. He seemed to have shed ten years. All the way back to Manly he chatted happily about the old times at Kingsford Lodge, recounting stories Jo had heard many times and others that were new, and Jo's heart sang. She'd square it with Dad somehow, and anyway, if it made the place run more smoothly, Dad'd have to swallow his pride.

Jo was delirious at finding Winks again and Winks was delighted to once more be part of Kingsford Lodge. Apart from reigniting their friendship, he was totally reliable, accurately recording the horses' times and never missed a track work, regardless of cold or heat. With the solid little team of Archie,

Pete and Winks, life at the stables jogged along. Charlie was slowly improving and had been transferred to a convalescent home but he was still paralysed down his right side and unable to walk, and no-one mentioned that he was still only speaking the one funny little three-word phrase which made absolutely no sense to anyone.

'Take each day as it comes, Mum,' said Jo as they proudly stood beside the gleaming brown three-year-old in the winning circle, Archie brandishing the gleaming plate above his head. It was his third win in a row.

Then that evening Simon rang in the middle of dinner announcing he was planning to fly out in September for a month.

'That's just over six weeks,' Jo cried happily.

'So it's good old wedding bells for the Pom and little sis, is it?' asked Bertie through a mouthful of strawberry cheesecake when Jo returned to the table.

'Don't call him a Pom!' Jo cried, throwing him a dark look. Nina suddenly became very involved with cutting the cheesecake. 'Damn you, Bertie,' Jo muttered under her breath. She felt thoroughly irritated with her brother. Recently he had taken to dropping in more frequently for meals, and last week she had barged in on her mother to find her handing Bertie some extra cash on top of his monthly allowance. Incensed, Jo had suggested her brother get a part-time job like other students instead of expecting everlasting handouts, but she hadn't been prepared for her mother's defensive reaction. Quickly the conversation had escalated into a huge argument, the first since the accident. Jo had come away feeling disappointed and angry with herself for upsetting her mother and even angrier with Bertie.

'Why don't you fly out and meet your young man

in Hawaii and have a bit of a holiday together?' suggested Elaine, down to visit for a few days, smoothing over the tension. When she had arrived in Sydney yesterday she had been shocked at how exhausted Jo looked. The girl needed a break. 'What's the name of those friends of yours and Charlie that own that resort on one of the islands? They'd be happy to put Jo and Simon up for a few nights, don't you think? That way we'd know you were safe and you could have a lovely break together,' she finished, turning to her granddaughter. Jo beamed.

'Connie and Will,' replied Nina looking uncertain.

Jo looked quickly from one to the other.

'Go on! Ring him back and suggest it. We can figure the rest out later,' ordered Elaine decisively, flapping her hands in Jo's direction. Jo didn't wait to be told a second time. 'And take that silly look off your face, Nina, the girl's lived away from home for long enough, whatever she might be going to do she's probably done already, and they are engaged, so stop worrying.'

'He thinks it's a wonderful idea. I said I'd phone again as soon as we'd sorted out the details,' cried Jo, bouncing back into the room and giving her grandmother a smacking kiss.

Chapter Eighteen

CONNIE AND WILL owned a resort with its own private lagoon on the island of Kauai. Landing shortly before midnight, wishing she could have seen more than the tantalising glimpse of the twinkling lights of Honolulu, Jo was quickly transferred to the small private plane waiting on the tarmac and whisked through the night to Outrigger Resort. When she met the flamboyant Connie and quietly successful Will she was immediately made to feel one of the family. Wondering how she would ever sleep for excitement, she fell into the soft double bed and was asleep before she knew it.

Waking up to the soft swish of the sea on the sand and the rustle of the trade winds in the palm trees, at first Jo couldn't think where she was. Then she sat up with a start and looked at her watch. She was in Hawaii and Simon was due to arrive on the island in forty minutes. Slipping out of bed she pulled back the curtains and gasped at the beauty of the brilliant green sea and startling white sands. A warm wind perfumed by a thousand tropical flowers grazed her cheeks. Dragging her gaze from this view of paradise she dived into her ensuite, showered and dressed in record time, her heart fluttering, and then sauntered into the dining area trying to suppress her mounting excitement. Finishing her breakfast she wandered onto the wide patio and her pulse started racing as she heard the faint buzz of a plane overhead.

'That'll be lover boy now. Come on! I'll get one of the boys to drive you out to the strip,' laughed Connie, brilliant in a dress splashed with Hawaiian orchids, seeing Jo fidgeting by the open doors.

Jo went bright red. Then she was at the strip and Simon was stepping out of the tiny plane, his dark brown hair glinting in the sun, and Jo was running towards him, shouting his name and she was in his arms, his lips pressed to hers, her head spinning wildly as he kissed her on and on.

'I think we might be holding a few people up,' laughed Simon, finally breaking away from their embrace, aware of the small crowd that had gathered around them.

'I don't care if I stop the whole world,' cried Jo joyously, never wanting him to stop, then gaped open-mouthed as a dark beauty stepped forward and placed a rich pink lei around her neck and then kissed her on each cheek.

'Aloha! Welcome to Hawaii,' smiled the girl, her perfect white teeth gleaming in her smooth brown face. Overcome, Jo stared up first at the smiling girl and then at Simon as the girl placed the fresh yellow and white island blossoms around his neck. Then others placed more leis around their necks until they had great collars of brilliant, colourful, sweet-scented flowers.

'What a great welcome,' sighed Jo, tears sparkling in her eyes. Glowing with happiness, she clung onto Simon's arm as they followed the little group back to the car and were driven back to the resort. 'I can't believe you're really here,' she grinned, giving his arm a sharp pinch as they walked into the foyer.

'Ouch!' yelled Simon taken by surprise.

'Just checking you really are real!'

'You're supposed to pinch yourself, not me,' laughed Simon, crushing her once more in his arms, every nerve in his body alive as he felt the full length of her warm soft body pressed against his. 'I want to stay like this forever,' he whispered, momentarily forgetting his surroundings, gazing into her dark violet eyes.

'I love you so much,' replied Jo, her lips ruby red from his kisses, her cheeks flushed with happiness.

'Did you like our Hawaiian welcome?' asked Connie, bustling up. Quickly the two parted.

'It was lovely,' cried Jo, brushing her fingers against the petals of her lei, her legs wobbly from Simon's embrace, one hand clasping his.

'We like to have young lovers at our resort. You'll have to come back for your honeymoon,' smiled Connie, clicking her fingers to a bellboy to take the bags to their rooms. Stepping inside Jo's room, shutting the door after the bellboy, Simon gathered Jo into his arms.

'It's so wonderful to hold you again. I can't believe this is really happening,' he murmured, burying his face in her hair. 'You smell so beautiful.'

'Then I was right to pinch you?' teased Jo, gasping as he covered her face and neck with kisses, surrendering to his embrace.

'I don't know about that but give me five minutes to shower and change and you can pinch me all you want,' Simon panted, regretfully letting her go.

Tingling with anticipation, Jo watched him slip from her room and then she stepped out onto the balcony. Staring out across the deep green lagoon, she breathed in the sweet scent of the leis and ran her fingers over her mouth, longing to feel Simon's lips against hers again. Turning she went back inside and jumped as she walked straight into his arms.

'You were quick,' she gasped, stroking the side of one cheek, breathing in his familiar aftershave. His dark hair, wet from the shower, was pressed smooth against his head and his cool shirt unbuttoned at the neck. She ran her fingers gently across his chest, fiddling with the buttons, the warmth of his touch spreading like fire through her veins.

'With you so close, did you expect me to take my time?' whispered Simon against her hair. Carefully he removed the leis and laid them on a nearby table then, drawing her back into his arms, he covered her mouth once more with his. The warm wind blew on them, the sounds of the sea a distant orchestra as they clung to each other.

'I love you so much.' Simon kissed her long and deep, tasting the soft salt of her lips, drinking in the heady perfume he remembered so well. Lifting his mouth from hers, he gazed into her beautiful face, running his fingers lightly across her lips, soft and warm from his kisses. 'God, I love you!'

Jo stayed fixed to the spot, her heart pounding, her legs like jelly as he kissed her again, harder, more insistently, lost in the passion of their embrace. Finally they drew apart, both thoroughly aroused. With a little laugh Jo dodged under Simon's arm and clasped his hand, leading him to the bed. Sinking down on the soft quilt she opened her arms invitingly, her eyes dark pools.

'I want to feel all of you next to me, my darling,' she murmured, her eyelids fluttering closed as he lay down beside her and kissed her again.

'Do you think we ought to go and say hello to our hosts?' he rasped after a very long time, wrenching his lips from hers, knowing that if they lay together like this much longer he would have to make love to her.

'In a while,' Jo replied huskily, unwilling to let him go. Gently he moved slightly away from her. 'In a while,' she repeated softly. Reaching up she stroked his cheek. Then she held her breath as Simon caught her hand and kissed the palm then lightly ran his finger across her lips and down her long creamy neck. Jo sighed, little shivers of anticipation running through her as his fingers played against her skin.

Slowly he slid his hand down the luscious curves of her breast, the neat dip of her waist and the rounded curve of her hip, fuelling her already awakened desire. Cupping one hand around her buttocks, he pulled her to him so his body was once more pressed close to hers. Her mouth opened at the insistent pressure of his lips, his tongue seeking hers. She could feel him harden against her. Eyes closed, she slid her arms around his neck and clasped him tight, letting the full excitement of his warm embrace flood through her, glorying in his kisses and responding with mounting passion. She had never felt such an overwhelming aching longing for him as she did now. Shakily she fumbled at the buttons of his shirt. One by one she undid them, her fingers refusing to work fast enough, the urgency inside her building. The last button undone, she slid her hands inside his shirt, stroking her fingers across his strong tanned chest and around his back. Shifting, she pressed her lips to his flesh, breathing in his strong male scent. Quickly pulling off her T-shirt and bra she pressed her warm breasts against his. She could feel Simon's heart racing against her own. Simon gasped. Holding her at arm's length he gazed at her beauty, the smooth creamy shoulders, the full olive breasts above her nipped-in waist, the ripe nipples hard with desire.

'God, you're beautiful,' he repeated. Cupping one breast in one hand, he kissed the warm firm flesh, gently brushed his mouth across her nipple. Jo jumped, her arousal making her nipples almost painfully sensitive. Simon's eyes flashed to hers. 'Sorry! I'll be gentle, I promise,' he murmured huskily, running his tongue down the valley between her breasts. Willing him to caress her all over, Jo closed her eyes and dug her fingers into his thick brown hair as a million sensations coursed through her veins. Covering one nipple with his mouth, Simon gently sucked on it. Jo gasped and then moaned, her whole body on fire, desire hot between her legs as he continued to suck first on one nipple then on the other.

'I want you, Simon. I want you so much,' she cried, fumbling for his zipper, her eyes wide, her pupils dilated. Simon clamped his hand over hers, holding it still. Jo's expression changed to startled surprise. 'Don't you want to make love to me?' she demanded.

'Of course I do, but are you sure? I didn't plan for it to happen now, so fast.' He faltered. 'You're so utterly desirable but I don't want to spoil anything before we are married.'

'I'm sure, my darling, you won't spoil anything. I went on the pill as soon as I knew you were coming out—just in case,' Jo replied boldly. 'And you're the first,' she whispered, half laughing in his ear.

'My darling girl,' Simon whispered, his voice thick with emotion. He cupped her face in his hands. 'You know I adore you. I have never loved anyone else the way I love you.'

'Then show me,' urged Jo, her nerves at screaming pitch.

With trembling fingers Simon helped her peel off her jeans and toss them on the floor and she lay before him naked except for a tiny pair of panties. Sensing a sudden shyness, he quickly undressed and, kicking the quilt from under them, lay down beside her. Then with the utmost love and tenderness, he took her in his arms. Gently he wooed her, running his hands over her body, covering her face, her neck, her breasts with kisses, fondling her young firm breasts so they ached with longing, sucking again on those glorious nipples until she wondered how long she could bear the exquisite pain, drawing out their lovemaking until she thought she would go mad with wanting him. Digging her nails into his back, she pulled him to her, arching herself into him, but he resisted, slowly bringing her desire to a peak. Stroking her thigh he slid his fingers between the soft cotton of her panties and fondled the silky mound of blonde hair. Sliding the panties quickly down her long slender legs, he tossed them away. Slowly he ran his hand up the inside of her thigh and she gasped as his fingers brushed the soft skin that was already wet and swollen with desire. Parting the sweet folds, he slid his hand between her legs, at the same time covering her mouth with his, revelling in her hot readiness while she moaned and writhed against his fingers, her body throbbing with passion.

'Now, Simon, now,' she begged, her fingers digging into his shoulders.

Unable to resist any longer, he lifted himself on top of her and gently entered her. Feeling her wince he stopped. 'Relax, my love, I'll go slowly.' Very gently he eased himself deeper inside her, moving slowly as she lay tense beneath him, kissing her and murmuring endearments so she gradually relaxed, her breath coming in little gasps. Then she felt the full force of his love, swept up in the rawness of his emotion and the answering desire of her own body. Clinging to him she arched her body against his as his gentle thrusting rhythm increased until she could hardly breathe. Twisting her head from side to side, she clenched and unclenched her fists, no longer able to control the sensations that consumed her. Her legs trembled violently and Simon responded to her passion. Racing along together he thrust faster and deeper into her, their bodies moving as one. Teetering on the brink, Simon crying out her name, she felt his release and her body responded with one last delicious shudder. Then she gave a sob and burst into tears.

Immediately Simon stiffened. 'I didn't hurt you, my love?' he cried, holding her close, stroking her hair, gazing anxiously into her lovely face, suddenly swamped with guilt that he had listened to his own desire and forgotten her innocence.

Clinging to him, Jo sobbed into his chest. Continuing to hold her close, for once in his life Simon felt completely lost. Gradually the sobs subsided and Jo looked up at him, her face bathed in a new soft radiance.

'I love you so much. I had no idea it could be like that . . . I didn't expect to feel so deeply,' she gulped, laughing through her tears.

Flooded with relief, Simon kissed her again, her lips still hot and swollen from his kisses. 'I love you, Jo, and I want to make you feel like that for the rest of your life.'

Jo kissed him again. Then, suddenly shy, she reached for the sheet. Helping her, Simon pulled the sheet around them and held her tight. Safely cocooned in his arms in the hazy aftermath of their love, Jo started to talk. As the sun hung high above the palm trees and sweet orchid scent wafted through the open balcony window, they talked of the future, their life together, when they would get married, the reality of Charlie's illness and the stables far away, then finally drifted off to sleep.

The next few days were idyllic as Jo and Simon explored the island. They hired a car and meandered through the lush tropical countryside. Discovering a secluded beach they made love under the palm trees and splashed in the clear green sea, their desire heightened by their exotic playground. The next day they visited the local markets and Jo bought some carved birds for Elaine, a T-shirt each for Bertie and Charlie, and a shell brooch for Nina, and they watched a group of Polynesian dancers in the local gardens. Each evening they were enchanted anew by the famous Hawaiian sunset, the sun's fiery tentacles stretching across the sky and turning the world red, orange and gold, then fading to purple before it finally dipped below the horizon.

They ate dinner in the open to the lapping of the waves and gazed into each other's eyes across the candlelit table, the gentle Hawaiian music playing in the background, the waiters silently piling their plates with fresh seafood delicacies and all manner of tropical fruits, the warm evening filled with the scent of frangipani. Dancing into the wee hours, their bodies pressed hungrily against each other, swaying to the gentle music, finally they returned to Jo's room where they made love again until the sun rose.

'There is an intoxication about you I want to capture and bottle,' whispered Simon, kissing Jo as they lay together in the big double bed while the sun filtered into her room on the last day of their stay, but she was fast asleep, her long fair lashes resting against her cheeks flushed with love.

Then it was time to leave. Thanking Connie and Will profusely, they climbed into the tiny plane to fly them back to reality.

'I love you so much. I'm so excited. I want to show you everything!' exclaimed Jo tired but happy, sinking back into the taxi taking them from Sydney's Kingsford Smith Airport.

'And I want to see everything,' replied Simon. He gave a long contented sigh. 'My darling, darling Jo,' he murmured, running his hands down her hair as the car rolled smoothly towards Coogee.

Nina, clutching Suzie Wong in her arms, greeted them at the front door. As she gave Simon a polite kiss on the cheek the fluffy white poodle squirmed out of her hold and licked his face, yapping furiously. Then old Sam came bumbling up the steps, barking, his tale thumping wildly, and the telephone added its shrill note to the confusion.

'Hello, Sam,' greeted Jo, bending down and hugging the old dog. 'I hope you feel suitably welcomed into the Kingsford household,' she shouted to Simon above all the noise and excitement. Straightening up she showed him inside. The aroma of fresh coffee and croissants wafted through the air.

'Totally,' smiled Simon as Suzie Wong leapt from Nina's arms and darted around, yapping excitedly running between everyone's legs and nearly tripping them up.

'Well, show him to his room, Jo. As soon as you've freshened up come and have a cup of coffee. I'm sure you're dying for one, I always am after a long flight,' chivvied Nina.

Twenty minutes later, showered and wearing fresh clothes, Simon and Jo gratefully downed several cups of piping hot black coffee and started to feel slightly less muddle-headed.

'I thought I'd take Simon down to the stables,' Jo said, finishing her croissant and suddenly realising how much she wanted to get back to the horses. 'Then if we're feeling up to it we'll go and visit Dad and take Sam down the beach for a run.'

'Sure, darling, but don't wear Simon out on his very first day. She practically lives in those stables,' Nina said, leaning conspiratorially towards Simon.

'He can handle it, Mum, can't you?' Jo slipped her arm around Simon and jiggled the car keys. Thanking Nina, Simon stood up and he and Jo disappeared out to the car.

Nina watched them thoughtfully as they drove away. On first acquaintance she was surprised how much she liked Simon. He was well mannered, well dressed and well spoken, and their obvious happiness in one another reminded her of how she and Charlie had been all those years ago. Yet underneath her happiness for her daughter, she hoped it wasn't the real love she feared it was. She dreaded the thought of Jo moving to live in England.

As soon as Jo walked into the stables it was as though a transformation had taken place. Watching her Simon felt a pang of fear as the sultry lover he had so adored in Kauai evaporated and an efficient, energetic businesswoman emerged. Listening to her talk with Pete as though she had never been away, watching her greet the horses and check out the racing itinerary with Gloria, he wondered whether he might ever recapture that precious butterfly that had quivered in his arms. But Simon knew the only way to keep his precious love was to throw himself wholeheartedly into her world, which he did to the best of his ability, joining her at predawn track work each day, working with her at the stables and accompanying her to the convalescent home to see Charlie.

By now Charlie was able to sit up in a chair for longer periods, but Simon was shocked at both his frailty and his mental state. Jo had never really spelled out how badly he had been affected by the stroke, nor had she told him that her father could only speak gibberish. Yet the love that flowed between father and daughter was almost tangible. Coming away from each visit Simon found he had to suppress feelings of envy at the incredible bond between them.

As the days streaked by Jo took Simon to different races both in the country and at the Sydney race-tracks, even flying him down to Flemington in Melbourne one weekend. Watching her at work he saw the enormous love she had for the horses and their response to her, yet he didn't really understand her passion. He also saw the respect in the eyes of the staff at Kingsford Lodge.

'She's a plucky one, our Jo,' said Archie, his Scottish accent heavier than ever, his lips hardly moving as he spoke. 'Not easy battlin' away with everyone picking on you because you're a woman, but she's not about to give up. Stubborn as a mule she is, just like her father.' Simon nodded; in many ways Archie reminded him of Neddy at the Orion stables. He had seen that same grudging respect in Neddy's eyes that he now saw in Archie's.

'Well, you're one woman determined to succeed in a man's world,' smiled Simon at the end of a particularly strenuous day at the stables.

'Do we have a chauvinist here? Who said it was a man's world?' asked Jo, giving him a quirky grin as she checked the stalls, the stables deserted except for the two of them, the horses snuffling in their boxes.

'Well, isn't it?' teased Simon, swinging her around and kissing her.

'No,' replied Jo moving out of his embrace, aroused as always by his nearness. 'I have to check the food bins. One of the girls ordered the wrong stuff and started feeding the horses with it.'

Suppressing his annoyance, Simon let her go. He followed her into the big barn where they kept the hay and grumpily watched her check the feed bags, ticking off her list. Unable to keep his hands off her he slid his arms around her waist and kissed her neck.

'There's no-one here and those hay bales look awfully inviting,' he said half joking. Jo gave a grunt and wriggled free. 'Damn it, Jo, don't you ever turn off? We haven't made love since I've been in Sydney,' he exploded. 'Where's that gorgeous girl I was with in Hawaii?'

Jo stopped, her pen poised. 'She's still here,' she said very quietly. The pen and pad slipped from her fingers and fell with a clatter on the concrete as she reached her arms up around Simon's neck.

'Is she?' rasped Simon, kissing her fervently. Jo returned his kiss with all the passion and love the frustration of being apart had built up in her, her body moulding to his, rejoicing in his arousal, and for a few fleeting seconds they were back in the tropical paradise. Then a horse whinnied in the nearby stall, jolting Jo back to the jobs she had to do before returning home. Sighing, she pulled away.

'I have a couple more things I have to do, my

darling, and then we'll take Sam down to the beach,' she murmured.

Reluctantly Simon released her. 'When in Rome . . .' he thought as he followed her up to the office. At least he had established for himself that the girl he loved still existed.

The next weekend Jo took Simon to Dublin Park. Persuaded by Archie that she needed a few days off and longing to be alone with Simon again, she decided to make it a long weekend. She was eager to introduce Simon to Elaine and she also wanted the two of them to go horseriding together.

'I want to ride with the wind with you at my side, not half a mile away from me like you were at Frances's hunt,' said Jo, grinning happily at him over breakfast on the Saturday, radiant at the thought of spending a whole uninterrupted day together.

'I'll be in that,' replied Simon, remembering how desperately he had fought the temptation to ride over to Jo on that frosty morning. He stood up, anxious to get away and be alone with Jo. Then Elaine, who was quite enchanted with Simon, suggested they take some sandwiches and ride up beyond the ridge.

'There are some nice trails there and the horses know them well,' she beamed, fussing around them as they saddled two ex-racehorses she rented out to the local pony club, delighted to see her granddaughter so happy. Jo had a new radiance about her, and if Simon made her look like that, then that was good enough for her gran.

The paddocks were lush and green as Jo and Simon walked the horses leisurely along. Dragonflies flitted across their path as they wandered, the hushed beauty of the countryside creating its own special haven. Stepping out of the sunshine they wound their way up the rocky trail between tall gum trees. Shafts of sunlight filtered through the leaves, catching on the branches and glinting on the undergrowth damp from recent rains. Birds warbled unseen from the trees. The snap of a whipbird echoed through the bush. Alternately trotting, then carefully stepping past big boulders, then trotting again, for the next half-hour, the sturdy sure-footed animals clambered up the hillside. Halfway up, the trail flattened out and the horses broke into a canter. In and out of the dappled sunlight Jo and Simon ducked branches and dodged muddy ruts, the horses' hooves pounding along the well-worn track, the treetops a green canopy overhead. Then Jo could see the open hillside ahead.

'Give them their head,' she cried, exhilarated. Breaking out of the shade into the sunshine, she urged her horse into a gallop. Her cheeks were flushed, tears streamed from her eyes as the wind caught in her face, every nerve was alive as she flew across the open pasture, the sound of Simon's mount thundering behind her. Simon caught up with her and together they galloped across the top of the ridge.

'Ride with the wiiiin . . . !' yelled Jo, the words snatched from her mouth, her love for Simon and the excitement of sharing this moment filling her with exquisite happiness. Reining in her horse then, she slowed to a canter and then a trot. They walked the last bit to the best view of the valley.

'Whoa,' Jo called, bringing her horse to a stop. Her chest heaving, her heart still racing, she turned to Simon, her face glowing with happiness. 'I've dreamed so often of riding up here with you. I wanted you to see all my world, not just the city, to see its beauty.' Across the valley patches of green caught in the sunlight; shadows from the small fluffy white clouds scurried across the ground, and great craggy outcrops glistened against the silver-grey of the gum trees.

'It's breathtaking,' exclaimed Simon, the reins slack in his hand. He scanned the horizon, his eyes following the hills that turned a hazy blue in the distance. The view was nice, yet in truth he could not see the beauty of the countryside. He could not see the subtle changes of colour in the bush Jo had pointed to as they had climbed the hill, nor appreciate the vast ancient grandeur of the craggy outcrops. He saw only ugly grey rocks jutting out from a hillside covered with endless gum trees, the only tree he believed existed in Australia. To him these rounded hills could never thrill him as much as the isolated beauty of Burnham Overy Staithe or the winding country lanes of Norfolk. There he knew he belonged, but he doubted he could ever feel the same bond for this ancient endless land. He glanced at Jo, whose face was blazing with happiness, and wished with all his heart he could love this place as she did. The two horses nuzzled each other, then his nudged forward to nibble the grass. 'Why don't we stop here for a while?' he suggested. Quickly dismounting, he walked his horse to Jo's, grabbed her reins with his and held out his arms for her to dismount.

'I can do it on my own, really,' said Jo, filled with love, kicking her leg over the saddle.

'I know. You can do an awful lot on your own. It's just that I can't keep my hands off you,' admitted Simon.

Laughing, Jo slid into his arms. She unstrapped her riding hat, took it off and shook her hair free. Simon ran his fingers through her locks and her heartbeat quickened.

'Finally we're alone,' said Simon. Then he kissed her slowly.

'We'd better tether the horses,' Jo said breathlessly, her knees trembling.

Taking the reins from Simon, she hobbled the horses whilst he laid a rug on the grass. Then once more they were in each other's arms. Slowly sinking onto the rug they undressed, their mouths hungrily seeking each other, their bodies aching to unite. Fumbling with the catch of Jo's bra, Simon ran his fingers over her breasts, his breath coming in fast pants. Giving up in frustration he pulled it over her head and hungrily took one breast in his mouth, feeling her quivering against him. Finally naked, they made love as passionate and abandoned as they had in Kauai, their bodies entwined so neither knew where one stopped and the other began. All Simon's fears vanished. She was still there, the beautiful open flower he had loved in Hawaii. As he entered her he felt a triumph he had never experienced before and Jo responded to his passion, laughing and moaning in turn. Holding Jo to him, he rolled over on his back and pulled her down on him so she rode him, their hips thrusting faster and faster, his hands moulding her breasts, until they came together in an explosion of love. Panting and sweating they lay back on the rug, the only sounds their racing hearts and the buzzing of the bees in the big yellow flowers. Turning over, Simon gazed down at Jo with such intense love she felt the tears prick her eyes.

'I love you so much, sometimes I think I will go mad with longing,' he said, his fingers wandering over her warm silky soft skin. 'I watch you every day and I can hardly bear to keep my hands off you. I want to make love to you every night in our own bed and wake up breathing in your scent, not skulk in corners and sneak in hay barns and paddocks.'

Jo stroked his chin. 'I hate it too, Simon, but please be patient. Give me a little more time. Dad's doing well in rehab but he still needs me. You do know I adore you?' she asked, suddenly fearful. Simon nodded. He kissed her again and flopped over on his back. Jo stared down at him naked and tousled and utterly desirable and she gave a deep throaty chuckle. 'Anyway, it's fun skulking in corners. Didn't I satisfy you?'

'No, I want more,' demanded Simon, grabbing playfully at her and missing.

Bending over, Jo tickled his chest and then his face with her hair. Simon caught her by the arm and she toppled onto him. 'No, no! You've had your lot!' she cried wickedly, only reigniting Simon's ardour, then suddenly she relaxed and grinned mischievously. 'Take me, I'm yours.' She flung her arms wide in surrender and once more they made love, the sun warm on their bodies, the horses chewing contentedly close by.

Afterwards, satiated, they lay back on the rug and Jo watched the clouds scud across the clear blue sky and felt more blissfully content than she could remember. Bees hummed in the clover and the wind shimmered across the grass, the spring sun warm but not burning. Smiling contentedly Jo snuggled up to Simon, who covered them both with his shirt and together they drifted off to sleep.

Waking two hours later, Jo sat up refreshed. Gazing happily down at the still sleeping Simon she stretched luxuriously, thinking about their love-making, her body still tingling. He made her feel complete, loved, content. She wriggled carefully out of his arms, pulled on her clothes and walked over towards the ridge edge, staring out at the beauty of the place. Her legs felt hot where the sun had caught them and the fluffy clouds were darkening in the distance. They could have a thunderstorm later today but there was still plenty of the afternoon left.

Woken by Jo's movements Simon watched her for a moment, his arms behind his head, marvelling that such a beautiful, exciting girl should love him so much.

Quickly he dressed and walked quietly up behind her, sliding his arms around her. She smelled deliciously warm and sexy. 'How's the gorgeous Mrs Gordon-to-be?' he asked.

Simon's words sent a shiver of happiness through Jo. Turning in his arms she slid her hands around his neck and gazed into his green eyes, filled with love and convinced that somehow their problems would be solved.

'Blissfully happy,' she murmured, nuzzling into his shirt, 'and starving. Let's have some of that lunch Gran gave us.'

After lunch, still in a haze of love, they remounted the horses and spent the afternoon wandering along the different trails, reluctantly turning homeward as the shadows lengthened and the world took on a golden glow. The trail down through the trees was, if anything, more magical than their earlier climb; as the sun set the world became crystal clear before the impending storm, the tall trunks silhouetted against the fiery sky, thunder rumbling in the distance. As they meandered back across the open paddock to Dublin Park the first drops of rain started to fall.

Jo was only half glad to find that everything had run beautifully smoothly at the stables whilst she had been away. Part of her also felt slightly let down, until Pete told her in a quiet moment that, although they had coped, things just hadn't been the same with her away.

'It's your drive and energy that keeps us on track, pardon the pun,' he said and Jo felt immeasurably better. She told Simon what Pete had said as they walked up to the house at the end of the week, both carrying bundles of files she needed to wade through.

'Everyone's dispensable. It's a measure of how well you've done your job,' said Simon more sharply than he had intended. Since returning to Sydney and the confines of separate rooms, his frustration had returned with increasing vigour. He had also become extremely irritated with Bertie who had lately taken to dropping in at the house more often and had made a couple of teasing remarks that had been too close to the truth for comfort. Simon had had enough of Australia. Despite some of the phenomenal sunsets and vast open spaces Jo had shown him, he knew he could never live here despite it being Jo's home. It was time for him to go and he wanted to take Jo with him.

'Why don't we cut all the wedding bells fuss and get married at the local registry office and you fly home with me? We could have a big second wedding at home,' he suggested, catching Jo's arm as she reached to open the front door.

Jo turned to him, laughing. 'You're not serious?' Then with a shock she saw he was. 'I couldn't do it to Mum. She's had too many awful things happen to her recently. I couldn't steal the wedding from her—she's dying to put on a grand affair. Anyway, I

thought you were happy with the December date.'
She felt her heart sink as she saw his mouth tighten.
'Why don't we go and discuss it with Mum now?' she
said briskly, turning the key in the lock.

'Hello, darling, we're in the sitting room,' Nina
called out cheerfully.

Simon and Jo walked in to find Nina and Bertie
enjoying a predinner drink.

'Hello, little sis. Still enjoying your early morning
starts, mate?' asked Bertie, raising his brandy and
ginger ale to Simon then helping himself to some
salted cashews from the bowl at his elbow.

'You can get used to anything if you try,' replied
Simon smoothly, smiling at Nina. He found Bertie
infuriating and had constantly to bite his lip so as
not to respond to his barbs.

'We were just talking about wedding dates,' Jo
jumped in quickly, sensing Simon's antagonism. 'We
were thinking of maybe early next year. Dad's
making good progress and should be able to cope
with the long day by then, don't you think?' She
waited expecting opposition from Nina because she
had not been consulted first, but instead was pleas-
antly surprised by her mother's reply.

'That sounds wonderful, darling, although I
wouldn't put too much hope on your father being
too fit. But that aside it would work in well with my
plans.'

'Plans?' asked Jo, puzzled. Simon was looking
increasingly more unhappy.

'Yes, darling. Come and sit down and talk to us.
Bertie, organise them both a drink.' She patted the
arm of the chair next to her.

Jo's stomach tightened in alarm. Her mother was
being far too calm and sensible. Dumping her files
and her purse on the floor, she sank into one of the

big armchairs and tried to look relaxed.

'We've had an offer on the stables and have decided to take it,' announced Nina, taking a sip of chilled white wine. Immediately Jo shot bolt upright. 'Now don't start bullying me,' Nina went on quickly. 'Bertie and I have discussed it thoroughly while you two have been away and don't go thinking we did it all behind your back because we didn't. I only got the offer on Saturday and this is the first time we've all been together. Bertie and I both agree that under the circumstances it's the best thing to do.'

'Sell the stables! You can't sell the stables, Mum!' Jo was stunned. Furious, she turned on her brother. 'You've put her up to this. You've always hated the stables. What kind of half-baked semilegal hocus-pocus have you been filling Mum's head up with this time?'

'Leave your brother alone, Jo. No-one's put anyone up to anything. I'm perfectly capable of making up my own mind and it makes a lot of sense, particularly with you now talking about marrying and hopping off to live on the other side of the world.'

'She's got a point,' said Simon, laying a steadying hand on Jo's shoulder.

Angrily she shook it off. 'No, she hasn't. Those stables are what keeps Dad going.'

'They're a bloody millstone round Mum's neck,' chipped in Bertie, stung by Jo's taunt. 'They're losing money. People don't have the confidence in Kingsford Lodge they had when Dad was running it.' He reached for some more nuts and stuffed them in his mouth, thinking about the lump sum he'd receive from the sale. Part of it would solve his immediate gambling debts and the rest, cleverly invested, would bring in far more than the measly addition to the allowance he had persuaded his father to give him each month.

'Shut up, Bertie!' shouted Jo. 'How would you know? You haven't been near the place since Dad's accident.'

'I hear things,' Bertie snapped back. 'Face it, Jo. Dad's never going to run the stables again. You're a girl and the money would be far better invested in different properties so that if Dad comes home Mum can look after him without all that extra worrying.'

'What do you mean *if*?'

'The doctors are talking about the possibility of putting him into full-time care,' explained Nina wearily.

'Why?' exclaimed Jo, sitting down, her shoulders slumping.

Agitated, Nina twisted her heavy silver bracelet around her wrist, avoiding her daughter's gaze. 'I was going to tell you after we'd talked about the stables, darling. The doctors are very worried about your father. It's his funny speech. They think he may never fully recover and be able to look after himself or speak properly.' She paused. 'No-one can be sure of the extent of brain damage he has suffered,' she added reluctantly.

'She means Dad may not be all there,' added Bertie helpfully.

Jo shot him a murderous look. 'You don't believe any of that rubbish, Mum,' she scoffed. 'You can't— he's going to get better.' Then another frightening thought struck her. 'You didn't accept the offer, did you?'

'My mind's made up. The stables have to go. We can talk about all the rest later,' replied Nina quickly, her face tense as she glanced briefly at Simon. Then the phone rang. 'That'll be Joan,' she cried, scuttling out of the room in relief.

'Bloody hell, Bertie! You didn't let Mum accept, did you?' fumed Jo leaping up and standing over him.

'I think it's the only sensible thing to do . . . Get off! No, I didn't!' he yelped as Jo shook him violently by the shoulders.

Simon took a sip of his drink, wishing he felt differently, but he had to agree with Bertie. Selling Kingsford Lodge seemed the sensible thing to do, and that way it would no longer be crucial for Jo to stay in Australia.

As though sensing Simon's thoughts, Jo took a step back from Bertie, the hairs on her arms rising. 'I need some fresh air,' she cried, the room suddenly too hot, and stumbled outside.

'What do you think, mate? You don't really think Jo can run a successful racing stable by herself, do you?' Bertie asked Simon, brushing bits of nut from his shirt.

'She's doing it,' replied Simon curtly. Resisting the temptation to thump Bertie for being such a twerp, he went in search of Jo. He found her marching furiously up and down beside the fish pond.

'She can't sell the stables! She can't! It'd kill Dad. The stables are what keeps him trying every day.' Jo clasped her arms tightly across her chest. 'They're talking about removing the one thing he lives for.' She looked up at Simon, her eyes tormented. 'What am I going to do, Simon? How am I going to stop them? Dad's doing fine. He understands everything I say. He just can't tell me yet, that's all. The doctors are wrong.' She grabbed both his hands and shook them, as if by doing so she would change things.

'Whether they're wrong or right doesn't matter. You have to get on with your own life and this is your chance,' said Simon, his eyes searching hers. 'You're so big-hearted, my darling girl, you want to fix up the world.'

Jo dropped Simon's hands as though they had burnt her. 'I thought there was something wrong in there. You think he's off with the fairies too, don't you? Not you, please not you as well.' She looked up at him in desperation. 'I can't leave him now. We're going to have to postpone the wedding until we've sorted this mess out.'

Simon shook her. 'Jo, stop!' he commanded. 'When are you going to think about us? When is it our turn? You can't undo what has happened and you can't live your parents' lives for them. They have to sort it out themselves. Marry me, darling. We were so happy in Norfolk. Let's get married as we planned early in the New Year. I could get time off work. Then we could buy the old rectory and get on with our lives. I'll even get my family to fly out here for it—the lot of them.' He gave a harsh laugh. 'That should frighten the living daylights out of you all.'

'You have to give me more time,' begged Jo, the words a death knell in her own ears. 'I have to convince Mum not to sell the stables. In another six months Dad'll be talking and more mobile. He could even be overseeing track work.' Her voice was suddenly hopeful.

Simon stiffened. 'How much time do you need? When he gets better will it be another six months? What if your dad never gets better?' he said angrily, releasing her abruptly.

'He'll get better,' she shouted at him. 'Why can't we live in Australia?'

'We've been over all that a thousand times. You know if I left the bank now it'd wreck my career,' replied Simon impatiently. 'Give me a few years, and if you still want to we'll up sticks and move to Australia.' He had already explained that he had verbally agreed to remain with the bank for the next three years even though the prospect didn't thrill him. His uncle was grooming him to be one of the bank's directors, but it was more loyalty to his father than enticement of the position that had persuaded him to agree to continue the family tradition. It was secure and would give them the lifestyle he wanted them to have and there were no obvious similar openings he could see for him in Australia. For a few seconds he vacillated, but being the youngest director ever did have its own appeal. Maybe in five years' time the opportunities would be there and he'd feel different about living in Australia.

Jo started to tremble. It was as though an invisible wall had come between them and it terrified her. 'So you don't mind if I leave my family and my career and live with you in your country, but you won't give up yours for me.' She folded her arms again and paced back and forth, trying to quell the rising panic.

'Oh come on, Jo, can't you see what you are doing to yourself? You won't let go. You've proved you can run the stables on your own, your dad's being cared for, now let's get on with our life together.' He attempted to take her in his arms but she pushed him angrily away.

'What d'you mean, I won't let go? What sort of an arrogant comment is that?' she demanded.

'If it sounded arrogant it was never meant to be. I love you so much I'm terrified I'm losing you,' he cried, his eyes tortured as he realised that selling the stables was not the escape he had at first seen it to be.

'How can you ever think that? Haven't I shown

you over and over that I love you? But I can't leave Dad, not now, not with all this mess.' Jo's eyes were filled with tears.

Simon hunched his shoulders and plunged his hands deep in his trouser pockets. 'I know that and I understand.' The truth he didn't want to see was now crystal clear in his mind. 'I wish to God I didn't. I wish to God I could be the selfish bastard I want to be and say to hell with them all. Choose. Leave your parents to sort out their own problems. Marry me tomorrow and we'll fly back to England and buy that old rectory and start a family and I'll build you a stable round the back, but I can't Jo . . . I can't, because I know if I did it would tear us apart.' He paused and Jo felt a sickening churning in her stomach. 'Right now, my darling, you don't need me,' he ended quietly.

'What d'you mean, I don't need you? You're the one person who has kept me sane through all of this.' She grabbed at his shirt, her knuckles white, cold fingers of fear clutching at her heart.

Simon kept his hands in his pockets. He stepped back, kicking a clod of dirt with one shoe. 'I've watched you, Jo. I saw it the first day you took me to Kingsford Lodge. You handle it all—your father, your mother, the stables, me, any crisis the world throws up at you. More than that, you love what you are doing.' His voice cracked. He reached out and then let his hands drop back by his sides in a gesture of hopelessness. 'If I forced you to choose between me and your dad and he died or you lost the stables, you'd never forgive me. Until all this is sorted out, there is no place for us and I can't sort it out for you. Only you can do that. You don't have a choice. I wish to God I didn't understand you so well.'

Jo had gone deathly pale. 'Don't say that, Simon. There is a place for us. I love you so much. I want to be with you, every part of me wants to be with you, to be your wife, to have your children, you know that.' The anguish in her voice cut Simon to the quick. 'But when I look into my dad's eyes I see life. We talk without words. I'm the only one that believes in him, Simon. He's just a bed number to the nurses. And you saw how Mum and Bertie feel. Dad knows that. If I leave him, he'll just give up.' Her last words came out as a stifled sob. Gently Simon picked up her left hand and ran his fingers over the emerald and diamond ring.

'I know, my darling girl, and that is why I'm going back home,' said Simon, the sadness in his voice breaking Jo's heart.

'What are you trying to tell me?' she whispered, twisting her engagement ring round and round, her voice barely audible.

'I'm telling you that right now it's not working, Jo. Don't hear this as blame, but until you have worked all this out, our love will only suffocate. I can't help you now and I need to go back to my job and get some semblance of normality into my life again. When you're ready, ring me and we can plan again.'

Jo's heart went cold as she heard the horrible ring of truth in his words. He was right. She didn't have a choice. She didn't have a choice because each time she walked into that convalescent home she saw that she was the reason her father kept fighting, and now she had to fight to save the stables. But underlying it all, even her love for Simon, was her deep need to win her father's approval, to prove that she was capable of keeping the stables running, to gain his respect and become a great trainer like him, despite being female. For an eternity Jo stared at Simon's hand. Then very slowly she slid the dazzling ring off her finger and held it out to him, her eyes filled with pain. 'I love you and I will go on loving you forever, but I don't know how much time I'm going to need and I can't stop your life too,' she said numbly.

Simon looked at her and then the ring and then back to her face. 'Don't be so final, my sweet girl. I'll always love you too and there may come a time when it's right for us to be together again. Ring me if you need me. I'll be there for you.' He gathered her protectively into his arms and kissed away the tears that spilled over and ran down her cheeks. 'Let's enjoy the last few days we have together.'

'You go in. I need to be alone for a minute,' she whispered shakily. Simon kissed her tenderly once more on the forehead and walked back into the house.

Wiping the back of her hand across her eyes, Jo watched him go, the pain in her heart unbearable. Curling her fingers round her engagement ring she crushed it so the diamonds dug into her flesh. He had said *may* not *will*. She pressed her fists to her cheeks and tried to stifle the sobs that pushed up from the very depths of her being. Such a short while ago they had been so happy, so full of joy for the future. Now that future was in tatters. She wanted to run after Simon and tell him that she would marry him, to jump on that plane with him and blow the consequences, but she kept seeing her father's face. She kept remembering the way his eyes lit up whenever she told him about the stables and the horses and the funny little day-to-day events, and how he clutched at her arm when she got up to leave, mumbling over and over the same incomprehensible three-word phrase that her mother saw as proof that he would never recover and that she was so convinced was just the beginning of speech, and she knew she could never walk out on her dad.

Chapter Nineteen

JO HAD LITTLE time to indulge her grief over Simon. The day after he flew out of Sydney, Arctic Gold chipped a bone in his off hind leg and Flighty Dame threw a shoe winding up to the gallops. Frantic at her mother's determination to sell Kingsford Lodge, furious at Bertie, and concerned that if word got out about her mother's intentions, more owners would take their horses away, Jo strode around the stable grim-faced, demanding higher standards at track work and snapping at everyone, refusing to explain even to Pete why she was so bad-tempered.

She ached to hear Simon's voice and feel his caresses. Each night in bed she wondered how she could get through another day without him and each morning she stared the same truth in the face that stopped her from picking up the phone. It would hurt too much. She daren't face the loneliness she knew would flood over her after they had spoken, and anyway, what could she say? 'I love you, I want to marry you, but we have to live in Australia'? What was the point until there was some hope?

Then, halfway through December, there was a

reprieve. Nina announced that the offer on the stables had been withdrawn.

'Stupid man. Why can't these silly people organise their finances before they start messing people around?' she said irritably. 'What's wrong with exchanging contracts on Christmas Eve anyway?'

Jo turned away to hide the relief that flooded across her face. 'I think I might just pop down to the stables and see how everything's going,' she said, trying to sound casual. Whistling to Sam, she helped him into the car and roared out of the driveway. Lately, on top of everything else, Nina had started to complain that he was pining for Jo while she was out, so she had begun taking him regularly with her to the stables. Winks had made the dog a wooden slat bed with a couple of old horse blankets on it, which he tucked in the corner under the stairs to his small flat above the stables, and from there Sam lay happily watching the goings-on or basked in a sunny spot in the courtyard.

'We're keeping the stables, Sammy old fella,' Jo cried jubilantly, hardly daring to believe it. She hooted at a truck that swerved in front of her. 'Someone up there must be looking after us.'

Shouting a greeting to one of the strappers leading two horses back from their afternoon exercise, Jo dived into the office to go through her messages with Gloria.

'Oh, and two Melbourne owners rang interested in joining the stables,' said Gloria, handing Jo their details. She looked up at Jo. 'You're very happy this afternoon.'

'It's a lovely sunny day,' said Jo brightly, reading the notes about the owners, glad that she had not mentioned the offer on the stables to Gloria. It would only have unsettled her.

With the sale of the stables no longer a threat hanging over her, Jo's longing for Simon intensified. Forgetting his lack of understanding about her passion for training and horses, she kept remembering how he had held her and kissed her and told her that he would be there for her. She longed to share all the little daily dramas with him, to laugh and tell him about the new horses, to find out what he was up to and maybe even dream a bit. She decided she was being silly refusing to ring him for fear of a loneliness and longing which surely could get no worse. Finally she rang him on Christmas Eve, her heart pounding as she tried to frame a sentence in her head.

'The Gordon household,' said a bright, very English female voice.

Jo could hear the sounds of revelry in the background. 'Hello, Mrs Gordon. It's Joanna Kingsford ringing from Australia.'

'Jo! What a surprise. How nice! How is everyone in Australia?' She pronounced it Awe-stralia.

Jo laughed. Mrs Gordon was such a cheery, welcoming person. For a few minutes they chatted and then Jo asked if she could speak to Simon. There was an awkward pause at the other end of the phone and Jo thought she detected a small sniff.

'I was hoping you wouldn't ask that,' said Mrs Gordon, her whole tone changed.

A tight pain gripped Jo's chest and she started to shake. 'I'm sorry, I didn't mean to intrude,' she said quickly, every imaginable scenario rushing through her head. Perhaps he was back with Lelia, or he was seeing someone else, or he had been killed.

'No, no. There's nothing wrong. It's just that no-one knows where he is,' explained Mrs Gordon quickly. 'I keep telling myself one would know if anything was really wrong.' There was another pause. Jo was convinced Mrs Gordon was crying. 'He came home and told us about, about well . . . how you couldn't leave Awe-stralia and all that sort of thing. I was so sorry to hear it, dear . . . Then he said he had to go away and do some thinking and that he'd be in touch and, well, basically he's just vanished off the face of the earth. I would have expected to hear from him by now, but not a word, but I'm sure we will.' Jo's heart missed several beats.

'It's really funny,' continued Mrs Gordon bravely. 'We bought this enormous bunch of mistletoe; you see, he always insisted on having it hanging off the big light in the hall. It's so strange not having him here for Christmas but, well, that's how it is . . . I'm sure everything will be fine,' she finished lamely.

Jo didn't know what to say. He said he'd be there for her and he wasn't. He wasn't there for anyone. 'Oh dear. Well, Merry Christmas,' she said, embarrassed, and put the phone down. Why had she ever believed their love could possibly last across the oceans? Maybe the whole trip was just a holiday romance. Yet the precious love they had shared had been real, she knew it. Deep down she was certain. If only she'd had a choice. Miserable, she went back to finish wrapping up her Christmas presents.

A few days later a desolate Jo stared across the garden from her seat at the table on the veranda, the summer sunshine hot on her cheeks. She had not shed a tear since ringing Simon, but the misery of Mrs Gordon's revelation ate away inside her. Her mother had dismissed the whole thing as typical of young people these days and vanished over to Joan's house. Beside Jo, old Sam lay sleeping, his muzzle resting across her feet, his warmth comforting.

She toyed wearily with a half-eaten roll already crisp in the sun's heat. Yesterday Archie had won five of his eight races, and two more owners had joined the stables in the last week, yet Jo could find nothing to be joyful about. She longed to be able to talk through her misery over Simon with Rick. He'd have jollied her out of it, put it in perspective. She hadn't thought about her brother for a while, but recently thoughts of him kept popping into her head. Once last week she had caught herself turning round to speak to him. She had felt foolish but oddly comforted. Sam was acting different too. Usually content to rest in the sun once she had fed him and given him his heart tablets and anti-inflammatories for his arthritis, he had taken to following her around, even in the house, hobbling close or, as he was this morning, resting against her as if he understood her intense suffering.

'I love him so much, Sam, you know,' she whispered, Simon's laughing face clear in her mind. Salt tears rolled silently down each cheek and splashed onto her lap. Sam lumbered up and pushed his muzzle in her lap, whining and licking at her hand. 'I'm fine, Sam, I'm fine, you silly old creature,' she choked, pressing her cheek momentarily against the dog's fur as he tried to lick away her tears, his actions only making the tears flow faster.

Patting Sam, Jo straightened and lifted her eyes to the big ghost gum, watching the breeze rustle through the long grey-green leaves, her fingers reducing the bread roll to a pile of crumbs. Turning round twice, Sam flopped back on top of Jo's feet with a grunt. Jo gave a half laugh, half sob. Then a flash of red caught her eye as a crimson rosella darted across the garden into the tree and hung precariously to one of its thin branches. Jo recognised the bird as one of the pair that returned each year to the garden. Joey and Chloe she had named them. That was probably Joey. Chloe, the female, was shyer. Tears blurred Jo's vision anew as she remembered showing Simon the birds and how he had mended the old tin tray that served as a bird table and hung it back up on the veranda away from the preying neighbourhood cats. She tossed some crumbs towards the rail and called softly. Joey flew over. Perching on the rail he cocked his head on one side and stared at her with one beady black eye.

Quietly Jo stood up and walked towards the bird, holding out her hand. Often he would hop onto her finger, but today he fluttered his wings and flew up into an overhanging branch, opening and closing his beak, calling to Jo in his distinctive ringing tone. Then Jo saw Chloe in the branches. One wing was hanging down obviously broken and she had lost some tail feathers. It was as though Joey was sharing his fears for his partner with her. Distracted from her own misery, Jo disappeared inside, rapidly reappearing with some bird seed which she shook onto the tin tray; then she waited, talking quietly. Joey was still hopping back and forth, watching her from the branch. After a few moments he darted down and pecked up a mouthful of seeds, flew back to Chloe and fed her. For the next ten minutes Jo watched him fly back and forth, feeding his injured mate. She felt enormously comforted by these two beautiful creatures. They were part of this place she called home, a place that moved her deeply even in her misery. How could she ever leave it for England?

At the end of December, just when Jo was starting to feel stronger, more optimistic, Nina agreed for Charlie to be put into an old people's home.

'Don't do this to him, please,' begged Jo, but nothing Jo said, or screamed, could stop her.

'You are young and loving but he's not going to get better. Your dad's never going to be the man we used to know,' said Nina tremulously. She had agonised over the decision herself but she did not have the blind faith in his recovery that her daughter had. 'The doctors advise it's for the best for all of us,' she said with finality.

The day Charlie was admitted Jo knew would haunt her forever. Something died in his eyes as they wheeled him into his neatly furnished room in the modernised home. Jo could hardly bear to meet his gaze as he stared up at them, helpless and bemused.

'They'll take really good care of you here, Charlie, darling. You'll be fine, and one of us will be in to see you as often as we can,' shouted Nina as though talking to some half-deaf child. Close to tears, she gave him a peremptory kiss on the cheek, her fingers nervously stroking his hands, Jack Ellis beside her, devastated to see his friend reduced to this but determined to support Charlie's family as best he could.

Leaning down to kiss her father, Jo choked back the tears.

'Don't you dare give up, Dad,' she ordered between gritted teeth, gripping his good hand so hard he flinched. 'Now you hear what I say, we'll get you out of here—soon,' she promised, anger churning inside her.

Returning home she stormed out onto the veranda, hating the world, wishing she didn't feel so helpless. As she stood, arms folded, trying to gather her thoughts, Joey swooped down and landed neatly on the old tin plate and started chattering at her. A few seconds later an entirely recovered Chloe alighted beside him, fluffing out her bright red feathers, and the two kissed, their beaks tapping against each other. Jo felt a lump rise in her throat at this obvious display of love and at the healing powers of nature. In that instant she vowed to get her father home by the end of the year.

Despite her pain, Jo's life quickly fell back into its regular routine with Archie continuing to win races and Pete helping to manage the stables. Although they were still down in horse numbers, Jo's schedule was full. Travelling all around Australia Kingsford Lodge collected wins in Brisbane, Tasmania and Melbourne, as well as in some of the smaller country races. With the winnings Jo purchased two top yearlings and fell in love with a gangly weanling called Sleeper. By Night Sky out of Lightning Strike, there was something in Sleeper's eye that reminded her of Outsider. Ugly, ungainly and from a relatively unknown stud, he cost Jo a measly two thousand dollars, yet his breeding was solid and she sensed a hidden power in him that even Archie found hard to believe. He also had the strangest habit. At track work, kept moving he streaked away, yet as soon as his training was over he reverted to a dopey, inelegant beast who appeared half asleep. The purchase of Sleeper became the butt of jokes around the other stables but Jo ignored them, believing in her own intuition. At Kingsford he quickly earned the stable name Dopey.

'What have we here, bloody Snow White and the

Seven Dwarfs?' boomed Freddy Zinman marching up to Arctic Gold. 'There's Grumpy here and that new one, The Doc, and Dopey.' A horse sneezed and Jo stiffled a giggle.

'And Prince Charming don't forget,' called a cheery voice Jo could have sworn she recognised. She turned in amazement as Phillip Gregg, the vet from Denman, strode towards them down the walkway between the stalls. Jo blushed a deep crimson remembering the last time they met.

'Ah yes, Jo. I'd like you to meet my new assistant, Phillip Gregg,' said Freddy pompously, rocking back and forth on his shiny leather boots. 'Bit of a wag but very thorough. From now on Phillip'll be your regular vet. I, of course, will continue to take an interest and if there are any dire emergencies, naturally you can call on me, but I am taking a bit of a back seat in the day-to-day routine.'

'Actually, we've met before, Freddy. I patched up this old fella when he was kicked by a horse at Miss Kingsford's grandmother's stud,' said Phillip quickly, seeing Jo's confusion. 'We're old mates, aren't we, Sam old boy?' He crouched down and fondled Sam who was wagging his tail and sniffing him.

Jo relaxed, seeing only friendliness in his gentle grey eyes. As tall and broad shouldered as she remembered, a healthy tan to his cheeks, and wide capable hands, Jo decided Prince Charming was not such a bad name for him. She also felt a strange sense of relief. Today was the first time in several weeks she had seen Freddy Zinman and it bothered her. When Jo had returned to Australia Freddy was still turning up religiously to the stables every morning at seven-thirty sharp to check the Kingsford horses as he had always done. However, over the last few months, as Charlie struggled in rehab, Doctor Zinman had become gradually more elusive, sending one or other of his assistants instead. It seemed no coincidence to Jo that after Charlie's admission to the home the vet was now bowing out of his responsibilities at the stables. It was hurtful, but at least now Jo would have a regular vet with whom she could consult and one whose skills she trusted.

'Well, I'll let you take over,' boomed Freddy. Giving Arctic Gold a pat on the rump, he swept grandly out of the stables.

'Hi, Jo, how are you?' said Phillip shyly after Freddy had gone. 'I was joking about the Prince Charming bit. The blokes gave me a bit of a hard time at the clinic, country boy and all that, so I just go along with it.' He went red. 'Don't worry, you aren't in any danger of me sweeping you up in my arms and riding off into the sunset, although with your colour hair Snow White's pretty spot on.'

'I'm just happy because I know you're good at what you do,' Jo stuttered, blushing deeply, an awkward silence falling between them as they both remembered their kiss.

'Well, I'd better do some work now I'm here. Tell me what's been happening with your horses,' said Phillip, rubbing his hands together, lessening the tension between them.

Jo relaxed. 'Let me introduce you to the whole family. We've got a few characters here,' she said cheerily.

Phillip proved just the tonic Jo needed. Excited to be working with such great horses, he always arrived early to do his inspections and often stayed to talk after he had finished. It gave Jo a lift to work with someone who so obviously loved and respected the animals as she did. Mostly they discussed the horses, but as they got to know one another better they started chatting about general things and Jo discovered Phillip was extremely knowledgeable about all sorts of topics. Happy to have someone so reliable to turn to, Jo gradually let down her guard, sharing more with him than she had ever shared with Pete, or could share with Simon because of his lack of understanding of horses and training. It was as though once more she had a brother to talk to and his gentle, teasing reference to her as Snow White when no-one else was around became a silly joke they shared that strengthened the growing bond between them.

'I just know Dopey's got enormous possibilities, but he needs a lot of patience. He's either up and gone or he's as dopey as his nickname,' she confided to Phillip at the end of track work one day early in March. He had taken to coming up two or three times a week to watch the horses at work and to help out with riding if Jo needed it. Jo found herself looking around for him in the mornings. 'Can you have a good look at his shoulders when you check him out this morning. I think there's some stiffness there that shouldn't be there,' she said as they headed towards the cars and the stables.

'Maybe we need to look at the food supplements. Sometimes a small change can make all the difference,' said Phillip, closing his bag. Jo called over to Pete to get the food chart, at the same time looking around for Sam.

'Let's have a cup of coffee in my office and we'll go over the food list in comfort. By the way, did Sam say hi to you this morning?' she asked, suddenly concerned. He had been very stiff this morning when she had helped him out of the car. Phillip shook his head. Jo glanced over to his usual spot under the stairway but he wasn't there. 'That's strange. Sam! Sam!' she whistled, her concern building. Looking around she strode into her office and saw him beside her father's big old leather desk.

'There you are, Sammy old boy. You frightened me. D'you want a bit of a hand,' she called, hurrying across to him as he struggled to get up, his back legs refusing to work. Then she saw the fear and bewilderment in his eyes. 'Oh God! Phillip!' she screamed, running over to Sam.

Phillip was already at her side. Gently moving Jo, he knelt down beside Sam and stroked him, his hands working swiftly over the old dog's body. 'Not feeling the best, eh, old fella?' he said massaging Sam's neck. Sam whimpered, his head resting on the floor, his eyes searching Jo's face. Phillip straightened up. 'It's his back legs. They've given out. See the swelling,' he said, trying to sound calm. He hated this part of veterinary work and seeing the anguish in Jo's eyes made it harder for him than ever before.

Jo stood beside him, her body controlled but her eyes wide with misery. She had dealt with horses in far greater pain than Sam was now, but he was too close to her. She bit hard on her bottom lip as Phillip gently explained what Jo had already guessed. Sam was an old dog and his body had finally worn out.

'Isn't there anything you can do?' she whispered. Yet she knew in her heart Sam's time had come. Phillip shook his head. Sam was still watching Jo, his eyes pleading for her help.

'It's the kindest thing you can do for him now. It's very quick and peaceful. He will just drift off to sleep. He won't feel any pain,' said Phillip. 'Do you want to stay with him while I give the injection?'

Jo nodded, her throat tight. 'You're such a great dog, Sam, such a great friend,' she said quietly, kneeling down and stroking the dog's head. Dry-eyed she held Sam's head in her hands as Phillip administered the lethal dose, her hand rhythmically stroking his soft yellow coat. Sam looked at her in absolute trust, the pain gradually fading from his eyes as the medicine took hold. Then he closed his eyes and she knew he had gone. For a long while she just sat gently stroking him and talking to him until, finally, her hands were still.

'He was a great dog,' said Phillip compassionately, bringing Jo back to the present.

She looked up. 'If someone had to do it, I'm glad it was you,' she said, her whole body tense. Sitting back on her heels she started muttering about the feed list and meetings.

Unable to bear the pain in her eyes, Phillip knelt down beside her and put his arm around her.

'It's all right, Snow White, you don't have to be brave all the time. Let it out. I know how much you loved him.' His words triggered a release in Jo. Turning to Phillip, she let out a howl of grief.

'He was part of the family for so long,' she cried, her shoulders shaking. 'He was the last little piece of Rick.' Then all the pent-up misery and despair she had kept locked inside for so many months poured out. Wrapping his strong arms around her, Phillip held her shaking body tight to him, stroking her and letting her cry until, finally, the sobs subsided and she slumped against him.

'You've had a rough trot for one person, Snow White.' He smoothed the hair back from her face, longing to kiss away her tears and to bring a smile back to her dear face. He had never stopped loving her since that first kiss, yet he was under no illusions that his love would ever be returned. Honest and up-front, Jo had explained her love for Simon and he had respected her for it and understood her hurt. He had his own pain loving her, but he would rather have her friendship than nothing.

'I'm just a cry-baby feeling sorry for myself,' said Jo at last with a sniff.

Phillip handed her his handkerchief. 'Blow,' he ordered and Jo did as he said. Then for a moment longer she allowed herself to rest against the warmth of his body. He was so loving and generous and he made her feel that she didn't have to carry the whole weight of life on her shoulders.

Straightening, she pulled away. 'You are such a dear friend, Phillip. I'm lucky. Thank you,' she gulped, 'Sam loved you too.'

After Sam's death Jo seesawed back and forth between good weeks and bad ones, yet felt more confident with Phillip around.

Running late she hurried into the house one morning to shower and change for an appointment and was surprised to find Nina already dressed and downstairs in the sunroom in a mood for action Jo hadn't seen since before she had left for England. Helping herself to a cup of tea and some toast she perched on the wide window sill and started eating quickly, the sun hot against her back.

'You're up early Mum. Something special on today?' she commented between mouthfuls, hoping her mother wasn't revving herself up for something crazily inappropriate.

'Not really, darling. I just didn't feel like sleeping in,' replied Nina brightly. Fiddling first with her spoon then the chunky gold bracelet Charlie had given her several years back, she clasped her hands together in a determined gesture and stared at her daughter. 'You're not overdoing it are you, darling? You've been working so hard since you got back from England. I don't know that I can do much with the stables but . . . Well, there's got to be more I can do to help. . . '

Jo stared at her mother in shock. The day had already started badly with Arctic Gold, who was supposed to be racing in Perth in three weeks, going lame at track work, then she'd had to sack one of the strappers, and she was flying interstate today. She had twenty minutes to shower, change, pack and get to a meeting she wasn't looking forward to. Now her mother was behaving alarmingly out of character. For a split second she almost unburdened the lot on Nina. Instead she said, 'You do help, Mum, and anyway you have to be with Dad. How was dinner? How's Joan?' She glanced at her watch. Nina's attitude change had shaken her, but she didn't have time to cope with her mother's problems right now.

'Dinner was interesting. Joan's up in Brisbane with the grandchildren.' Nina paused, looking steadily at her daughter. 'I've never really told you how grateful I am at the way you've kept the stables going since your dad's accident, darling.' Her fingers worked harder on the thick gold links, her eyes growing moist. 'It's been so hard for us all since Charlie . . . since . . . but, I . . . Do you think I send out wrong messages sometimes . . . ?' she gulped. Jo tried to stay calm, aware the seconds were ticking away.

'About what, Mum?'

Nina shook her bracelet down her arm and smoothed her hair, blinking back the tears. 'Oh nothing, darling. It was just something Jack said last night but it doesn't matter. Sometimes it takes a close friend to shake you out of yourself. More importantly, are you packed and ready to go?' She stretched out her hand to Jo.

'I haven't even started and I'm supposed to be the other side of Sydney in forty minutes,' Jo replied agitatedly, not even wanting to think of the implications of her mother's words. 'You couldn't . . . ?'

'You jump into a shower, darling, I'll see to it,' Nina cut in, raising her hand as Jo started to talk. 'No, trust me for once, darling. I'm your mother and I know what looks good on you. Go and organise yourself for your meeting. I'll get your luggage to the airport in time for you to catch your plane.'

'Thank you, Mum, I love you,' cried Jo, amazed. Fifteen minutes later, feeling strangely relieved, grateful and fearful all at the same time, Jo gave her mother a hug, checked she had her ticket and left. Nina watched her go, resting her fingers where Jo's lips had brushed her cheek. Until today she had not realised how much she took her children's love for granted. As she had sorted through Jo's clothes and packed them neatly in the suitcase, she thought again of last night.

The evening had started strangely. Nothing tangible, just a feeling Nina had. For want of a better explanation, once in the restaurant the energy between her and Jack had felt different. Desperately lonely and drained from the constant strain of watching Charlie go steadily downhill, coupled with her financial worries, Nina hadn't noticed how much she had come to rely on Jack. A natural party animal, with the wine and muted glamour of her surroundings, she had enjoyed her meal, glad of the extra energy emanating around them. Talking about their children, laughing over inconsequential things, she allowed herself a tiny oasis amidst the present misery of her life and thought nothing of it when Jack invited her back to his house for a nightcap. Then as they sat together on the veranda drinking coffee and liqueurs, listening to the frogs in the dark and enjoying the night air, Jack had slid his arm around her and tried to kiss her. For a moment she couldn't believe what was happening. Then she pulled away, incredulous. She was even more shocked at his reaction.

'Well that was what you wanted. Don't deny it. You've been sending me these signals all evening, Neene.' The use of Charlie's pet name was the final affront. Leaping up from her seat Nina swept towards the door, but not before Jack had grabbed her again.

'Only Charlie calls me Neene,' she gasped, eyes glittering.

'Stop playing games, Neene, you're a grown woman. If you didn't want what I can offer...' Impatiently, Jack let her go and stood back, shoving his hands deep in his pockets. Nina's hand flew to her mouth, her eyes wide with consternation that she could have led him so completely astray.

'Jack, I'm so sorry, I had no idea. I never meant to send any signals. I'm sorry, I'm really sorry,' she said shakily. She took a step towards him. 'You are such a great friend, Jack, I'm so grateful to you. I just enjoy your company. I feel safe with you, but I never meant you to think I wanted anything more. I'm so sorry.' For a few moments the two stared at one another. Jack shrugged and relaxed slightly.

'You're a very beautiful woman, Nina. I'm a grown man with feelings. What was I supposed to think?' Then he had picked up his keys and driven her home.

Nina snapped the catches shut and lifted the

suitcase onto the floor. For a moment she stared at the photo on Jo's dressing table, one of the whole family when Rick was alive. A lump rose in her throat as she thought of the girl and all she had been through, and how she had kept the family going while her mother flailed around for someone to lean on. Nina was no longer under any illusions about her own behaviour since Charlie's accident. She had a daughter who had more courage and strength of spirit than she had ever had. Jack had made that quite clear. It was what he hadn't said that had hit home the most, but she was grateful. She was a grown woman and it was time to take the brunt of the load.

The racing at Ascot in Perth was going well. Phillip had examined Arctic Gold thoroughly before Jo left Sydney and had deemed him fit to race. The horse had acclimatised quickly and Archie had already won one race and been beaten by a nose in his second. With three strong horses in the next race and Archie in top form, Jo thought the day was going to be a real winner. Then eight hundred metres from the finishing post Jo watched in horror as, sabotaged by another jockey, Archie fell. Although his injuries were not severe he was confined to bed for two months, during which the wins at Kingsford Lodge dropped dramatically and the media, who were showing an increasing interest in Jo's activities, leaped on the misfortune.

Ignoring the snipes about Archie being the one running the stables and Jo being the token head, Jo continued to train, barking out orders at track work, struggling to find good jockeys to tide her over while Archie was out of action, thankful that at least in amongst all of the business of getting her father settled in the home there had been no further mention of selling Kingsford Lodge. Archie struggled back to fitness and put himself through a punishing training programme. Long months later but once more back in the saddle and confident on Flighty Dame, a newcomer to the stables they were trying out at a country meeting, horse and jockey leaped out of the barrier. Jo crossed her fingers. Seconds later the crowd gasped in horror as the highly strung thoroughbred went berserk and tried to vault a fence. Misjudging the height, the terrified animal smashed into the rail, throwing Archie who was knocked unconscious. Flown back to Sydney with three broken ribs, a broken leg and broken pelvis, he announced to Jo when he was fit enough to be visited that he intended to retire from racing.

'Nothin' personal, Jo. I'm just getting too old for this game,' he explained sadly.

Jo nodded, hiding her despondency. The press would have a field day.

'That's it! I've had it up to here with those darned horses,' cried Nina, throwing her hands in the air, when Jo broke the news to her. 'First Rick, then Charlie, now Archie. With him gone we'll be lucky to get half the price that other silly man offered. I'm putting the stables on the market while we can still sell it and I'm doing it this minute.' She reached for the phone.

Jo clamped her hand over her mother's outstretched fingers. 'Mum, these things happen in racing. It's a risk you take, you know that. It's all part of the sport.' She didn't need Nina to tell her the struggle she faced without Archie.

'Sport! You call it a sport—crazy horses killing

people!' She felt oddly calm and in control, despite her outburst and fear of what lay before her. 'It was only because Archie stayed with us that I didn't sell the stables before,' she said shortly, removing her hand. She started to dial. Jo blanched. Her lips tightened, her mother's calm was panicking her, her words salt on an already open wound. 'This is not an impetuous decision, you know Jo,' continued Nina, seeing Jo's reaction. 'I have given a lot of thought to what this family should do and there are a whole lot of reasons why selling the stables is the best way to go.' Her face softened as she looked at her daughter. 'One of the main ones being you need the chance of a life of your own.'

'But this is my life, Mum! I run the stables, not Archie. I buy the horses, I supervise the training, I am responsible when things go wrong. Archie is an employee and I knew one day he would want to retire. Please, Mum—don't sell!'

'You may think that but I've heard what they really think at the track. I lunch with their wives, remember. They're saying your efforts are a joke,' retaliated Nina, incensed by the way Jo dismissed her opinion, the receiver hovering limply in her hand. Then she saw Jo's stark expression and wished with all her heart she could take back her words. She wanted to support, not hurt. 'No, no, darling, what I mean is we don't need any more people sneering at this family right now. . . ' she stumbled, but Jo wasn't listening. All she wanted was to make her mother delay the call. Searching frantically, she kept coming up with blanks. Finally she took a deep breath.

'Mum, I know that this is unreasonable and I can't think of any good reason why you should, but give me one more chance. I'm off to see Dad now. Wait until I get back before you phone anyone about selling the stables, please. Let me ask Dad first,' she pleaded.

Nina stopped, shocked. 'You poor child. You really believe he's going to get better, don't you?' she whispered, dropping the phone back onto the hook. Slumping against the bench she rubbed her fingers across her aching forehead. Her own daughter was in total denial. The doctors had warned her it could happen. 'All right darling. You talk to your father first,' she said quietly, reaching over and squeezing Jo's arm. Her eyes filled with tears. She would have to pick up the pieces later.

Jo let out a long sigh of relief, praying that by the time she returned she would have thought up another delaying tactic.

'I love you, Mum,' she gasped, hugging Nina tightly, the panic still hard in her chest. 'You never know, Dad might answer me this time.' Releasing her clasp, she grabbed her car keys and the latest copy of *Turf* and was gone.

The smell of stale food and hospital-strength anti-septic grabbed at Jo as she stepped into the home, dragging her down, and the hearty greeting of a uniformed carer made her cringe. It was a year to the day since Charlie had entered the home, a year since she had vowed she would get him out, and he was still here, still unable to talk. He had regained a lot more mobility in his right side, but it was the look of quiet desperation in Charlie's eyes that always cut Jo to the quick. An overwhelming sense of failure swept over her. She had let him down. Anger at herself, at the world, at his lack of willingness to keep fighting smouldered inside her as she marched into his room and sat down next to him. Dozing in a chair by the window, cushions supporting his back, a dull grey rug over his knees, he opened his eyes as Jo pressed off the chattering radio and kissed him on the cheek.

'How's things today? The nurses giving you heaps?' she said with forced cheerfulness and pushed the copy of *Turf* onto his lap. She started her usual chatter. Normally calm and positive, today she felt edgy and abrupt. A beefy nurse bustled in with a tray of tea and biscuits.

'Are we ready for our tea, Mr Kingsford? Now, no spilling it on the rug today.' She spoke loudly as though to some delinquent child, cutting across Jo's talk.

Jo's rage boiled over. 'I'll take that,' she snapped, leaping up and relieving the woman of the tray. 'You don't have to treat him like an idiot, you know; he's not six years old.'

'My, my we are sparky today. I understand your concern, dear, but they have to be given encouragement to try harder or they never improve,' the nurse replied with a sympathetic glance and left the room.

The pity in the woman's eyes was too much for Jo. Something in her snapped. Suddenly she was pouring out all her anguish to her father, not caring if he could understand or even hear her. Like a river bursting its banks her emotions spilled out—how Simon had broken off their engagement and Archie was resigning and Sam was gone and all the hurtful negative talk between other trainers and owners and even her own mother thought she was a joke and now Nina was threatening for the second time to sell the stables, only this time Jo knew she couldn't stop it happening.

'I hate them, Dad, I hate them all. I hate you being here, I hate myself for not getting you out of here but I don't know what to do next. I don't even know if you can understand a word I'm saying, but just this once please say more to me than that funny little sentence. Tell me what I'm going to say to Mum to stop her from selling Kingsford Lodge. Dad, I need your help, I can't do this on my own.'

Desperate she lifted her violet eyes to her father's face, struggling to stop the tears from spilling over, and her heart missed a beat as she saw in her father's usually impassive face an answering fury. Clutching Jo's arm with both his hands, Charlie heaved himself upright in the chair and for a split second she saw the father she had known before the accident. Leaning towards him to hear his words, she watched his lips moving, the flash of hope already evaporating as she waited for the funny little three-word phrase. It never came. Very slowly and unmistakably her father said two words.

'Don't sell.'

Chapter Twenty

JO COULDN'T STOP herself from grinning as she walked towards the stables' office with Phillip, the morning veterinary inspection finished, the worried frown she had worn for so long dissolved. The sun glinted on the slate tiles and caught on the polished brass fittings on the stable doors. Sparrows twittered in the stalls above the munching horses, and the sweet smell of fresh hay filled her nostrils. Since Phillip had made the feed adjustments all the horses seemed to have picked up. Last weekend had proved remarkably successful considering the mishmash of jockeys she had finally managed to round up for her mounts, but financially the stables were still looking decidedly rocky. Numbers of horses coming through had fallen off dramatically since Archie's retirement. Now half the stalls were empty and no-one wanted to ride her horses. She might have to offer jockeys extra money. It went entirely against the grain with her, but it might be the only way. Yet despite all her concerns about Kingsford Lodge, nothing could wipe the smile off her face. Yesterday Charlie had come home.

'I just can't believe it, Phillip,' she said, her eyes

sparkling, flopping down in the big leather chair in the office where Charlie had spent so many hours. 'Today I kissed Dad on the way out to track work and he said "Atta girl!".' Pictures of her father's racing wins hung all around the room, now joined by some of hers. She reached for a small photo in a silver frame on the desk. It was of her as a little girl walking proudly beside Charlie as he led his first Melbourne Cup winner from the ring. 'One day we'll do it again, Dad,' she whispered.

'You're a pretty impressive lady,' said Phillip watching her. Her hair was tangled and windblown after working out on the track; her jodhpurs were splattered with mud and there was a smear of dirt on the tip of her nose, but nothing could dampen her glowing beauty. He longed to take her precious face in his hands, wipe away the mud and see her eyes melt with love as he kissed her warm soft lips, but he had long ago accepted that would never happen. At least she had removed the picture of Simon that had been such a thorn in his side and today was the third day in a row she hadn't worn her engagement ring. He patted his pockets and searched for a pen.

'What d'you mean?' asked Jo, surprised but flattered by his words. Carefully she replaced the photo and sipped the hot coffee brought in by Gloria.

'He wouldn't be on the mend and the whole racing industry wouldn't be talking about it if it hadn't been for you,' said Phillip. Jo blushed with embarrassment. 'How's your mum coping?' Phillip continued quickly, seeing her discomfort.

'She's gradually settling down now they've got a routine going and a full-time nurse helping. I dunno, Mum's changed. I can't quite explain it. She's more settled about everything and she seems to be coping with Dad much better than I would have thought. She still gets in a dither about things, of course, but we don't have the same rows, and there's been no more mention of selling Kingsford Lodge,' explained Jo. 'We had a long talk together which made me feel heaps better. Although she didn't say so, I think she was hideously embarrassed at the whole dreadful timing of it all—but she really wants to do the best by us.'

Since that day Charlie had spoken those two magical little words 'don't sell' he had steadily improved. Still confined to a wheelchair, he struggled to get his tongue around words, or scribbled with his left hand. Watching her father's confidence return, the fight back in his eyes, Jo spent as much time as she could talking with him. Teasing, cajoling and discussing important aspects of running the stables, Jo finally discovered what he had meant by the funny little phrase that had driven them all crazy.

With surprising clarity he explained how he had been trying to tell her he believed in her, that he could see she had the get up and go to keep the stables afloat until he was back, but all he could ever manage was 'got to go'. It moved Jo to tears when he confided how he had wept for a week after she had misinterpreted his pitiful attempt at speech as an attack on her. Only able to guess his frustration at being trapped in a body that wouldn't work with his mind wholly intact, Jo risked questioning him further, wanting to know how much he had understood while they had all chattered round him, but he shut up like a clam, his eyes watering, the memories clearly too painful to voice. Respecting his need for privacy, Jo had let him be, rejoicing she had her father back.

'You'll have to come over for a meal so Dad can meet the vet that's been caring for his horses. He's asked me enough about you,' she said, grinning up at Phillip, her diminutive figure lost in the big chair, and saw more than polite acceptance in his eyes. Flustered, she fumbled for her notepad and knocked a pile of letters to the floor. Quickly bending to pick them up, she replaced them on the desk and ignored her rapid pulse rate.

'Well. Tell me the worst. How d'you think that tendon's mending in Picasso?' she said, clearing her throat, once more the efficient trainer. For the next twenty minutes they discussed the performance of the horses and their various ailments, Jo's concerns about finding jockeys and some of her other worries. Outside, horses clattered on the stone as they were led back to their stalls, bridles clinking. Grooms swept and hosed down and tidied up, and Les, a groom in his early forties in charge of feeding the horses, prepared the next feed.

Glancing at his watch, Phillip reluctantly stood up. 'I hate to do this to you but I've got some more visits to make, so I'd better get moving.'

'I'm sorry, I've kept you too long, again,' said Jo guiltily, standing up with him. It was such a relief to be able to share so many of her worries with Phillip. 'You're such a good friend,' she said gently.

Phillip felt like a gauche schoolboy, his throat suddenly dry. 'Fancy grabbing a bite to eat and seeing a movie tonight?' he asked quickly.

Jo glanced up at him and for a moment her eyes locked with his, the intensity in their depths setting her heart racing. Colour flooded her face.

'I'd love to,' agreed Jo rather too brightly, her cheeks hot, chiding herself for being silly. He was her vet and a good friend and she was acting like she was being asked out on her first date. 'Come up to the house about six and I'll introduce you properly to Mum and Dad.' She gave him a brilliant smile and firmly turned her mind back to stable concerns. 'I need jockeys I can rely on,' she said, continuing their earlier conversation. 'It's the chicken and the egg, isn't it? You have winners, you get good jockeys; good jockeys give you winners.'

'I'll have a scout around the traps. There are a couple of friends I can have a word with. Don't you worry, Snow White, we'll come up with something. See you tonight,' he replied, his heart thudding. Picking up his bag, he swaggered jauntily out of the stables.

Jo watched him go from the office door, startled at the reaction he had caused in her. She knew how lucky she was to have him as a friend and she trusted him implicitly, but they were just pals, no more. They both knew where they stood—and she'd told him all about Simon.

Her heart gave a lurch as she thought of Simon and his continuing silence. She had rung his home again shortly before her twenty-first birthday and had got the daily help who had assured her Simon was fine and that Mrs Gordon had most certainly passed on her good wishes. That had hit her like a blow. It didn't matter how many times she told herself to forget him, the pain and disappointment she felt at his continuing silence was still as raw and fresh as ever, her love for him as strong. Yet she could not bring herself to condemn him. He had said he would be there when she was ready to marry him, but she was still in Australia running the stables.

The clatter of a shovel pulled her out of her daydream. Looking towards the noise she saw Sally, one of the strappers, talking to someone in the shadows halfway down one of the walkways. Wondering how the visitor could have slipped into the stables without her noticing, Jo walked over to investigate.

'Everything okay, Sally?' she asked, taking in the scruffy, underfed individual standing next to the strapper.

'This just walked in, miss. I was about to send him over to you,' replied Sally with a look of distaste.

'Right. Thanks, Sally.' Jo nodded dismissively. Sally was a funny girl, sharp-faced and sometimes extremely abrupt, but Jo could not fault her hard work and she was a very useful person to have around the stables. The girl went back to helping Les sort the food bins for the next feed and Jo turned her attention back to the young lad who now held out his hand. 'How can I help?'

'Damien Cardelli, miss. I'm an apprentice jockey and I heard you were looking for riders.' Jo looked at him curiously, wondering why he had sought her out, and shook hands.

'I'm eighteen, miss, and I've worked all me life wiv horses and I learn fast.' He stepped out of the shadows and Jo smothered a small gasp. His left eye was puffy and swollen from a recent knock, brown and yellow bruising already discolouring his skin around the eye. He was the height of a twelve-year-old boy, but the deep lines etched in his face showed a lifetime of experience, belying the cocky tilt of his head, and he was favouring one arm.

'You don't look fit to ride,' she said before she could stop herself.

'Had a bit of a run-in wiv a barn door, miss. I'll come good.'

'That was bad luck,' replied Jo evenly. She didn't believe his explanation about the barn door for one second—she had seen enough beaten-up jockeys in

384

England to know the difference between walking into a door and a hard swipe from a fist—but there was an appeal in the cocky weather-beaten face Jo couldn't resist. 'Come into the office and tell me why you want to work at Kingsford Lodge,' she said kindly.

'One day I'm going to be the greatest Australian jockey of all time. You won't regret taking me on,' started Damien, wrapping his fingers around the steaming cup of coffee Jo handed him.

'I haven't agreed to yet!' replied Jo, who had not missed his wince of pain as he'd sat down. 'Who are you apprenticed to?' Gradually, as Damien talked, his bravado lessened and Jo learned of his passion to become a top-class jockey and how he had been working at a number of stables across the countryside struggling to make a crust, before finally becoming apprenticed to Rosy Roesinger at his stables, Phantom Lodge; Rosy was a long-time friendly rival of Charlie.

'Some of them horses were real rogues,' he finished.

'And there are a lot of barn doors in his stables,' said Jo lightly, surprised that trouble should have come from Rosy. Stories filtered through to Jo from time to time about mistreated lads and horses, but on the few occasions she had run into Rosy, although she had found him the ultimate chauvinist, he had always appeared fair in his dealings. While he had a reputation for being cold and calculating, there had never been any talk of him being vicious to his staff.

'That's right, miss,' said Damien bravely, shifting in his chair as pain stabbed his emaciated body. Weakened by fear, lack of sleep and proper food, and unaccustomed to kindness in any form, the understanding in Jo's voice was too much for him and he burst into tears. 'The flamin' mongrel he just came at me. I hadn't done nuffin'. Just done me track work but the rotten bugger, beggin' your pardon miss, he just flew at me. He had to take his anger out on someone and I was the smallest.' He wiped a grimy hand across his eyes.

Jo's heart went out to the lad.

'Who's "he"?' she asked cautiously, her opinion of Rosy Roesinger sinking lower.

'Mr R's new foreman, Kurt summat foreign. They call him the iron man from hell.' He looked up at Jo, rage and misery spilling from his battered, tear-stained face.

Jo tensed in alarm. 'Kurt Stoltz?' she asked, everything suddenly making sense. This looked like his handiwork all right.

'That's right, miss. Just got back from England. He keeps telling me I'm a no-hoper . . .' He stopped, suddenly appalled at his own indiscretion. 'I never said anything bad about him, miss. Please.' He scrambled to his feet, wobbling slightly, gripping the desk till the dizziness that swamped him passed. 'I'd best be off. You won't be wanting me to stick around knowing all that and me snivelling like a three-year-old too. Dunno wot made me spill me guts to you but thanks anyway, miss, you're a real lady.' He doffed his cap and turned to go.

'Don't worry, Damien, I never heard you say a bad word. And you're quite wrong. I would like you to stick around. I could use someone with your grit and determination. It took courage to stride in here looking for something better. It shouldn't be difficult to transfer your indentures across to Kingsford Lodge.' She nodded, trying to stifle the anger she felt towards Kurt. So much for the damp squib

Simon had called him. She'd do her damnedest to make Kurt pay for this. Suddenly she felt very, very good. She might not be able to turn Damien into the greatest Australian jockey of all time, but she would enjoy every second of organising his transfer across to Kingsford Lodge and she'd give him every possible opportunity to prove himself. Damien sat down in stunned amazement. Walking to the door Jo called through to Gloria.

'Could you organise some more hot coffee and two large hamburgers in here? We're feeling a bit peckish.' The tap of the typewriter stopped. Jo turned back to Damien. 'You do understand that you'll be apprenticed to Mr Kingsford, don't you? You'll just be taking your orders from me.' Damien nodded. 'Now let me tell you how we work at Kingsford Lodge and what I am looking for in my jockeys.'

'I'm not sure it's a wise move hiring young Cardelli,' Pete said quietly to Jo in the stripping sheds the following morning. 'People don't like their dirty linen aired around the countryside and that's just what that young fool's done. You'll make enemies, Jo.'

'All I know is he walked into a barn door. If you know anything different, spit it out, Pete. Damien's got the sort of fire in him that makes great jockeys. I want to give him a chance.'

Pete gave Jo a long look and went back to organising the horses and riders, knowing there was no point arguing with her.

Having hired Damien, Jo insisted he see her doctor who confirmed her suspicions that he had a broken collarbone. He also had two broken ribs and several nasty bruises on his back and legs. She started him on light work around the stables to give his battered body a chance to heal but as soon as he was fit enough she shifted him across to track work. Damien was ecstatic. Worshipping the ground Jo walked on, nothing was too hard or too much trouble for him to do for her. In return Jo saw her instincts were right. He knew how to handle horses and he learned fast. Trying him out on several solid goers she finally put him on Sleeper. Immediately she could see the natural bond between rider and horse. With each week both jockey and horse improved, Damien settling into a natural rhythm with Sleeper that put a gleam in the horse's eye and gave him a taste for victory as they pounded around the track. The only behaviour Damien couldn't change was Sleeper's habit of reverting to a dozy unprepossessing creature as soon as his work was done or whenever he had to stand around and wait.

Over the next six months Jo took Damien and Sleeper around the country racetracks. As the horse settled in, Jo saw a new confidence emerge in the cocky Damien that was more than empty boasting. Energetic and cheerful, he transferred his eagerness to his mounts and quickly started pulling off wins. Gradually the odds shortened as horse and rider kept galloping across the finishing line ahead of the field, word of Sleeper and Cocky Cardelli spreading. Much-needed prize money started coming into Kingsford Lodge and, more cautiously, new owners followed.

'You picked a winner there, little sis,' said Bertie over a barbecue one Sunday. Happily he pulled out a wad of notes and fanned them in Jo's face, then squashed them into an already overstuffed wallet. 'Not bad for an afternoon's pickings.' Now a quali-fied lawyer working for a well-known firm, he swaggered even more than before. He was also living at home again and took every chance to needle Jo.

Today, flush with her latest success, Jo refused to let him ruffle her feathers. 'Then you can pay back the money you owe me,' she said, holding out her hand, wondering why she had been stupid enough to lend him the money in the first place. But he had sounded so desperate that she had given in.

'Um, slight problem. I've got one or two people to pay first, but I promise I'll pay you back at the end of the week,' he said quickly.

'Come on, Bertie, I'm one of those people. That's what you said last week,' insisted Jo.

'Ssh, Dad'll hear,' hissed Bertie.

'What? Does he think you've given gambling up for Lent or something?' she retorted sarcastically and walked over to the table laden with food and started peeling the Gladwrap off the salad. Glancing over at her father chatting with two mates, a beer in his hand, Jo thought what a long way they had come in this last year. His legs might still be weak but his mind was as sharp as ever and heated discussions about training thoroughbreds were now commonplace between the two of them, despite being hampered by his speech problems and sometimes, for his part, entirely conducted on paper. He was as frustrating as all heck, yet her heart warmed as she watched him. He was the dad she knew and loved of old, irascible, terse yet, despite his slow mumbling speech, still passionate about his horses. One day when she was feeling brave she'd raise the spectre of England with him to clear the air, but not yet. Today was the first time he had allowed any of his friends to the house. The last thing he needed right now was worries about Bertie's gambling habit.

'D'you want to come to Sleeper's debut at Rand-wick on Saturday, Dad?' she asked later that afternoon.

'The next time I go to the track I walk, my girl. That's what I said when I came home and that's how it's going to be.' He smiled up at her but she caught a glimpse of sadness in his eyes. He was a proud man and he had been a great trainer, but the initial lack of faith in his recovery from all except Jo and the veiled comments about his sanity had left their own scars, particularly where Neene was concerned.

Trapped in a body that refused to work, Charlie had understood everything that was going on around him. God! How he had longed to wrap her in his arms and convince her he was sound in mind and body, to tell her how much he loved her and to trust their daughter. Jo knew what she was doing. But he hadn't even been able to tell the stupid nurse to move him out of the sun. Then when Neene had walked into that depressing home with her nervous chatter and he had sensed her guilt, all the punch had gone out of him. He had felt so desolate. If it hadn't been for Jo, he'd have given up altogether. One day when the raw edge had worn off he'd tell her how much he admired her courage and tenacity. How fiercely he loved her for not abandoning him.

Charlie ran his hand shakily across his eyes, think-ing of Nina and sighed inwardly. Since returning home their relationship had changed. Everything had changed. It had been a long day and he realised he was far from ready to face the racing community.

'Fine, Dad, if that's how you want it,' replied Jo used to his gruffness. But she was disappointed. She dearly wanted to share this moment with Charlie. There was absolutely no doubt in her mind that, with the consistent record of wins Sleeper had built up over the past twelve months, the horse would romp home. Her mind wandered briefly to Simon, wishing he were here to share her triumph. It had been almost four years since they had parted. Time and time again she told herself she was over him, yet she knew if he were to walk through that door tomorrow, she would rush straight into his arms without a second thought.

Saturday dawned bright and warm. Having already put Sleeper through a trial the week before to make sure he was confident at the barrier at Randwick, Jo, outwardly bubbly, was tense and keyed up. Wearing her most extravagantly outrageous hat and a bright green pant suit that set her neat figure off to perfection, she insisted on saddling up Sleeper herself. Giving Damien a leg-up in the mounting yard she squeezed his hand and then watched him trot Sleeper out towards the barriers, the bright yellow and pink Kingsford silks glinting on his back. This was her proudest moment since her return to Australia and Dad would be watching it all on television.

'You can take all the credit for this one yourself,' said Phillip quietly as she followed the horse's progress to the starting stalls through the powerful compact binoculars he had given her for her twenty-third birthday. Sleeper had drawn barrier number three, close to the inside rail, giving him an ideal position to get away right at the start.

'What are they doing?' she muttered, half to herself, half to Phillip, watching the horses still milling around the barrier, wishing her stomach didn't churn so before each race. Pete already had Sleeper in the barrier. 'Those darned Kiwi horses, they're dithering about ... Get them in the barriers!' she shouted, waving an arm. A group of racegoers stared disapprovingly at her.

'Just cool it, Snow White,' nudged Phillip.

'I'm cool, I'm cool!' cried Jo, feeling anything but, greatly comforted as always that Phillip was beside her. Then the final horse was in and the clerks of the course retreated. Jo held her breath as the barriers opened and the horses leaped out.

'Go, Dopey!' yelled Jo, her words drowned by the race caller.

'And it's Rosy Roesinger's Rain Maker leading, with Red Rogue in second place and My Girl in third and, oh dear! What's happened to the favourite? He hasn't come out of the barrier. Has he collapsed? No! There's no sign of the horse ambulance, maybe Sleeper's finally lived up to his name and had a nap,' laughed the commentator.

Jo's hands shook as she trained her lenses back at the barrier, the caller's voice grating on her nerves. Sleeper! What was wrong? Around her the crowd groaned with anger and disappointment. Then she saw him leap out of the barrier, Damien perched on top like a bouncing ball. The crowd urged him on momentarily but it was too late. The other horses were halfway down the track. Even such a great galloper as Sleeper had no hope of catching up. Devastated, Jo watched as Rain Maker crossed the line to take first place, with Sleeper coming in fifth. It was a monumental effort to have closed the gap so much but cold comfort to Jo and the many angry punters who had bet heavily on the horse. Fighting back tears of frustration and disappointment, Jo shoved her way through the crowd and raced down to the enclosure.

'What happened?' she hissed, grabbing the reins

off the strapper as the horses were being led away, panting to keep up with Damien. But he was too distraught to speak. All Jo could do was stifle her frustration until after Damien had been weighed in.

Examining the horse back at the stalls, neither Jo nor Phillip could find anything wrong.

'What happened at the barrier?' Jo demanded again when Damien reappeared. But the jockey couldn't explain.

'He just wouldn't move till it was too late,' was all he could tell them.

Back at the stables Jo got Phillip to do another urine swab to check that the horse hadn't been slipped something that had somehow missed the scrutiny of the course vet, but it was clear as a bell. At track work the following Monday Jo watched him closely but he worked perfectly, falling into his characteristic dopey state when he wasn't being worked.

'Well I don't know. Maybe we were just on a lucky streak and now we've fallen off it,' she said but she didn't believe her own words. That horse was healthy and it could gallop the pants off any of the others on the field. It had proved her right over and over again on any track in any condition over the past year.

It wasn't until the following Friday that the mystery was finally unravelled. Working twenty horses and with one rider sick, track work took longer than usual. Concentrating on Let's Talk, a classy show-off she had bought at last year's Easter sale, Jo was standing next to Winks who was clocking the horses' times from the top of the octagonal Pizza Hut.

'I can't see a darn thing wrong with that horse, can you?' Jo muttered, bemused.

Winks looked across at Sleeper standing quietly and gave a chuckle. 'The cheeky beggar's dropped off. My granddad had a horse used to do that. Never cottoned on for months. Drove us daft. Look at him. Fast asleep.'

Training her binoculars on the big gelding, Jo gasped. 'He can't be! I know we joke about him, but . . .' About to yell at Damien to wake Dopey up, instead she clambered down the stairs and walked quickly over to the horse. Beckoning to Phillip in disbelief, she pointed to Sleeper. 'You're absolutely right,' she yelled up to Winks, who was leaning out of the window.

Then everyone else gathered round in amazement. Sleeper, bored with waiting to work, had genuinely fallen fast asleep.

'Get that horse moving!' yelled Jo. A quick nudge from Damien and Sleeper was awake, ears forward, ready for work. Jo looked at Phillip and Phillip looked at Jo and Damien looked extremely embarrassed, and Winks chuckled.

'What a cheeky beggar!' exploded Jo. Then they all started to swear and then to laugh. Sleeper must have fallen asleep at the barrier. It was the only explanation that made sense. How Emma would laugh, thought Jo, suddenly reminded of her old friend. She would write and tell her the whole amazing story tonight.

Chapter Twenty-one

POURING HERSELF A large Coke and lemon from the kitchen fridge, Jo flopped down into a chair at the end of one of the most exhausting weeks of her life. Still smarting from the dressing down she had received from Charlie at not picking up Dopey's habit of falling asleep. His comments merely added to her own feeling of stupidity over the whole incident. The whole week had had the air of a farce. If it hadn't been so serious it would have been hilarious. The media, latching onto the story, had been all over her and the stables like a swarm of wasps, some of them even screaming foul play, despite her protestations that both the Australian Racing Association and her own vet had checked for any drug traces. Wits from all areas of racing came up with smart comments every time she showed her face anywhere and reporters, unable to find a new angle, invented new stories of Jo's life and work at the stables. Jo had no choice but to accept that she was the flavour of the month and to try and capitalise on all the publicity to lift the profile of the stables, which she did with remarkable success.

Far more alarming than all the hype and brouhaha were two very disturbing phone calls she had received threatening dire consequences if she 'pulled a stunt like this again'. Having Sleeper lose from such a favoured position had made a lot of people poorer and very angry, but she could not be accountable to everyone. What made it doubly bad was that Damien's girlfriend, Hope, had come home from the race with a fistful of notes. Superstitious from childhood, Hope had always bet on the horse running against Damien, as well as the one he rode, and had put money on both Sleeper and Rain Maker. While this was not public knowledge, within the racing industry it pointed a very bad finger at both Jo and her jockey.

'It's the nature of the racing game,' she told herself, trying to brush the calls off as overreaction from angry punters. But the longer she sat sipping at her drink the more unsettled she felt. Knowing Charlie slept badly and found the evenings long and tedious, she decided to go and talk the whole incident over with him. Entering his study where he often escaped to mull over blood lines and catch up on the latest in the thoroughbred industry, she found him surrounded by books and magazines, engrossed in a crossword.

'Never mind any phone calls. What the heck's got into you that you could have been so stupid?' The words were mumbled and unclear but his meaning was made blatantly obvious as Charlie picked up a handful of cuttings from national newspapers and waved them in Jo's face.

Jo went bright red, taken aback by the angry glitter in his eyes, his biting words inflaming her own feelings of inadequacy over the Dopey farce. 'Come on, Dad, we've been over all this,' she cried defensively indignant at this second attack, her eyes travelling across the notepad on which he was now scribbling with his left hand. The shaky writing attacked her approach to training, the publicity the stables were getting and her not checking the obvious and remembering every detail of a horse's behaviour. 'Dad, that's completely unfair, I'm doing the best I can!' Jo cried as Charlie underlined the last word with a shaky flourish.

'It's not good enough. You can't afford mistakes like these,' Charlie said slowly, stumbling over the consonants.

'Hey, back off, Dad. I'm the one out there every morning, fighting the troops. Not you. I don't need criticism from my own father of all people. How about some support for a change?' shouted Jo. Stung, she hunted around for more ammunition to hit him with and thought of the latest depressing figures from the stables accounts. 'It's not like I'm asking for much from you, just a few words of advice now and then, a bit of understanding, not handouts like Bertie got left, right and centre for years without anyone blinking.' Charlie gave her a withering look, but in her hurt Jo kept going. 'Why did you keep dishing out all that money to Bertie, Dad? You never did to either me or—' She was going to say Rick but stopped herself just in time. 'You must have known I'd find out about the money from the stable accounts,' she finished, still boiling mad.

Charlie put down the newspaper and looked at Jo over his dark-rimmed glasses. 'I'm not prepared to discuss anything with you until you change your tone,' he said slowly and turned back to the crossword puzzle. Her words had dug deep. Lying in the hospital as any hope of ever living a normal life again had slowly faded, Charlie had thought a lot about Bertie and money. Bertie had been his most infrequent visitor and the least supportive. His own son had tried to sell the stables from under them, without a word to his father, despite Charlie having fished him out of trouble over his growing gambling excesses. He was going the very way Charlie had dreaded, following his Uncle Wayne downhill, but in loyalty to Nina, Charlie could not and would not discuss the problem with Jo. Seven down three across—loanshark. He scribbled angrily into the tiny squares.

'Bloody hell, Dad! You could at least explain. I'm the one working the horses every day,' exploded Jo.

'So you keep saying,' said Charlie coldly. 'Your brother and I came to an agreement before the accident that was between him and me. The lump sums were one-offs and of no concern to you.' He returned to the crossword, but Jo could see his hand shaking and suddenly his vulnerability made her heart go out to him.

'All right, Dad. Look, I'm sorry. It's just that . . . well, I didn't expect you to be so hard on me.' Fighting her father would get her nowhere. She needed his trust and his advice and, damn it, he was right about Dopey. He had his pride too. He had come so far on his long journey to recovery and while little was said, Jo sensed his frustration at no longer being in the thick of the action. 'Could we go over some of the training points and ways I could improve things; better still, will you come to track work with me?' she asked quietly.

'Not until I can walk onto that field, head held high. Now, what about those phone calls?'

Heaving a sigh of relief, Jo unburdened herself, and her father quieted her fears, then they talked about the stables and the horses, using the notepad when words became a struggle, their relationship back to one of open friendship and understanding.

However, later, as she was making herself a hot chocolate before going to bed, Jo's anger towards her brother resurfaced and as a result she was in no mood to be friendly when the back door opened cautiously and Bertie crept in.

'Mum and Dad?' he hissed, his eyes wild. Dishevelled and dirty, his tie gone, his shirt open at the neck, she could smell the rum from where she stood.

'Upstairs,' snapped Jo, helping herself to some sugar. It wasn't the first time he'd crept home drunk after a day of celebrating his winnings.

Bertie lurched across the floor, his finger to his lips. 'Can you lend me a few quid? I've got myself in a bit of a jam,' he slurred, sliding up to Jo and putting his arm around her.

'What have you done this time—bet the stables and lost?' she retorted with a mirthless laugh.

'You'll help your big brother out of a little jam, little sis, I know you will,' Bertie said softly, ignoring her taunt. He put his arm around her, whispering the amount in her ear and attempting to give her a brotherly kiss.

Horrified, Jo wriggled free. 'You're joking!' Bertie shook his head and tried to hug her again. 'I'm not lending you another red cent, Bertie. Grow up and solve your own problems.' Shaking, she stormed to the other side of the kitchen, spilling her chocolate on her pyjamas. 'God, now look what you've made me do. Go to bed, Bertie.'

'Well, well, well, we are the little high and mighty miss,' sniggered Bertie. 'Then I'll just have to put the stables up as collater-collat- whatever instead of the cash.' He smirked, unable to get his tongue around the word.

Jo whirled round, panic in her eyes. It was just the

sort of damned fool thing Bertie was capable of doing. 'Don't be a bloody idiot, Bertie. If you want to throw your money away, go ahead, but you're not throwing mine away too. What are you trying to do— milk the stables dry?' To her amazement Bertie slumped down and started sobbing.

'How could you do this to me? How could you let me down?' he blubbered. 'Why didn't you tell me your horse was a dud? Little sis, I need your help. I'm in serious trouble,' he pleaded, clutching at her.

'Oh, for God's sake, Bertie, shut up and start acting your age,' she hissed, shaking him off. She had to be strong. She had to make a stand or she'd be giving him handouts for the rest of her life. This was typical of compulsive gamblers, they just kept taking and taking, only no-one would admit that was what Bertie was. 'If you've got yourself in a mess, it's not my fault. Get yourself out. You never lift a finger to help and now you expect me to fish you out like Dad used to. Well, I won't do it. No-one's going to any more, anyway I don't have that sort of money.' She started towards the door but Bertie, smarting at her attack, blocked her way, a shiftiness creeping into his eyes.

'Jesus! When your own brother asks you for help . . . You always were the favourite, Daddy's precious little girl looking after his wonderful horses. What about my feelings? All I ever got was money from him. Well, don't come crying to me when it all falls in a heap.' He stumbled to the fridge and pulled out a beer.

'It's not going to fall into a heap,' said Jo, halted by his words. A shiver of concern ran down her spine. Bertie mixed in very strange circles sometimes. Blackjack and poker players were not always the most honest and neither was every bookmaker.

Bertie took a slug of beer. 'How long are you going to keep up this pretence of a game? The old man's never going to get back to running the stables, the blokes in racing don't want you, Mum doesn't want you to keep at it. That's part of my inheritance you're messing with.'

'You're drunk and you're being a total pain in the butt. Go to bed, Bertie,' ordered Jo, her eyes blazing, giving him another push.

Bertie leered at her, almost losing his balance, catching at the kitchen table at the last moment. 'Legally, little sis, I could make you sell the lot tomorrow. So don't you go telling me what to do,' he snarled, shoving his face close to hers, his eyes bloodshot, the alcohol fumes overpowering.

'Bulldust you can. Go to hell! And don't call me little sis!' shouted Jo, shoving him aside, and stormed off to bed. Soon she heard the backdoor slam, followed by the roar of the car leaving the driveway. 'That's right, go and gamble away some more money you haven't got—if you don't get done for drink driving.' She flopped into bed. Pulling the bedclothes tightly around her, she stared at the ceiling. He was just stirring her up about that legal stuff. He had to be, but lawyers were cunning and Bertie was adept at twisting life to make it work his way. She'd talk to the family solicitor tomorrow. Firmly she turned over and went to sleep.

At one o'clock in the morning she was shaken violently awake by Nina.

'What? What?' cried Jo sitting up in alarm.

'Jo! Jo! Wake up! It's Bertie! He's in casualty. He's been mugged,' cried her mother white-faced. 'The police just rang.'

Jo was on her feet in a flash, her brother's words

a terrible taunt in her ears. Leaping into the car with Nina, she raced to the hospital, her heart racing with fear. Bertie was lying in one of the cubicles, his face a mass of bruises, one eye swollen and almost completely closed.

'He's very lucky he's no worse. Whoever attacked him must have been scared off. Some of these beatings that come in from the Cross are pretty nasty,' explained one of the casualty staff, referring to Kings Cross, the redlight district of Sydney. 'Then one of our regulars phoned and we brought him in. The police want a word with you. I hope they catch the dirty bastards who did this.'

'If they don't I will,' growled Jo. She and Bertie might not always see eye to eye but this was different. He had pleaded and she hadn't heard.

'I didn't think he was serious,' admitted Jo, riddled with guilt, to the police officer who interviewed her and Nina later.

'He may not have been, but whoever attacked him certainly was. They found this pinned to his shirt.' The police officer produced a transparent plastic bag containing a crumpled bloodstained piece of paper which he spread out on the table in front of Jo and Nina. Jo's flesh crawled as she read the childlike capital letters. *This is a warning—pay up or move out.* Heavens! Who was Bertie involved with and how much was he in debt?

Nina gave an involuntary gasp. Immediately Jo leaned over and clasped her mother's hand. 'It's okay, Mum,' she said softly.

'How could this happen, Jo? Oh my God, this is all so terrible,' whispered Nina. Quickly she pulled herself together, and her fingers answered Jo's handclasp. 'I'm all right, darling.'

'I realise this is very distressing for both you and

your daughter, Mrs Kingsford, but there are a few more questions I have to ask,' said the police officer kindly. Numbly Nina nodded while Jo answered the questions, torn between guilt and fury that her brother had brought this on them all.

'I'm sorry, little ... I'm sorry, Jo, I didn't know what to do,' sobbed Bertie after they brought him home the next day. 'They were threatening me so I said they could have the stables if Dopey didn't come good. He was such a sure thing I thought I was in the clear. Part of it'll be mine anyway.' For a moment his eyes blazed at Jo through the bruises. Jo looked away, torn between disgust and remorse.

'Bertie, how could you?' said Nina. 'Whatever happens, not a word of this to your father. I'll borrow the money from the bank and sell one of my properties in Neutral Bay and you can pay these people off,' decided Nina, grim-faced, as soon as she and Jo had extracted the amount owed from a chastened and very scared Bertie.

'You'll do no such thing, Neene,' barked Charlie staggering into the room, dragging his right leg, supported by his two walking sticks. 'Why don't you make your mother a cup of tea, Jo. Bertie and I have some talking to do in private.' Shooing the two startled women out of the sitting room Charlie sat down heavily in the big armchair opposite Bertie, tossing his sticks on the floor.

'You will ignore everything your mother said,' he began firmly, his dark eyes boring in to Bertie. 'It's time to grow up, son.' Bertie seemed to shrink in stature, the colour draining from his face, the purple and yellow bruises livid against his parchment cheeks as his father gave him the dressing down of his life. Charlie's words were slow and carefully pronounced, and sometimes he stumbled, making the agony longer for Bertie, but when his father compared him to his Uncle Wayne, it proved too much for Bertie.

'I've just been beaten up, Dad. I don't have to listen to all this,' he cried leaping up, but Charlie grabbed him with his good hand. For a moment father and son stared at one another. Then Charlie let go of Bertie's arm.

'Now you sit down and listen to me until I've finished, son.'

Caught between his father's rage and the impossible weight of the debt, Bertie gave up all attempt at a further fight and slumped back into the chair, scowling at his feet.

'A good decision, son,' continued Charlie with satisfaction. 'You can pay off this debt but you will borrow the money. I'll square the loan with the bank but it's your loan and you will pay back every cent you borrow, with interest. You're a lawyer for God's sake, Bertie, a respected member of the community committed to helping keep law and order.' Charlie paused an instant. 'What you'll also do is keep your mouth shut and stay away from racetracks and card games until you've learned some self-control. Go on then, we're done. You can get me a stiff whisky and then go and see what your mother and sister are up to.'

Exhausted, Charlie leaned back in his chair and watched Bertie slink out of the room. The boy's pride was badly battered and he wondered if anything he had said over the last half hour had made the slightest impression. Somehow between them they had to persuade Bertie to seek help before he ruined his life. The boy reminded him so much of Wayne, it was frightening. Yet even if not one word had been heard by Bertie, the effort Charlie had been forced to muster to confront his son had done something quite extraordinary. Charlie felt whole again. For the first time since the accident he had been in charge, yet physically there was no way he could have restrained the boy. He rubbed his chin with his good hand, feeling the way his mouth still sloped down one side from the stroke, and suddenly he realised that somehow none of that mattered any more. It was as if out of the whole darned mess Charlie had rekindled his fighting spirit.

'I tried to shelter you from all of this, Charlie darling, but what could I do?' cried Nina, wringing her hands in the privacy of their bedroom a few hours later. Nina was terrified of the effect the whole issue was having on Charlie. He looked worn out.

Charlie put down the stud book he was reading and took off his glasses. 'We need to do some serious talking, Neene, my love,' he said heaving himself up in the big double bed and patting the bedclothes. Like a frightened bird Nina sat down on the other side of the bed.

'I tried to be a good mother,' she sobbed.

'Shh . . . Shh, and so you have been to all my children,' murmured Charlie. He ran his fingers down her hair and around her cheek. 'I've been the one at fault. I should have said no the first time Bertie asked for money but I didn't want to see he was just a younger version of Wayne. I couldn't accept it. It would have meant somehow I had failed, but now it doesn't matter. I have told Bertie he has to borrow the money from the bank, and pay back the debt and the loan himself. Then we have to help him. He's sick.' He paused. 'As for you, my darling wife.' He lifted her chin with his finger and gazed into her eyes. Nina pulled away and started fiddling with the covers, but he clasped her trembling fingers. 'I know you, Neene my love. I could always . . .' He paused again, the words coming out with difficulty. 'I always used to be able to read you like a book, but there's something bothering you that I can't fathom.'

Nina gave a little gasp and burst into tears. Falteringly, through her sobs she explained how Jack had tried to kiss her and the guilt that consumed her at having led him astray, and how once Charlie was home she dared not mention the incident though it weighed her down, convinced Charlie would think she had purposely led Jack on and that it would destroy their love. As she continued her voice grew stronger as she admitted her fear and emptiness while Charlie was so ill, her shame at not having the same courage and belief as her own daughter, and how dreadfully she'd missed him and longed to feel his strong arms around her, holding her and sheltering her from the buffetting of the world.

'All the time I wanted you. I needed you so much. Yet I had to show you I really have grown up and can manage on my own . . .'

'I hope not all the time, my darling, else what job do I have?' interrupted Charlie huskily, opening his arms. Sometime later he'd work out his feelings about Jack. Now all he wanted was his wife.

'Oh! Charlie, I love you so much,' shuddered Nina from the depths of her being, moving into his embrace. Then, with infinite tenderness and with her assistance, for the first time since the accident they made love.

Chapter Twenty-two

GLAD TO BE away from Sydney for a few days, Jo stared around at the small crowd of elegantly dressed and hatted men and women at the Tamworth race meeting, wondering for an instant what it would have been like if she had continued with her modelling career. Although she refused to admit it, the incident with Bertie had shaken her badly. Strange noises at night made her edgy. Jumping every time the phone rang, she kept walking into the office expecting to find threatening letters. Though no more arrived, the media got hold of the story and soon the whole world knew of the Kingsfords' crisis. Then Jo was greatly cheered to receive a letter from Emma.

She and Emma had remained close even though they rarely wrote or phoned more than twice a year; Jo regularly saw her friend's face and luscious body leaping out of the glossy magazines. Fleetingly, as the horses moved into the barriers, Jo thought of Emma's letter. Her friend's happiness bubbled through her words—her career was going strong, she had never been happier in her life and she was madly in love with a rock star. Then Jo remembered the jolt of pain that had shot through her as she read how Emma had run into one of Lelia's friends and learned that Simon was off travelling the world and that the family were being very tight-lipped about his behaviour.

'You didn't mention him in your last letter, so I guess you haven't heard either . . .' The kind words that followed had blurred before Jo's eyes. Furious with herself for letting him get under her skin again, she had stuffed the letter back in its envelope and gone out and bought herself a new hat, the fetching bright red and white one she was wearing today.

Now, as the horses leaped out of the barrier, Jo's full attention was back on the track. Watching Sleeper leap in front from the start, Jo's heart lurched and she jumped up and down, urging him on.

'Go, Dopey! Go!' she yelled, all thoughts of Emma and Simon pushed into the far recesses of her mind. Sleeper is back on form, she thought bursting with pride as he stormed ahead of some of the best sprinters in the country. Her heart racing, she watched him streak past the finishing post three lengths ahead of the impressive field. Jubilant, Jo whirled round and hugged Phillip, giving him a smacking kiss on the mouth which he returned with equal fervour. Looking slightly startled afterwards, they stared at one another.

'Isn't he amazing?' cried Jo breathless, then dashed over to Sleeper and Damien to congratulate, be congratulated and collect yet another winning sash. While the race meeting was relatively small, many influential people had attended it and Sleeper's win, along with two other wins and one second place for the Kingsford stables, had at last established Jo as a force to be reckoned with.

'Mum and Dad seem to be much happier these days,' Jo remarked to Phillip as they drove back home, Sleeper and the other horses safely heading for Sydney in the float under the watchful eye of Pete. 'God, I'm tired.' Stretching, she laid her head against Phillip's shoulder and shut her eyes. A happy smile hovered around her lips, music from the cassette player gently soothing as they rumbled along the country road. It had been a long hard month for Jo, scratching away, struggling to get new owners, to keep the horses up to scratch, always with this sense of unease following her and the bank balance reminding her how perilously close they had come to having to sell the stables.

Then there had been all the scenes with Bertie as they tried unsuccessfully to get him to seek counselling for his gambling problems, reducing Nina to tears on several occasions. With Charlie now much more like his old self, Jo felt more confident. She supported his insistence that Bertie had to pull himself out of this one by himself and not come crying to the family, yet there was an undercurrent of tension and she worried just how strong her father really was.

She worried about Bertie as well. At least, though, in the space of a five-minute conversation she had established with the solicitor that Bertie had been talking absolute nonsense in threatening to sell the stables from under her. But he had not forgiven her for ignoring his cries for help before the mugging and a couple of times she had walked in on phone calls which he had abruptly ended. He had also hit her for a couple of small loans. Riddled with guilt and terrified of a repeat of the mugging, though all her instincts screamed out not to give him the money, Jo had found refusing him face to face nigh impossible. Sometimes she felt unbearably weighed down with the responsibility of everything. But then a day like today came along and made it all worth-while, Jo thought, happily breathing in Phillip's warm male smell. She scratched her nose, the soft cotton of his shirt tickling her, and snuggled closer. Phillip was another of her problems but then again, maybe he wasn't. She drifted off.

Bumping along the scenic Putty Road, always watchful for kangaroos as the shadows lengthened, from time to time Phillip glanced down at Jo breathing gently beside him, her warm perfume wafting over him when she stirred, her long hair straying like seaweed along his arm. His body ached with longing as he relived their brief kiss when he had swung her around in his arms and tasted the sweet salt of her lips, both flushed with Sleeper's victory. It had all felt so natural, so sweet, as though they were meant to be together. Gently he moved his arm and placed it around her shoulder so she lay in the curve of his arm. She gave a muffled grunt and snuggled closer, only increasing his longing. Country races always made him feel good; away from the city a special intimacy sprang up between the two of them. They could almost have been husband and wife, he thought restlessly, irritated with himself for dithering for so long in showing Jo his true feelings. She always seemed relaxed and happy with him, yet ever lurking in the shadows was the spectre of Simon. Jo never mentioned him but Phillip knew he was still there in her heart. How Phillip hated the man, hated and envied him at the same time, that he could command such deep love for so long. Yet of the two, Phillip told himself sternly, he had to be the luckier. Simon was on the other side of the world, invisible, silent, and Jo was here warm, vibrant and lying in his arms. He pulled the car off the road and stopped near a paddock gate.

'Wake up, Snow White. It's time for a break and cup of tea,' he said, shaking her gently.

'Where are we?' asked Jo sleepily as she stretched and pulled a face.

'Two more hours and we'll be home,' said Phillip, getting out of the car and stretching his cramped legs. The sun was sinking on the horizon, the paddocks bathed in gold. A kangaroo watched from the tall grass, stock-still and almost invisible. Jo handed Phillip a cup of tea from the thermos and a biscuit and leaned against the car, nibbling at the corner of her biscuit. She gave him a sidelong glance, watching his strong chiselled face, following the full contours of his lips. His roughened hands clasped the cup and her pulse quickened as she wondered what it would be like to feel them caress her body, and suddenly she longed for him to hold her. A fat kookaburra stared down at them from a telegraph wire, then lifted its fat beak in the air, cutting the evening stillness with its raucous call and breaking Jo's mood.

'What am I going to do about Damien's girl-friend?' she asked abruptly.

'You mean Hope?'

'More like Hopeless,' nodded Jo with a grin, sipping her tea. 'She looked dreadful again today. She's got a lovely nature but absolutely no idea how to dress. Damien's getting too high a profile to drag someone looking like that around with him.' Slightly taller than Damien, the plump seventeen-year-old had turned up dressed entirely in black, her heavy pendulous breasts stuffed into a too-tight cotton jumper, the skimpy skirt stretched over her ample backside, black laddered tights showing beneath, her feet squashed into badly scuffed high heels. With her peroxide blonde hair and eyes

411

outlined in thick black kohl and plastered with mascara, she looked like a tiny blinking owl. The whole outfit was capped with a cheap, overpowering perfume.

Phillip put his cup down on the car bonnet, a frown puckering his brow. At this moment he didn't give a fig about Hope. The only person he wanted to talk to or think about was Jo. 'Rope your mother in. She's had enough practice with this sort of thing,' he said more abruptly than he meant.

'Hey, why didn't I think of that?' replied Jo. 'You're always so practical. How come I miss the obvious? Have I said something to upset you?' she asked, seeing his frown.

'I don't want to talk about Hope, Faith, Uncle Jo Bloggs or any other lame ducks you want to rescue,' said Phillip, trying to keep his tone playful. 'The only person I want to talk about is you.' He took the cup from her and placed it beside his on the bonnet. 'You are the most perfect woman I have ever met. Beautiful, gutsy, intelligent . . .' Jo grimaced. Her heart started hammering. 'We're like an old married couple, Jo. We do everything together, we discuss, we plan, we work everything out together. The only thing we don't do is this.' He pulled her to him with one hand, pushing away the platinum strands from her face with the other. Then he kissed her warm pink lips.

'That's twice,' he laughed shakily as they broke away.

'Make it the magic three,' whispered Jo breathlessly, her face still upturned to his, sliding her arms up around his neck, the contours of her body moulding to his.

'If you insist,' murmured Phillip. Covering his mouth with hers, he kissed her long and hard,

412

sending little thrills of delight through her, reawakening sensations she had kept buried for too long. Then, sweeping her up in his arms, he carried her to the gate where he gently sat her on the top bar, his hands clasping her knees to steady her. 'Have you any idea how much I love you and how long I have wanted to do that?' Jo's laughter was warm and low, her body tingling from his touch. Phillip picked up her left hand, the fingers ringless, and pressed the soft palm to his lips and Jo stiffened. Suddenly she was back in Norfolk and it was Simon kissing her and he was sliding the ring on her finger and they were promising to love each other till the end of time. Phillip looked at her in consternation as her eyes filled with tears which came tumbling down her cheeks.

'What's wrong, Snow White? What did I do wrong?' he stuttered.

Quickly Jo slid from the gate. 'I'm sorry!' she cried, her hands to her face, and ran to the car. Phillip ran with her, cursing himself for being such a clumsy fool. Curling up in a tiny ball Jo buried her face in the leather of the seat, her body racked with sobs. Unable to bear watching her misery, Phillip slid into the car beside her and took her once more in his arms. Burying her face in his broad chest, Jo sobbed out all the pain and longing Simon's silence had built up inside her, which she had so wrongly thought she had conquered.

'I'm over him, Phillip, I really am,' she kept insisting. 'I'm just so tired. It's been so hard, all this stuff with Bertie and Mum and Dad and the phone calls and that horrible note. I'm so tired.'

Phillip listened, stroking her hair, and quietened her sobs, any hope of gaining her love vanishing forever.

'Why do you put up with me crying and carrying on like this?' hiccuped Jo, red-eyed, fiddling with a lock of his brown hair.

'Because you need someone to take care of you,' he said gently, kissing her hair.

Neither of them spoke much for the rest of the journey. Returning Jo safely home Phillip went out and got very drunk, then a few days later he rang up an old girlfriend.

Popping into the stables shortly before the horses were due to be walked one afternoon, Jo was surprised to hear clattering coming from the food barn. Striding quickly down the walkway and round the corner, she pushed up the roller door and caught Sally emptying feed from one of the buckets into another. Startled, Sally looked up, alarm in her eyes, which was quickly replaced by friendliness.

'Les asked me to redo some of the feed,' she said before Jo could question her. Businesslike, she finished pouring the feed into the bucket. For a moment Jo believed her. Then she looked back at the bucket in Sally's hand; something about the girl's attitude and the situation struck her as very odd.

'Whose feed is that?' Jo asked sharply, glancing at the neat rows of numbered buckets and then at the corresponding names of horses on the whiteboard on the wall.

'I told you, Les asked me to redo the feeds,' the girl retorted defensively, trying to hide the number on the bucket.

Jo grabbed it from her, a horrible thought occurring to her. The bucket belonged to Let's Talk. Then Jo noticed a blue plastic bucket containing

414

more feed. Thinking she was just being neurotic, she was about to go back outside when the penny dropped. Twenty-five contained anti-inflammatories for another, recently injured, horse and Sally had been pouring the contents into bucket twenty-four—Let's Talk's bucket. Let's Talk was racing tomorrow. If he had eaten the wrong feed his swab would have shown up to contain a prohibited substance and he would have been disqualified after the race. To be accused of doping her horses was the very last thing Jo needed after all the recent bad publicity over Bertie.

'You swapped the feeds round, didn't you?' accused Jo, grabbing the girl by the wrist as she tried to make a dash for the door. 'You were setting me up! Why you, Sally? I thought we got on fine.'

'I don't know what you're talking about,' spat Sally, her demeanour changed. 'Let go, you're hurting me.'

Jo released her wrist and pulled the name tag viciously off the girl's shirt. 'You won't be needing this. You're fired and you know exactly why,' she snapped furiously, eyes hard as granite.

'It's your word against mine and who's going to believe a stupid bitch like you with too much money and taking orders from a cripple?' snarled the girl. Grabbing her jumper she kicked over the offending feed bins, knocking over two others as well, and ran from the stables.

Trembling all over, Jo cleared up the mess. Calling Les, together they redid the feed for all the horses. Then, slumping down in her office, Jo tried to work out why Sally of all people would do that to her, and came up with a blank. Did the world really see her as the poor little rich girl playing at training horses? She shook her head. She was getting maudlin, but the barb had cut deep.

Jo wished she could pick up the phone and pour out her hurt to Phillip, but things had changed between them since that drive home from Tamworth. Phillip continued to treat Jo the same way he always had—with respect and care—and his gentle strength and solid commonsense continued to make her feel safe and secure. Yet she sensed he had withdrawn from her. It was nothing she could put into words, cheerful and efficient as ever, if anything he worked harder with her than before. But he was quieter and more serious and a couple of times she caught him staring out into the distance, a new wistfulness in his eyes. Not sure where she stood with him Jo continued to confide in him and ask his opinion on matters to do with the horses, but she could not deny their relationship had altered.

'I heard Sally boasting to one of the other strappers she's been seeing Dennis Cook who does a lot of rides for Rosy,' said Pete sombrely after Jo had explained Sally's sudden dismissal. 'Probably just a coincidence, but you never know.'

'Probably,' nodded Jo, walking away grim-faced. The disaster had been averted but it had undermined her trust in her own workers.

'Who do you trust, Winks?' Jo asked the old man tiredly as she helped him lock up at the end of the day.

Winks shook his head, equally mystified. 'You've upset someone, that's for sure. Just watch your step, girl.'

'I thought I was,' she said, trying to sound unruffled, determined not to let this get to her, yet unable to stop wondering pessimistically what would be next. Her answer came three weeks later, knocking her sideways and stopping her dead in her tracks.

First Damien was suspended for three months for interference on consecutive Saturdays, and as if that wasn't enough, stirred on by bad publicity and rumours of Charlie's demise, owners started leaving the stables in droves, complaining that they had come to Kingsford Lodge to have their horses trained by Charlie, not one of his kids—and a girl to boot.

'Why didn't they leave ages ago if they felt like that?' stormed Jo, striding up and down Charlie's study, her frustration growing with every step. 'You may not be there in person but we're winning races and ... and ...' she swivelled round to face her father. 'Damn it, Dad, how long do I have to prove I'm good before they'll accept me? I'm sick of bloody hearing Pete's the one who's the real foreman. For God's sakes, am I any good?'

'You know the answer to that, Jo. It's just a handful who've shot through, and good riddance to them. There'll be others who'll want to train with us. The Kingsford name is still good, father or daughter. Get on with what you have to do and leave the rumour-mongering and temper tantrums to the others.'

'It's easy enough for you to say, Dad, but I have to get out there every day ... and another thing. I know Damien has been warned on a few occasions for shifting ground, but I had a look on the video. It was quite obvious on both rides that the other jockey forced him over.' Neither horse had come from Phantom Lodge but the jockey the second time had been Sally's boyfriend Dennis Cook. It all seemed too coincidental.

'Calm down, chicken,' said Charlie, placing his hand over Jo's. 'We can be cleverer than the rest of them.'

Jo's eyes softened. 'Dad, you haven't called me chicken since before ... before ...' She gulped, squeezing his hand tight. His words were clearer today too.

'None of that teary stuff now, Jo. Keep it for later,' retorted Charlie quickly but the significance of her words was not lost on him, his memory was intact and his pride and love for his daughter knew no bounds. 'What you do, Jo, is you let the interference thing run its course. You let them win this round.'

'What?' screeched Jo in horror. 'You're asking me to sit back and do nothing when they're in the wrong and meanwhile the stables go down the gurgler?'

'Trust me on this one,' said Charlie, looking her square in the face. After a long pause Jo reluctantly agreed. 'Good girl. Maybe it's time I put in an appearance at the stables to restore a bit of faith in the tenacity of Charlie Kingsford—not to mention seeing what you've been doing to my horses in the interim,' he added casually with his lopsided grin, but there was a steely glint in his eyes, his mind already planning ahead as Jo flung her arms around him and hugged him. It was time to call in some favours. One person who could help bring back custom with a few words in the right ears was Jack Ellis. Charlie and he had been skirting around one another ever since Nina had confessed to him about Jack's advances—the business Jack brought the stables was worth hanging onto, and damn it he still liked the man, but Jack definitely owed him one.

Overjoyed that Charlie had finally agreed to visit the stables, nevertheless Jo's frustration built over the next three months as she sweated out the wait, with Damien out of action, determinedly working the horse but only getting places in minor races in small country areas, acutely aware of the focus of criticism aimed at the lodge. The stables and bank account continued to empty out at an alarming rate, with only a few stalwarts believing in her ability, loyally hanging on. Compounding her misery she watched Damien, his suspension over and desperate for rides, win the Moonee Valley Stakes on one of Rosy's horses.

'When does it ever stop?' cried Jo, flopping down on the swing sofa on the back veranda one still sweltering afternoon, having just finished another phone call with the accountant. Her heart was set on entering Let's Talk for the Melbourne Cup this year but at the rate they were going she'd run out of time to clock up the wins the horse needed to qualify.

A big dark chestnut, Jo had loved Let's Talk from the moment she had laid eyes on him. Noisy, demanding, cheeky, he had gained his name by skitting about the stable yard and whinnying whenever he felt he was not getting enough attention. Paraded into the hushed bidding ring by a young strapper, the only sound the auctioneer's call, Let's Talk suddenly stopped dead in his tracks. No matter what the girl did the horse wouldn't budge. Grinning, Jo entered the bidding with a vengeance and was surprised when it was all over in seconds and the horse was hers. While others beside her muttered about dubious lineage and apparent wilfulness, she had never felt so excited nor so sure about a horse. She could see the potential in his young sturdy frame and spirited streak. But still the horse stood firm. In desperation the strapper started clapping. Let's Talk eyed the crowd and took one step forwards. Then someone in the crowd started clapping. Let's Talk took another step forwards. Quickly cottoning on, everyone else joined in cheering and clapping too. Responding with a quick bow of his head, the horse pawed the ground twice. Letting out a loud whinny he then trotted happily out of the bidding ring, tail held high, amidst much mirth, and to the red-faced strapper's relief. Later out on the track, Let's Talk's powerful stride and seemingly effortless gait confirmed Jo's faith in him even more. He had cost her a mere three thousand dollars and he just kept improving.

'I know I can do it if I can just get past all this garbage.' Her shoulders slumped and she scraped her feet against the deck, picking at the fringe on the Indian cotton blanket in despair. The swing groaned in complaint.

At twenty-five Jo's life was on hold, her whole career hanging in the balance, the stables' bank balance plummeting; her greatest unspoken fear that trust in her father and patience were simply not enough. Yet right now what other choice did she have? The heat was stifling. Beads of sweat trickled down the inside of Jo's cotton blouse, the humidity sapping her last drop of energy. Bertie had once more been pressuring Nina to sell and if they didn't get back into the game soon, Jo would have to declare them bankrupt. God, where was her life going? A sulphur-crested cockatoo shrieked across the hazy blue. Too restless to sit still despite the heat, Jo walked out to check the mail, wondering what other disasters awaited her.

Unenthusiastically she flipped through the junk mail and the magazines her mother regularly received from overseas and suddenly her heart missed a beat as she recognised the unmistakable writing on a brown paper package at the bottom of the pile. In shocked disbelief she ran back to the house, tossed the other mail on the kitchen table and ripped open the fat package pulling out a manuscript labelled *uncorrected proofs* and with it an envelope and the flat cover of a book. Heart pounding, Jo stared at the cover—a solitary bird lifting into flight against a backdrop of the Norfolk mudflats, the words *The Oystercatcher* and *Simon Gordon* leaping out at her. Trembling from head to toe she fumbled with the envelope, her hands shaking so violently that it slipped to the floor. Stomach churning, she retrieved the envelope and tore it open, her eyes racing across Simon's all too familiar handwriting.

My darling Jo
It is now several years since we said goodbye and even though I have kept out of your life I have been watching as you have grown and blossomed. Always I kept hoping for that phone call but I promised you time and I have and will always give you time and space. I did call once but you never rang back.

Jo's heart lurched, a confusion of emotions bombarding her. What phone call? Why had he suddenly written? Why had he never responded to any of her calls? The words kept blurring as she read and she had to keep wiping away the tears.

Where your life has been very much in the public gaze, mine has been quite the opposite. When I got back home I wondered how I would go on living without you. All I wanted to do was to run away, which is exactly what I did. Cowardly I know, but I had to. My family were amazingly understanding. I think Mum at least understood that I needed to work out who I was and what I wanted to do, but I know they didn't find it easy. I'd always vaguely dreamed of becoming a writer but it was only after we separated that I discovered I had to write.

They say writing can be cathartic and for me that has been true. Writing The Oystercatcher, *I believe, saved me from going insane.*

Jo turned briefly to the book cover, tears streaming unhindered down her cheeks. In her mind she was back in Simon's arms amongst the sea lavender. She could hear the call of the birds, feel the soft salt wind against her cheek and the warm pressure of his body next to hers. She would never forget the distinctive cry of the oystercatcher nor the catch in Simon's voice at sharing his joy of his special place with her.

I wanted you to read The Oystercatcher *first, before the world sees it, my darling Jo. I'm sure you have guessed by the title that it is the story of our love. I have dedicated it to you and it comes as a statement of my undying love for you, to thank you for the richness you gave to my life while we were together, a richness and love that I have never ceased to long for and to pray for its return. Jo, I love you and I want so much to be with you again. Reading about your father's progress, I wonder if maybe now there is once more hope for us . . .*

The rest of the letter explained that *The Oystercatcher* was to be published in two months' time and that, although Simon was an unknown author, because of his connections in Australia his publishers had agreed he fly out for a short Australian tour around the beginning of November. He promised that he would call her very soon.

Her throat tight, Jo turned to the dedication. It said simply 'To the person who is and always will be the centre of my being.' Gathering up the manuscript, letter and cover, she stumbled blindly back out to the swing seat on the veranda. For the next two hours she sat on the seat, the heat and humidity unnoticed as she devoured Simon's words. She kept brushing away the tears but her eyes kept filling, fresh hot tears tumbling down her cheeks and splashing onto the pages. The passion she had felt in Simon's arms flooded back to her as she turned the pages, the aching longing and the emptiness inside her as vivid as ever. Why had he never told her this was what he had been doing? Why the need for such a long silence? She would have understood.

Turning over at last to the final page she covered the words with her fingers, sliding her hand down the page, revealing each line one at time, the poignancy of his words almost too painful to bear.

It is winter now. The biting wind stings my face as I shiver alone on the flat Norfolk wetlands. The other birds have long since migrated south. For an instant I believe she will come rushing back into my waiting arms. As I watch, a solitary bird climbs, circles and dives, its familiar distinctive cry echoing across the ebbing tide flooding me with memories. Hovering, it swoops down one final time as though it understands my pain. Then it too leaves the marshes. The sea lavender stirs and as the water laps at my cuffs my last hopes flee with the oystercatcher.

With a great shuddering sob Jo shut her eyes and lay back against the soft cotton, hugging the manuscript. Her eyes stung from so much crying and she felt wrung out but still the tears stole out from under her eyelids and poured down her cheeks.

'Oh, Simon. It didn't need to be like that,' she whispered, desolate.

Chapter Twenty-three

OVER THE FOLLOWING two weeks Jo found it almost impossible to talk civilly to anyone. Struggling with a confusion of anger, disappointment and longing, she buried herself in her work, thoughts of Simon too exhaustingly painful to dwell on. She found her father's occasional visits to the stables intrusive and their discussions invariably ended in argument. Even Phillip couldn't get close to her. Finally one morning, walking back to the car with Phillip chatting beside her after a particularly unsuccessful track work, she let down her guard.

'Men are very peculiar,' she announced, interrupting his flow.

'Not as peculiar as women,' retorted Phillip with a lopsided grin, hoping to jog her out of the strange mood she had descended into recently. 'What's brought this on?'

'Well they are, let's face it. They do things and they say things and then they ... well ...' Jo could feel his eyes searching her face. 'I heard from Simon last week,' she blurted out. A horse and rider clattered past in the gloomy dawn.

'Oh!'

'What d'you mean, "Oh"?' demanded Jo, quickening her stride.

'Nothing really,' replied Phillip, speeding up beside her. 'I wondered why you'd gone a bit off lately.'

Jo glanced up at him sharply. 'What's that supposed to mean? I haven't gone off.' Phillip said nothing. Jo started talking very fast. It seemed easier to tell him in the semigloom. 'He's written a novel.' She plunged her hands deep in her jacket pockets. 'It's about these two people, well of course it's about two people. It's set in Norfolk where he used to take me.' She shrugged, her stumbling words hanging in the air between them. 'Oh, it's just that, well, he writes amazingly well but it stirred up all these emotions I didn't want stirring up.' They were nearly at the car. 'He said he's coming out here in November to do a promotional tour of his book.' There, now it was out. She wasn't sure why she needed to explain it all to Phillip, but she didn't want any lies or deceit between them.

'Good for him. That's not a bad start for an unknown,' said Phillip. He pulled the car keys from his pocket, keeping a tight grip on his emotions; the thought of Simon reentering Jo's life plunged him into a mixture of anger and despair.

'Yes, it is, isn't it?' replied Jo. More relaxed now, she slid into Phillip's car and started talking shop again. By the time they reached the stables Phillip had his emotions back under control.

The next few months for Jo were completely draining. Refusing to accept defeat as the media's attention swirled around her—alternately proclaiming her and the stables doomed, then challenging her to prove herself one of the big league by becoming a trainer in her own right—she ploughed her energy into working the thoroughbreds, picking her father's brains, demanding peak performance from her riders and hiding her fears for the future of Kingsford Lodge. At the same time she struggled to come to terms with Simon's sudden reappearance in her life and the knowledge that he would be in Australia later in the year. Numbed by all the other disasters in her life she no longer knew how she felt towards him; Charlie was still not strong enough to take on the running of the stables, and she had no idea what to do about Phillip.

She felt too vulnerable, too emotionally raw to let anyone come near her, least of all the man she refused to accept she was falling in love with. She knew she took him far too much for granted. Yet the tenderness he had shown when he had held her and comforted her on their return from Tamworth had touched her deeply. It had not mattered that she was crying for a lost love, or that she had hurt him, which she knew she had. He had been there. He was always there. He gave her the courage to keep going when life was at its blackest. It wasn't that he made decisions for her, it was just that he was her sounding board, a man who was nonjudgemental and demanded nothing in return. With Simon about to descend upon Australia she had to sort herself out. She frowned as Phillip examined a horse who had been having problems with one of his hooves.

'It's mending nicely,' said Phillip, gently rubbing the horse's flanks. Then he broke the news that Doctor Zinman had insisted he go to Hong Kong for the next month with another client and he would be sending another vet along to look after Kingsford Lodge. 'I know this couldn't be worse timing but I can't get out of it. Freddy gets these bees in his bonnet and he has insisted it has to be me.' He gave her a crooked grin. 'I'll be back, Snow White, no worries, riding my charger right into the stables in plenty of time to get Let's Talk purring along.' He stepped back as the strapper led the dark chestnut horse back to his stall, hooves clattering across the concrete.

'Too right it's bad timing. Can't he get someone else to run after his special clients?' snapped Jo. Phillip gave Jo a long look. 'I'm sorry. That was uncalled for,' she apologised quickly.

'You won't have any worries with Alison. She's good. I've been through everything with her in detail,' said Phillip briskly, picking up his bag and walking with Jo to the gate. Her gaunt look worried him. She had lost far too much weight recently. 'Take care . . . and eat. I'm going to miss you.' He gave her a quick hug.

Jo smiled briefly but her shoulders sagged as she walked over to the tack room to check the stirrup leathers. Damn Freddy Zinman. Right now she didn't need the extra worry of working with a different vet, quite apart from having her best friend whisked away from her. She rubbed her finger over a bit, the steel cold to the touch, noting with satisfaction that the saddles were now polished and shiny after she had yelled at everyone at the beginning of the week. She was getting obsessive again and over-sensitive. This was not the way to get through all the muck and confusion that surrounded her.

Alison proved to be remarkably easy to get on with, pleasant and efficient at her work, but she was not Phillip. Jo missed him far more than she could possibly have imagined. Each time the phone rang she expected it to be him and then remembered with a jolt that he was away.

Trying to snatch a midmorning nap at home one day, Jo tossed and turned, thoroughly unsettled. How she longed to turn back the clock and replay the journey back from the Tamworth races, respond to Phillip's kisses instead of dredging up old memories of Simon. Now it was too late. She picked up *The Oystercatcher* and flicked through the loose pages. Tossing them to one side she got up and made herself a cup of coffee. Let's face it, my personal relationships are a disaster, she thought despondently. She rang a couple of clients and then arranged to meet Dianne for lunch.

Sitting in a corner of the restaurant at the hotel where Dianne worked, Jo unburdened herself to her friend, relieved to talk to someone who wasn't involved in her turbulent and sometimes extremely public life. She shared her frustration at Phillip being whisked away to Hong Kong then told Dianne about Simon and his novel.

'Do you still love him?' asked Dianne, cutting into her open Danish sandwich.

'Who?'

'Simon, who else?' said Dianne, eyebrows raised.

Jo poked her food with her fork. About to reply she was interrupted by a gruff male voice.

'You want to do more lunches and less messing with horses. You're giving the industry a bad name, you are.' Outraged, Jo looked up and stared into Kurt Stoltz's mean dark eyes. Taken by surprise she gaped at him, her fork frozen in midair. 'That's right, gawk at me as if you don't know what I'm on about,' snarled Kurt, shoving his face so close Jo could smell his breath. 'You want to watch your step, my girl, or you might find yourself in some real trouble.'

Snapping out of her stupor, Jo scraped back her

chair and leaped up, shoving him out of the way.
'Don't you threaten me, Kurt Stoltz! I could tell
people a thing or two about you that wouldn't sound
too pretty,' she spat back. Instantly she regretted her
words as a flashbulb popped and a microphone was
stuffed under her nose.

'I could have you up for assault and intimidation,'
cried Kurt loud enough for the hungry newspaper
reporter to hear. Jo tried to escape but the reporter
and his cameraman pressed forward. Leaping to her
feet Dianne forced her way between Jo and the inva-
sive media men, calling for the restaurant manager,
but it was too late. They had their headlines and
Kurt had melted from the room.

Shaking from head to toe, Jo let Dianne usher her
quickly out of the restaurant and into the staff
quarters.

'I should have had more sense than to sit us in
such a public place,' apologised Dianne.

Jo shook her head. 'You weren't to know that
creep was going to set me up like that,' said Jo biting
her trembling bottom lip, far more shaken than she
wanted to let on. The incident brought home to her
how much Kurt hated her and it made her break
out in goosebumps. She wished again that Phillip
wasn't overseas. On the rare occasions she had
glimpsed Kurt on the track she had kept out of his
way. Vicious and mean his rumour-mongering skills
were sharper than ever, but until today she had
managed to keep him at bay.

Kurt's attack only intensified Jo's sense that her
life was disintegrating before her very eyes. Nothing
seemed to be going right. She felt tired and
weighed down and she missed Phillip far more than
she wanted to admit. Then like the sun coming out
after torrential rain, business began to pick up. In

the one week Jo took three enquiries from owners wanting to put their horses with the stables.

'Three owners in one week,' she squealed, staring at the notepad where she had scribbled down the names. The phone rang. It was Charlie.

'Get any interesting callers today, Chicken?' His speech always seemed much clearer over the phone.

'You could say,' Jo replied as calmly as she could and then chattered out her excitement down the line. 'I love you, Dad. How on earth did you do it?'

'Patience and trust, Chicken, patience and trust,' he replied. He'd been confident Jack would come through with the goods.

'Dad . . .!'

'Put it this way, someone wanted to be extra specially nice to us. Have a nice day.' The phone went dead.

Jo stared at it for a moment, grinning from ear to ear, then replaced the receiver and switched on the office television for the latest race results. Her dad was a complicated person, but whatever he had done was working. The door opened. Jo looked up and gasped in delight.

'Phillip! I thought you were still in Hong Kong.' Leaping up she rushed over and hugged him as if her life depended upon it. Stepping back they stared at one another, both momentarily speechless. Collecting herself, Jo grabbed her notepad and waved it in his face. 'I'm back in business,' she cried, all her pent-up feelings bubbling to the surface. Determined this time not to make a complete idiot of herself and blub all over him, she swallowed hard and stepped back. 'How was your trip?'

Phillip glanced at the notebook and grinned at Jo. 'Lonely,' he said and stared at her so she blushed crimson. A clock chimed in the distance. 'I read about you and that weasel Kurt. Bloody sleazebag reporter should be sacked. I wish I'd been there. I'd have punched his lights out.'

'That would really have helped. Oh Phillip, I've missed you,' Jo laughed, happy he had missed her too. 'I'm just so glad the tide's finally started to turn. Dad's of course had a hand in all this, but one thing's for sure, Snow White's still alive and kicking! Alison's been great looking after the horses too, thanks. Come and say hi to them all again.' She grabbed his hand and urged him towards the horses, not wanting to dwell on thoughts of Alison and Phillip. She had heard talk that they were almost an item.

'Alison said everything was all pretty straight-forward. So what's your next plan of attack—I've never known you not to have one,' asked Phillip, rubbing Let's Talk's muzzle as the horse tried to chew his way through the padlock on his door, longing to gather Jo in his arms yet sensing that invisible fence still in place. She looked stunning, her face tanned, shirt open at the neck, jeans cling-ing to her rounded hips, her hair pinned back with a comb.

'If only I could enter this fella in the Melbourne Cup,' Jo declared, reaching up and scratching the horse's nose, enjoying the soft warmth of his breath.

'I've been sick with worry about the money I need to enter him in the Cup. I dare not put the stables further into debt but it breaks my heart not to enter him. Dammit, I am going to get the money,' she cried, with all the vibrant energy that had kept her going over the past few months. 'I'm going to wish it here. Heck, the horses are starting to come back, why not the finance?' She looked up at Phillip, her face alight with excitement.

'You never give up, do you,' he exclaimed admiringly. 'And knowing you, you'll find the perfect syndicate partners.'

'Yes, they've got to be part-owners with me, on a sixty-forty split, who spend most of the year out of the country and just let me get on with things. I'll take the sixty and they can work out between them which part of the horse each of them owns. That'd solve all our problems. And wouldn't that just sock the delightful Kurt between the eyes? Especially after the creep called Let's Talk an old flea bag in front of me and most of the Randwick trainers.' Jo grabbed Phillip and gave him a shake. 'I don't care what anyone thinks, I'm convinced Let's Talk has it in him to win the blessed thing. In fact, the more rumours spread about how hopeless he is, the better. That way no-one will be expecting the sudden onslaught.' She grinned wickedly at Phillip. 'Imagine ferret-features's face if Let's Talk came flying past his horse, winning by a length and a half. Wouldn't that make his blood curdle?' Her grin widened, the picture made her start to giggle. Catching her mood Phillip threw in a few choice ribald comments and soon the two were rolling around laughing like schoolkids, the tears streaming down their faces while Let's Talk kept nibbling away at his door.

'I haven't laughed like that since I can remember,' gasped Jo, clasping her hands to her aching sides, wiping her eyes. Then their laughter ceased and Phillip, drawing her into his arms, stepped back into the shadows and kissed her. For a long time neither of them moved. Dizzy from the kiss, so firm and strong yet so gentle, and utterly unlike any other sensation she had ever experienced, she let the feelings wash through her like a wonderful cleansing balm. It was as though every jangling nerve first tingled and then calmed as he kissed her on and on. Reluctantly they parted as a strapper clattered past.

'I didn't think it possible to miss anyone as much as I've missed you,' whispered Phillip huskily.

'Me neither,' breathed Jo. Reaching up she stroked his cheek. 'Especially when he's my best friend,' she added softly, her eyes moist. She stepped back into the sunlight, her body still throbbing from his embrace, almost colliding with another strapper leading two horses back to their stalls.

'Seriously though, we've got to come up with more ways to entice owners back,' she grimaced as she and Phillip strolled through the stalls, trying to seem as though their whole worlds hadn't suddenly been rocked from their axes.

'Have you thought about changing things around a bit?' suggested Phillip gently, wishing everyone would vanish from the stables so he could keep on kissing her.

'What d'you mean?'

'If I were an owner I'd want to know what was happening with my horses and not to be kept so much at arm's length,' he said, linking arms with her and wandering back down the walkway. 'I've heard a number of people complaining about not being involved enough. Is there any way you could attract owners to Kingsford Lodge because you offered something different?'

Jo grabbed both his hands, her face lighting up in amazed disbelief that they could be so much on the same wavelength. 'This is crazy. I've been playing with an idea while all this other stuff has been happening. It's been gnawing away at me. I ran it past Dad but he thinks it's a terrible idea "Waste of time, energy and money," he said. We had a bit of a row about it actually, but I really think it could work. I can't think of another way and I've got to do something drastic to get the stables back on its feet. We seem to teeter from crisis to crisis.' She took a deep breath. Charlie still got very tired and only spent small amounts of time at the stables, his support being mostly in his daily briefings with Jo. 'What do you think about Sunday champagne breakfasts, sort of open house to owners and prospective owners?'

'Go on,' said Phillip cautiously.

Excitedly she explained her ideas of meeting with owners on a regular basis, allowing them to see what was happening to their horses and explain why they did certain things, make them feel a part of the whole training process. 'I'm convinced it could work,' she cried, her cheeks flushed.

'It's different, so don't be surprised if you cop some flak,' warned Phillip.

'After the last few months, why would I care?' Jo's mind was buzzing with ideas. 'I'd want some of the jockeys to be there too, especially Damien now he's so well known. Once it's up and running I'll have another go at Dad and see if I can get him to come to one.' She hesitated. 'Would you be willing to explain the veterinary side of the business?'

'You're like an express train. I don't know how you do it. Throw you an idea, next thing you're charging full pelt down the track with it,' he smiled. 'It's good your dad's getting so involved again by the way, even if he doesn't like this idea.'

'Well, what do you think?' persisted Jo, brightening at his comments.

'Sure, I'll be in that. It can't hurt to give it a go, can it? On one condition . . .'

'Which is?'

'That you let me kiss you again, just to make sure

it really did happen the first time.' Jo threw back her head and laughed and he caught her again and crushed her in a bearhug, kissing her firmly on the lips. Breathless, they pulled away.

'You're so beautiful,' Phillip said and kissed her tenderly on the forehead.

As they parted Jo gave a deep contented sigh. 'We'd better at least pretend to look as if we're doing something constructive,' she laughed, leading him back into the sunshine. For the first time in months she felt incredibly relaxed as she nattered on about all the tiny little incidents she had not been able to share with anyone else whilst Phillip had been away. Jo felt as though a part of her had come home.

Two weeks later, the syndicate they had dreamt of became reality, and Let's Talk's training for the Melbourne Cup started in earnest.

Back into the full pressure of training and racing, the number of horses at Kingsford Lodge rising, Jo had one more concern but she decided to let it sort itself out. Striving to get the best riders for their mounts, trainers and owners vied for the top jockeys. Whilst most of Damien's wins had been on Kingsford horses, he had recently had successes at other stables as well, and Joe was unsure how far his loyalty towards her stretched. The answer came from an unexpected quarter at the first champagne breakfast. The stables looked spotless but it was a disappointing turn-out with only five owners turning up and one disgruntled owner from another stables, however Jo was heartened to see Damien had shown up with his girlfriend, whom everyone still called Hopeless.

'It's a start,' said Jo, talking to Pete and Phillip with forced cheerfulness, and was nearly bowled over by Hope, cheeks flushed, transformed in appearance through Nina's skilful guidance and in awe of Jo who had organised it all.

'I know you're really busy, miss, but I just wanted to let you know, Damy'll never forget what you did for him to get him started,' she bubbled, the champagne loosening her tongue. 'He's as loyal as a blue heeler. He'll never tell you but he worships the ground you walk on. If it weren't for you he wouldn't be where he is, we both know that, and he wants to win this cup for you as much as for himself.' Hope gulped down some more champagne.

'Thank you, Hope, that's sweet of you. I think we've got a great team,' smiled Jo, noticing the dark plum nail varnish which she guessed was not one of her mother's ideas.

'I'm ever so grateful to you too, miss,' Hope rattled on. Glancing about her, slightly tipsy, she lowered her voice. 'If you're wondering why Damy's been taking so many rides with Mr You-Know-Who at the You-Know-Where stables it's because he wanted to shove it up their noses that he's the best jockey in town and that he's working for you. Damy says winning all them races has rattled them good and put the wind right up Dennis Cook. So thank you, miss, and if I can do anything . . .' she tailed off as Damien, placing his arm possessively around her waist, doffed his forelock at Jo and dragged Hope away.

Turning to an owner at her elbow Jo listened to his questions, her mind still half on Damien. The jockey's skills were proving legendary around the tracks. He and Dennis Cook were now the two top

Australian jockeys and if Damien was as loyal as Hopeless promised then Jo had a definite advantage, but jockeys were funny animals and the name of the game was winning on the best horse. Still, until proven otherwise, Jo decided to believe Hopeless who stood staring adoringly at Damien. All they had to do was get Let's Talk up to scratch.

Now an experienced four-year-old, Let's Talk had lived up to Jo's expectations in every way. Attractive but not outstanding in looks he had developed the power Jo had suspected he possessed when she bought him. She had concentrated on building the strength in his shoulders, and his deep chest gave plenty of room for powerful lungs, but the trump card for the cheeky show-off was his now legendary showbiz antics.

Damien had experienced a repeat performance of the bidding ring fiasco after riding Let's Talk to his second win. Walking down the straight, as the crowd applauded, Let's Talk bowed and pawed the ground. When the crowd began clapping for the runner-up horse, Let's Talk stopped dead in his tracks and continued to bow and paw, despite every attempt by Damien to move him on. The crowd burst out laughing at these antics and clapped even harder, which only encouraged Let's Talk further. He continued for several minutes until he considered he had received enough applause, then he walked on, Damien very red-faced astride him. At the next race he repeated the whole performance, this time tossing his head, whinnying and rearing up on his haunches, but this time Damien was ready for him and played up to the crowd as well. Likened to Gunsynd, the famous Goondiwindi grey foaled in 1967, Let's Talk won the hearts of the crowd wherever he went so people came to watch him and bet on him as much because of his character as for his racing performance.

Jo, of course, was delighted with all this publicity but, even better, she could see he was developing into a great stayer. Despite his dubious parentage there was a lean strength about him that sent shivers of excitement down Jo's spine every time she watched him stretch out on the track.

'He's a sure thing on a long haul,' nodded Winks one morning, reading out the horse's time.

Jo gave the old man's arm a squeeze. 'We better check those padlocks on his door. I don't want anyone getting in at night and nobbling him.' The mental scars left by Sally's betrayal were still fresh and there had been a number of doping scams recently in racetracks around the countryside. Yet her hopes climbed as each day she watched the horse's performance improve inch by inch.

'Look at him. He's hardly raised a sweat. Take him round once more, Judy,' she shouted to the rider, leaning out of the window of the Pizza Hut.

Today was a fast day and great clouds of steam billowed from the sweating horses as they were led back to the stripping sheds after their gallops, their riders moving on to the next horse. Darting from window to window, listening to the sounds of the horses breathing, Jo watched the dim figures galloping round the track, checked times with Winks and yelled instructions to her riders. There were forty horses in the stables now—partly thanks to the champagne breakfasts which had become increasingly popular—but there was still plenty of hard work ahead to get Kingsford Lodge back to its former glory.

When the morning's work was over, Jo went home for a well-earned breakfast. In the kitchen she made herself some toast and jam and a cup of tea and carried it into the sunroom where her father was reading up on the latest breeding techniques.

'Let's Talk just keeps going and going,' Jo told her father proudly. Soon they were embroiled in a heated discussion over training.

'Come to track work and then you can see for yourself,' said Jo after a particularly niggly comment from Charlie. 'You've come to the stables before and you can get around pretty well with those,' she said indicating his two walking sticks. 'Swallow your pride, Dad. Phillip and I'll help you into the Pizza Hut.' She knew half his pickiness came from his own frustration and he looked particularly tired this morning.

'The day I come back on the track I walk on my own two pins,' growled Charlie, his weak hand clasping the book on his lap. He had made a pact with himself and he would keep it. It was part of his own self-motivation. Already he was managing with one stick a lot of the time. 'I see the results on the television. You just keep on listening to me and we'll be right.'

'It's not the same, Dad. Why do you have to be so stubborn?' she was tired too and longed to have her father see her in action. Besides, much of the training these days was based on her initiative and understanding of the horses and his criticisms cut deep. For a while they sat together lost in their own thoughts.

'About Phillip . . .' began Charlie, breaking the silence, a teasing note in his voice. 'I never stop hearing the bloke's name. It's Phillip this and Phillip that. Have you forgotten to tell me something?'

'He's my vet and a good friend, that's all,' said Jo yawning and firmly shut her mouth.

'Is that a fact?' stirred Charlie.

'Yes. I'm going to have a rest,' she stood up, blushing furiously.

'And you call me stubborn and proud,' Charlie shot at Jo as she stomped out of the room thoroughly irritated, wishing her father didn't understand her so well.

Day after day, week after week with Phillip by her side, Jo worked Let's Talk, running him in races where he would win easily, building his confidence, and then testing him against some of the big names in racing. Slowly but surely the two watched the gallant horse build up the wins he needed to qualify for entry into the Melbourne Cup, his antics continuing to win the hearts of racegoers across Australia, drawing increasingly big crowds. Jo also felt secure in Glen, the strapper she had put in charge of Let's Talk. He was as much in love with Let's Talk as Jo was and she felt very confident in his handling of the big chestnut. Her own relationship with the horse was similar to the one she had had with Outsider and she used all the techniques she knew to keep the animal fit and calm and less likely to get spooked over nothing.

Watching the horse cope with all types of track conditions Jo could not fault the big chestnut except for one point. No matter what she did, he never really settled going around the track the opposite way as he would need to do when running at Flemington. It worried Jo a lot but she kept pressing on.

Then Jo's attention was diverted away from Let's Talk at a major race at Rosehill when Hope, decked out in a beautiful little outfit complete with fluffy white hat, came running up to Jo, her eyes wide with fear.

'It's Sleeper! He's come all over strange. You've gotta come!' she burst out, interrupting Jo who was chatting with one of the course stewards.

Jo had already checked all the horses and Sleeper's strapper was one of her most reliable employees. She set off at a run back to the stalls. Pushing through the crowd that had gathered around the horse, she paled at the sight of Sleeper staggering in the stall, his powerful legs wobbling, his eyes filled with pain. Sleeper's strapper turned to her, his own eyes glistening with tears.

'He started scouring a few minutes ago. Someone's hit him with something,' the young man choked as the valiant horse struggled to stand.

Jo started shaking as the course vet hurried over and confirmed that the horse had been doped. Five minutes later, her heart like lead, Jo helped the suffering animal into the horse ambulance while the course announcer boomed out that Sleeper had been scratched from the race on veterinary advice.

As soon as he was strong enough Jo sent Sleeper down to Dublin Park for a spell, but his doping had shaken Jo to the core and the fear would not go away. Every day she checked with Winks that there had been no intruders or strange incidences. She went through her list of staff over and over again, yet they had been with her so long and were so utterly devoted to her and the horses that she couldn't believe one of them could be betraying her. Even Glen, the relative newcomer, was too much in love with his flamboyant charge for Jo to believe he could be bribed by someone from another stables. Always in the back of her mind was Kurt and the hate she saw in his eyes every time they met at the track which, as the Melbourne Cup grew closer, was far too often for her liking. Becoming increasingly more jumpy as November approached, Jo refused to allow any vet except Phillip near her horses, particularly Let's Talk.

'Why don't we grab a bite to eat, go and see a soppy movie and forget all about horses and racing for a couple of hours? You've got to make it through the Melbourne Cup Carnival too,' suggested Phillip after a particularly exhausting day at the beginning of October.

'I'll probably fall asleep,' admitted Jo with a wry grin, grateful for Phillip's thoughtfulness. The Melbourne Cup was held each year on the first Tuesday in November, but the carnival ran from the Saturday to the Tuesday, involving a grand ball on the Friday night beforehand, two other big races, the Victoria Derby and the MacKinnon Stakes, as well as several other high-profile races. The pressure was mounting and Jo could feel it. Driving herself harder and harder she ignored the warning signs her body gave her and charged on, snapping at her loyal stable staff, uncharacteristically letting little niggles become blown out of proportion and getting progressively more uptight. Then Emma called one day out of the blue. It was just what she needed to lift her flagging spirits.

'Emma rang today—you know, my famous model friend. She's been invited to present the Fashion in the Field prizes on Derby Day,' she cried excitedly to Phillip. There was a lilt in her voice that had been missing for too long, although it sounded somewhat raspy because of a sore throat she had developed three days previously.

'Hey, that's great! I'll finally get to meet this goddess in the flesh,' he replied cheerfully.

Jo pulled out a throat lozenge and popped it in her mouth. 'She's been invited to the Derby Eve Ball but she said she'd only attend if we were included in their party. Will you be my partner? She's dying to meet you and I'd hate to disappoint her.' She looked up at him from under her long lashes. 'I promise I won't get uptight and start yelling or throwing champagne glasses or anything, and I do know some very influential people.'

'Are you trying to bribe me?' Phillip asked huskily.

'I might be. Please say yes.'

'You realise I've got two left feet.'

'I don't mind. I'll lead,' grinned Jo, her eyes beguiling. She looked so soft and appealing, Phillip wanted to drag her off to bed then and there.

'You would too. When you look at me like that, how can I refuse?' replied Phillip, his heart pounding, wondering how he was going to survive with Jo in his arms for a whole evening without going crazy.

For a long time now Phillip had longed to take their relationship further, but the stress and pressure of work in the build up to the Melbourne Cup had forced them both to put their personal lives on hold.

With three weeks to go before the Melbourne Cup, three days before Jo and Phillip were due to fly down to Melbourne, Phillip turned up for his usual vet check ten minutes late to find Jo tearing strips off one of the strappers, her fingers clenched round a pitchfork.

'Where the bloody hell have you been?' screamed Jo, turning on Phillip in the middle of berating the ashen-faced girl.

'Pull your head in and calm down,' ordered

Phillip. Grabbing the pitchfork from her, he tossed it to the girl, who scuttled off into a stall where she started forking hay ferociously.

Trembling from head to foot, Jo stared at Phillip, her eyes glittering with fury. 'Don't you dare do that to me in my own stables ever again,' she hissed through clenched teeth.

'What the hell was all that about anyway?' demanded Phillip, grabbing her by the shoulders, ready to shake her, only to be shocked at the heat emanating from her.

'The stupid girl nearly gored the horse with the fork,' raged Jo.

'You're not well, Jo.' She was burning up with fever.

'I'm perfectly well,' cried Jo and promptly passed out.

Too late Phillip leaped to catch her as she slid to the ground, her head hitting the concrete with a resounding thud. Shaking, he knelt down beside her and felt her burning cheeks and frozen fingers.

'Jo! Jo, can you hear me?' He tapped her gently on the cheeks; her eyes were wide open, staring blankly straight ahead. Slowly coming round, Jo mumbled incoherently and tried to get up. 'Don't try to move,' ordered Phillip. Heart pounding, he gently gathered her up in his arms and carried her into the office where he laid her on the bed she sometimes used for catnapping and called Gloria to get the doctor. Pronouncing Jo had roaring tonsillitis the doctor prescribed penicillin and two weeks' rest.

'Don't be absurd,' croaked Jo to herself, grey-faced.

Twenty-four hours later, with the world no longer

spinning round her, she rang Gloria to check her plane ticket was booked and then persuaded Jackie the housekeeper to help her pack for Melbourne. Jo then rang Pete to ensure that everything was in order for the horses to be flown down to the stables they had rented at Flemington. Finally she rang Phillip.

Knowing there was no point in attempting to stop her, he reassured her that they were as prepared as they would ever be, that Let's Talk would be fine and that he'd drive her to the airport. At least he'd be there to catch the pieces, he thought as he stuffed the last pair of socks in his suitcase and snapped it shut.

'You're looking after me again,' Jo said huskily as the seatbelts warning light came on in the aircraft, feeling much improved now the medicine had started to work.

'Like I said, someone has to,' Phillip smiled, his eyes filled with love. Leaning close so she could hear him over the roar of the engines, he gave her a peck on the cheek, his eyes twinkling mischievously. 'You know, I can't decide if you're a classy thoroughbred or just a plain old stubborn mule.'

Chapter Twenty-four

ONCE IN MELBOURNE Jo's biggest concern was settling the horses in and working them in their new surroundings. Although they were used to travelling they nevertheless needed a period of adjustment to the new stables and track conditions, particularly with so much hanging on the upcoming races.

The full force of the penicillin quickly kicked in, making Jo feel much better, and while she fell exhausted into bed each night, the anticipation of the carnival, the excitement in the air and her nervous energy gave her plenty of drive. With each day she could see the horses felt more at home and Let's Talk, twigging he had a new audience, demanded attention on the track with even greater audacity than ever, winning more hearts and creating hilarious diversions at track work. Once at work, responding to the atmosphere of excitement, he pounded the track, his long measured strides covering the ground in record time, his powerful limbs glistening in the early morning sunlight. Jo was still concerned about him riding the wrong way round the track, so she and Damien kept working him steadily. Back in his stall she used all the calming methods that had worked so well for Outsider, whispering to the big horse, rubbing him with herbs, soothing him and pampering him so he rolled his eyes in ecstasy and nuzzled her in return.

'He managed the heavy track surprisingly well today,' said Pete to Jo on the eve of Derby Day as they watched Phillip examine Let's Talk while Arctic Gold shrieked for his feed in his stall.

'As long as he gets the crowd working for him he'll be right,' said Jo, her hands clutching a steaming cup of coffee. Over the past two and a half weeks Jo had fully recovered from her bout of tonsilitis, but the damp overcast morning made her shiver.

She had done all she could, now it was up to Damien and Let's Talk. She pulled her jacket closer around her and let out a gasp of delight as she caught sight of a tall, willowy young woman dressed in an old pair of jeans and a sweater, who had just stepped into the stables.

'Emma!' she shrieked shoving her coffee mug at a strapper, rushing over to her friend and hugging her close.

'I told Davie the only way to catch you was to get up in the middle of the night,' laughed Emma hugging Jo back. The two stepped back, staring at one another, hands still clasped.

'You look great. Thinner but great,' cried Emma, taking in Jo's drawn, pale face yet amazed at the aura of energy and excitement radiating from her.

'You don't look half bad yourself. You found the place all right? Oh, it's so good to see you! What have you done with your rock star?'

'I left him snoring in the hotel. He's definitely not a morning person,' she laughed, flashing the gigantic rock on her finger at Jo. Squealing with delight, Jo hugged Emma again, their laughter echoing through the stables. Horses shoved their noses inquisitively over their half doors to find out what all the commotion was about.

'Come and meet some of my favourite two- and four-legged friends, then we'll vanish,' cried Jo, dragging Emma towards Phillip who was talking to Pete. Quickly introducing Emma to both men she then took her round the stables, the horses eyeing her over, some reaching out to nibble her, others sniffing her inquisitively or staring at her with their big dark eyes while Emma stroked their soft noses.

'Meet the comedian,' said Jo, lovingly stroking Let's Talk who, seeing a stranger, immediately tossed his head up and down and started pawing the ground. 'You have to clap,' laughed Jo. Emma obeyed. Satisfied, Let's Talk bowed to Emma, settled down and, lifting his top lip, chewed at Jo affectionately. Emma laughed again, joining in with her friend's happiness.

Jo told Phillip and Pete she would ring in an hour, then whisked Emma off in a taxi to the privacy of an out of the way cafe in Melbourne. Over cappuccinos and cake they talked nonstop for the next two hours. Excitedly Emma told Jo how her career had skyrocketed and she was in demand all over the world, and Jo described some of her successes and frustrations.

'But I'm doing what I want. We both are,' said Jo, her eyes alight.

Emma nodded, flicking her long chestnut hair back off her face. 'The US is fun but hard work. A bit like a jungle, what with all the different egos floating around ... Well, it was till I met Davie,' she explained with a laugh. 'We kind of fell over each other at a party celebrating a new designer and we just clicked. I couldn't believe it. Oh Jo, I've never been so happy in my life. Even the media gives us a good time, mostly. You'll meet him at the ball tonight.'

'I'm longing to meet him. Whatever he's doing to you is working.' Good old down-to-earth Emma. She hadn't changed a bit. Except that the glimmer of sadness in her eyes had been replaced by a vibrant radiance and Jo felt a tug of envy.

'What about you?' asked Emma, sensing the fleeting mood change in Jo.

'I don't know,' she started. 'Well, I do, sort of. Oh Emma, I'm so hopelessly mixed up at the moment. Phillip's so lovely. He's kind and gentle and thoughtful and everything you could ask for and it was going swimmingly and then ...' She paused and fiddled with her coffee cup, her emotions unexpectedly choking her. Slowly she looked across at her friend. 'Simon's coming out and I don't know what to do. Part of me longs to go back to the past and the way things were between us and the other part ... The trouble is ... I don't know ... I loved Simon so much ...' she faltered. Tears sparkled in her eyes.

'You'll sort it out,' said Emma softly, gently squeezing Jo's hand.

'I know. I'm just a bit twitchy, that's all,' said Jo, wiping the corners of her eyes, trying to sound convincing.

'Think about what you want for yourself. You deserve to. You've worked hard enough. Look what you've achieved and you obviously love it.' Emma glanced at her watch. 'Oh golly, Jo, I wish I didn't have to do this but I've got to get to an interview. They've given me a schedule thick as toffee.'

'We'll catch up tonight at the ball,' smiled Jo, relaxing, glad to be off the topic of her love life.

Hiring a taxi she whisked Emma back across Melbourne to her hotel.

'See you tonight in something sexy and slinky,' grinned Emma, leaping out and flying up the hotel steps.

'You betcha!' grinned back Jo. 'The Grand Hyatt, please,' she said to the back of the taxi driver's head, waving to Emma as she disappeared into the hotel. Her old friend was indeed the consummate model, yet underneath she was still the Emma Jo knew and loved. It was great to see her so happy, yet the mention of Simon had set Jo trembling all over. If only she didn't feel so emotionally confused, but it had all been so long ago ...

Splashing a final dash of perfume on each wrist, Jo picked up her evening bag and stole and stepped from her room into the hotel corridor, her simple figure-hugging gold and cream ball gown shimmering as she moved, her shoulders bare except for the tiny string straps, a single enormous pearl gleaming against her creamy skin. Pressing the ground level button she was suddenly aware that her heart was pumping furiously.

'You look amazing,' said Phillip materialising from the crowd.

Jo felt an unexpected jolt at the sight of his powerful frame squeezed into a dinner jacket, his thick brown hair for once neatly combed. There was an air of raw sexuality about him she had never noticed before. Always likening him to a big cuddly teddy bear, tonight he promised far more than just hugs. 'It must be lack of sleep and tension making me light-headed,' she thought and gave him a dazzling smile.

Phillip kept staring at her. Pulling himself out of his trance he proffered his arm and walked her to the hotel taxi stand. Throughout the journey to the Hilton-on-the-Park and while Jo introduced him to His Excellency Prince Satu and the Michaelsons from Toorak, he couldn't keep his eyes off her. She dazzled. Her neat figure curved voluptuously. Her young firm breasts peeped enticingly over the top of the shimmering gold and cream, her whole being exuding an aura of unsophisticated sensuality that sent waves of longing through him. He could hardly believe she was the same woman who worked alongside him day after day in mud-splattered jeans and oversized men's shirts. She looked more enticingly beautiful than he could ever have imagined.

'Phillip, where are you?' sang Jo, shaking his arm as Emma, dressed in a dramatically simple black and gold evening dress, joined the party with her rock star lover. Focusing back on the party Phillip nodded politely while they were all introduced. Lifting two glasses of champagne from a waiter's tray, he passed one to Jo and fell into polite chit chat.

Davie lived up to Emma's description of him—larger than life, with dark mysterious eyes, a lived-in face and shock of dyed red hair, he soon set the party at ease cracking stupid jokes with everyone and making enough noise for ten, while allowing the world to see he was utterly besotted with Emma. His cockney accent somehow complemented Emma's aristocratic English accent and soon the whole party were chatting like old friends.

'I don't know what you're hesitating about. Your vet's absolutely gorgeous,' Emma whispered in Jo's ear.

Jo felt the blush spread from her cheeks down her

neck and across her shoulders. 'He's nice,' she agreed quietly.

'Just nice. Oh, I see—you really are taken with him,' whispered Emma knowingly.

Dinner announced, they walked on the arm of their partners through a magnificent tunnel of perfumed spring flowers into the dining room. Jo gasped in delight at the spectacle. No expense had been spared. Bedecked with crisp black linen table cloths and intricately folded white napkins, the tables sparkled with crystal and polished silver. Great November lilies spilled out from tall glass vases to head height, the whole room a vision in black and white. In one corner a twenty-piece band played soft music behind the polished wood dance floor.

For Jo the whole evening sped past in a whirl of good food, fun and laughter, and for the first time since she could remember she relaxed. It was impossible to stay serious with Davie and his unbelievably loud laugh, and Emma and Phillip were getting on like a house on fire. Jo kept stealing glances at Phillip, outrageously handsome in his dinner suit, and every time she looked at him she caught him looking at her, setting her heart racing.

Finally unable to ignore the craving to hold Jo that had been driving him mad all night, Phillip leaned over and whispered in her ear. 'Would you do me the honour of dancing with me and my two left feet,' he asked, kissing her hand, his eyes full of mischief.

Jo pushed back her chair and walked into his arms, surprised to find she was trembling all over. For the first half of the dance they stumbled around apologising and standing on one another's toes, with Jo issuing instructions that made them both extremely confused. Then gradually they both relaxed and Phillip's arm tightened around Jo's waist.

'You know, you are the most beautiful woman here,' murmured Phillip. Jo didn't know what to say so she concentrated on dancing. Somehow they fell in step and then he was gliding her round the floor until the dance ended. Shocked, they both stood still.

'We did it,' laughed Phillip, feeling the tension in Jo's body. He gave her a little shake. 'Loosen up. I'm your friend, remember.'

'You can talk,' cried Jo suddenly tremendously happy. The band broke out into a rumba.

'Now's our chance—I actually know this one,' laughed Phillip, his hips moving, lithe and supple, to the music. Quickly Jo fell in step with him, her hips swayed with his, the champagne, the intoxicating beat of the music and the challenge in his eyes sending the blood thudding through her veins.

'You lied to me,' she laughed huskily as they danced.

'I might have,' he replied, wanting to crush her to him, but instead, when the music stopped, he led her back to the table, his hand lingering in hers. With Derby Day only hours away neither Jo nor Phillip wanted to make it a long night. After a couple more dances they excused themselves from the party.

'Have fun with the Fashion in the Field tomorrow. There'll be some wild hats there,' said Jo, giving Emma a goodnight kiss and laughing at Davie who swamped her with an enormous hug. Sauntering down the stairs with Phillip's arm lightly resting around her waist, Jo felt as though she were floating. Inside the taxi she snuggled against him and he slipped his arm around her.

Then, back at the hotel, he escorted her up to her room.

Fumbling for her keys, Jo turned to thank Phillip. 'It's been such a lovely evening. Would you like a nightcap?' she asked with a yawn. She swayed gently towards him.

Shaking his head, he wrapped her in his arms. 'It's only because it's Derby Day tomorrow that I'm allowing you to escape now.' Jo gave a low laugh and let her head fall back, her eyes closed. Gently he kissed her cheeks, then her eyelids, then her waiting mouth. His lips burned against hers, reigniting in her the fire he had started when they had kissed at Kingsford Lodge and that had smouldered with increasing intensity throughout the evening. Drowning in the warmth and love of his kiss, for an instant she was tempted to drag him into her room, but the night was half over and she knew she had to be fully alert tomorrow. Reluctantly they drew apart.

'I'll see you in a few hours,' whispered Phillip huskily, their fingers still entwined. With one final kiss Jo slipped into her room and shut the door. Phillip straightened his bow tie and walked jauntily to the lift. In his room, leaving the lights off, he strode to the window, pulled back the curtains and stared out across the bright city lights.

He could still smell Jo's perfume and he hung onto the memory of her body pressed against his as they danced. His whole body throbbed with longing, but his heart sang. There had been no mistaking the answering passion in Jo's kisses and he had sensed that if he had pushed one fraction harder he could now be lying in bed with her, but he had made a pact with himself that he would put no personal pressure on her until after the Cup race and he was determined to stick to it. For a long while he stood and stared out across Melbourne city, his mind centred on the woman he had loved for so long. Finally he undressed and slid between the cool sheets, dropping into a fitful sleep filled with erotic dreams of Jo, cut short by the jarring shrill of his wake-up call.

Derby Day dawned brilliant and sunny. The crowd poured into Flemington racecourse, many of the women elegantly dressed in the traditional Derby Day black and white, the men in top hats and tails and sporting a blue cornflower in their breast pockets. At first a bundle of nerves, Jo calmed down as the day progressed. Everything went smoothly with Kingsford Lodge horses being placed in three races and Damien winning on Arctic Gold. Then Jo listened proudly as Emma presented the Fashion in the Field prizes.

'Did you enjoy the ball?' said a soft voice behind her. Jo spun round and stared stunned at Elaine, dressed in a new designer suit, matching gloves and a neat matching hat, and her eyes filled with tears.

'Gran!'

'How are you, dear? I got picked to go in the Fashion in the Field. Fancy that at my age,' said Elaine opening her arms and giving Jo a hug. 'You look lovely. I wish we'd managed to persuade your silly, stubborn father to fly down, but I never could change his mind once he'd made a decision.' She pulled a hanky from her purse and hastily wiped the corners of her eyes.

'Gran! You darling, wonderful . . . what a surprise!' gulped Jo, laughing as she too wiped her eyes.

'Well, someone had to represent the family. It's not every day we Kingsfords have a horse running in the Cup,' said Elaine, regaining her composure. 'I had a lovely chat with Emma. Now tell me, dear, which horse should I back for the next race? Perhaps your young man has a good tip,' she said smiling at Phillip. 'Good to see you again, Phillip.'

Jo blushed. 'Phillip's my vet, Gran.'

'I know, dear, and doing very well in Sydney, I hear,' said Elaine, scrutinising her race book and then tucking her arm through Jo's. 'Now tell your gran everything that has been happening.'

Jo's happiness on seeing Elaine largely took the edge off her disappointment when Let's Talk only managed to come fourth in the Derby. But her abiding disappointment and hurt, exacerbated by the sudden appearance of Elaine, was that neither Charlie nor Nina had shown the slightest interest in attending this year's carnival. But at least Nina had phoned to wish her good luck.

'You'd have thought Mum could have persuaded Dad to come down here. No-one would have cared about his stupid walking sticks,' Jo muttered to Elaine, who gave her arm a quick squeeze. Then Jo's spirits soared again when Let's Talk came third in the MacKinnon Stakes, convincing her he had the courage and tenacity demanded of the big one.

'If he keeps in the middle of the field I'll be happy,' Jo admitted to Phillip after she had paid the final acceptance fee and Let's Talk was safely ensconced in the Melbourne Cup.

'I don't want to scare you but Damien mentioned he and Hope were followed back to their hotel last night. He said it was a white car that drove off in a big hurry when they turned into the hotel parking,' said Phillip as they closed up the stables. Jo went pale. 'It's probably nothing but Damien thinks he's seen the car before while we've been down here. He looked quite shaken. I think we should have someone with him all the time till this race is over.'

'I'll tell Pete to stay glued to him,' Jo replied grimly. In a lot of ways she'd be glad when Tuesday was over. Catching Damien as he left the racetrack she told him of her plan but he wasn't happy.

'I'd feel a right dill being babysat by Pete. All this wasting and fasting gets to you after a while and I haven't seen the car again. Maybe I just imagined it. Look, I'll be fine really, Jo. Anyway Hope's always around. Let's forget it, okay? I shouldn't have said anything.'

Torn between overvigilance and upsetting the already highly-strung jockey, Jo let Damien persuade her against her better judgement. Accepting an invitation to a society luncheon with one of her owners in Toorak on the Sunday, she put her worries aside for a few hours. She returned to the hotel halfway through the afternoon, desperate for some sleep and time to herself, then on Monday was back on the track, only to learn that someone had tried to mug Damien and Hope as they were walking out of a restaurant. The car had not been a figment of his imagination.

'It was Hope's blood-curdling scream that scared 'em off,' laughed Damien, wincing as he wrapped his arm around his girlfriend's waist. He could laugh now but yesterday had been anything but funny. He rubbed his side where one of the muggers had struck him. Shaken to the core and racing through the day with a million things to worry about, Jo was wound up like a tight spring by the evening. She rang Damien at his hotel to ensure he was safe before she went to bed, then she tossed and turned all night, waking early, stomach churning, and leaped into the shower. Melbourne Cup day, the day each year that a horse race stopped the nation, had finally arrived.

Jo could feel the buzz of excitement in the air long before she drove into the stables. By seven a.m. people were already camped out at the racecourse, dressed in all their finery, tucking into their champagne breakfasts. Hats of all shapes and sizes bobbed on heads, from the sublimely elegant to the outrageous and ridiculous—feathers, lace, fruit, anything went when it came to the Melbourne Cup. The media were everywhere looking for a story, a tip, a notorious personality, anything to spin out and build up this national day. Cool but sunny, the weather looked promising, the famous Flemington roses a stunning display of colour.

Striding down to the stalls with Phillip to where Glen was busy grooming Let's Talk, Jo could hardly believe the big day had finally arrived. Bleary-eyed from his nights guarding the horse, Glen greeted Jo with a cheery grin.

'Guess who just dropped in,' grinned Glen as Winks materialised from the shadows.

'I never thought I'd be a part of this, but I wouldn't miss it for quids,' said the old man emotionally, chewing hard on the remains of an unlit cigarette. He stopped, unable to say more. Jo's jaw dropped and her heart gave another jolt. Then she wrapped her arms around the old man and hugged him tight, her heart full. They had all come to cheer her on, her friends, her family—she had even caught a glimpse of Bertie hovering near the bookies' stands before he had quickly moved away— all of them except Mum and Dad, and Charlie was the one person she really wanted to see her horse race.

'Thank you,' she whispered. Then she moved across to Let's Talk. Having thoroughly checked the horse, she went through the details of getting the animal to the stalls before the race with Glen for the final time. Still nervous, she had spoken to Damien on the phone before she headed down to the stables. He wasn't due on the course till early afternoon but she was confident the jockey had got himself together after the mugging. But despite her confidence in Damien, every nerve was taut.

As she watched the last race before lunch she felt more keenly her disappointment that her father was not here to share her moment of triumph. For triumph it was. Despite moments when she could have cheerfully thrown the whole battle away, Kingsford Lodge had proven it was still a stables to be reckoned with. Kingsford horses were getting placed at this prestigious racing carnival and whether Let's Talk came first or last she, his trainer, albeit officially only the foreman, had entered him in Australia's most famous race. She gave a sigh and hurried over to the stall.

The course vet having already passed Let's Talk as fit to race, Jo talked gently to the horse while she saddled him up, her fingers shaking as she fussed over the girth buckles and ensured the weights were properly strapped in position, while Glen checked from the off side. Always punctual, by now Damien would hopefully be safely weighed in and waiting in the jockeys' room in his freshly washed silks, the incident of the white car and attempted mugging ancient history. Nervous but satisfied she had done everything possible, Jo left Glen in charge and went over to talk to Let's Talk's other owners in the mounting yard, glancing around for Hope who should be able to confirm that Damien really was in the jockeys' room. Captured by two national television racing commentators demanding to know her opinion on her horse's chances, after what seemed to her forever, Jo caught sight of Hope tottering towards her on four-inch stilettos, breasts squeezed into a tight-waisted brilliant orange suit. Quickly excusing herself, Jo hurried over to the girl.

'I've given Damy his lucky button, he's been weighed in and he's going to look smashing in his silks,' cried Hope in a stage whisper, bright orange smeared across lips stretched in an enormous grin. Heaving a sigh of relief, Jo gave the girl's arm a quick squeeze and walked towards the group milling around Let's Talk.

The band struck up 'Waltzing Matilda' and the crowd swelled in song. Goosebumps breaking out on her arms, Jo felt a rush of national pride, and when the jockeys for the Melbourne Cup were announced over the PA system and then paraded on the dais, their silks glistening in the sun, she felt her heart might burst with excitement. Palms sweating she strode across to Glen who was holding Let's Talk steady for Damien to mount. Coat gleaming, ears alert, flanks shivering with anticipation, the horse looked stunning. Her mouth dry, Jo rechecked the saddle and lead weights for the last time, went through her final instructions to Damien and then gave him a leg-up onto Let's Talk.

'This one's ours,' Damien hissed, leaning down to Jo, his jaw set tight, his body a wound coil ready to explode. He slipped his feet into the stirrups, the sunlight catching on his pink and yellow silks, strain etched in his face.

'Go for it,' said Jo, briefly clasping Damien's hand and in the tradition of horseracing superstition avoiding the L word—luck.

Nodding to Jo, Damien patted Let's Talk's neck and then nudged the horse forward, the large yellow number displayed clearly on his saddlecloth. Her heart in her mouth Jo ushered the other owners of Let's Talk towards the members' stand. Out of the corner of her eye she could see Kurt talking to the steward of the course. Grimacing, she blotted out the chatter in her head that demanded to know what the evil little man was plotting now. Then her heart missed a beat as she heard her own name blared out across the PA system summoning her to the stewards' room. Terrified she had left some detail undeclared that could disqualify them, she left the other owners in a froth of panic and sped across to the stewards' room. Anxiously she stepped into the gloom only to be greeted by a grinning young man holding her binoculars that in her haste she had earlier left on one of the seats. Her legs turned to jelly with relief. Charging back, feeling silly at committing such a blunder, she quickly soothed the owners and joined Phillip and Elaine in the members' stand.

Jo had never felt so keyed up in her life. Turning her attention to the horses parading before the excited crowd, she watched with mounting excitement. This was the moment the whole nation had been waiting for. Already hyped up and full of champagne, the crowd was ready to cheer and clap at anything, so when Let's Talk stopped with his accustomed aplomb and started pawing the ground and demanding applause everyone went wild. Loving every minute of it, the more the crowd cheered, the more Let's Talk performed, the whole scene flashed live across the nation on radio and television.

News of the attempted assault on Damien had spread like wildfire so the crowd's sympathies were already with the young jockey and somehow everyone sensed Let's Talk's antics were more controlled today, as if he knew the rider he was carrying needed extra care. While the favourite was Rosy's Valiant ridden by Dennis Cook and no-one really expected Let's Talk to be placed, despite all the prerace hype, the horse's compassion sent the crowd to fever pitch. Cheering and whistling, clapping and stamping, they shouted out his name, some were even dabbing at their eyes, and for the next five minutes Let's Talk accepted everything they gave. Anxiously Jo trained her binoculars onto Damien, watching him sitting quietly as the horse went through his act; then, with a final acknowledging toss of Let's Talk's mane, horse and rider moved down to the other twenty-three horses at the starting barriers.

Jo had drawn barrier twenty which put Let's Talk at a definite disadvantage in getting ahead quickly but Jo had faith that his long strides and powerful heart would keep him to the centre of the race.

'Just keep praying Damien keeps his nerve. He looked pretty pale,' whispered Jo in Phillip's ear, anxiously chewing at her nails. The attack on Damien had profoundly shaken them all.

'If they work together like they've been doing . . .' Phillip gave her shoulders a quick squeeze and she held her breath as the barrier gate closed behind the last horse.

Then twenty-four horses burst from the gates to a giant roar from the crowd. The air was electric. Fingers crossed, Jo watched the horses charge down the straight, shouting with the rest, urging Let's Talk and Damien on. As they jostled for position Ruby

Red was in front with Valiant in second place and Damien and Let's Talk well back in the field. Avoiding a muddle as they passed the winning post for the first time, Let's Talk pulled out into fifth place, coming up on the outside, but there was a length and a half between him and the next horse. The crowd had quietened as the horses raced away from the grandstand. Jo tore her eyes from the horses for a second as a cheer went up when two red-coated clerks of the course staged a mock race to the winning post. Then her eyes were back, her binoculars glued to the horses on the far side of the course, sweat trickling down her back. Let's Talk was coming up wide.

'This is a phenomenal effort from Let's Talk but he's too far back and Valiant is now well in front . . .' shouted the race caller.

Jo was trembling from head to foot as they came round the bend and into the final stretch. The roar of the crowd was deafening, and Let's Talk had shifted himself up into fourth place. His great strides thundered across the track and he was in third and then, unbelievably, in second place behind Valiant.

'This is phenomenal,' repeated the race caller. 'The power . . . This course has never seen anything like it, this horse is unstoppable. We're watching history in the making.'

Jo could hardly breathe. Her vision kept blurring as the horses pounded the turf. Then they were neck and neck and Jo could almost hear Damien urging Let's Talk on as the big, courageous horse tired in the gruelling race. Impossibly he lengthened his stride, inching ahead, and the crowd roared again. Then a great gasp of horror went up as Dennis Cook on Valiant deliberately swerved, charging into Let's Talk. But it was too late, Let's Talk broke away in the nick of time and Valiant lost his rhythm.

While the nation watched, the great stayer stretched his powerful limbs in one last remarkable act of courage, pulling ahead to win, not by a head but by an incredible length and a half. As Let's Talk crossed the finishing line Jo's throat ached from screaming. Her fingers balled into tight fists, she punched the air, unable to believe what she was watching. Then she turned to Phillip and hugged and kissed him, her whole body trembling, tears streaming down her face, while an unknown Double Trouble came in second, followed by Kiwi Lad in third and Valiant limped home in fifth place.

'We did it! By golly, we did it! We won!' she cried. Kissing Phillip on the mouth she turned to run down the steps to greet horse and rider, her legs like jelly, and froze at the sound of a voice she knew so well.

'I always knew you could do it, kiddo.'

'Dad!' she shrieked in disbelief, watching her father, leaning heavily on a single walking stick, walk towards her, a grin splitting his face from ear to ear, with Nina beside him beaming proudly. Running up she hugged Charlie, unashamedly letting the tears tumble down her cheeks and splash onto his jacket, smiling up at her mother, while the crowd in the members' stand looked on in sudden awe and then burst into spontaneous applause.

'Go on then. Go on, you've got a horse and a jockey to see to,' said Charlie abruptly to hide his emotions as Jo kissed her mother who was openly crying.

'I love you both so much,' cried Jo, her laughter echoing through the stand as she ran out to greet Damien who was walking the sweating Let's Talk off the field, tears streaming down his face too.

464

Triumph blazed from his eyes through the sweat and mud. Exhausted but elated he leaped from the horse, victorious, his whip held high in salute, the bruise in his ribs forgotten while bulbs flashed and microphones appeared from nowhere. About to grab the reins Jo reeled sideways as Kurt, puce with rage and reeking of alcohol, rushed at her from the side and hurled himself at her.

'You fucking bitch, you slipped him something before the race. You fucking cheating bitch . . . Your stupid jockey don't know how to ride. He purposely crossed over into Valiant's track. You saw! Everyone saw! I've been set up. I'm going to protest!' he screamed, beside himself with rage and disappointment, and swung a left hook at Jo. Roughly pushing her aside, Phillip stepped forward, shielding Jo from Kurt's blow and collected it on his own cheek instead.

'Fucking bastard!' Kurt screeched, lunging back at Phillip, furious that he had failed to get rid of Damien. Immediately security guards grabbed both men and led them away, but not before the media had caught it all on camera.

Still shaking from head to toe, as much from having won as from the unexpected attack, Jo straightened her clothes and walked over to Let's Talk proudly wearing the winner's rug, stroking him and thanking him for his great courage, and hugging Damien. By the time they were ready for the presentation, Phillip had reappeared.

'I thought for a horrible moment you might have had to spend the night in the lock-up,' Jo whispered, relief flooding over her. 'Did he hurt you badly?'

'Hardly tickled me,' replied Phillip, gingerly moving his jaw. 'You won't have to worry about Kurt any more. Losing it like that at such a prestigious event—the ARA'll almost certainly ban him for life. They've been after Kurt for a while now. He and a few who shall be nameless have been arranging all sorts of nice little rorts. Doping, fixing races, bribing jockeys ... mugging jockeys,' he added pointedly. 'Quite a colourful man is our Kurt.'

Jo grabbed Phillip's hand as everyone assembled for the presentation. 'I love you and I want you with me to collect the cup.' Beaming with pride Phillip stepped up onto the dais and stood next to Damien and Hope who were behind Jo and Let's Talk's co-owners. Accepting the coveted three-handled cup with Phillip, Elaine and her father and mother beside her, Jo felt this was the proudest moment in her life. Nearby, Let's Talk calmly flicked his tail.

But then Charlie stepped forward, and Jo thought her heart would burst with happiness.

'Many of you think of Jo as the daughter who had to give up a successful modelling career to take over Kingsford Lodge when her dad had a bit of a run-in with a tree,' Charlie began, his words slow but clear.

The crowd gave an uncomfortable titter not sure what to expect from the man around whom so many rumours had sprung.

'But I know Jo as a young woman of immense courage, love and tenacity. Today you have seen her achieve her greatest dream and no-one could be more proud of her, nor more grateful, than me.' Jo felt the tears prick the back of her eyes. 'It is a triumph for anyone to win the Melbourne Cup but I'm not only talking about Jo's ability to produce great racehorses or suss out great jockeys,' continued Charlie, turning briefly to Damien, 'I'm talking about winning in that other great race, the race of life, the race in which I was very nearly a casualty.' He shifted his position; Nina watched anxiously at his elbow and Elaine's eyes were fixed on his face, her gloved hands clasped tightly in front of her.

'We Kingsfords are a proud, stubborn lot but none more proud or stubborn than Jo who refused to believe that her old dad would be confined to a wheelchair for the rest of his life or had lost his marbles when he could barely mutter a few words.' He paused, the crowd silent as though captured on film, every ear poised for Charlie's next words. Even the breeze had dropped. Faint in the distance a car horn beeped.

'I don't know where I thought I had to go but Jo knew. Jo was determined the only place I was headed was back to Kingsford Lodge and she'd drag me there whether I liked it or not.' This time the ripple of laughter was one of sympathy and admiration. Charlie turned to Jo, love and admiration spilling from his eyes. 'I vowed I wouldn't put in a public appearance until I could walk unaided, but today, Jo, I bow to your wishes. I salute you for the way you handled yourself when your twin brother Rick was so suddenly taken from us, for the support you gave your mother and elder brother in our family's hour of crisis, and for your courage in taking on Kingsford Lodge. But most of all I salute you for your stubbornness, because without it I would not be standing here today, sticks or no sticks.' He stopped, gripped by emotion. People in the crowd were wiping their eyes; Nina pressed her hankie to her lips.

'It's rare a father gets an opportunity to acknowledge in public the admiration he has for his children, and I've never been one to get sentimental, but today, Jo, I want you to know how incredibly proud your mother and I are of you. Your stubborn old father would never accept you had the same love and understanding of horses that he has nor that you have been blessed with that special gift that turns them into winners, but you have finally made me see you have everything it takes to do just that, and more. Because of you I am back in the world I love. As for the future of Kingsford Lodge, well . . .' He turned to the crowd. 'I guess I'd better ask the boss here.' Everyone started clapping but Charlie held up his hand then clasped Jo's hand in his. Jo fought back the tears, biting her bottom lip to stop it trembling, hardly able to comprehend his words. Everything she had wanted to hear for so long he was saying.

'Jo, you have never faltered or swayed in your belief in me or your support for your family. Both I and your mother congratulate you on your win today. It is your win. Today is your day. Enjoy it. We love you,' he finished, his voice thick with emotion. Then he stepped back, acknowledging Jo. There was a stunned silence followed by a loud burst of applause. Holding high the cup, Jo smiled through her tears first at her father then at the crowd. Then she hugged him while the crowd kept clapping.

'I love you, Dad,' she whispered, tears splashing onto the cup.

Stepping down from the dais after the ceremony was over Jo hugged Charlie and then Nina and Elaine, and then everyone hugged everyone else and made a big fuss of Let's Talk.

'I meant every word I said,' said Charlie as Jo wiped the tears from her eyes.

'Thank you, Dad, and thank you for being here. I love you so much. You don't know how much I wanted you to be here.'

'I never had any intention of missing it,' he said,

a catch in his voice, wiping a tear from his eye. 'Let's Talk's not the only one who likes to make grand entrances, you know—and by the bye, I think you'd better get your own trainer's licence. I've had my eye on a stables that could suit you very well.'

Chapter Twenty-five

THE RESTAURANT IN South Yarra was packed as the celebrations stretched late into the evening. Radiant from her win and deeply moved by her father's words, Jo kept repeating the awe she felt not only to have won the Cup with a great jockey, but the joy of having her father stand beside her to receive it.

'I had no idea Dad felt like that about me. Look at him and Mum, it's like they've just met,' she said to Phillip for the umpteenth time that night. 'I've never seen them so engrossed in one another. Mum looks positively gorgeous.'

'Eclipsed by someone else I know,' murmured Phillip, longing to take her in his arms.

Jo laughed. 'Flattery will get you everywhere. I must have talked to everyone in the room.' She gave a big sigh and smiled into Phillip's eyes. Suddenly she didn't want to be in the crowded restaurant any more, chatting to acquaintances, she wanted to be in Phillip's arms, to feel his mouth on hers, to finish what they had started the night of the Derby Ball.

'D'you think we'd be missed if we slunk off?' she whispered mischievously, her heartbeat quickening.

'You are the main attraction, you know . . .' replied Phillip.

'Not any more. The journos've got enough shots of us all to fill a month's worth of papers.'

'Well, I don't want to talk to anyone else except you,' grinned Phillip.

'That's settled then,' decided Jo, finishing her glass of white wine and grabbing Phillip's hand. Kissing Nina and Charlie, on the pretext of tiredness they said their goodbyes and slipped from the restaurant. Once outside they ran like naughty children towards a nearby taxi rank. Jumping into the waiting cab they directed the driver to their hotel. Only the cab driver's excited chatter when he realised who his passengers were stopped Phillip from pulling Jo into his arms and smothering her with kisses. Laughing, they tumbled out of the taxi as it pulled up in front of the Grand Hyatt. Pouring a wadful of notes and silver into the astonished driver's hand, Phillip grabbed Jo and they ran into the hotel, across the foyer and dived into the lift.

Jo's fingers were shaking so much when she tried to unlock her suite door that Phillip had to take over. Marginally better than her, he fumbled around, finally opened the door and they fell inside. Slamming the door behind him, Phillip pulled Jo into his arms. Kissing her, he dragged off his tie and unbuttoned his shirt while Jo tossed her hat and jacket aside. Unbuttoning Jo's blouse he kept kissing her hard. Without a word they clung to each other, scrambling out of their clothes, Jo bursting out laughing and helping Phillip when he got stuck frantically trying to pull his hands out of his shirtsleeves without removing the cufflinks. Leaving a stream of discarded garments across the room, they fell naked onto the bed.

Intoxicated with happiness they kicked aside the bedclothes and clung to each other, their bodies seeking release from the tension of the race and the excitement of the win. Running her hands over Phillip's strong broad back, Jo surrendered to his passionate advances, allowing his love to swamp her as he smothered her with kisses and ran his hands over her warm silky-smooth skin. She gasped when his fingers brushed her nipples and ran down her tummy to the warm wet mound between her legs, feeling the heat of his passion burning into her. There was an urgency about their love-making that precluded words, a desperation that made them cling more tightly to each other as their desire mounted.

Winding her legs around Phillip, Jo laughed in ecstasy as he ran his tongue down her neck and between her breasts and they rolled together falling in a heap on the floor on top of the blankets. Then he was on top of her and she was drowning in deliciously intense longing. Panting and sweating, their bodies moved rhythmically together with increasing speed. Moaning, Jo dug her nails into Phillip's back, clinging to him, her desires urging her on, and Phillip responded to her, plunging deeper into her until, with a simultaneous shuddering cry, they consummated their love. His heart still racing, Phillip slumped down on her and for a moment neither of them moved, bathed in the wonderful aftermath of spent passion.

'You are an amazingly exciting woman,' Phillip sighed, rolling over. He lifted himself on one elbow and gazed into her lovely flushed face.

'And you are my Prince Charming,' she murmured, caressing the bruise on Phillip's cheek where Kurt had managed to clip him in the scuffle.

She moved her fingers down his neck and onto his chest, marvelling at the intensity of the love she had just experienced. She had felt a glimmering of it at the ball, raw passion tightly restrained, yet in the last ten minutes he had unleashed an ecstasy of love on her that had taken her entirely by surprise. She sighed, wondering that such depths of feeling could be hidden in so outwardly calm and gentle a man.

'Penny for them?' said Phillip quietly, his eyes never leaving her face.

'Not on your life. You'd get far too big-headed,' she retorted, her eyes laughing. She started to giggle, realising they were lying in a heap on the floor. 'How did we get down here? I don't remember falling off the bed.'

'Wild passion from a man-eater, that's what did it,' laughed Phillip. Then his face softened. Running one finger down her cheek, he cupped her face in his hand. Gently he kissed her lips and Jo surrendered to him again, this time their lovemaking gentler yet every bit as passionate. 'I love you, Jo,' he sighed after a long time.

'And I love you,' whispered Jo. 'I don't know if I could have kept going without you.' She raised her hand and pushed aside a wayward lock of hair that had fallen across one eye, then pulled him to her and gave him another long, lingering kiss. Lying back feeling voluptuously decadent, she let herself float unthinking, enjoying the sensation of his fingers playing on her body. For a while neither said anything, basking in the new-found intimacy between them.

'You've made it, Snow White,' Phillip said softly, breaking the silence. 'After all your hard work and battling, you've really made it. You deserved today.'

Jo sighed contentedly, smiling in the gloom. 'You mean *we've* made it. I still can't believe it! We actually won. We won the Melbourne Cup. The race that stops the nation. I'm so happy!' She rolled over and kissed Phillip again, the glow from the streetlights enough to make out his face.

'You've made it, but I don't know that we've made it quite yet,' he said, letting his fingers trail down her neck to the top of her breasts.

Jo tensed, cold tentacles clutching at her heart and spreading through her veins. 'What d'you mean, we haven't made it yet? What was that we've just been doing?' she demanded, drawing away.

'Forget it. Let's order a bottle of French champagne and make love some more,' said Phillip, instantly regretting his comment. He hadn't meant to bring up the subject of Simon now, not while Jo was so happy with her success and they were so close. The words had just slipped out.

'Let's!' replied Jo quickly, determined to keep the wonderful intimacy between them alive. Just then the phone jangled harshly from across the room, making her jump. 'Room service by telepathy,' she laughed and stumbled to her feet. Picking up the receiver she switched on one of the wall lights and her whole body went rigid. Quickly she turned her back to Phillip.

'Hello? Oh . . . How lovely to hear you. However did you track me down?' Her voice sounded artificial and the blood pounded in her ears as she listened. 'Yes, it was a bit of a shock. I was amazed too and excited. Where are you ringing from?' She scribbled down a number. Chatting on for a few seconds she abruptly finished the conversation. 'Look, I'll ring you when I get back to Sydney. Okay? Bye.' Quickly she replaced the receiver, her palms sweaty.

Suddenly she felt exposed. Grabbing the bed sheet she wrapped it around her.

'That was Simon,' she announced, trying to sound casual. 'Jackie gave him the hotel number. Silly old Jackie's been trying to marry me off since I turned eighteen. She was devastated when we broke up and always hoped we'd get back together.' Jo knew she was gabbling. 'You don't have to worry. I'm not going to see him when he gets here. I made that decision on the plane. It's over between us. It's just that well I . . . It just felt awkward right then.'

'You don't have to justify what you do to me, but for both our sakes I think you have to see him,' said Phillip walking over to her, his firm tanned body once more aroused, and kissing her gently on the top of her head. He poured himself a glass of iced water from the jug in the fridge.

'Oh Phillip!' cried Jo and sank into a chair by the window. The tension in the room was tangible. Jo watched him drink the water as she twisted her arms in the sheet. 'I keep telling you, it's over between us. I love you, not Simon.'

'And I love you, Jo. You just don't know how much I love you and how long I've wanted to make love to you.' He turned to face her, his grey eyes intense. 'I have loved you since you walked into the surgery at Denman and I forgot I was a vet and you were only sixteen. You were irresistible then and you still are. I love you, Jo, and I want you to marry me, but for it to work you have to see Simon. I can't live in his shadow, wondering which of us you really love, living with the question that if you had seen him, would you have gone back to him?' He ran his fingers through his tousled hair and poured himself another drink.

Jo swallowed, unwanted tears welling up in her

eyes, Phillip's words hanging in the air between them. Damocles's sword, she thought with a shiver, misery and shame creeping over her. She didn't want to face Simon. It was the coward's way out she knew, but it was also the easiest, or so she had thought until a few seconds ago. Now she had no choice. The scariest part was that she just didn't know how she would react meeting him again. She gave Phillip a quick glance from under her lashes, unable to meet his gaze.

Phillip sat down on the edge of the bed his arms resting on his thighs. His heart ached as he spoke. 'The syndicate that invited me to Hong Kong want me to fly to Japan with them when we get back to Sydney. I told them I'd give them my answer after the Melbourne Cup. I'm going to accept.' He took a deep breath. 'You need some time to sort yourself out, Jo, so I'm going to get out of your life for a bit. Whatever you decide I will know that you have done it from your heart and you need never fear I'll bother you afterwards. I hope that you'll be here for me when I get back, but if you're not . . .' He opened his hands, his eyes filled with pain. 'I can't bear the thought of life without you, but sometimes in life you have to close a door or go through it,' he finished thickly.

Jo sat staring unseeing at her fingers, tears splashing onto her hands. 'I promised myself I'd never hurt you again,' she mumbled, lifting red-rimmed eyes to him.

Phillip strode over and gently pulled her to her feet. 'No-one can take away what we had tonight but you have to do this. We both know it. For our love to survive, you have to see him.'

'Whatever happens I want you to know that you are a wonderful man and that tonight was the most special . . .' She couldn't go on. She started shivering violently, despite the warmth of the room. 'Oh God, life is such a muddle.' She let her head fall on his shoulder and burst into tears.

Phillip wrapped her in his arms. 'My beautiful Snow White, don't cry,' he whispered, lifting her face to his, kissing her once more, tasting the salt of her tears as they tumbled down her face. 'I'm such a big clumsy fool. I never meant to make you so miserable, today of all days. Today is your day, my darling. Let's worry about all this tomorrow.' Tenderly he unwound the sheet and drew her back to bed. Pulling the covers over them he hugged her close, stroking her and soothing her as she did her wonderful horses until she relaxed and, with a shuddering sigh, slid her arms around his neck.

'Oh, Phillip, I don't deserve you,' she cried, closing her eyes, letting him kiss her again long and deep. This time her shivering was from her arousal.

'Definitely a classy thoroughbred but with certain mulelike tendencies, I'd say,' whispered Phillip, nibbling at her ear.

Startled, Jo opened her eyes and stared into his grinning face. 'Mulelike tendencies!' she exclaimed, giving him a shove. Then they were laughing again and making love, the excitement and wonder of the day and the warm intimacy between them recaptured, the pain of tomorrow put off for a few more hours.

The day Phillip was due to fly to Tokyo Jo set off to meet Simon in the late afternoon, catching him after a spate of radio interviews. Heart racing, her palms sweaty, she tried to work out how to greet him as the taxi drove through the Sydney rush hour.

Clambering out of the car, a smile plastered firmly on her face, she walked towards the wide glass doors of the Hilton hotel, butterflies in her stomach. Then she saw him racing across the foyer towards her, the same man she had loved and missed so desperately for so long, and suddenly all her fears evaporated.

'Simon!' she cried, running into his outstretched arms.

'Jo!' He lifted her off her feet in his enthusiasm and hugged and kissed her. 'You look and smell as wonderful as ever,' he gasped, setting her feet back on the ground. 'How are you? You've done so brilliantly well. I've just been reading all about you all over again. I couldn't believe it when I saw my girl splashed all over the newspapers.' Jo laughed up into his face. There were tiny lines around his eyes that had not been there five years ago and there was a new maturity about him, but otherwise he was exactly as she remembered him. As devastatingly handsome as ever, his sea-green eyes dancing in his face, his smile hypnotically captivating. She felt as though she were being drawn back into a comfortable world that she had never really wanted to leave.

'I loved *The Oystercatcher*. I cried buckets,' she said, the lilt back in her voice.

'Did you really?' said Simon, his eyes soft on her face. 'I've got a real copy for you in my room.' Tucking her arm under his, Simon led her to the lift and they chatted about this and that as they walked the long corridor to his suite. As he closed the door Jo let him draw her into his arms and kiss her. Sighing, he let her go and handed her a copy of *The Oystercatcher*. She felt his eyes hot on hers as so many wonderful memories came flooding back.

'We're quite a pair, you and me. You winning international horse races and me with my book,' exclaimed Simon, breaking the silence that had sprung up between them. 'Since I spoke to you last I've got some more exciting news to tell you. Only I wanted to keep it until I saw you in the flesh, the very beautiful flesh, I might add,' he finished, running his hands down Jo's body and clasping her round her neat waist.

'Full of flattery as ever,' Jo laughed, giving him a peck on the cheek. Their meeting was just as warm and wonderful as she had hoped, yet beneath her happiness another tiny voice tugged at her. She looked up into his face, tuning into his excitement. 'Well, come on, tell me!'

'My agent called and the book's gone ballistic,' grinned Simon. 'One of the big American publishing companies has bought the American rights and we're in the process of negotiating a contract for a major film. This has all happened in a matter of days. I'm still reeling from the shock. Oh Jo! One minute I'm an unknown, the next I'm an international author. I mean, this is really going to happen. The film company are hopping up and down with excitement and can't wait to start filming. As well as that, my English publishers are talking about a three-book contract with translations into German and Swedish,' he finished breathlessly.

Jo hugged him again, kissing his cheeks and smelling his familiar aftershave. As he kissed her on the mouth it was as though she were transported back five years. 'Oh, Simon, I'm so happy for you,' she cried, unexplained emotions welling up.

'Let's go out and celebrate,' declared Simon, shoving his wallet in his back pocket and grabbing the room key. 'You tell me the most special place you can think of and we'll go there.'

'What about that seafood restaurant I took you to

after we came back from Dublin Park?' suggested Jo. His news had stunned her. Simon the famous author. It didn't seem real. But then neither did winning the Melbourne Cup and Dad saying all those wonderful things.

All the way to the restaurant they gabbled non-stop. There were so many questions she wanted to ask, so many explanations, so much to share and catch up with.

'Why didn't you ever contact me?' Jo asked as they tore into Balmain bugs and peeled away the shells from monster king prawns.

Simon put down his prawn, rinsed his fingers in the water bowl and wiped them on his napkin. 'But I did call. I spoke to Bertie and left a message for you to call me back and to be sure to tell you about Neddy, which he obviously never did. Neddy sold the Orion after another bad bout of bronchitis and his hip gave out and moved to live with his sister in Bournemouth. Got a tidy sum for the Orion, thanks to your efforts. He gave Winnie to the young lad who used to help you with the stables, d'you remember him? I think she's still around . . . "Her'll outlast me, ticker stronger'n a three-year-old",' Simon laughed, doing a bad impersonation of Neddy.

'Ohh . . . ! Dear Neddy, he's such a sweetie,' sighed Jo, laughing too, then her expression changed. 'You know Bertie's got a gambling problem, although he doesn't think so. Mum and Dad've had an awful time. He's still livid with Dad for forcing him to take out a massive loan to pay off his debts. The repayments eat up most of his pay packet each month, it's wrecked his social life, and he's never forgiven me for refusing to lend him money after Dad said he had to pay off his debts himself. God, that was hard! He swore he wouldn't come down for the Melbourne Cup, but he did, although at the time I didn't care much because Dad was pretending not to be interested either; but after I won Bertie just made this really mean comment about having another cup I could hock to buy my next horse. If it had been anyone else I'd have been hurt, but I knew it was his jealousy talking. He's still got this thing about being the one no-one cares about in the family. I wish he'd get over it. He could be a great lawyer if he tried. It's not as if he hasn't got the brains.'

'I'm sorry to hear that,' said Simon frowning as he refilled Jo's wineglass. 'Bertie's jealousy of you was always as plain as day, but I didn't think he'd purposely fail to tell you I'd phoned. Anyway, just to confuse things further, I never found out either for months that you'd called me, and by the time I did, I'd convinced myself you weren't interested any longer. Mum was so distraught when I just took off without a word that when I got back somehow your phone call got forgotten. I don't think Mum meant to forget on purpose. I think it was just one of those things. I'd given her such a hard time already I couldn't really blame her.'

He leaned across the table and covered Jo's hand with his. 'I've missed you so much. I think I poured an awful lot of the pain and loss I felt at being away from you into the novel.' He kept her hand in both of his, staring deep into her dark violet eyes. 'You're the reason why the book's such a success. Without knowing that pain and loss I could never have written it.' Jo opened her mouth to speak but he kept going, her hand still tightly wrapped in his. 'I read about your father's recovery. I was so delighted for you but more selfishly for us. You've done everything you set out to, Jo, and I really admire you.

You've bred and trained horses, won races, become a national hero. Now, my darling, I want you to come back home with me to England and be my wife. With all this happening and me becoming this big international success, the world is our oyster. It's what I've always wanted, my darling, and I want you by my side. I want to let the world know that you are the reason for my success and that your beauty shines through *The Oystercatcher*. Will you marry me as we always planned?' he asked urgently.

Jo looked across at the man she had loved so desperately and for so long and a cold panic swept over her. The small voice that had been niggling her since she had stepped into the taxi that afternoon started screaming and she could hardly hear herself think. Pulling her hand back she took a gulp of champagne and wiped her palms on her linen serviette, her panic rising.

'I love you, Simon, and a part of me will always love you,' she started.

'I know, darling. Just say you'll marry me,' interrupted Simon, alarmed by the sudden tension between them.

'Just hear me out.' She watched him, wishing she could make it work, longing for him to understand the great love she had for her horses, wanting him to say he could never take her from the life she had so painstakingly built up, sticking to his own promise that after a few years he would be willing to marry her and live in Australia and make their dream come true. But he hadn't. He hadn't changed at all. He was still the Simon who couldn't understand what drove her to get up at three in the morning, to fight the overwhelmingly male domain to succeed. He couldn't comprehend that breeding and training horses was like breathing to her and without it she

482

would only ever be half alive. If she faced the rugged truth, however much she longed for it, this man whom she had loved so deeply, who had touched her to the core, simply didn't understand who she was. But there was someone else who did and if she didn't act quickly she might lose him forever.

'Simon, I love you and I'm so excited by your success, you have no idea,' she said, jumping out of her seat. 'I think *The Oystercatcher* is the most moving story I have ever read and I will follow your rise to fame with great interest, but we have to leave the ending in real life as you wrote it. *The Oystercatcher* is our love to the last scene. It was a first love, a great love that will stay with me forever but ... Simon, I wish you every success in your life but we're not meant to be together any longer.' She was gathering up her bag and her jacket. 'I have to go. I know this is terribly rude and strange but I ... There's someone ...'

Simon was on his feet. 'The vet! The one by your side in the photos, the one who hit that chap,' he exclaimed, his eyes haunted. 'I've lost you, haven't I?'

Jo nodded, her cheeks hot. 'Forgive me. It's better this way, Simon, really. One day you'll understand and you'll write more wonderful stories. You're so talented, Simon. I'll always cherish our love and now I have to catch a plane.' She ran round and hugged him, for once dry-eyed, and though the pain in his eyes pierced her to the core, she knew she was doing the right thing. 'I'm sorry, I'll write and explain everything to you. Maybe you could turn this into another bestseller.' She smiled tenderly.

'It was always a risk that I had lost you before I came out,' said Simon, squaring his shoulders, not wanting to let her go. 'I think I knew it the moment we kissed in the bedroom. I just didn't want to accept the truth.' Jo looked at him puzzled, aware the time was ticking away. 'Part of you was somewhere else,' explained Simon. 'He's a very lucky bloke.' He gave a wry grin at his attempt at Australian jargon.

'Oh Simon, thank you, thank you for understanding,' sighed Jo and kissed him hard on the mouth. 'I will love you till the end of time. Have a wonderful life.' Then she was outside running along the pavement, searching frantically for a cab, but there wasn't one in sight so she kept running. She nearly jumped out of her skin when she felt an arm around her waist and Simon was holding her and pulling her towards a cab speeding round the corner.

'I called one from the restaurant. Just wanted to make sure you got there,' he panted, helping her in and slamming the door. With a lump in her throat she waved goodbye watching his forlorn figure, poignantly reminded of the end of *The Oystercatcher*. Then the car turned the corner and Simon was gone and they were speeding across town to Coogee. Telling the driver to wait, with the clock still ticking, she raced upstairs, changed into a shirt and jeans, threw some make-up, wash things and a change of clothes into an overnight bag, grabbed her passport and dashed back out of the house.

'International terminal!' she cried. 'As fast as you can!'

The journey to the airport seemed never-ending. Sitting on the edge of her seat Jo kept praying she would get there in time. Phillip had said he was booked on the Qantas evening flight that left around ten o'clock, but she still had to buy a ticket. She pulled at a loose thread in her jeans and crossed and uncrossed her arms, chastising herself for being an idiot like this, tearing after Phillip like a mad-woman. What if there were no seats left on the plane? What if she got there too late? What if he really didn't want her to come with him? She broke out in a sweat and almost stopped the taxi. Then she remembered how Simon had called her 'my girl'. It was then that the penny had started to drop but, like him, she hadn't wanted to face the truth. He was wonderful, glamorous, romantic and an utter gen-tleman, but he didn't understand her. Horses and racing were just another Saturday sport to him. He had no idea of the skill or dedication or the sheer joy Jo got out of what she did. He just couldn't see it, but Phillip, kind, loving, gorgeous Phillip could. All the way to the airport she kept seeing the pain in Phillip's eyes after he had told her he was getting out of her life for a while. Out of her life. Cold panic gripped her again.

'Please God let me catch the plane,' she prayed as she thrust the fare at the driver and without waiting for the change raced into the international terminal. The place was awash with people. Fighting her way through the crowd to the Qantas counter, she waited impatiently, watching the minutes tick by until finally it was her turn at the counter. By a miracle there was a last-minute cancellation. Grab-bing her ticket and boarding pass she craned up at the arrivals and departures board and saw they were already flashing up the Qantas flight for Tokyo. Her whole being trembling, she rechecked the gate number. Flying down the moving walkway, she charged through the departure door and up to the boarding gate just as they were announcing the final boarding call.

'Nearly missed your flight, lady. Oops, evening, Jo

Kingsford! How ya going, ma'am. I won a heap on Let's Talk, thanking you. Enjoy your flight,' grinned the ticket clerk whom Jo regularly met on her international flights.

Smiling stiffly Jo dived into the plane, her heart pounding. Searching the cabin she squeezed past the other passengers down the aisle and stopped in front of a man heaving his hand baggage into the overhead compartment.

'Excuse me. Could you put mine up there too?' she asked quietly, her heart hammering in her chest. The man whirled round, nearly clouting her in the ear.

'Jo!'

'I'm coming with you,' she cried, staring into Phillip's eyes. Then she was in his arms, her overnight bag falling from her fingers.

'Jo. My darling adorable wonderful . . . Does this mean . . . ?'

'I love you Phillip Gregg. I love you so much and I don't want you to get out of my life even for a second.' Her words were smothered as he covered her mouth with his. Around them the whole cabin sighed and then erupted in applause. Jo and Phillip looked up, grinning like Cheshire cats.

'I've shut one door and come through another,' whispered Jo, her face alight with happiness.

'Thank God.'

'Do you still want me?'

'I'm not even going to dignify that with a reply,' rasped Phillip, crushing her to him and kissing her on and on.

'Could you take your seats please and fasten your seatbelts ready for takeoff,' said the flight attendant in his ear. 'We'll be serving champagne once we're airborne.' He gave them both a big wink as they broke away. Jo, blushing furiously, moved towards her seat.

'You very happy child, please, seat,' said a middle-aged Japanese businessman tapping Jo on the shoulder. Bowing, he pointed to the seat next to Phillip which he had just vacated. Bowing back gratefully, Jo sank down next to Phillip and fastened her seatbelt as the plane roared into life and taxied out for takeoff. Eyes shining, Jo tucked her arm through Phillip's.

'I love you, Snow White,' mouthed Phillip, covering her hand with his, his words drowned out by noise as the plane tore down the runway and lifted effortlessly into the sky.

'I love you too,' Jo murmured, snuggling up against him, as they stared out at the rapidly vanishing lights of Sydney. She had one change of clothes, no idea how long they would be away and had forgotten to leave any messages to say where she was, yet for once in her life she simply didn't care. Later she would contact Pete, ring home and tell Phillip about Simon and her dash to the airport, but for now she was content just to hold onto Phillip and dream of their future together. Of one thing she was absolutely sure, right now in the whole world she had to be the happiest woman alive.

Reach for the Dream
Anne Rennie

From the black soil plains of Australia to the rolling hills of England comes an uplifting tale of passion, courage and determination ... and a love as enduring as the land itself.

Alice Ferguson is eight years old when a savage bushfire brings her idyllic childhood to an abrupt end. Alice's father takes her and her brother Ben to live with his sister's family in the tiny country town of Billabrin ... and then walks out of their lives forever.

Spurred by an indomitable spirit, Alice dreams of one day breeding the best wool in the country. Only the belief that she can reach this dream sustains her through tragedy and disaster ... but nothing can prepare Alice for the treachery of her jealous cousin or the betrayal of the only man she ever loved.

Kal
Judy Nunn

Kalgoorlie. It grew out of the red dust of the desert over the world's richest vein of gold. Like the gold it guarded, Kalgoorlie was a magnet to anyone with a sense of adventure, anyone who could dream. People were drawn there from all over the world, settling to start afresh or to seek their fortunes. They called it Kal; it was a place where dreams came true or were lost forever in the dust. It could reward you or it could destroy you, but it would never let you go. You staked your claim in Kal and Kal staked its claim in you.

In a story as breathtaking and sweeping as the land itself, bestselling author Judy Nunn brings Kalgoorlie magically to life through the lives of two families, one Australian and one Italian. From the heady early days of the gold rush to the horrors of the First World War in Gallipoli and France, to the shame and confrontation of the post-war riots, Kal tells the story of Australia itself and the people who forged a nation out of a harsh and unforgiving land.

The Dark Dream
Lilly Sommers

From the bestselling author of *The Glass House* and *The Bond* comes a gripping story of passion and survival.

Who is Ella Seaton? Waking face-down in the mud by Seaton's lagoon, her head throbbing from an ugly wound, a young woman struggles to come to terms with an unfamiliar world. Who is she? Why can't she remember? Was she on her way to the goldfields at Bendigo? Or escaping from them?

All she has are snatches of a dark dream, a dream which holds memories she is too terrified to face.

Adam, a handsome young goldfields merchant, befriends her on the road, but Adam is a man with secrets of his own.

As she travels from the danger and excitement of the goldfields to polite Sydney society, Ella begins to unravel the threads of her past to confront the startling truth. A truth that will change her life forever.

The Burning Land
John Fletcher

The land out there has been burning me as long as I can remember. All these years I've been getting ready for this moment. I'm going out there to take hold of it . . .

Raised by struggling Scottish immigrants in the sparsely inhabited mountains of the Port Phillip District, Matthew Curtis dreams of the vast unexplored spaces of inland Australia.

Defying his stern foster-father, he leaves home— and the warm grey eyes of Catriona Simmons—at sixteen. His journey takes him first to the brawling life of the goldfields with the beautiful Janice Honeyman, then north into the burning wilderness of the unexplored outback.

An engrossing historical saga in the tradition of Evan Green and Wilbur Smith, *The Burning Land* bursts with life and the passion and daring of the Australian pioneers.

This Time Forever
Lynne Wilding

Laura McRae is beautiful, gifted, madly in love—
until at eighteen her life is shattered in a few brief
moments.

All she can cling to is her talent for fashion and
her determination never to be poor again; a talent
and determination that take her into the glamorous
salons of Sydney high society.

But soon it is wartime, a time of racketeering and
high stakes—and impulsive marriages. Falling into
the arms of Eddie Ashworth seems to be the love
Laura has dreamed of . . . but is her new husband
the man he seems?

As her business climbs from success to success, her
creations become the toast of the town, her custom-
ers the rich and powerful.

Then Captain Jack Beaumont walks into her life.

This time, can Laura truly find happiness? And
this time, could it be forever?